VIRAGO
MODERN CLASSICS

Victoria Mary Sackville-West

Victoria Sackville-West (1892–1962) was born and educated at Knole, the family home that was to be an abiding passion throughout her life. During a brief spell at school in London she met Violet Trefusis with whom she would later have a passionate affair. A distinguished critic, biographer, award-winning poet and gardener, her novels include the acclaimed *All Passion Spent* (1931, dramatised by the BBC in 1986) and *The Edwardians* (1930). Her close friendship with Virginia Woolf is celebrated in Woolf's novel, *Orlando* (1928). In 1930, Vita and her husband Harold Nicolson bought Sissinghurst Castle in Kent, where they created their famous garden. Vita Sackville-West died at home, after an operation for cancer, aged seventy.

THE EDWARDIANS

Vita Sackville-West

Introduced by Juliet Nicolson

virago

VIRAGO

This edition published by Virago Press in 2011
Reprinted 2011, 2013

First published in Great Britain by the Hogarth Press in 1930
Published by Virago Press in 1983
Reprinted 1984, 1987, 1988, 1990, 1991, 1992, 1993, 1995, 1996,
1998, 2000, 2003, 2004, 2006, 2007, 2008 (twice), 2009

A CIP catalogue record for this book
is available from the British Library.

ISBN 978-0-86068-359-9

Typeset in Goudy by M rules
Printed and bound in Great Britain by
Clays Ltd, St Ives plc

Papers used by Virago are from well-managed forests
and other responsible sources.

MIX
Paper from
responsible sources
FSC
www.fsc.org FSC® C104740

Virago Press
An imprint of
Little, Brown Book Group
100 Victoria Embankment
London EC4Y 0DY

An Hachette UK Company
www.hachette.co.uk

www.virago.co.uk

CONTENTS

AUTHOR'S NOTE

No character in this book is wholly fictitious

INTRODUCTION

Vita Sackville-West was in love with Knole. The huge house in Kent, where the novelist, poet, gardener and romantic grew up, mattered to her more than any other thing and at times more than any other person. *The Edwardians* is my grandmother Vita's love letter to that place.

Vita Sackville-West was born at Knole in 1892, the only child of Lord and Lady Sackville. The house sits in a thousand-acre deer park and, with its 365 rooms, 52 staircases, and the 'square turrets and grey walls, its hundred chimneys sending blue threads up into the air',[1] the entire structure resembles a small village. Indeed Vita's friend and sometime lover Virginia Woolf hazarded that 'the conglomeration of buildings' was probably 'half as big as Cambridge'.[2] Knole had belonged to the Sackville family since the death of Elizabeth I and, according to Victoria Sackville, its early twentieth-century chatelaine and Vita's mother, it united 'the beauties of Windsor Castle with the comforts of The Ritz'.[3]

On Lord Sackville's death in 1928, due to the ancient rules of primogeniture, or what Vita called 'a technical fault', the ownership of Knole passed at the beat of a funeral drum to her male cousin. Later that year Knole, in all its romantic, feudal, and aristocratic complexity, would be symbolically returned to a grieving Vita through the pages of Virginia Woolf's semi-biographical fantasy *Orlando*. Virginia's gift 'dazzled, bewitched, enchanted'[4] its recipient. Vita finished writing her own memorial to Knole during the spring of 1930, making Knole 'Chevron' and *The Edwardians* an autobiographical fiction, prefaced with the author's teasing caution to her readers that 'No character in this book is wholly fictitious'.

When Queen Victoria died in 1901 Vita Sackville-West was eight years old and the British aristocracy was delighting in the regal turnaround. The hefty paperweight of widowed restraint, held in place for so long by the old Victorian plutocracy, was lifted with the death of the old queen and replaced by the hedonistic excesses of Edward VII's court. For the following decade the ruling class, licensed by royal example, remained hell-bent on pleasure. It was an existence maintained by inherited riches and dozens of servants, and led without a thought, let alone desire, that these circumstances would ever alter. In houses like Knole the air hummed with gossip and fizzed with double standards. Infidelity was taken for granted as night-time corridor creeping, from one velvet-draped four-poster to the next, was permitted only as long as the deceitful creepers were never caught. Bilious, rich meals, games of bridge and changes of clothes punctuated interminable stretches of boredom and vacuity. Every empty day yawned with a hopeless conviction that it might bring more lasting fulfilment than the day that had either preceded or would succeed it. These were the moral tenets of Vita Sackville-West's upbringing.

But any complacent acceptance of the unthreatened

continuity of such a life was ill founded. In *Pepita*, Vita's biography of her grandmother, published in 1937, she wrote of how pre-war life had been idyllic only for those 'who were blessed with money and possessions and whose ears were not tuned to catch any sound of ominous cracking going on around them'. Lurking just the width of a duchess's calling card below the peacetime surface of the country was a slow-burning dissatisfaction waiting to erupt. The story of *The Edwardians* begins in 1905 during the reign of Edward VII and ends in 1911, a year after his death. In those six years Britain moved from an era of apparent national tranquillity into one of flux and fragmentation. The poor, the servant classes and women were among those beginning to shake their collective fists at the establishment of a hundred years ago. The sound of rumbling discontent grew ever louder, eventually releasing the trigger that unravelled centuries of unchallenged aristocratic dominance. The poor were no longer prepared to accept their poverty in silence. Dockworkers, miners and railwaymen joined fledgling trade unions as they engaged in ever more disruptive protest at uncertain employment and pitiful wage levels. Children of servants refused to follow their parents into domestic service. The head carpenter in *The Edwardians* is confused and tearful at his son's decision to abandon centuries of inherited carpentry skills and to join the new motor trade instead. Suffragettes were upping their efforts to win the vote, while in private women were loosening the laced-up, corseted taboos that governed sexual relationships, and heading for the divorce courts to untie themselves from unhappy marriages. The fictional world of *The Edwardians* is balanced on that cusp of change; it is a story that plunges down into the murky self-satisfied lives of the rich with their lack of compassion and intellectual curiosity, but which on occasion tips steeply in the other direction towards those increasingly desperate for a new way of doing things.

Sebastian and Viola, brother and sister, are symbols of the duality of Vita's own nature, spiritually, historically, culturally, socially and sexually. At times in umbilical thrall to her heritage, Vita also raged against the devious behaviour practised within Knole's thick walls. Just as Sebastian swings from emotional embrace to fierce rejection of his birthright, so Vita teetered between those two sensibilities. Both author and hero are subject to a contrasting mixture of affection and revulsion, an addictive see-saw that both sustains and damages them. It is Viola and the enigmatic explorer Leonard Anquetil who offer the emotional, sexual and intellectual honesty that is such a seductive and enduring alternative. The Edwardians is Vita's response to an ambivalence that was to pull and push at her throughout her life.

By the time The Edwardians was published more than a decade had elapsed since the end of the Great War, and many of the hypocrisies and inequalities of the Edwardian age had receded. The servant class was no longer intact, the constructive power of the trade union movement had been recognised, women had won the vote, and the pre-war Chevron-like life of luxury had all but ceased to exist. This change of circumstances was reflected in Vita's own life. Her three-year love affair with Violet Trefusis had ended in 1921 (the intensity of the relationship is described in all its powerful depth by her younger son, my father Nigel Nicolson, in his masterly book Portrait of a Marriage[5] and also by Vita herself in her novel Challenge). Both women had temporarily deserted their husbands and children, and planned a permanent life together, but Vita eventually realised the emotionally thrombotic consequences involved in that decision, and drew back. The prospect of losing her husband threatened to be as damaging as the loss of Knole, even though Vita continued to crave, and indulge, the exhilarating thump of the extramarital pulse for the rest of her life.

I knew my grandmother as an intimidating figure. We would often visit her and my grandfather Harold at Sissinghurst in Kent where together they had made one of the most beautiful gardens in England. Many thousands of visitors still come every year to admire its breathtaking creativity.[6] As a child, I remember resisting Vita's grasp as she reached down a long way (Vita was a tall woman) to take my four-year-old hand and guide me through the intoxicatingly bitter-smelling hop fields that surrounded Sissinghurst. If I had then been aware of the meaning of the word romantic, I would not have used it to describe her, and yet what did I know then of the astonishing secrets of her emotional life?

The Edwardians is a novel skewered to a moment that preceded the imminent death not only of an age but also of hundreds of thousands of young men who would be killed during the Great War. As she began the book in the spring of 1929 Vita wrote to Virginia Woolf of her plan to describe 'The smell of the bus that met one at the station in 1908. The rumble of its rubberless tyres. I find that these things are a great deal more vivid to me than many things which have occurred since.' The reader is immersed in a lost world in which the infinite minutiae of life from flowers to food, bicycles to banquets, and courtships to a coronation are vividly recaptured with infallible accuracy: the eyewitness account of the ancient ritual of the crowning of George V, to which Vita travelled in

1911 in the creaking hearse-like Sackville coach, has the clarity of a contemporary television documentary; the glittering description of a fashionable duchess preparing for dinner is based on the evening toilette of Vita's mother. This remains perhaps the most surprising scene of all to me, as I remember the author as a fashion-phobic grandmother dressed in work-aday breeches and boots and who, finding herself one day hatless in the late 1950s, was grateful for the loan of a neighbour's felt beret to wear to a formal party at Buckingham Palace. Her appearance in later life rarely changed, inviting the view that above the waist she resembled a perpetually pearl-festooned Lady Chatterley, while remaining clothed in the costume of a gamekeeper below.

Vita intended *The Edwardians* to 'make my fortune'. She finished the novel on 4th March 1930. On 5th April she went with her husband Harold to visit a ruined Elizabethan house not far from Knole. It was for sale and Vita wrote in her diary that night that she had 'fallen flat in love with it'. By 6th May Sissinghurst Castle was theirs. *The Edwardians* was published by Virginia and Leonard Woolf's Hogarth Press on 29th May and by June it was selling so well that Virginia reported to her nephew Quentin Bell how she and Leonard were 'hauling in money like pilchards from a net'. Leonard was delighted if surprised at the commercial success of the book. In his autobiography he described Vita as not much more than a 'competent' writer. Vita herself was not proud of the novel, writing to Virginia, 'Oh that bloody book! I blush to think you read it.'[7] Despite the misgivings of the author *The Edwardians* sold thirty thousand copies in the first six months and the magic of Sissinghurst gradually began to ease the pain that Vita felt at the loss of her childhood home.

However, Vita's fierce attachment to Knole never wholly left her. When Knole was slightly damaged by a bomb during the Second World War, she wrote to Harold, 'I always persuade myself that I have finally torn Knole out of my heart [but] I cannot bear to think of Knole wounded and me not there to look after it and be wounded with it.'[8] For Vita the legacy of Knole, immortalised in *The Edwardians*, brought with it 'the weight of the past' and that, as Sebastian says, 'is a real atrophy of the soul'.

Juliet Nicolson, 2011

1 *The Edwardians* by Vita Sackville-West (Virago).
2 Virginia Woolf, 5 July 1924. Quoted in *Inheritance* by Robert Sackville (Bloomsbury).
3 *Lady Sackville* by Susan Mary Alsop (Weidenfeld and Nicolson).
4 VSW to VW, 11 October 1928. *The Letters of Virginia Woolf*, edited by Nigel Nicolson and Joanne Trautman (Hogarth Press).
5 *Portrait of a Marriage* by Nigel Nicolson (Phoenix).
6 Both Sissinghurst and Knole are now owned by the National Trust and are open to the public between April and October.
7 *Vita, The Life of Vita Sackville-West* by Victoria Glendinning (Weidenfeld and Nicolson).
8 VSW to HN, 11 February 1944, quoted in ibid.

I

CHEVRON

Among the many problems which beset the novelist, not the least weighty is the choice of the moment at which to begin his novel. It is necessary, it is indeed unavoidable, that he should intersect the lives of his dramatis personae at a given hour; all that remains is to decide which hour it shall be, and in what situation they shall be discovered. There is no more reason why they should not first be observed lying in a bassinette – having just been deposited for the first time in it – than that the reader should make their acquaintance in despairing middle age, having just been pulled out of a canal. Life, considered in this manner from the novelist's point of view, is a long stretch full of variety, in which every hour and circumstance have their peculiar merit, and might furnish a suitable spring-board for the beginning of a story. Life, moreover, as we continue to consider it from the novelist's point of view, life although varied is seen to be continuous; there is only one beginning and only one ending, no intermediate beginnings and endings such as the poor novelist must arbitrarily impose; which perhaps explains why so many novels, shirking the disagreeable reminder of Death, end with Marriage, as the only admissible and effective crack in continuity. So much for the end; but there are obvious disadvantages to starting the hero off with his birth. For one thing, he is already surrounded by grown-ups, who by reason of his tender and inarticulate age must play some part in the novel, or at any rate in the first chapters of it, and whose lives are already complicated in such a fashion that it is no true beginning for them when they are hauled ready-made into the story. For another thing – but I need not enlarge. The arbitrariness of choice has already been made sufficiently evident, and no further justification is necessary to explain why we irrupt into the life of our hero (for so, I suppose, he must be called) at the age of nineteen, and meet him upon the roof a little after midday on Sunday, July the 23rd, nineteen hundred and five.

He had climbed on to the roof not only because for years such exercise had been his favourite pastime but because it was now his only certain method of escape. Escape was a necessity; otherwise, his mother expected him to play the host, which meant that the men chaffed him and that the women rumpled his hair. Even at that early age, he liked his hair to be oiled and tidy. Even at that early age, he resented any intrusion, however genial, upon his privacy. So he escaped; sprang upstairs through the rich confusion of staircases and rooms; and finally reaching the attics pushed his way out through a small door which opened on to the leads. Nimble in tennis-shoes, he went up an angle of the sloping tiles, to sit astride the peak of the roof; tore his shirt open, fanned his flushed face, and drank the air in large draughts. Arrived there, his surroundings supported him in the most approved fashion. A cloud of white pigeons wheeled above him in the blue sky. Acres of red-brown roof surrounded him, heraldic beasts carved in stone sitting at each corner of the gables. Across the great courtyard the flag floated red and blue and languid from a tower. Down in the garden, on a lawn of brilliant green, he could see the sprinkled figures of his mother's guests, some sitting under the trees, some strolling about; he could hear their laughter and the tap of the croquet mallets. Round the garden spread the park; a herd of deer stood flicking with their short tails in the shade of the beeches. All this he could see from the free height of the roof. Immediately below him – very far below, it seemed – lay a small inner court, paved, with an immense bay-tree growing against the grey wall, and as he peered down, feeling a little giddy, he saw a procession emerge from a door and take its way across to a door opposite. He grinned. Well did he know what this procession meant. It meant that at a given moment in the servants' dinner, the flock of housemaids had risen from their seats in the servants' hall, and, carrying their plates of pudding in their hands, were retiring to their own sitting-room to complete their meal. So the procession came, one, two, three, four, five, six, seven, eight, one behind the other, in print dresses and white aprons, carrying their plates, each plate with a dab of pudding on it and a spoon laid across, as though they observed the ritual of some ancient and hierarchical etiquette.

It must, therefore, be a quarter to one. The servants' dinner began at half-past twelve, and the punctuality of the house was as reliable as the sun himself. Sebastian grinned; then he sighed. For the approach of luncheon meant that he must abandon the roof and its high freedom, with the surveying glance it gave him of house, garden, and park, and go downstairs to be engulfed once more in the bevy of his mother's guests. Week-ends were always like this, throughout the summer, though he, Sebastian, who was at Oxford, suffered from them only during his summer holidays. For his sister it was different; she was always at home, and even now probably was having her hair tweaked and frizzed, till, as her brother said, she could hardly shut her mouth. On Monday and Tuesday – unless it rained – her hair would still be curly; by Wednesday it would again be lank.

But although it was easy to get up it was not so easy, as Sebastian found, and was to find as life went on, to get down. He hung for a long time in perilous hesitation over the well of the little court. He could not make up his mind to jump. Supposing he missed his footing? shot between the battlements and crashed into the depths below? The air was good, warmed by the sun; and the ground was good, when the foot was on it; but he hung now in a false position between the two; a tenta-tive movement made a tile slip. It slipped with a single, cautionary rattle. The heraldic leopards watched him sarcastic-ally, holding their shields. Overhead, the clock suddenly struck One, and the sound reverberated all round the roofs, coming to rest again in the clock-tower, after its journey of warning in that solitary punctuation of time. The pigeons rose in a scatter, only to settle once more on the gables, and there to resume their courtships. There was nothing for it but to jump. Sebastian jumped.

He was late for luncheon, and his mother looked at him dis-approvingly as he slipped into his place at one of the little tables. His mother was annoyed, but she idolised her son, and

could not deny that he was very good-looking. His good looks
were of the kind that surprised her afresh every time he came
into the room. He was so sleek, so dark, and so olive-skinned.
So personable. Potini, that sly, agreeable, sensuous Italian, hit
the nail on the head when he murmured to her that Sebastian
enjoyed all the charm of patrician adolescence. Patrician adolescence! Yes, thought his mother, who could never have found
the words for herself; yes, that's Sebastian. He could be half an
hour late for luncheon, and one would still forgive him.

There were thirty people to luncheon; but two places
remained empty; they were destined for two people who were
motoring down from London and who, naturally, had so far
failed to arrive. The duchess never waited for motorists. They
must take their chance. And, to-day being Sunday, they would
not be able to send the usual telegram saying that they had
broken down.

Conversation stopped for a moment when Sebastian came
in, and one or two people laughed. They were amused; not
unkindly. Luncheon was laid in the banqueting-hall at small
tables of four and six, the formality of a long table being
reserved for dinner. The hall was large and high, with a flagged
floor; coats of arms stained the windows, and the heraldic leopards stood rampant in carved and painted wood against the
panelling; antlers of stags ornamented the walls, opposite the
full-length Vandycks; two Bacchanalian little vines, dwarfed
but bearing bunches of grapes of natural size, stood in gold
wine-coolers on either side of the door; they were a well-known
speciality of Chevron. Sebastian found himself at a table with
Sir Harry Tremaine, Lady Roehampton, and the old Duchess of
Hull. He liked Lady Roehampton, and was faintly troubled by
her presence; in her large Leghorn hat, with nestling roses and

blue velvet streamers, and a muslin fichu like that of Marie Antoinette, she looked exactly like her own portrait by Sargent, which had been the sensation of that year's Academy, and it was not difficult to believe that she was popularly accepted as a professional beauty. The old Duchess of Hull he could not abide. She was heavily but badly made-up, with a triangle of red on either cheek, and, since her sense of direction was no longer very sure, she made bad shots with her fork which wiped the enamel off her face all round her mouth, and left the old yellow skin coming through. But her tongue was as sharp and witty as ever, and moreover she played an admirable hand at Bridge. No hostess could afford to omit her from a party. 'Well, young man?' she barked at Sebastian; but Lady Roehampton murmured, 'Well, Sebastian?' and smiled at him as though she knew exactly what he had been doing.

Lady Roehampton, though no one seeing her would have suspected it, had a marriageable daughter.

And now the rest of the day must be got through somehow, but the members of the house-party, though surely spoilt by the surfeits of entertainment that life had always offered them, showed no disposition to be bored by each other's familiar company, and no inclination to vary the programme which they must have followed on innumerable Sunday afternoons since they first emerged from the narrowness of school or schoolroom, to take their place in a world where pleasure fell like a ripened peach for the outstretching of a hand. Leonard Anquetil, watching them from outside, marvelled to see them so easily pleased. Here are a score or more of people, he thought, who by virtue of their position are accustomed to the intimate society of princes, politicians, financiers, wits, beauties, and other makers of history, yet are apparently content with desultory chatter and make-believe occupation throughout the long hours of an idle day. Nor could he pretend to himself that on other days they diverted themselves differently, or that their week-end provided a deserved relaxation from a fuller and more ardent life. All their days were the same; had been the same for an eternity of years; not only for themselves, thought Anquetil, but for a long dwindling procession of their ancestors. By God, thought Anquetil, waking up to a truth that hitherto had not occurred to him, Society has always existed. Strange hocus-pocus, that juggles certain figures into prominence, so that their aspect is familiar to the wife of the bank-clerk, and their doings a source of envy to the daughter of the chemist in South Kensington! With what glamour this scheme is invested, insolent imposture! and upon what does it base its pretensions? for Anquetil, for the life of him, could not see that these people were in any way remarkable, nor that their conversation was in any way worthy of exciting the interest of an eager man. He listened carefully, tabulating their topics. They were more interested, he observed, in facts than in ideas. A large proportion of their conversation seemed to consist in asking one another what they had thought of such-and-such an entertainment, and whether they were going to such-and-such an other. 'What was Miriam's party like, Lucy? sticky, as usual?' 'No,' said Lucy, 'quite a good party for once, but of course nothing will ever make poor Miriam into a good hostess.' 'Millions don't make a salon.' 'Are you lunching with Celia to-morrow, Lucy?' 'Yes, – are you? What fun. Who else is going, do you know?' 'Tommy, you're going, aren't you? How too deevy. We'll all be able to laugh at Celia in a corner. And let me see – tomorrow evening is Stafford House, isn't it? Deevy parties at

Stafford House, always. And Millie looking like a goddess, with a golden train half-way down the stairs. The charm of that woman! Everybody will be there.' 'Violet really ought to be stopped from giving parties. There ought to be an Act of Parliament about it. Friday was ghastly.' 'Ghastly! Horribilino! And the filthiest food.' 'Where are you going to stay for Ascot?' ... Anquetil nearly got up and wandered off, but he was fascinated and amused. These parties of theirs, he thought, were like chain-smoking: each cigarette was lighted in the hope that it might be more satisfactory than the last. Then investments bulked heavy in their talk, and other people's incomes, and the merits of various stocks and shares; also the financial shrewdness of Mrs. Cheyne, a lady unknown to Anquetil, save by repute, but who cropped up constantly in the conversation; Romola Cheyne, it appeared, had made a big scoop in rubber last week – but some veiled sneers accompanied this subject, for how could Romola fail, it was asked, with such sources of information at her disposal? Dear Romola: what a clever woman. And never malicious, said someone. No, said someone else; too clever to be malicious. Then they passed on to other house-parties, and Anquetil learnt how poor Constance had made the *gaffe* of her life, by inviting Sophie and Verena together; but who Sophie and Verena were, or why they should not be invited together, Anquetil did not discover. And would Constance's girl marry young Ambermere? she would be a fool if she refused him, for when his father died he would come into thirty thousand a year – incomes again, thought Anquetil, who happened to know young Ambermere and had once had the pleasure of telling him exactly what he thought of him. He felt sorry for Constance's girl. Then for a space it seemed good to them to play at being serious. Politics flitted across the conversation, and these ladies and gentlemen spoke with a proprietary and casual familiarity, somewhat as though politics were children that they entrusted to the care of nurses and tutors, remembering their existence from time to time, principally in order to complain of the inefficient way the nurses and tutors carried out their duties; but although they were careful to give an impression of being behind the scenes, like parents who go up to the nursery once a day, their acquaintance remained oddly remote and no more convincing than an admirably skilful bluff. It was founded, Anquetil discovered, on personal contact with politicians; 'Henry told me last week ...,' or 'A. J. B. was dining with me and said ...,' but their chief desire was to cap one another's information. So this is the great world, thought Anquetil; the world of the élite; and he began to wonder what qualities gave admission to it, for he had already noticed that no definite principle appeared to dictate selection. He was not really very much interested, but the study would do well enough as an amusement for a Sunday afternoon under the trees of Chevron, listening to chatter in which he could not take part. This organisation puzzled him, for, so far, he could perceive no common factor between all these people; neither high birth nor wealth nor brains seemed to be essential – as Anquetil in his simplicity had thought – for though Sir Adam was fabulously rich, Tommy Brand was correspondingly poor; and though the Duchess of Hull was a duchess, Mrs. Levison was by birth and marriage a nobody; and though Lord Robert Gore was a clever, ambitious young man, Sir Harry Tremaine was undeniably a ninny. Yet they all took their place with the same assurance, and upon the same footing. Anquetil knew that they and their friends formed a phalanx from which intruders were rigorously excluded; but why some people qualified and others did not, he could not determine. Some of these women were harsh-faced, and lacked both charm and wit; their only virtue, a glib conversance with such topics as came up for discussion and a manner of delivering themselves as though the final word had been uttered on the subject. If this is Society, thought Anquetil, God help us, for surely no fraud has ever equalled it. These are the people, or a sample of them, who ordain the London season, glorify Ascot, make or unmake the fortune of small Continental watering-places, inspire envy, emulation, and snobbishness – well, thought Anquetil, with a shrug, they spend money, and that is the best that can be said for them. Lying in his long wicker chair, he could see some of them strolling about the lawn, and so low did he lie that the green lawn appeared to stand up behind them, like a green cloth stretched on a wall, with the little domes of the parasols moving against it, and the trim waists cutting their hour-glass pattern above the flowing out of the skirt.

Down in the steward's room the butler offered his arm gravely to the Duchess of Hull's maid, and conducted her to the place at his right hand. Lord Roehampton's valet did the same by Mrs. Wickenden the housekeeper. Mrs. Wickenden, of course, was not married, and her title was bestowed only by courtesy. The order of precedence was very rigidly observed, for the visiting maids and valets enjoyed the same hierarchy as their mistresses and masters; where ranks coincided, the date of creation had to be taken into account, and for this purpose a copy of Debrett was always kept in the housekeeper's room – last year's Debrett, appropriated by Mrs. Wickenden as soon as the new issue had been placed in her Grace's boudoir. The maids and valets enjoyed not only the same precedence as their employers, but also their names. Thus, although the Duchess of Hull's maid had stayed many times at Chevron, and was indeed quite a crony of Mrs. Wickenden's, invited to private sessions in the housekeeper's room, where the two elderly gossips sat stirring their cups of tea, she was never known as anything but Miss Hull, and none of her colleagues in the steward's room would ever have owned to a knowledge of what her true name might be. It is to be doubted whether Mrs. Wickenden herself had ever used it. Mrs. Wickenden and Vigeon the butler, between whom a slightly hostile alliance existed, prided themselves that no mistake had ever been made in the Chevron steward's room, and that consequently no disputes had ever arisen, such as were known to have happened, most distressingly, in other houses. The household at Chevron was indeed admirably organised. For one thing, any servant who had been at Chevron for less than ten years was regarded as an interloper; at the end of ten years' service they were summoned to her Grace's presence and received a gold watch with their name and the date engraved upon the back; a few encouraging words were spoken by her Grace and henceforward they were accepted as part of the establishment. But for this one, brief, intimidating occasion, the under-servants rarely came into contact with her Grace. It was to be doubted whether all of them knew her by sight, and it was quite certain that many of them were unknown to her. Various anecdotes were current; one to the effect that the duchess, meeting the fifth housemaid at the foot of a stair, had asked whether Lady Viola were in her room and had been completely routed by the reply, 'I'll go and see, madam; what name shall I say?' Then there had been that other terrifying incident, when her Grace, taking an unusually early walk in the park on a Sunday morning, had observed the black-robed, black-bonnetted procession setting off for church, and had descried a white rose coquettishly ornamenting a bonnet. The white rose had bobbed up and down across the grass. It was a gay little flower, despite the purity of its colour, and to the shocked eyes of the duchess it had represented insubordination. Mrs. Wickenden, summoned on her return from church, was equally scandalised. She explained the whole matter by a deprecatory reference to 'those London girls,' and the culprit had been discharged from Chevron by the afternoon train.

It was, however, seldom that any complete stranger obtained a situation at Chevron. The system of nepotism reigned. Thus Mrs. Wickenden and Wickenden the head-carpenter were brother and sister; their father and grandfather had been head-carpenters there in their day; several of the housemaids were Mrs. Wickenden's nieces, and the third footman was Vigeon's nephew. Whole families, from generation to generation, naturally found employment on the estate. Any outsider was regarded with suspicion and disdain. By this means a network was created, and a constant supply of young aspirants ensured. Their wages might range from twelve to twenty-four pounds a year. To do them justice, it must be said that the service they one and all gave to Chevron was whole-hearted and even passionate. They considered the great house as in some degree their own; their pride was bound up in it, and their life was complete within the square of its walls. Wickenden knew more about the structure than Sebastian himself, and Mrs. Wickenden had been known to correct her mistress – with the utmost tact and respect – on a point of historical accuracy. Such disputes as might arise between them – and the household was naturally divided into factions – were instantly shelved when any point concerning the interest of Chevron arose. Shelved, perhaps, only to be renewed later with increased but always dignified animosity. A vulgar wrangle was unknown, and indeed it was only among the upper servants that any such thing as a jealous friction existed. Such small fry as under-housemaids and scullery-maids and the like were not supposed to have any feelings: they were only supposed to do as they were told. The severest discipline obtained. But it was known that an occasional clash occurred between Mrs. Wickenden and Mr. Vigeon; and when that happened, in however dignified a privacy, the repercussion was felt throughout the house, and the ragtag and bobtail might be observed scurrying with additional diligence through hall and passage about their tasks, and many an eye might be furtively wiped under the stimulus of an undeserved scolding.

But when the steward's room was full of guests, and the table had been extended by the addition of several leaves, no indications of any schism were allowed to appear. Mrs. Wickenden and Mr. Vigeon, presiding at opposite ends of the table, were held to be models of their profession. They treated one another with immense ceremony, so that a foreigner, unversed in the ways of English service after the grand manner, might well have refused to believe that they had lived side by side for five-and-twenty years in the same house. Mrs. Wickenden was small, prim, and birdlike; when she moved, she rustled. In cold weather she wore a black shawl tightly drawn around her shoulders; her steps were quick and precise; her nose was sharp, and her manner slightly deprecatory, even mournful. Vigeon, on the other hand, though correctness personified in his professional capacity, was inclined to be facetious in private life. The duchess did not know this, but Sebastian and Viola did. As children in the house, they had of course been on terms of familiarity with the servants, especially when their mother was away, and as a small boy Sebastian had counted among his treats a particular game that he played with Vigeon. Vigeon could not always be coaxed into playing it – 'No, I can't be bothered now,' he would say – but sometimes he condescended, and taking Sebastian in his arms he would lift him up to a painting that hung in the pantry. Sebastian in his sailor suit would squeal and wriggle with excitement. The painting represented a still-life of grapes and lemons beside a plate of oysters. Vigeon would make passes before the picture, finally making the gesture of picking a grape off the canvas, when lo! a real grape would appear between his fingers, and with a final triumphant flourish he would pop it into Sebastian's mouth. 'Pick off an oyster, Vigeon!' Sebastian would cry, 'pick off an oyster!' but only on one occasion, never to be forgotten, had Vigeon obliged.

Grapes were on the steward's room table now, for Mrs. Wickenden controlled 'the fruit' from her lair behind the still-room, and no one troubled as to the exact number of bunches ordered daily from the kitchen garden. It was all part of the system of loose and lavish extravagance on which the house was run. Everybody, from Sebastian downwards, obtained exactly what they wanted; they had only to ask, and the request was fulfilled as though by magic. The house was really as self-contained as a little town; the carpenter's shop, the painter's shop, the forge, the sawmill, the hothouses, were there to provide whatever might be needed at a moment's notice. So the steward's room, like the dining-room and the schoolroom, was never without its fruit and delicacies. More especially when visiting maids and valets were there to be entertained by the domestic deities of Chevron, for snobbishness must be satisfied, and only by extravagance and waste could the honour of Chevron, in the opinion of Vigeon and Mrs. Wickenden, be maintained. They would not have Miss Hull and Mr. Roehampton go away on the Monday morning, and relate at their next weekend that Chevron fell below the proper standard.

Sebastian's mother tapped at Lady Roehampton's door an hour before dinner. She had not remembered exactly which room had been allocated to Lady Roehampton, for she had settled such matters with Miss Wace at least a week earlier, but she knew that she would find her in one of the best bedrooms, and in any case the name of each guest would be neatly written on a card slipped into a tiny brass frame on the bedroom door. This question of the disposition of bedrooms always gave the duchess and her fellow-hostesses cause for anxious thought. It was so necessary to be tactful, and at the same time discreet. The professional Lothario would be furious if he found himself in a room surrounded by ladies who were all accompanied by their husbands. Tommy Brand, on one such occasion, had been known to leave the house on the Sunday morning – thank goodness, thought the duchess, that wasn't at Chevron! Romola Cheyne, who always neatly sized up everybody in a phrase – very illuminating and convenient – said that Tommy's motto was 'Chacun a sa chacune.' Then there were the recognised lovers to be considered; the duchess herself would have been greatly annoyed had she gone to stay at the same party as Harry Tremaine, only to find that he had been put at the other end of the house. (But she was getting tired of Harry Tremaine.) It was part of a good hostess' duty to see to such things; they must be made easy, though not too obvious. So she always planned the rooms carefully with Miss Wace, occasionally wondering whether that upright and virtuous virgin was ever struck by the recurrence of certain adjustments and coincidences. She knew that she could trust Wacey to carry out her instructions; nevertheless, looking for Lady Roehampton's room, she glanced critically at the name-plates. Wacey had done her work well. Lord Robert Gore was in the Red Silk Room; Mrs. Levison just across the passage. That was as it should be. Julia Levison was the duchess' bosom friend; indeed, it was largely owing to her friendship that Mrs. Levison was admitted into such society at all. The Archbishop's Room, the Queen's Room, the Tapestry Room, Little North, George III.'s, George III.'s Dressing-room – she passed them all; they all bore names she did not want. Their counterparts would hang on cards beside the bell-indicator outside the pantry, for the information of the visiting maids and valets: the Tapestry Room: the Duchess of Hull; the Queen's Room: H.E. the Italian Ambassador – thus the pantry indicator would read. Little North – a humble room, a bachelor's room – Mr. Leonard Anquetil; but Anquetil, she reflected, would have no valet; he would be valeted by a Chevron footman. Anquetil was the lion of the moment; an explorer, he had been marooned for a whole winter somewhere near the South Pole in a snow-hut with four companions, one of whom had gone mad, but for some reason it was difficult to make him talk of his experiences; a pity, for they had been reported in all the papers; still, Polar sufferings were perhaps on the whole a bore, and, since one must certainly have the lion of the moment at one's parties, it was perhaps just as well that he should not boringly roar. So she passed by the rooms, and found Lady Roehampton in the Chinese Room. 'How nice to see you alone for a moment,

Sylvia,' – as the experienced maid withdrew. The professional beauty was moving idly about the room looking like a loosened rose: she was wrapped in grey satin edged with swansdown. 'How attractive you look, Sylvia; I don't wonder that people get on chairs to stare at you. I don't wonder that Romola Cheyne gets uneasy. But seriously, no one would believe that your Margaret was eighteen.' 'Nor your Sebastian nineteen, Lucy dear.' They were intimate friends; they had known the undeniable facts, dates, and current gossip about each other's lives from their youth upwards. Lucy sank on to the sofa. 'Oh, these parties! Sylvia, dear, how very nice to snatch a moment with you alone. Really that old Octavia Hull is becoming too terrible for words; did you see how she dribbled at tea? She ought to be put out of the way. Sebastian nineteen – yes. Absurd. To think that you might be his mother.' 'Or his mother-in-law,' thought Lady Roehampton; it was an idea that had occurred to her more than once. She did not utter this aloud, nor the supplementary remark, 'Or his mistress,' which had entered her head for the first time that day. Instead, she said, 'Speaking of Romola Cheyne, wasn't she staying here last week?' Lucy knew from her tone that some revelation was imminent, and when she saw Lady Roehampton take up the blotting-book she instantly understood. 'How monstrous!' cried Lucy, moved to real indignation; 'how often have I told the groom of the chambers to change the blotting-paper, in case something of the sort should happen? I'll sack him to-morrow. Well, what is it all about? It makes one's blood run cold, doesn't it, to think of the hands one's letters might fall into? I suppose it's a letter to . . .' and here she uttered a name so august that in deference to the respect and loyalty of the printer it must remain unrevealed. 'No,' said Lady Roehampton, 'that's just the point: it isn't.

Look!' Lucy joined her at the mirror, and together they read the indiscreet words of Romola Cheyne. 'Well!' said Lucy, 'I always suspected that, and it's nice to know for certain. But what I can't understand, is how a woman like Romola could leave a letter like that on the blotting-pad. Doesn't that seem to you incredible? She knows perfectly well that this house is always full of her friends,' said Lucy with unconscious irony. 'Now what are we to do with it? The recklessness of some people!'

The two friends were both highly delighted. Little incidents like this added a spice to life.

Lady Roehampton carefully tore out the treacherous sheet. 'There's no fire,' she said laughing; 'for the moment I'll lock it up in my writing-case. I daresay I'll find some means of destroying it safely to-morrow.' Lucy laughed too, and agreed, knowing well that Lady Roehampton had no intention whatever of destroying it. She might never use it, but on the other hand it might be useful. 'But meanwhile is it safe?' asked Lucy. 'You're sure your maid hasn't a key of your writing-case? Servants are so unscrupulous, one can't trust them a yard. However long they have been with one, – even if one looks on them as old friends, – one never knows when they will turn nasty. You're sure you hadn't better give it to me?'

Lucy expected no answer to this, and Lady Roehampton gave none. That was consistent with her usual manner. She had a way of suddenly dropping a subject; it was a trick she had often found convenient, and since she enjoyed all the assurance of a beautiful woman, she was able always to impose her own wishes upon her audience. So now she could abandon the subject of the letter, and revert to Sebastian, who had aroused her interest: 'That dark romantic boy of yours, Lucy, – tell me about him. When does he leave Oxford? Is he going into the Guards?'

Lucy was never reluctant to talk about Sebastian; moreover, Lady Roehampton had no son, only a daughter of whom she was reputed jealous. 'My dark romantic boy, Sylvia! how absurd you are, he's only an untidy schoolboy, – a colt, I tell him, – I hope he won't get spoilt, if women like you take too much notice of him. He's a nice boy, I admit, though he's apt to be moody.' 'But that's his charm, my dear Lucy: Sebastian sulky is irresistible. Promise me you will never ruin him by persuading him to appear good-tempered.' 'How perverse you are, Sylvia; I believe you really like people to be disagreeable. So that you can win them round. You would like Sebastian to snarl at you for half an hour, if at the end of forty minutes you were sure of having him at your feet.' 'What nonsense you talk, Lucy; I knew Sebastian in his cradle. But you needn't shut your eyes to the fact that he will have great attraction for women. That casual, though charming manner of his . . . I doubt if he knows so much as my name.' 'My dear Sylvia, you are one of his favourites; when I tell him you are coming, he says, Thank goodness for that.' 'That means,' said Lady Roehampton, gratified at having caught the fish for which she was angling, 'he is bored by most of our friends.' 'Worse than that, Sylvia,' said Lucy, settling down to a grievance, 'sometimes I think he really dislikes them. He says such sarcastic things, – quite unlike a boy. Cutting things. They make me quite uncomfortable. At other times he seems to enjoy himself. I can't make him out.' 'Adolescence,' said Sylvia, blowing a long thread of smoke from her cigarette, for although she never smoked in public she could enjoy a cigarette in the privacy of her bedroom. 'If I could really think that!' sighed Lucy; 'if I could be sure he was going to turn out all right! It's a great responsibility, Sylvia.' 'You could always marry again, Lucy,' said Lady Roehampton, looking at her friend. 'Yes,' said Lucy, instantly on her guard, 'I could, but I prefer keeping my difficulties to myself, on the whole. I am quite prepared to run Chevron for Sebastian until he marries. But, Sylvia, we must dress.' 'Dinner at half-past eight?' 'Dinner at half-past eight. What are you going to put on? The Nattier-blue taffeta? I always think you look better in that than in anything else. Don't hurry, darling. I shall be late anyhow.'

One half of Sebastian detested his mother's friends; the other half was allured by their glitter. Sometimes he wanted to gallop away by himself to the world's ends, sometimes he wanted to give himself up wholly to the flattering charm of pretty women. Sometimes he wished to see his whole acquaintance cast into a furnace, so vehemently did he deprecate them, sometimes he thought that they had mastered the problem of civilisation more truly than the Greeks or Romans. 'Since one cannot have truth,' cried Sebastian, struggling into his evening shirt, 'let us at least have good manners.' The thought was not original: his father had put it into his head, years ago, before he died. But this brings us to Sebastian's private trouble: he never could make up his mind on any subject. It was most distressing. He had, apparently, no opinions but only moods, – moods whose sweeping intensity was equalled only by the rapidity of their change. He could never accustom himself to their imper-manence; whatever state of mind was upon him at the moment, he instantly believed to be his settled outlook upon life. Momentarily alarmed when it deserted him, he changed over at once in oblivious optimism. Between-whiles, when no particular mood possessed him, he worried over his own in-stability. Something, he thought, must be wrong with him. He contrasted himself with the people he knew: how calm they were, how certain, how self-assured! With what unfaltering determination did they appear to have pursued their chosen path from its beginning right up to its end! – No, not yet right up to its end. Most of the people he knew at home were in their middle age; some certainly were old, the old Duchess of Hull, for instance, progressing, though still indomitably, towards her grave; but it was obvious that as they had begun, so did they mean to conclude. The world would be with them, late, as soon. They had known their own minds; they had stuck to their opinions. They had made their choice. How enviable! They had settled their scheme of values. How reposeful! But was it, he wondered, a very good choice? Were those values so very valuable? His mood underwent a violent revulsion. He wanted suddenly to be up on the roof again, this time under the stars. Sulky and critical, he shut his disappointed spaniels into his bedroom and went downstairs to obey his mother's summons.

On leaving Lady Roehampton, Lucy went to her own room: the great house was quiet; all the guests were safely shut into their rooms till dinner; no one was about, except a housemaid beating up the cushions or a footman emptying the waste-paper basket. Along the passages, the windows were open, for it was a warm July evening, and the pigeons cooing on the battle-ments made the silence murmurous as though the grey stone of the walls had itself become vocal. Lucy hurried through the empty rooms. She detested solitude, even for half an hour; the habit of constant company – it could scarcely be called com-panionship – had unfitted her for her own society, and now she sagged and felt forlorn. She ought to look into the schoolroom, she thought, and say good-night to Viola, who, in dressing-gown and pigtails, would be eating her supper, but the idea, no sooner than conceived, filled her with boredom. She decided to summon her favourite Sebastian instead. Reaching her room, where her maid, Button, was laying out her dress, she said, 'Send word to his Grace, Button, that I should like to see him here for a few minutes.'

Oh, the weariness of life, she thought, sitting down at her dressing-table; and then she remembered how Leonard Anquetil had looked at her when she had shown him the garden after tea, and a slight zest for life revived. She sat with lowered eyes, smiling a downward smile, while her thoughts dawdled over Leonard Anquetil and her fingers played with the jewels laid out on the dressing-table. She had recently had the family jewels reset by Cartier, preferring the fashion of the day to the heavy gold settings of Victoria's time. The top of the dressing-table was of looking-glass, so that the gems were dupli-cated; rubies to-night, she thought idly, picking up a brooch and setting it down again; last night she had worn the emeralds, and her depression returned as she reflected that some day she would have to give up the jewels to Sebastian's wife. She did not want to become either a dowager or a grandmother; she did not want to renounce her position as mistress of Chevron. Its luxury and splendour were very pleasant to her. Perhaps she would end by marrying Sir Adam after all, before Sebastian and his bride could turn her out; it would be a come-down to marry a Jew, and physically Sir Adam was not appetising, but then his millions were fabulous, and she could make him buy a place quite as imposing as Chevron. Not as beautiful, perhaps, but quite as imposing. Her hands strayed over the rubies; yes, and he would buy jewels for her too; her own, this time; no question of heirlooms. Besides, Sir Adam could do whatever he liked with the King. If only Sir Adam were not physically in love with her, she might really consider it.

Sebastian came in, and Lucy became brisk again.

'Give me a wrap, Button. You can start doing my hair. Sebastian, give me the plan of the dinner-table. On the table there. No, silly boy. Button, give it to his Grace. Now, Sebastian, read it out to me while I have my hair done. Oh, George Roehampton takes me in, does he? *Must* he? Such a bore that man is. And Sir Adam the other side. Don't pull my hair like that, Button; really, I never knew such a clumsy woman; now you have given me a headache for the rest of the evening. Do be more careful. Well, I am not going to enjoy myself very much, I can see: Sir Adam and George Roehampton. However, it's inevitable. Or no, let me see for myself. That Miss Wace is such a fool that she may quite well have made a muddle of the whole thing. Come and hold the plan for me to see, Sebastian. Button! you pulled my hair again. How many times must I tell you to be careful? Once more, and I give you notice, I declare I will. Tilt it up, Sebastian; I can't see.'

Sebastian stood beside his mother holding the red leather pad, with slits into which cards bearing the names of the guests were inserted. As she stood holding it, he watched his mother's reflection in the mirror. With her fair hair and lively little crumpled face, she looked extraordinarily young for her age as a rule, but now she was busily applying cream and wiping the cosmetics from her face with a handkerchief, at the same time as Button removed the pads from under her hair and laid them on the dressing-table. 'Rats,' her children called them. They were unappetising objects, like last year's birds-nests, hot and stuffy to the head, but they could not be dispensed with, since they provided the foundation on which the coiffure was to be swathed and piled, and into which the innumerable hairpins were to be stuck. It was always a source of great preoccupation with the ladies that no bit of the pad should show through the natural hair. Often they put up a tentative hand to feel, even in the midst of the most absorbing conversation; and then their faces wore the expression which is seen only on the faces of women whose fingers investigate the back of their heads. Sebastian had watched this hair-dressing process a hundred times, but now seeing it take place in the mirror, he observed it with a new eye. He stared at his mother's reflection, with the pool of rubies in the foreground, and the uncomely 'rats,' as though she were a stranger to him, realising that behind the glitter and animation in which they lived he had absolutely no knowledge of her. If he had been asked to describe his mother, he must have said, 'She is a famous hostess, with a talent for mimicry and a genius for making parties a success. She is charming and vivacious. In private life she is often irritable and sometimes unkind. She likes bridge and racing. She never opens a book, and she cannot bear to be alone. I have not the faintest idea of what she is really like.' He would not have added, because he did not know, that she was ruthless and predatory. 'Why are you staring like that, Sebastian? You make me quite shy.' Her hair was about her shoulders now, and Button was busy with the curling-tongs. She heated them first on the spirit lamp, and then held them carefully to her own cheek to feel if they were hot enough. 'Bless the boy, one would think he had never watched me dress before. Now about that dinner-table, yes, it's all wrong; I thought it would be. She has clean forgotten the ambassador. Button, you must call Miss Wace – no, Sebastian, you fetch her. No, ring the bell; I don't want you to go away. Why on earth can't people do their own jobs properly? What do I pay Wacey a hundred and fifty a year for, I should like to know? Oh dear, and look at the time; I shall be late for dinner. I declare the trouble of entertaining is enough to spoil all one's pleasure. It's a little hard, I do think, that one should never have any undiluted pleasure in life. Who's that at the door? Button, go and see. And Miss Wace must come at once.'

'Lady Viola would like to know if she may come and say good-night to your Grace.'

'Oh, bother the child – well, yes, I suppose she must if she wants to. Now, Button, haven't you nearly finished? Don't drag my hair back like that, woman. Give me the tail comb. Don't you see, it wants more fullness at the side. Really, Button, I thought you were supposed to be an expert hairdresser. You may think yourself lucky, Sebastian, that you were born a boy. This eternal hair, these eternal clothes! they wear a woman out before her time. Oh, there you are, Miss Wace. This plan is all wrong – perfectly hopeless. I don't go in with Lord Roehampton at all. What about the ambassador? You must alter it. Do it in here, as quick as you can. Sebastian will help you. And Viola. Come in, Viola; don't look so scared, child; I can't bear people who look scared. Now I must leave you all while I wash. No, I don't want you now, Button; you get on my nerves. I'll call you when I want you. Get my dress ready. Children, help Miss Wace – yes, you too, Viola; it's high time you took a little trouble to help your poor mother – and do, all three of you, try to show a little intelligence.'

The duchess retired into her dressing-room, from where she kept up a flow of comments.

'Viola, you must really take a little more trouble about your appearance. You looked a perfect fright at luncheon to-day; I was ashamed of you. And you really must talk more, instead of sitting there like a stuffed doll. You had that nice Mr. Anquetil, who is perfectly easy to get on with. You might be ten, instead of seventeen. I have a good mind to start you coming down to dinner, except that you would cast a blight over everything. Girls are such a bore – poor things, they can't help it, but really they are a problem. They ruin conversation; one has to be so careful. Women ought to be married, or at any rate widowed. I don't mean you, of course, Wacey. I'm ready for you, Button.'

Button vanished into the dressing-room, and for a while there was silence, broken only by irritable exclamations from within. These inner mysteries of his mother's toilet were unknown to Sebastian, but Viola knew well enough what was going on: her mother was seated, poking at her hair meanwhile with fretful but experienced fingers, while Button knelt before her, carefully drawing the silk stockings on to her feet and smoothing them nicely up the leg. Then her mother would rise, and, standing in her chemise, would allow the maid to fit the long stays of pink coutil, heavily boned, round her hips and slender figure, fastening the busk down the front, after many adjustments; then the suspenders would be clipped to the stockings; then the lacing would follow, beginning at the waist and travelling gradually up and down, until the necessary proportions had been achieved. The silk laces and their tags would fly out, under the maid's deft fingers, with the flick of a skilled worker mending a net. Then the pads of pink satin would be brought, and fastened into place on the hips and under the arms, still further to accentuate the smallness of the waist. Then the drawers; and then the petticoat would be spread into a ring on the floor, and Lucy would step into it on her high-heeled shoes, allowing Button to draw it up and tie the tapes. Then Button would throw the dressing-gown round her shoulders again – Viola had followed the process well, for here the door opened, and the duchess emerged. 'Well, have you done that table? Read it out. Louder. I can't hear. Yes, that's better. I'm sorry, Sebastian, you'll have to take in old Octavia Hull again. Nonsense, she's very amusing when she's not too fuddled with drugs. She'll be all right tonight because she'll be afraid of losing too much money to Sir Adam after dinner. Now, Wacey, off you go and rearrange the cards on the table. And you too, Viola. There are too many people in this room. Oh, all right, you can stop till I'm dressed if you like. Button, I'm ready for my dress. Now be careful. Don't catch the hooks in my hair. Sebastian, you must turn round while I take off my dressing-gown. Now, Button.'

Button, gathering up the lovely mass of taffeta and tulle, held the bodice open while the Duchess flung off her wrap and dived gingerly into the billows of her dress. Viola watched enraptured the sudden gleam of her mother's white arms and shoulders. Button breathed a sigh of relief as she began doing up the innumerable hooks at the back. But Lucy could not stand still for a moment, and strayed all over the room with Button in pursuit, hooking. 'Haven't you finished *yet*, Button? Nonsense, it isn't tight. You'll say next that I'm getting fat.' Lucy was proud of her waist, which indeed was tiny, and had changed since her girlish days only from eighteen to twenty inches. 'Only when your Grace stoops,' said Button apologetically, for Lucy at the moment was bending forward and peering into her mirror as she puffed the roll of her hair into a rounder shape. '*There*, then,' said the Duchess, straightening herself, but reaching down stiffly for the largest of her rubies, which she tried first against her shoulder, but finally pinned into a knot at her waist. Then she encircled her throat with the high dog-collar of rubies and diamonds, tied with a large bow of white tulle at the back. 'You must choose a wife who will do credit to the jewels, Sebastian,' she said as she slipped an ear-ring into its place, 'because, of course, the day will come when your poor old mother has to give up everything to her daughter-in-law, and we shan't like that – eh, Button?' – for she was in a better humour now, again completely adorned and clothed – 'but we'll put up with it for the joy of seeing a bride brought to Chevron – eh, Button? eh, Wacey? oh, no, of course Wacey has gone to do the table – and you and I, Button, will retire to the Dower House and live humbly for the rest of our lives, and perhaps his Grace will ask us to the garden-party – eh, Sebastian, you rogue? – will you, if your wife allows it?' Lucy was herself again, adjusting her frock, clasping her bracelets, dusting her throat with powder – for she was one of those who used powder, to the disapproval of her elders – and everybody except Sebastian was radiant with responsive smiles. She flicked her handkerchief across Sebastian's lips. 'Sulky boy! but Sylvia Roehampton says you are even more attractive when you sulk than when you are amiable, so I suppose I must believe her. Now Viola, my darling, I must run. Kiss me good-night. Go straight to bed. Do I look nice?'

'Oh, mother, you look too lovely!'

'That's all right.' Lucy liked as much admiration as she could get. 'Now you'll run away to bed, won't you? Dear me, I quite envy you the quiet of the schoolroom instead of that noisy dinner. Don't you, Sebastian? Good-night, my darling. Come along, Sebastian. I shall want you to wait up for me, Button, of course. You go in front, Sebastian, and open the doors. Dear, dear, how late you children have made me. Sebastian, you must apologise to old Octavia at dinner, and tell her it was all your fault. My fan, Button! good heavens, woman, what are you there for? One has to think of everything for oneself.'

Those meals! Those endless, extravagant meals, in which they all indulged all the year round! Sebastian wondered how their constitutions and their figures could stand it; then he remembered that in the summer they went as a matter of course to Homburg or Marienbad, to get rid of the accumulated excess, and then returned to start on another year's course of rich living. Really there was very little difference, essentially, between Marienbad and the vomitorium of the Romans. How strange that eating should play so important a part in social life! They were eating quails and cracking jokes. That particular dish of the Chevron chef was famous: an ortolan within the quail, a truffle within the ortolan, and *pâté de foie gras* within the truffle; by the time all the disembowelling had taken place, there was not much left of any of the constituents. From his place at the head of the table, Sebastian watched the jaws going up and down, and wished that he did not always see people as though they were caricatures. There was Sir Harry Tremaine, the perfect courtier, with his waved white hair, turning his head rigidly above his high collar, rather like a bird; there was Mrs. Levison, with her raucous voice and her hair like a frizzed yellow sponge. They were all people whose names were familiar to every reader of the society titbits in the papers. Sebastian saw them suddenly as a ventriloquist's box of puppets. Fourteen down one side of the table, fourteen up the other; with himself and his mother at either end, that made thirty. Then his vision shifted, and he was obliged to admit that they were very ornamental. They seemed so perfectly concordant with their setting, as though they had not a care in the world; the jewels glittered, the shirt-fronts glistened; the servants came and went, handing dishes and pouring wine in the light of the many candles. The trails of smilax wreathed greenly in and out among the heavy candelabra and the dishes of grapes and peaches. Yes, he must admit that his mother's friends were ornamental; he liked the bare shoulders and piled hair of the women, their pretty hands, and the bracelets round their wrists; the clouds of tulle, and the roses clasped by a brooch against the breast. His mother herself, whom he had so lately seen as a mask within her mirror, looked young and lovely now, so far away down the table; for a curious instant he imagined her, no longer his mother, but his wife. Then leaning towards her he saw the long nose of the Jew. 'A tip for the Stock Exchange!' he thought; for his mother had explained to him, with unusual candour, exactly why she wanted him to be polite to Sir Adam. This passion for money was a thing Sebastian could not understand; he was rich; his mother practically controlled the spending of his fortune until he should be twenty-one; where was the need for more? It was simply part of her creed and the creed of her friends. Creed, greed; they rhymed. He was paying no attention to what his neighbour was saying. Yet Sebastian was said to have charming manners.

After dinner, primed by his mother's discreet signals, he moved round to talk to the Italian ambassador. He rather liked old Potini, a crank on the subject of the English character. Sebastian, depressed now and disgusted – for he suffered acutely from his moods – would have welcomed any argument, and knew he would get entertainment from old Potini, who was always bursting with things he wanted to say. Among the ruins of the dinner-table, Sebastian drew a chair up beside him, holding a glass of port under the light, and old Potini began at once, rubbing his cigar between his fingers: 'Ah, you young man! you fortunate young man! home from Oxford, I suppose? Yes, Oxford, that strange university where you young men live in segregation; a town of masculine citizens.' The ambassador's English was faultless, if a trifle elaborate; the only thing which betrayed him was the rolling of his r's. 'Now such a thing, my dear duke,' he said, drawing his chair a little nearer to Sebastian and talking confidentially, 'would be unthinkable in Italy. Or, indeed, in any Latin country. The English have no interest in women – in Woman, that is to say. What do you care about a pretty ankle? You think a lot about the fetlocks of your polo ponies, but when you look at a woman you rarely look below her face. Oh, I assure you. You yourself are nineteen – twenty? And what part do women play in your life? What do you do in the evenings at Oxford? You sit with your friends, hugging your knees and smoking your pipe, and you talk about – what? Sport, politics. Woman might not exist; she is Bad Form. An evening in London now and then, I daresay,' – and his chuckle made Sebastian feel as though the ambassador had given him a dig in the ribs, – 'then back to this male life among a thousand other young men, as though nothing had happened. Yes, you are a strange race, a secret race, ashamed of being natural. Now in Italy, at your age ...' The ambassador's words threw Sebastian into an ill humour; he was stung, disturbed; he was ashamed of his virginity. People were not very real to him, and women least real of all. Little did he foresee, as he sat scowling at his wine, the adventure that was about to befall him. He wondered only how soon he might interrupt Potini, and suggest joining the ladies upstairs.

*

'Nothing ever happens,' said Sebastian violently; 'day after day goes by, and it is always the same.'

'Happenings go in series,' said Lady Roehampton, 'nothing happens, as you say; and then several things happen in a quick, odd succession. It is as though life had been gathering strength over a long period for an effort. Notice that for yourself. It is no good my telling you. One never believes other people's experience, and one is only very gradually convinced by one's own. Oh, my dear Sebastian,' she said – and she ceased to quote Mrs. Cheyne and spoke for once in all sincerity, remembering a young lover who had died – 'think of all the people who have died too young to have learnt their own wisdom.'

They were walking in the garden after dinner, up and down the long path that ran parallel with the house. From the windows of the house streamed yellow light, and the sounds of music. Overhead, the sky was black and starry, and the trees of the garden were massed darkly against the faintly lingering light of the horizon. The summer air was warm and scented. Sebastian had forced her to come out; still disturbed by the veiled sneers of Potini, he had felt it necessary to make a determined gesture, and in this company of strangely artificial standards he could think of nothing more drastic than to deprive his mother's bridge-tables of Lady Roehampton's presence. He smiled inwardly and ironically at the inadequacy of his caprice; it had created so much annoyance, an annoyance, he felt, which in other company would be reserved for something of real emotional importance; yet it was an annoyance discreetly controlled, with the perfect manners of those well-bred people. Lady Roehampton herself had alone displayed graciousness; she had smiled on the boy who, suddenly masterful, demanded her society. She had risen with a great billowing of blue taffeta skirts – a graceful, warm uprising of her beauty, conscious that many eyes were curiously and speculatively turned towards her. Sebastian was intensely aware of her quality as she strolled beside him; her quality of a beautiful woman exquisitely finished, with a perfect grasp on life, untroubled, shrewd, mature, secret, betraying her real self to none. Compared with her, he felt vague and raw, incapable of coming to terms with life. Yet he felt he could talk to her. She was charming, dangerous; he could talk to her. The knowledge that she was wholly unworthy of his confidence added a spice of pleasurable pain to the humiliation of giving himself away. For Sebastian liked to pour vinegar into his own wounds.

THE EDWARDIANS

II

ANQUETIL

On the Monday morning they were all disposed of; the carriages came round to the front door, and they were all stowed away safely inside – the men into the station bus, with its fusty smell, its rattling windows, and the rumbling of its rubberless wheels on the gravel; the women into the rubber-tyred broughams, the windows making a frame to the pretty veiled faces and waving hands. Sebastian came out to the door, smiling, his two little spaniels at his heels, the flag floating from the tower as it would float until the day it flew at half-mast for Sebastian's death. So they were all gone, all but Leonard Anquetil, who had been asked to stay till after luncheon. Sebastian turned, and crossed to the inner court, whistling; he enjoyed the sensation that the house was once more empty. He would force himself to forget Lady Roehampton. These parties might please his mother; they did not please him. He enjoyed another life – the life of Chevron. His mother did not altogether relish his interest in the estate; he could not help that.

The estate was his, and he loved it. At these moments, he forgot that 'nothing ever happened.' He felt, on the contrary, that in the placid continuity of Chevron lay a vitality of an order different from the brilliant excitement of his mother's world.

It came now to him as an audible hum. The whole community of the great house was humming at its work. In the stables, men were grooming horses; in the 'shops,' the carpenter's plane sent the wood-chips flying, the diamond of the glazier hissed upon the glass; in the forge, the hammer rang upon the anvil and the bellows windily sighed; in the slaughter-house, the keeper slung up a deer by its four feet tied together; in the shed, an old man chopped faggots. Sebastian heard the music and saw the vision. It was a tapestry that he saw, and heard the strains of a wind orchestra, coming from some invisible players concealed behind the trees. His thoughts turned to the house itself, and there also found their satisfaction, for there also was activity; the pestle thumped in the kitchen; the duck turned sizzling on the spit; the laundry-maids beat the linen in the coppers; the garden-boy dumped a basket of fruit on the dresser; and in the stillroom the maid stirred a cauldron of jam upon the fire; Mrs. Wickenden counted the sheets in the linen cupboard, putting a bag of lavender between each; Vigeon, having stored away the plate, turned the key in the lock of the strong-room door. Sebastian's thoughts strayed out again, over the park where the bracken-fronds were uncurling; and went beyond, running up and down the paths, to *this* farm where he had granted a new Dutch barn, to *that* cottage where the damaged tiles were already half stripped from the roof. Ladders and mallets, and men tossing up the tiles: Sebastian was a good landlord. He would walk over to Bassett's cottage that afternoon, and see how things were getting on. Or he would ride over. He had leisure, a whole week before him. Even his mother was going away to London. Next Saturday the house would again be filled with people – people who were so well equipped, so sure of themselves, so supercilious, that they ruffled and confused him, and made him say the biting things that so disconcerted his mother – but until then there was nothing but leisure hung with tapestry and filled with the sounds that were as music.

All was warmth and security, leisure and continuity. An order of things which appeared unchangeable to the mind of nineteen hundred and five. Why should they change, since they had never changed? There were a few minor changes, perhaps; no armourer was beating out a new pair of greaves for his young master; but in the main the tapestry had changed very little. The figures were the same, and the background was the same: the grey walls, the flag on the tower, the verdure of the trees, the hares and the deer feeding in the glades – even to the laundry-maid hanging out the washing. Court-baron and audit; heriot and peppercorn; the rope flapped idly against the flagstaff. Sebastian became aware that he was still standing in the middle of the court. He looked across the grass, to the bronze replica of the dying gladiator, upon whose shield his ancestor had caused his own coat of arms to be embossed. Superb insolence! thus to impose upon the classic statue the heraldry of an English milord. Nor did he realise that that insolence found a counterpart in his own youth and lordly security. He simply shook himself out of a dream, and went indoors to his own room. Sarah and Henry trotted after him.

There, he was undisturbed; the centre of all the life that hummed around him. Plenty of work awaited him, for when he was at home he insisted on looking into all the estate business himself. It was the only thing that made him really happy. He knew only three kinds of people: his Oxford friends, who thought him aloof and unsatisfactory; his mother's friends; and his own dependents. Between his dependents and himself the best of understandings existed, an understanding due partly to the fact that he had grown up amongst them, standing beside the wood-cutters as a small boy to watch them fell a tree; begging a new rabbit-hutch from Wickenden; leading his pony himself down to the forge to be shod; partly to their innate sense of tradition; and partly, we must concede, to Sebastian's own manner, which in such relationships was both simple and charming. He might puzzle his mother and his mother's friends; he might even puzzle himself, with the revulsions of his moods; but his own people, who saw him only in the one mood, his most serene, found him nothing of an enigma. Furthermore, he was open-handed, as he could well afford to be; money was a thing about which he never needed to think. There had always been plenty of money at Chevron, and there still was, even with the income-tax raised from 11d. to 1/- in the pound; that abundance was another of the things which had never changed and which had every appearance of being unchangeable. It was taken for granted, but Sebastian saw to it that his tenants benefited as well as himself. 'An ideel landlord – wish there were more like him,' they said, forgetting that there were, in fact, many like him; many who, in their unobtrusive way, elected to share out their fortune, not entirely to their own advantage – quiet English squires, who, less favoured than Sebastian, were yet imbued with the same spirit, and traditionally gave their time and a good proportion of their possessions as a matter of course to those dependent upon them. A voluntary system, voluntary in that it depended upon the temperament of the squire; still, a system which possessed a certain pleasant dignity denied to the systems of a more compulsory sort. But did it, Sebastian reflected, sitting with his pen poised above his cheque-book, carry with it a disagreeable odour of charity? He thought not; for he knew that he derived as much satisfaction from the idea that Bassett would no longer endure a leaking roof as Bassett could possibly derive, next winter, from the fact that his roof no longer leaked. He would certainly go over and talk to the man Bassett. Bassett should see that he took a personal interest. Together they would stand and watch the wooden pegs being tapped into the sound new tiles. 'Very much obliged to your Grace, I'm sure,' the man Bassett would say – he was always known as the man Bassett, nobody knew why – but the last thing Sebastian wanted was gratitude. He would instantly think with apologetic shame of his own roof, the roof of Chevron, seven acres of it, no one inch of which would be allowed to leak for more than a single hour after its discovery by Wickenden. – Wickenden. He must see Wickenden. There was a note laid on his table: 'Wickenden would be glad if he might see your Grace for a few minutes.' He rang the bell and sent for Wickenden.

Wickenden came, a small apple-faced man with keen blue eyes, a foot-rule sticking out of the pocket of his baize apron. He had served his apprenticeship in the Chevron shops under his own father, and now had succeeded to the position of head-carpenter. He had started by rough-hewing the timber-ends for gate-posts, and now delegated all but the most delicate work to his underlings. Eight Wickenden children came annually to the Christmas tree, there to receive a toy, an apple, and an orange, but Wickenden had no passion in his life but Chevron. 'Well, Wickenden, what can I do for you?'

Sebastian had anticipated some apprehension about an inse-
cure chimney, a flaking gable – the structure which had resisted
the weather since the days of Henry the Seventh was in need
of constant supervision and repair – but Wickenden picked at
his cap, keeping his eyes bent down upon it, in a way which
indicated a deeper trouble. It was evident that he would bring
out his words with difficulty. 'Well, Wickenden, what's tumbling down now?' Wickenden raised his eyes. 'Everything! as it
seems to me, your Grace.'

Sebastian was startled; the man's eyes were swimming in
tears.

'It's my boy, your Grace – Frank, my eldest. Your Grace
knows that I was to have taken him into the shops this year.
Well, he won't come. He wants to go – I hardly know how to
tell your Grace. He wants to go into the motor trade instead.
Says it's the coming thing. Now your Grace knows', said
Wickenden becoming voluble, 'that my father and his father
before him were in the shops, and I looked to my boy to take
my place after I was gone. Same as your Grace's son, if I may
make the comparison. I never thought to see a son of mine
leave Chevron so long as he was fit to stay there. And Frank *is*
fit – a neater-handed boy I seldom saw. That's what draws him
to engines. Now what is engines, I ask your Grace? What's
screwing up a nut beside handling a nice piece of wood? Such
nice pieces of wood as I have lying out in the timber-yard, too;
will be as ripe as a violin in forty years or so. Just right for Frank
to handle by the time he's sixty. He could make panelling out
of them – anything! I picked the oak for the grain myself; Mr.
Reynolds, he wanted to saw them up for firewood, but I
wouldn't let him. I said, it'd be a shame. Oak that came down
in the gale three winters ago. I cut it into planks and left it out

in the yard to weather. I showed it to Frank, and "Frank," I said, "when you're sixty and need a nice piece of wood, you'll find it here, and don't you forget your father put it there for you." And now he wants to go into the motor trade. I don't know if it'd be any good your Grace talking to him. Telling him he's giving up a sure job for a shadow. Telling him he's breaking his father's heart. I don't know, I'm sure. The young is very set on their own ideas. But it seems to me that everything is breaking up, now that my eldest wants to leave the shops and go into the motor trade.'

Leonard Anquetil woke late, and lay for a while with his hands laced behind his head, very much amused at himself for being in such surroundings. It tickled him exceedingly that, because one had tried to reach the South Pole, one should be invited to Chevron. Chevron! that anachronism! the duchess' guests, those figures of cardboard! Anquetil was not impressed by such things. Yet he owned – he must own – that both were picturesque in their way. The picturesqueness of Chevron pleased him best; he had not much historical sense, but such historical sense as he had, recognised the morsel of English history. But Chevron was dead, he thought; or at all events moribund; or, to say the least of it, static. It was a rock at which waters were nibbling. He was not at all sure that the duchess' guests, for all their fantastic unreality, were not more permanent as a type in the world, outlasting the dignity of Chevron and continuing to exist independently of it; prosperous or ruined, a snobbish society – he sneered – was an inevitable component of the human system. They might carry on in rags; still there would exist always a group affecting elegance and superiority, preserving their jargon establishing their internal freemasonry, excluding the unwanted aspirant, admitting for a brief space and according to the accepted caprice of the moment such outsiders as himself. He had no illusions; so few illusions, that he did not even despise himself for being there. He had wanted to see the cream of English society from the inside; well, he had seen it. He would not want to see it again, and it would afford him but the very slightest amusement to elude their pursuit in future.

Anything but fatuous, he could not help being unpleasantly aware of the interest taken in him by the duchess. At first she had merely given him his turn of flattery; had played the impresario – 'Fancy, Sir Adam, Mr. Anquetil was left behind by his ship for a whole winter in the Arctic Circle, and lived in a snow-hut on nothing but biscuits'; had tried to make him talk; had asked him to tell them how he got the scar on his cheek; then, thinking she had awarded him enough attention, had mercifully passed on to somebody else; but at a given moment, as she strolled down the herbaceous border with him after tea, he had felt that she suddenly ceased to regard him as an exhibit and began to think of him as a man. He had felt it as definitely as though he had heard an audible click. He had been gazing at her in wonderment, fascinated by the incredibly foolish flow of remarks that she was pouring forth, and she had happened to look up at him, catching his eyes fixed upon her. Thereafter, and much to his embarrassment, her manner had changed towards him; subtly she had suggested – oh, not by a word – that some understanding existed between them. Thank goodness, he had been very careful. He had not played up to her in any way. The last thing that he, Leonard Anquetil, wanted was an entanglement with a lady of fashion. He was not the man to play tame cat to any woman. But the incident, if incident it could be called, had suggested various speculations to his surprisingly unsuspicious mind, and he had looked with a fresh eye full of an amused curiosity at his fellow-guests. With fashionable gossip he was utterly unfamiliar, therefore he must observe and deduct for himself if he was to arrive at any discoveries. 'Fast' – he remembered that he had heard this particular set called 'fast.' Outwardly, he must admit, they behaved with perfect correctness. Although they were all upon terms of easy intimacy, and although he imagined that they were in the habit of meeting constantly in each other's houses throughout the year, even the practice of Christian names did not appear to be very general amongst them; the women, naturally called each other by their Christian names, but such was by no means the rule between the men and the women. Indeed, he would have said that a good deal of formality was observed. Yet, once his very fleeting and contemptuous interest had been aroused, he had become conscious of many undercurrents whose significance he was unable to disentangle. Half-smiles and flickers of confederacy; he felt acutely that he was the only outsider in a company of which every member was privy to the origin, developments, and existing state of its complications. He wondered how many *faux pas* he had committed, and hoped he had committed a great many. His fellow-guests, he felt sure, were far too well informed ever to commit one in the whole course of their careers.

Why on earth, he asked himself, returning to actuality, had he accepted the duchess' invitation to stay till after luncheon?

Then he remembered: the children. He liked young people, and furthermore he had been curious to see this household left to itself, when the flock of macaws and magpies had retreated. He began to look forward to lunching alone with the duchess

and the boy and girl. He had been put next to the girl yesterday, and although he had not been able to get many words out
of her, he had been interested by the shy, trapped look in her
eyes. The boy, too – a handsome, angry boy. There was a resemblance between the brother and sister. But that was only youth,
he thought; they would very soon be broken in. The pressure
on them would be too strong. What else could be expected of
them? He lay in his comfortable bed, and allowed the warm
luxurious silence of Chevron to sink into his bones.

The duchess, also lying in bed, was thinking pleasantly of
Leonard Anquetil. It was now some months since she had
begun to tell Harry Tremaine that she was tired of him, and she
was wondering whether Anquetil would make a good substi-
tute. But could she force Anquetil on her acquaintances? Yes,
surely – they might grumble, but she knew she was a power:
they would tolerate any of her whims, even if they jibbed at
first. (That Anquetil himself might decline to conform never
entered her head.) She was glad she had asked him to Chevron.
He was rather a rough diamond; he had led a terrible life, poor
boy, and it must be a nice change for him (after that ice-hut)
to come to a comfortable house and enjoy the society of
civilised people. It was nice to give people a treat. Lucy was
filled with a sudden benevolence. She could make Anquetil
very happy. She would spoil him. She was sure he had never
been to the Opera; or, at least, only in the gallery. She was sure
he had no cuff-links; or only bone ones. True, he did not shine
in conversation, but then, in compensation, he had the kind of
personality that made you conscious all the time of his presence; nor was he good-looking, though he reminded her rather
of one of the pictures upstairs – not at all a modern face; that,

in itself, had a certain distinction; she must ask Sebastian which picture it was, so that she might instance it, if anyone made derogatory remarks. He was very dark, even sallow, with two puffs of frizzy black hair standing out from either temple, bright black eyes, and a sword-cut running from chin to ear. A startling face; pocked, moreover, by little blue freckles, where a charge of gunpowder had exploded, as though an amateur tattooist had gone mad and had made freckles with his needle instead of making an anchor, or a monogram, or crossed cutlasses, whatever it might be. It would increase her reputation for originality if she calmly imposed Anquetil upon the world, her world, as her lover. 'Amant de coeur,' she murmured, stretching her limbs between the linen sheets and forgetting her original impulse of benevolence.

Lucy seldom came down until luncheon, but this morning she wandered into the garden at midday, a lacy parasol slanting between her fair head and the sun. The silence of the house oppressed her, nor had she been able to find Anquetil either in the solar or in the library, and, spoilt, she was already out of temper at not having found him where she had expected to find him. Her heels made little round marks as she sauntered across the turf. Miss Wace watched her from an upper window, with feelings compounded of resentment and adoration. How neat the duchess looks this morning, to be sure, she reflected, in that tailor-made which shows off her figure to such advantage, and which indicates that she is going to London, after the muslins of Sunday; but still she keeps the country touch in her parasol, and has perched no hat as yet on the curves of her coiffure. Miss Wace, who herself affected a dress of heliotrope serge with a stiff petersham belt, and who scraped her hair angrily back from her ears, lived in a constant dilemma between disapproval of Lucy's frivolity, and rapturous fascination before her femininity. She never could grow accustomed to this being who at one moment would goad one into such a paroxysm of indignation as could culminate only in giving one's immediate notice, and who next moment would charm one into such a state of subjection that one would gladly have sat up all night, boiling hot milk against the hour when a tired Lucy would be pleased to go to bed. Some people, thought Miss Wace, working herself up, think that everything is permitted them; for although she found great satisfaction in formulas she had never quite arrived at the formula that everybody imposes their own valuation. It was impossible to take serious exception to anything the duchess said, she thought now, as she watched Lucy twirling her parasol, a coloured butterfly flitting across the grass; impossible to be really offended; but then again she remembered how Lucy had flown at her for something that was really not her fault, and she decided that sooner or later the day must come when she would pack her boxes and go. 'There is such a thing as Self-respect,' was one of her favourite phrases. In her heart of hearts she knew perfectly well that she would cease to exist – would peter out – away from the thrilling and dangerous excitement of Lucy's proximity; and besides, she knew equally well that she would never bring herself to leave a house where the King came so often. 'I am not a snob, my dear,' she was fond of confiding to an intimate friend; 'I pride myself on that, I simply don't know the meaning of snobbishness, I am indeed a Republican and proud of it,' and it was only with a great show of reluctance that she could be induced to describe the latest royal visit. 'Such a terrible lot of extra work it means for me,' she would sigh, and then she would go on to relate how she must look into every detail, even to seeing that the strip of red drugget was properly laid across the court and the Royal Standard ready to be substituted for the ordinary flag on the tower. 'You would think the servants by now were accustomed to this sort of thing – six visits we had, I think, last year – but would you believe it, something is always forgotten.' It was fair to assume, however, that there were compensations for her extra trouble, for upon the left side of her thin and Republican bosom hung a mauve enamel watch from a true lover's knot of mauve enamel ribbon. 'I have to wear it face outwards,' she would explain, 'because of the initials on the back. So silly. Such a pity. It would have been so much nicer plain,' and then she would turn the watch over and display the interlaced E.R. VII, and the crown on the back. 'Of course I don't *like* it,' she would say, 'but it's a good little timekeeper, and so I wear it.' In point of fact everybody knew that it was not a good little time-keeper at all, but gained about an hour a day.

Lucy disappeared round the corner of the house and Miss Wace went severely back to her accounts. Lucy was not look-ing for Anquetil, or at any rate she did not acknowledge to herself that she was; she was merely strolling in the garden. But she found Anquetil where she least expected him – in the summer-house talking to Viola. The summer-house served as an outdoor schoolroom; the walls were scribbled over with sums and childish drawings, the table-edge carved into scollops by an idle penknife. Annoyance surged up in Lucy, which she rapidly attributed to the fact that Viola was looking so plain. According to Lucy's ideas, the child was looking her very worst, for Lucy liked her hair to be frizzed out and tied with a large black bow, also she liked her to wear girlish frocks, fussed over with little ruches and trimmings; but to-day Viola's hair was straight and sleek, and lay like black satin against her forehead, making her small face yet paler and more oval; also she wore a severe red dress, which in Lucy's opinion became her not at all. Her hair was curled yesterday, thought Lucy, and the weather is dry; she must have been putting water on it. Lucy, with her taste for fidgety ornament and the feminine graces of the piquante woman, was incapable of appreciating her daughter's smooth line and glossy delicacy. The child had good eyes, she admitted that; and there was something to be said for her winged eyebrows, that always looked as though they had been brushed over with oil; but why must she be as pale as a saint and do her hair like the Madonna?

Both Anquetil and Viola looked up as the duchess came round the corner, for she threw a shadow between them and the sun. Lucy knew instantly that she was in the way. This small circumstance increased her annoyance beyond all measure; she might have forgiven another woman, say Sylvia Roehampton, for engaging Anquetil's attention so easily and lightly in the summer-house with the dragon-flies darting over the flowers in the sunk garden, for then she could have entered into rivalry with the other woman and they would both have begun to spar with weapons whose use they well understood; but Viola she could not forgive for having crept into Anquetil's confidence, so to speak, by the back door. It was because Viola was a child, of course, that Anquetil had unbent to her, he who had stood so on his guard from Saturday to Monday. Innocence had succeeded where skill had failed. But she pretended to be surprised to see him there, and said, 'Dear me, Mr. Anquetil! Why, I thought you were still sleeping off the effects of your bridge last night. What a lovely morning, isn't it? I so enjoy a little quiet walk before luncheon. I do hope, Viola, you haven't been boring Mr. Anquetil. And what about your lessons, my dear child? Surely you ought to have been doing those? Why, the table is littered with your books. What *will* Miss Watkins say? I must really take you away, Mr. Anquetil, and let Viola go on with her lessons, or the poor child will get into trouble – I always wonder whether Miss Watkins isn't a little *too* strict, but one doesn't like to interfere too often; governesses have their own methods, haven't they? and it's scarcely fair to make them feel one doesn't trust them.'

Anquetil had been waiting for a chance to speak, and now he took it. 'That's quite all right, duchess. I am the culprit. I squared Miss Watkins, on condition that I might tell Viola stories till luncheon. I explained that it would be good for her geography. And it has, hasn't it, Viola? What she doesn't know now about the Orinoco isn't worth knowing. That's the way to learn geography,' he went on, seeing that Lucy was about to speak; 'talk to somebody who's been there instead of learning paragraphs out of a repulsive little primer like this. Or spend an hour with a globe. Now you, duchess, couldn't tell me what places you would pass through if you drew a line round the world on the latitude of Madrid. Try!'

The duchess was amazed; this was a very different Anquetil from the hard, unwilling man she had tried to lionise and whom she had thought she might eventually conquer. He sparkled; he was laughing at her. Viola watched them both, between alarm and fascination. Anquetil's presence gave her an extraordinary support; she knew, somehow, that her mother would not lose her temper before him. Afterwards ... but her mother was going to London after luncheon, and by the end of the week, when she came back, she would have forgotten.

*

Lucy intercepted Sebastian in the library before luncheon. She put on her fondling manner, smoothing back his hair in the way he particularly disliked. Suave though she was, he knew that something had occurred to put her in an ill-humour; he knew, too, that her first remarks were but a preliminary to what she really wanted to say. So he was not surprised when she finally said, 'Oh, by the way, about Mr. Anquetil . . .' Which picture upstairs, she wanted to know, was so like Mr. Anquetil? She had been too lazy to go upstairs and look for it. But Sebastian knew the pictures so much better than she did. He knew so much more about Chevron altogether. Which picture was it? An ugly man, Mr. Anquetil; but not an entirely unin-teresting face – didn't Sebastian agree? – that funny scar, those funny blue freckles, those funny puffs of hair. Not a modern face. He might be hanging among all those historical Tudor portraits in the Brown Gallery, all in the same frames, with their names written on festoons swooping from corner to corner: Drake, Howard, Raleigh – which was it? 'No particular picture,' said Sebastian; 'he's like any Elizabethan sailor.' 'Any Elizabethan pirate,' said Lucy. 'Most Elizabethan sailors were pirates,' said Sebastian. Lucy laughed her most silvery laugh, the laugh that had made several men believe that she under-stood what they said.

Lucy had arranged in her own mind that Anquetil should accompany her to London, but to her intense irritation this plan was thwarted, not by Viola, but by Sebastian, who sur-prisingly proposed that Anquetil should come for a ride with him in the afternoon and take an evening train. Sebastian had never been known to do such a thing before – usually he did nothing but express his impatience that everyone should clear out of Chevron as early as possible – so that his mother's dismay was equalled only by her astonishment. She was now filled by the unpleasant suspicion that she herself was *de trop*, and that Anquetil, no less than her own children, looked forward to the hour of her departure, when they might all three be left alone together. Still, she doted too much upon Sebastian to resent even the consequences of anything he might do; if scapegoat there must be, that scapegoat should be Viola. Should she take Viola to London with her? she wondered; pretending to herself that she would then have the girl handy if she wanted a safety-valve for her ill-humour – for thus far she could be frank with herself – but refusing to acknowledge that her real wish was to prevent any growth of the companionship between Anquetil and Viola. Then she decided that it would be too much of a bore to have Viola in London. She felt uneasy sometimes under the girl's unspoken criticism, and in London, she knew, the house would be full of people at all hours of the day, people at whom the girl would glance once before going out of the room – let them stay together; she washed her hands of Anquetil; fool that she had been, even to have thought of him! She would take Wacey with her instead. Still, she had been baffled; she took the thought away to London with her, as irritating as a stone in the shoe.

They rode, all three of them, with the two dogs, that afternoon, and Anquetil found himself happy and at ease in the society of the two young creatures. More than that: he felt himself exhilarated, as he seldom was, save in the anticipation of some new adventure. He was approaching that age when the contemplation of the very young is in itself a source of wistful happiness; that is to say, he was nearing forty – twenty-two years older than Viola, twenty years older than Sebastian. Necessarily in good condition, thanks to the arduous life he had always led, he was yet aware of a difference between his own austere fitness and their simple animal spirits. If he enjoyed their opening gallop, it was partly because it undid the softness of two full days in London, and could be put down to the credit of his account with bodily health, but for them it was no more than a natural expression of exuberance, as they loosed their horses and tore, racing each other, up the valley, wildly waving their caps and shouting at one another as they raced neck-to-neck up the final lap between the banks of bracken. Side by side they sat their horses waiting for him to come up with them, a great view of fields and distant hills opening behind them, but he slackened his pace into a trot, for he liked to look at them and thought that he should carry away for ever this image of the two sitting so gay and slender in the clearing of the bracken, with the English view behind them and their horses pawing the turf, and Sarah and Henry stretched panting on the ground. They reminded him of a picture by Charles Furse. It seemed to Anquetil that he caught a moment exactly at its passing. Earlier in the morning he had thought of Chevron as a dead thing, an anachronism, an exquisite survival, and his democratic instincts had brought a slightly sardonic smile to his lips; now he modified his conception, and smiled again, but this time he also sighed for the passing of something so characteristic, so intrinsically real, and so gracious. It must go, he thought, go with all its absurd paraphernalia of servants and luxury; but in its going it would carry with it much that was dignified, traditional, and – though he laughed at the word – elegant. His opinions turned over, and he felt suddenly regretful as a man of letters might feel at the debasing of literature, or as a lover of dogs might feel at the coarsening of the greyhound. An anachronism certainly, but many fine things were anachronisms, most indeed; he would like to raise the wall round the park, and keep Chevron with all its inhabitants as a national museum, but then they should never change or grow older, least of all Sebastian and Viola; all should be transformed into a palace of Sleeping Beauty, only they should not be touched as with a sleep of death, but should move immortal about their immemorial activities. For his own part, he felt convinced that he would never see Chevron again; the incident would be isolated in his life; he was too active for England ever to hold him long, and already he had other plans in preparation, but the short incursion into this strangely segregated world had surprisingly enriched him, as one is enriched by any experience one had believed to be entirely outside the scope of one's sympathies, and which unexpectedly acquires a life of its own in a new reach of one's comprehension.

If Anquetil had been surprised at himself for remaining at Chevron till after luncheon, and then still more surprised at his acceptance of Sebastian's invitation to remain until the evening, how much more and finally surprised was he to find himself agreeing to remain until the following morning! But he was now no longer the duchess' guest; he was Sebastian's and Viola's. He was no longer a member of a house-party, an outsider, an onlooker, alternately bored, contemptuous, and amused; he was one of a happy trio, light-hearted in the absence of the grown-ups. He had noticed the change that came over the two children (for as children he regarded them) as soon as their mother had left the house. She had gone in a flurry of cushions, handbags, dust-coats, dozens of little unnecessary things that had to be carried out by hand and stowed away on the back seat of the brougham; the servants had scurried like rabbits; everything seemed to have been forgotten at the last minute; Button and Miss Wace had been harried and chivied, the former remaining commendably imperturbable, the latter getting visibly flustered, for tears came into her eyes, her nose turned red, and she dived for a handkerchief into the pocket concealed in her petticoat; poor Miss Wace looked remarkably plain, with a flat tweed cap on her head and a long dust-coat of brown holland. Over the whole scene of departure hung the probability that the duchess would miss the train. Anquetil reflected that he could have departed for the South Pole with less agitation. Off she had gone at last, alone in the brougham, while Button and Miss Wace followed, jerking and swaying, in the noisy wagonette. 'Back on Saturday!' she had cried to the children through the window; and 'Perhaps I shall find you still here' she had cried to Anquetil, who was not sure whether he ought to regard this as irony or as an invitation. So he had smiled and shaken his head, but the duchess was already engaged in rescuing a slipping parcel and next moment the brougham had carried her beyond the reach of any answer. Anquetil was glad to have witnessed the whole of this little comedy; he liked seeing how other people lived, provided he was not obliged to follow their example. 'Now!' said Sebastian; and Anquetil knew that only his natural good manners prevented him from adding a great deal more.

What charming children they both were, he reflected; natural, unspoilt, and so good to look at. Simple? He would not go so far as to say that, though they were certainly simple in what he called the right way; that is to say, they were easily amused, laughed readily, and enjoyed the pleasures of their physical well-being. Anquetil, who held definite views, did not like young people to be blasé, and blasé these two were not, though they had certainly had enough to make them so. But simple? He came back to that question and thankfully decided that he might reject the word. He had not much use for exaggerated simplicity, except in the men with whom he pursued the adventure of his perilous voyages. These men, however, knew nothing of him beyond his qualities as a cheerful, resourceful, and reliable companion; it was a curious relationship, in which a very special kind of intimacy, begotten of common hardship and necessity, was allied to complete ignorance of one another's private life and character. Anquetil reserved that relationship for those men, of whom he scarcely knew whether he was fond or not. From other people, in the rare intervals of life in England – which he thought of almost as life on dry land – he demanded something different. He would not have wasted his time over Sebastian had he felt that Sebastian could be summed up as a young aristocrat, charming because his breeding made him so, and very little else except the dash of romance which he could scarcely avoid, and which he owed to his birth, his wealth, his youth, and his personal good looks. This dash of obvious romance, indeed, had almost sufficed to prejudice Anquetil against the boy from the start. Even the additional qualities of a good landlord, of a good country gentleman in fact, inherited but respect-worthy, would not have added much to Sebastian's interest in Anquetil's eyes. He would have taken such qualities for granted; and, as it happened, had been given an opportunity of observing them for himself, for after their gallop they had ridden over to several farms and cottages undergoing improvement or repair, where Anquetil had recorded Sebastian's easy manner with his tenants and his evident familiarity with their affairs. So far so good, but it was not enough. On such attributes, Sebastian might be comfortably pigeon-holed with other young men in an equally fortunate position, and dismissed from Anquetil's mind. But, fully expecting to arrive at some such conclusion, he had watched the boy, and still had found his expectation unsatisfied. This colt was not really broken to the bridle; perhaps never would be. Though, to be sure, he might carry his rider tamely for a year or more before bucking him off.

Moreover, Anquetil, who was sensitive in such things, had discerned in Sebastian that day something which he took to be a special wildness. Of course, he knew the boy so little that it was difficult for him to gauge the shade between his usual manner and some extra, suppressed excitement. Nevertheless, he could not rid himself of the idea that the boy had just passed through, or was actually passing through, some definite crisis. He speculated vaguely as to what this crisis might be, only to come in vexation to the conclusion that it could be nothing but a love-affair. As Anquetil arrived at this conclusion, Sebastian dropped by several points in his eyes. Anquetil was not interested in love-affairs. He had had too much experience of their deadly sameness. He could not forgive them for being, at one and the same time, so promising and then so monotonous. They were to him but an expense of spirit in a waste of boredom; and the sooner they were over the better; so he thought. By this time he was disposed to rate Sebastian as a commonplace young man. Poor Sebastian, he thought, condemned by the very circumstance of his situation to be nothing more, ever, than a commonplace young man; as commonplace as a king; for even his rebellions, were he to rebel, must be on ordained lines; there was nothing for him to rebel against, except his own good fortune, and that was a thing he never could evade. His wealth was secure – though Anquetil had but the vaguest ideas about entail – his house was secure, this mellow, majestic Chevron; and as for his great name he must carry it to the grave; all these things were tied on to him like so many tin cans to the tail of a poor cat. With them went the romance of his whole make-up. Poor Sebastian, condemned to be romantic; condemned always to be romantically common-place! What were the wild oats of such a young man? An inevitable crop, sown by his bad godmother at his christening. Not sown even by his own hand, but anticipated on his behalf. Poor Sebastian, his traditions were not only inherited, they were also prophetic. They stretched both ways. It was an unfair handicap.

Anquetil was not changing for dinner; he was merely washing. This state of affairs had been brought about by Sebastian, who, as they returned from their ride, had said, 'Look here – don't let's change – it's such a lovely evening – we'll go out after dinner.' Viola had concurred. Anquetil had realised with amusement that in this suggestion lay a whole implication of daring innovation. He knew quite well that had Sebastian and Viola been dining alone together in their mother's absence they would have changed for dinner in each other's company as scrupulously as in the company of thirty guests. He knew also that in his own alien presence Sebastian found an incitement for such an act of unconventionality. And he was proportion-ately amused. But, unaccustomed to the ways of such houses as Chevron, he had not realised the full daring of Sebastian's innovation until he met the butler in the library and detected the quick glance at his tweed jacket followed by a quick, almost imperceptible, glance at the clock. He gave a tribute of admir-ation to Vigeon's tact. No one, he thought, but a butler reared in such Chevronesque traditions could have conveyed so subtly, so delicately, the suggestion that it was time for him to go and dress. An impulse of explanation rose in him, instantly and mischievously checked. 'His Grace,' he felt impelled to say, 'told me not to change,' but just for the pleasure of disconcerting Vigeon he refrained in time from saying it. He preferred to let Vigeon think that he, Anquetil, the scallywag adventurer that her Grace had been pleased to pick up somewhere, did not know how to behave. At that moment he heard the quick patter of Sarah and Henry on the boards, and Sebastian entered the library, still in his shirt and riding-breeches.

During dinner, Anquetil revised his view of Sebastian, reverting to his second impression. He suspended criticism; he allowed himself to fall under the spell of the boy's charm. Vigeon and his trained myrmidons waited on them, and Anquetil had the pleasure of feeling Vigeon's disapproval pricking at him through every nerve. Vigeon held him responsible; responsible not only for Sebastian's unwonted attire – the outward and visible sign, thought Anquetil, of an inward and spiritual emancipation, for he had already, if almost unconsciously, arranged for himself the place of mentor in Sebastian's spiritual life – but also for Sebastian's unwonted discourse and lack of reserve. Not that Sebastian talked much himself, but that he forced him, Anquetil, to talk. Sebastian lounged there, at the top of the table, in the small dining-room where his ancestors had entertained Drake and Frobisher, Pope and Dryden – as attested by the portraits that hung on the walls; – Sebastian lounged there, in his blue shirt, dallying with a glass of wine, ridiculously handsome and romantic, enticing Anquetil to talk of things he never talked of: his piercing up tropical rivers, his stagnation among ice-floes, until Anquetil (losing his head a little under the influence of wine and historical portraits, and also of Sebastian's personality, lounging there, half callow boy and half patron) expanded as he never expanded either to his intimate friends or to flattering women. He could not explain, satisfactorily to himself, why he thus expanded to Sebastian's drawing out. Was it something atavistic in himself, he wondered, that responded to the potential patron? By Gad, he said, looking at the silent portrait of Frobisher, is it possible that I want Sebastian to finance my next enterprise? His relation to Sebastian became suddenly too complicated for human disentanglement. Was it self-interested, or disinterested? Was it cynical, or impartial? Was it half-mischievous, or wholly benevolent? Did he want to confuse the boy, or to free him, or merely to make use of him? Were his motives pure, or mixed? Were motives not always mixed? Why, anyhow, had he become so preoccupied with Sebastian? Bah, he said to himself, he might be useful to me; and next he said to himself, It would serve his mother right if I coaxed him away from all this; and lastly he said to himself, I like the boy, and if I can save him from wasting himself I will.

Viola contributed very little to the conversation, and only once or twice did Anquetil turn aside to wonder what was going on in her head. He had not noticed Viola much, beyond registering briefly that she was at the slim, swaying age of girlhood, as tremulous as a plant in a stream. It was an age that had its own loveliness, but Anquetil's appreciation was impersonal; his taste in women was for something more sophisticated. Not for women of fashion; no! remembering the duchess. But there were deep, wise women, with whom he could talk; women who knew life; those were the women that Anquetil liked.

It was Sebastian's suggestion that they should go up on to the roof.

He shut Sarah and Henry into the library, and, taking a candle, led the way. Anquetil was moved by this vision of the boy passing, candle in hand, through the shadows and splendours of his inheritance. For the great rooms had lain in darkness till the candle disturbed them; the great rooms of state, that were never used now, but preserved their ancient furnishings, their gildings and velvets, and seemed in the light of the candle to flutter still with a life that had but barely departed from them. Such illumination was far more suggestive than the light of day, by which Anquetil had first seen them. Then, the silver tripods, the portraits, the tapestry, the long, polished floors, had stood out plainly visible, silent and motionless, with no mystery attaching to them – nothing except the very obvious interest of their age, their survival, their state of preservation, and their intrinsic beauty. As dead as a museum, Anquetil had thought, in the resistant mood that then possessed him. He had looked, he had admired, but it had been a dutiful admiration; he had not been touched. Now, he saw the old rooms quiver in the uncertain light thus unexpectedly imported, and learnt that some things gained through being indistinctly seen, things that were too delicate and frail to stand the full truth of day. For not seeing is half-believing. That he should make such an admission was a proof that he had travelled a long way since the morning, when he believed himself to be a matter-of-fact man, concerned only with the hard outlines (as he conceived them) of objects, relationships, and situations. Now, he perceived that aspects might alter, and that actuality was a fiction, dependent solely on the observer, his mood, and his prejudice. The old rooms, in the candlelight, inspired him with a tenderness he would not by daylight have credited. Their beauty, which he had thought to be exterior, became significant; they were quickened by the breath of some existence which they had once enjoyed, when no eye regarded them as a museum, but took them for granted as the natural setting for daily life; and that applied to their furnishings too, to the mirrors into whose dim pools women had stolen many a frank or furtive glance; to the chairs whose now faded velvets had received the weight of limbs regardless of mud on the boots. Nevertheless, Anquetil still strove against them. He would not be deluded into sentimentality about things that were dead, merely because it was possible to convince oneself that they had once been alive. This dead beauty inspired him again almost with horror, as he reacted against his own momentary softening, and the resolution returned to him to save Sebastian if he possibly could. The boy, he thought, is already lying in state in a splendid tomb. We will see if we cannot make the effigy jump up and run.

The gleam of the candle mounted the dark stairs and stirred the shadows of the long low attics. There was no colour up here, neither velvets nor gilding; nothing but plaster and grey oak the colour of ashes. Anquetil preferred this bareness to the sumptuous rooms downstairs; he thought he saw the bones of the house stripped of their flesh; and indeed these silvery galleries recalled the pallor of a skeleton. In certain tombs, he reflected – his mind still running on dissolution – in certain tombs, the skeleton lies exposed beneath the monument, a humble and yet terrible reminder; but here it is otherwise; the house is dying from the top; this uppermost floor is deserted wholly, and all the cheerful bustle has departed from it; it lies stretched in the ashen hues of mortality, immediately below the roof that thinly divides it from the sky. The tiles are no thicker than paper. And he thought that when he had come downstairs again, and was in the living-rooms with their deep curtained windows and comfortable sofas, rooms a degree less dead than the state rooms on the middle floor, he would remember the attics at the top of the house, silent and blanched and empty, the shadow of the lattice faintly chequering the boards, attics, stretched horizontally beneath the roof-line, like an old skeleton that has been laid to rest out of sight and whose presence everyone has conspired to ignore.

It was evident that neither Sebastian nor Viola had any such feelings about their home. This frightened Anquetil, by now strung up to an unusual pitch of sensitiveness: he felt that they *ought* to rebel against the oppression of the past. According to his ideas, they were in no healthy condition if they did not so rebel. He himself was in a state of violent and alarmed resistance; warring emotions tore him; he was determined not to sink under enchantment, but in order to preserve his safety he must keep all his faculties critically on the alert – the only inhabitant of the palace of Sleeping Beauty able to stick pins into his flesh and startle himself from the overtaking sleep. In two days the spell had worked to this extent! and he recollected the mood that had passed over him at dinner, when he glanced up at the portrait of Frobisher, and saw himself in the light of the impecunious adventurer, and Sebastian in the light of the potential patron, whose capricious sympathy might be turned to good account. Such revolution had a bare two days worked in him! Such a spell was the spell of Chevron and the past! But Sebastian and Viola, they had had, respectively, nineteen and seventeen years of it, added to centuries of it in their blood: it was a wonder that they were still alive – awake – at all.

He moved between them, Sebastian with his candle going on ahead, Viola gliding behind. They were the two natural inhabitants of this exquisite sepulchre, moving amongst its shadows as freely as nocturnal visitants amongst gravestones, and Anquetil revolted against their assumption of franchise, their ease, in these (to him) suffocating surroundings, lethal for all their beauty.

Sebastian blew out the candle as they emerged on to the roof. The night-breeze ruffled their hair. The stars were thickly sown overhead in a black sky. Anquetil, as his eyes grew accustomed to the darkness, made out the square crenellation of the battlements and the shapes of the towers rising square across the chasm of the courtyards. It was not possible to see anything very distinctly, but he had the impression of a vast, broken roof-line, and of being at a great height above the lawns and tree-tops of the sleeping garden. He saw that the short ridges of the battlements and the longer ridges of the roofs were outlined in a clarity that could not be called light, yet sufficed to distinguish them from the mass of darkness that suggested, without entirely revealing, the intricacies and bulk of the structure. His resentment against the house again vanished, now that it had become part of the night air which cooled him and which was a thing he could understand. He liked Sebastian better, and with less complication, for having brought them up here. But ardently, ardently he wished Viola away.

They stood upon the leaded flats, but with a gesture Sebastian invited him to climb; he was himself already springing up the pent of the roof like a young feline animal. Anquetil followed. He liked Sebastian for having forgotten the twenty-

odd years of difference in their ages. He liked this roof adventure, with the possibilities involved in a false step. He liked
Sebastian's boyishness, freed from his mother. So up they went,
the two of them, Anquetil not willing to admit that he was less
agile than the boy or less practised in this kind of exercise, for
Sebastian's personality had so inspired him with romantic
notions that he now knew that as a sailor and an adventurer he
would be expected to display an agility acquired amongst the
rigging. Over the roofs he went, scrambling up and sliding
down, under the guidance of one who was intimately
acquainted with the house's intricate geography, until Anquetil
had completely lost his bearings among the chimney-stacks, the
battlements, and the gables, and would have been incapable of
finding his way back had Sebastian elected to disappear and to
leave him up there, waiting for the dawn. Never once did
Sebastian look back to see if his companion still followed him,
but climbed and leapt and ran as one possessed by genius, or as
one that puts another man to the test, mischievous, unmerciful, and mocking. Anquetil was hard put to it to keep up with
him, but he would sooner have broken his neck than cried out.
It was a duel between them; from a mere prank, it had turned
into an affair of honour. Or was it flight and pursuit? – for the
most fanciful ideas now crowded into Anquetil's head, under
the stars – was Sebastian flying from him, conscious of some
conspiracy? was he making an ally of his house, using its jumble
of roofs as a protection against his pursuer? And as though
Anquetil had spoken his thoughts aloud, he cried suddenly over
his shoulder, 'You haven't caught me yet.'

He was invisible in the darkness as he spoke, but next
moment he appeared, sitting astride a long ridge of roof, gaily
waving his hand to Anquetil below. Thus defied, Anquetil

went up, hand over hand, creeping on his knees up the sloping tiles. Cautiously he got astride the ridge and began edging his way along, but Sebastian with a ringing laugh receded from him, enticing him on. Anquetil was now seized with the determination to triumph; he felt that something extremely important depended upon it. But to his horror, Sebastian, seeing himself overtaken, rose to his feet, swayed for one moment against the stars, and fell.

Anquetil caught him, though how he did it he never knew. He caught and held him, hanging above the black pit of the courtyard below. 'Well,' he said, looking down into the boy's upturned face, 'now, at any rate, I have you at my mercy. What if I let you go?' 'I shall crash, that's all,' said Sebastian; 'pull me up. How long are you going to keep me dangling here?' 'That depends,' said Anquetil, settling himself more firmly. He was holding Sebastian by both wrists. 'You have had your fun with me, my young friend; now I think it's my turn. You look very foolish, let me tell you, lying there spread-eagle on the tiles of your ancestral home. Pride has had a fall – very nearly a nasty fall. But you seem quite calm. I see that the patrician can face death with dignity – even a ludicrous death. I congratulate you.'

'Well, you are a queer sort of fellow, to be sure,' said Sebastian.

'Do I seem queer to you? I assure you, you seem equally queer to me. There are several things I have been wanting to say to you. Shall we talk?'

'Like this?' said Sebastian.

'No, not like this,' said Anquetil, and pulled Sebastian up so that they sat facing one another. 'But we will remain here, if you please. After all, consider: the accident of birth has given you a great many advantages over me, it's only fair that I should make the most of the only occasion when I am likely to be in an equal position. Your personal safety is assured, and my personal vanity is satisfied. You shall not be bored. I will entertain you with some remarks about your life and mine.'

'You are a jester, evidently,' said Sebastian, 'but I like your humour. Talk away.'

'I am a man of the people,' said Anquetil. 'My father owned a fishing-smack in a little village in Devonshire. I wanted to go to sea, but they sent me to school instead, and I was sensible enough not to run away. I am, you see, eminently sensible and practical. I worked hard; I had brains; I got a scholarship; I finally went to Oxford. All the time I continued to think about going to sea, but I was patient enough to wait and shrewd enough not to underrate the value of education. When I had done with Oxford I fell in with a man who was taking an expedition to Siberia; he asked me to go with him. We were to look for mammoths. We found fossilised mammoths in the banks of frozen rivers, and by the remains of food still adhering to their teeth we were able to throw some interesting light upon their diet. We were away for a year and a half; and as our researches had met with some success, I have never since lacked employment. You know quite enough about my various undertakings for me to spare you any account of them now. I only wanted to emphasise the difference between our lives.'

'Wait,' said Sebastian. 'I am at Oxford now. I am where you were twenty-odd years ago. How do you know what my life will be after I have left?'

Anquetil laughed. 'My dear boy, your life was mapped out for you from the moment you were born. You went to a preparatory school; you went to Eton; you are now at Oxford; you will go into the Guards; you will have various love-affairs, mostly with fashionable married women; you will frequent wealthy and fashionable houses; you will attend Court functions; you will wear a white-and-scarlet uniform – and look very handsome in it, too – you will be flattered and persecuted by every mother in London; you will eventually become engaged to a suitable young lady; you will marry her in the chapel here and the local bishop will officiate; you will beget an heir and several other children, who ought to have been painted by Hoppner; you will then acquire the habit of being unfaithful to your wife and she to you; you will both know it and both, out of sheer good manners and the force of civilisation, will tacitly agree to ignore your mutual infidelities; you will sometimes make a speech in the House of Lords; you will be given the Garter; you will send your sons to a preparatory school, Eton, Oxford, and into the Guards; after dinner you will talk about socialism and the growth of democracy; you will be worried but not seriously disturbed; on the twelfth of August you will go north to shoot grouse, on the first of September you will return south to shoot partridges, on the first of October you will shoot pheasants; your photograph will appear in the illustrated papers, propped on a shooting-stick with two dogs and a loader; you will celebrate your golden wedding; you will carry a spur or a helmet at the next coronation; you will begin to wonder if your son (aged fifty-one) wants you to die; you will oblige him by dying at last, and your coffin will be borne to the family vault on a farm cart accompanied by a procession of your employees and your tenants. And during all those years, you will never escape from Chevron.'

'But I don't want to escape from Chevron,' said Sebastian.

'No,' said Anquetil, shifting his position a little, 'you don't want to escape from Chevron. You think that you love it, that you give it glad and happy service, but you are really its victim. A place like Chevron is really a despot of the most sinister sort: it disguises its tyranny under the mask of love. Would you like to know what a man like me thinks of a place like Chevron? It fascinates, horrifies, and shocks me. Remember, I come from a cottage myself, and have been accustomed to see families living overcrowded and poor, for so long as I can remember. But it is not the contrast which shocks me. It is not the fact that you employ fifty servants and can choose your room amongst three or four hundred rooms, when parents and children elsewhere are sleeping together in a bed. No. It is the effect on you yourself. You are not allowed to be a free agent. Your life has been ordained for you from the beginning. I will give you the benefit of the doubt. I will agree that probably you will do your duty according to your lights, you will befriend your tenants, rule justly over your servants, take the chair at meetings, earn the respect of your equals – all this when once you have ceased to be a wild young man – but you will be dead, you will be a stuffed image.'

'You are very eloquent,' said Sebastian, 'and your sarcasm makes me uneasy, but are you right? Surely one might lead a worse life.'

'Then,' pursued Anquetil, taking no notice, 'there is another danger which you can scarcely hope to escape. It is the weight of the past. Not only will you esteem material objects because they are old – I am not superficial enough to reproach you for so harmless a weakness – but, more banefully, you will venerate ideas and institutions because they have remained for a long time in force; for so long a time as to appear to you absolute and unalterable. That is real atrophy of the soul. You inherit your code ready-made. That waxwork figure labelled Gentleman will be forever mopping and mowing at you. Thus you would never forget your manners, but you would break a heart, and think yourself rather a fine fellow for doing it. You would not defraud others; but you will defraud yourself; you will never take your conventions and smash them to bits. You will never tell lies – avoidable lies – but you will always be afraid of the truth. You will never wonder why you pursue a certain course of behaviour; you will pursue it because it is the thing to do. And the past is to blame for all this; inheritance, tradition, upbringing; your nurse, your father, your tutor, your public school, Chevron, your ancestors, all the gamut. You are condemned, my poor Sebastian; you are beyond rescue. Even should you try to break loose, it will be in vain. Your wildest excesses will be fitted into some pigeon-hole. That convenient phrase, "wild oats," will cover you from twenty to thirty. That convenient word, "eccentric," will cover you from thirty until death. "An eccentric nobleman." That's the best you may hope for. But though you may wobble in your orbit, you can never escape from it.'

'Nor can the planets,' said Sebastian, looking up at Jupiter.

'Another misleading analogy,' said Anquetil, also looking at Jupiter; 'the firmament has magnitude and possibly organisation in its favour, but mankind, though puny, has independence and an undeniable boldness. I like mankind. I prefer a small, bold astronomer to a big, decorous star. But we are getting away from you and Chevron and your common past; further away than you will ever get. You will never jump as far as a planet; never even further than the limits of your own park. You are fenced in – fenced in with oak planks cut from trees several centuries old.'

'Another misleading analogy,' said Sebastian; 'you are simply losing yourself in a lot of words.'

'Ah, but remember,' said Anquetil, 'I have had my head turned. Not only am I keeping you here in this very peculiar situation, but I have been invited by your mother into surroundings well calculated to make me lose my head. Consider my past. I come from the humblest of homes; I depended for my supper upon the catch of a few miserable herrings; I often did not know whether my father was drowned or still alive; my wits were my only fortune; when I go home from time to time to-day, I have to readjust my ideas, even my speech, until I scarcely know who I am or where I belong. But my week-end at Chevron has shown me one thing: I don't belong here. I don't mind admitting to you that these two days have disturbed me more than I should have thought possible. I have perceived a certain beauty where I expected to find nothing but farce. There have been moments, even, when I was bewildered and recreant, and was inclined to go back upon all my fiercest convictions. Your Chevron soothed and charmed me. You, yourself, were a thing new to my experience. You, and your Chevron, were different from your mother and your mother's world; you had a different quality. I try to be open-minded, you see; I recognise the small particular quality that is your speciality. It breathes from you like an aroma. I don't suppose that it is peculiar to you personally. I daresay I should recognise it in many young men of your class. You don't like to hear me say that,' said Anquetil; 'it embarrasses you, you think me class-conscious. It is one of your taboos, never to mention class; I am offending against good manners. I don't care. This is my hour and I am making the most of it; and as for you, you must endure hearing the truth for once in your life. Besides, I am not insulting you. I am saying that I perceive the charm of a young man like yourself, master of a great estate, easy, full of grace, with centuries of easy, graceful ancestors behind him. You affect me very strongly – I, who thought myself beyond being affected by such things – so strongly that at dinner for an instant I imagined myself and you in the roles which your personality (oh, quite unconsciously!) was creating for us both. I saw you as the patron and myself as the parasite. You, of course, are quite unaware of the effect you produce; you are quite unaware of your own easy assumptions; that is part of the charm, but it is also your danger. Lofty young man that you are, splendid and insolent, no uneasiness has ever crept like a louse between your shirt and your skin. Remember always, to my credit, that I did my best to put it there.'

'Well, but what do you want me to do about it?' said Sebastian at last.

Anquetil considered him. To Sebastian's eyes, accustomed by now to the darkness, he looked almost diabolic, with the two tufts of the fuzzy black hair sticking out on either side of his face, and the scar running from his mouth to his ear. He knew, however, that he liked Anquetil better than anyone he had ever met in his life. 'What do you want me to do about it?' he repeated.

'Come away with me,' said Anquetil. 'I am sailing next week, and I may not return to England for two years or more. Come away with us and forget who you are, forget Chevron, forget your carpenters and your blacksmiths, forget society, forget your safety, forget the whole paraphernalia. Learn another point of view. This is your opportunity. Look, you're hanging over a big drop. Down there, you die; but up here, beside me, you breathe and live. Which is it to be?'

'Do you mean that you will push me over if I refuse?' asked Sebastian. He was not frightened, but interested; he thought that Anquetil, in his exalted state of mind, was capable of anything.

'Oh, no,' said Anquetil contemptuously, 'I shan't push you over. I wouldn't commit a murder for the sake of an allegory. But, metaphorically, you will fall if you refuse. I shall look down, and I shall see a little black speck twirling, twirling down until it disappears into greater blackness, and that will be the free spirit of Sebastian gone for ever. An empty husk of a body will then politely lead me back across the maze of roofs.'

'And you'll despise me.'

Anquetil did not answer.

'I can't do it,' said Sebastian desperately, after a long pause. 'Why didn't you say all this yesterday? Then, I might have listened to you; to-day, I can't. You simply torture me, and all for nothing. It's too late.'

'Ah?' said Anquetil. 'Then I was right. Something has happened to you; I have known it all day. I suppose you imagine that you have fallen in love.'

'I *have* fallen in love,' said Sebastian sulkily.

Anquetil laughed. 'What an anti-climax! My poor boy, you evidently have a genius for the commonplace. I see I was mistaken in you. Forget all that I have said.' They sat there, hostile, absurd, facing one another. 'I am indeed unfortunate,' said Anquetil, 'to have come upon the scene twenty-four hours too late. For since you tell me that yesterday you might have listened, I can only imagine that this cataclysm overtook you late last night. What happened? Did some fair lady appear in your bedroom? Was it ...'

'Shut up!' cried Sebastian, 'I won't stand this.'

'Of course you won't,' said Anquetil, 'I forgot you were a gentleman. I apologise; you see, I'm only a common man, and

I rather resent having given myself away to you as I have been doing for the past hour. But you see that one of my prophecies about you has already come true; I told you that you would have a series of love affairs with fashionable married women. You are already at the beginning of one, it seems; perhaps the first? I hope you will enjoy it. I hope it will be a long time before you discover the ghastly sameness which attends all such adventures. I hope ...'

'Shall we go down now?' said Sebastian in a voice of ice.

'By all means,' said Anquetil instantly; 'let us go down.'

III

SYLVIA

Anquetil left England and was heard of no more, but he left it unaccompanied by Sebastian. His image very quickly faded in Lucy's memory, whether as a cause for annoyance or for regret. On the other hand, she began to notice a change in her son, and upon her asking him fondly one day what had come over him, he replied that she might attribute anything she chose to Leonard Anquetil. Lucy was surprised by this, and unconvinced, since she would have expected Anquetil's influence over Sebastian, if any, to work in quite a different direction. She wished that Sebastian were not always so uncommunicative. She, who revelled in confidences, could never indulge the taste with her son, probably the only creature in the world of whom she stood in any awe, for he was not a person of whom one could ask many questions, and indeed she knew very well that she would be wasting her breath in asking questions which from the outset he did not intend to answer. Moreover he was daily growing more forbidding and more masterful, and arranged his life as it pleased him without seeking advice or encouraging interference. Lucy sighed, but her distress was greatly modified by the fact that he was developing in exactly the way she most desired. According to her ideas, he was growing up into an exemplary son, and conducted himself precisely in the way that his mother considered suitable for a young man of his position. He made friends with all the right young men, he brought them home to Chevron, where they became acquainted with Viola; he went to balls in London and danced with all the right débutantes, he flirted with all the right young married women; he organised parties on his own behalf, both at Chevron and elsewhere – was it not he who chartered a liner and spent a turbulent week-end with forty friends, steaming up and down the river from London to Gravesend, and from Gravesend to London, while the strains of his orchestra floated out to the astonished crowds upon the banks? – he bought the fastest motor on the market and drove it himself, he squandered money, he was picturesque, extravagant, wild. Yet withal he was wary, and showed no disposition to marry, though every mother in London did her best to trap him. Finally he appeared one day at Chevron, announced that he had been sent down from Oxford, had no intention of returning there, and proposed to enter the Household Cavalry as soon as possible.

Privately, Lucy thought that Leonard Anquetil was less responsible than Sylvia Roehampton. She could not imagine Anquetil – 'that rude man, my dear' – as encouraging Sebastian to his present career of dissipation. Sebastian's liaison with Lady Roehampton was, of course, notorious. She was seen everywhere with him, and though some people said it was a pity, Lucy did not altogether agree; Sylvia would teach the boy a lot, and meanwhile she kept him from less desirable entanglements; also, thanks to Sylvia's medium, it was often possible for Lucy to trickle into Sebastian's ear suggestions which could certainly not have been made by any more direct method. Sylvia, superb and triumphant, was commendably amenable, even if she occasionally annoyed Lucy by her air of superior privity. (Lucy's passion for her son, probably the most estimable thing about her, inevitably carried with it a certain degree of jealousy.) Many and long were the conferences that Lucy held with Sylvia, for Sylvia, even if not contributing much beyond an 'Ah!' or a 'Quite,' was content to let Lucy talk while she herself reclined on a sofa, stitching at an end-less piece of needlework which well displayed the grace of her little, white, exquisite hands. They were tiny hands, that col-lapsed, boneless as a kitten, when one grasped them. Lucy, who had scarcely noticed these hands before, now often looked at them and thought with a curious complicated pang how much Sebastian must love them. She, who was as a rule unappre-ciative of women apart from their clothes, learnt to appraise Sylvia very closely in those days. She looked at the other woman with all her own feminine experience coming to her aid. Sylvia, the beautiful Sylvia, she had always thought, had always been something of an overblown rose, loose, generous, lovely; now she recognised an additional luxuriance, as though the rose were putting forth all its lavishness before the petals fluttered finally to the ground. There was a bloom on her cheeks, a light in her eyes, a softness on her mouth, which even Lucy must attribute to some influence working from within. Then, immediately, she began to wonder. Was Sylvia really in love with Sebastian? or was it only a final blossoming of her vanity? Impossible to answer! and, needless to say, no allusion was ever made between the friends as to Sebastian and Sylvia's real relationship. 'How kind you are to that boy of mine,' Lucy would say, playing the grateful mother; 'so good of you, Sylvia dear, to be bothered with a boy who might be your son – and so raw and uncontrolled, too; so uncivilised. I never know what he will do next. There seems to be no sense in him. I wonder that George doesn't get annoyed, to see him perpetually storming into the house. Send him back to me, if he becomes a nuisance.'

But she was amused, not dismayed. For a young man to start his career with a love affair with an older woman was quite *de rigueur*, and in choosing Sylvia, Sebastian had certainly given proof of his fastidiousness. Lucy respected the instinct that went straight for the best. It did not distress her in the least that they should exhibit themselves together as they did, for she considered it quite cynically: Sebastian *affiché* with the most beautiful woman in London, Sylvia *affichée* with the most dashing and eligible young man. Such aesthetic sense as she possessed was gratified by such an association. Of course, it must not go on for too long. An apprenticeship was a very different thing from a career. Meanwhile she was quite content that Sebastian should become tanned in the rays of Sylvia's Indian summer.

About Sylvia, her dear friend, she did not trouble her head at all. Sylvia had had enough experience, and could look after herself. Still, she wondered. Was Sylvia merely amusing herself with the boy, or was she really in love with him? Anyhow, however much in love she might be, Sylvia could be trusted to see that no unpleasantness resulted. Supposing that George, for instance, suddenly unsealed the eyelids that had been so conveniently stuck together for all these years, and put his foot down as he most certainly would? What would Sylvia do then? Lucy's knowledge of her friend and of her world gave the instant answer: prevent a scandal. The code was rigid. Within the closed circle of their own set, anybody might do as they pleased, but no scandal must leak out to the uninitiated. Appearances must be respected, though morals might be neglected. Sylvia knew and had always obeyed this unwritten law. Lucy had no cause to be uneasy, though she might perhaps have felt a tremor had she known how very passionately Sylvia had fallen in love with Sebastian.

The way in which Lucy had originally discovered her son's infatuation perhaps deserves remark and record.

Houses such as Chevron enjoy not only their traditions but their minor habits. Raisins and almonds appear during Advent, when the last bunches of white grapes shrivel yellow like the skin of an old woman and are no longer decorative though still palatable; raisins and almonds, with oranges and bananas, are typical of the winter season when the home produce, but for the humble apple, gives out; yet there are certain imported fruits which persist irrespective of season throughout the year. Such a foreigner is the French Plum. Black, glossy, he remains a plum so long as he is offered in a bottle labelled J. & C. Clark, Bordeaux – his most expensive and luxurious form; in more modest households he is bought by the pound from the grocer, is stewed, served with custard, and becomes a Prune, even as a sheep becomes mutton once it is dead, or the deceased relict of a baronet, in the column headed Latest Wills, becomes Dame. The distinction between French plums and stewed prunes is thus not to be overlooked by those sensitive to these nice shades. French plums, then, were a constant adjunct to the Chevron dinner-table, though stewed prunes never. French plums appeared regularly, in their squat tubby little bottle labelled J. & C. Clark, Bordeaux, and Viola, who detested them, had from her childhood upwards been enjoined to eat them – 'So good for you, darling; another one, just to please mother' – but by the usual irony of life, Sebastian, whose complexion mattered less, had always consumed them in large quantities of his own accord. He had, indeed, been known to finish off a bottle at a single sitting, and to tell the chaplet, Tinker, Tailor, Soldier, Sailor, Gentleman, Apothecary, Ploughboy, Thief, several times over in the garland of stones arranged round the edge of his plate. What more natural, therefore, than that his mother should notice that he now never ate more than four? or, if pressed, was consistent in bringing the tally up to nine? She tested him more than once, dining alone with him and Viola at Chevron: always four stones, or nine. 'This year, next year, now, or never?' she twitted him; that fitted the four, but not the nine. Then it dawned on her: *Elle m'aime, un peu, beaucoup, passionnément* – and she saw the arithmetic which would bring it to *pas du tout*. Then, being committed to numbers, how could she fail to put two and two together? Sebastian's secret was hers.

It was also the property of the Chevron servants. Correct, distant, reserved, it was not to be supposed that they were without eyes in their heads, and it may also be imagined that they had their views upon the subject. This strange behind-the-scenes domestic world, indeed – so sharply segregated, yet so intimately concerned – had been thrown into a muddled state of mind upon observing the new complication in the affairs of their master. The upper servants, who regarded themselves as the discreet guardians of the house and family, suffered most from this confusion of their feelings, for they brought to the consideration of the matter two entire but conflicting systems of opinion, the one learnt in youth in a home decently regardful of the moral virtues, the other acquired through years of experience in an atmosphere where self-indulgence was the natural law. What was their own existence but one long pandering to this self-indulgence? Printed cards, with a list and time-table of duties, hung in all the under-servants' bedrooms. Wood must be cut and carried, hot-water bottles put into beds, inkstands filled, breakfast trays prepared, blinds raised or lowered; housemaids must vanish silently if surprised at their tasks, hall-boys must not be allowed to whistle, Vigeon must wear London clothes in the country, no noise must be made anywhere lest her Grace should hear it and be annoyed – all this long creed was handed on and taken absolutely for granted in its observance. In a word, life for the great and wealthy must be made as pleasant as possible. Their pleasures came under the same heading; traditionally, the lords of Chevron had kept their mistresses for so many hundreds of years, that the charming cohort of the shades of these ladies peopled the corridors and insinuated their suggestions into ears well attuned to listen. If the fifth duke had made a scandal in the reign of Queen Anne, why shouldn't his Grace make one now, if he was so minded? Thus thought Mrs. Wickenden stoutly; and tried to crush the small voice which said that this was not precisely the lesson she had learnt at her mother's knee. Her mother had implied that married ladies cast down their eyes when in the presence of gentlemen other than their husbands, and that young gentlemen reserved their attentions for the young ladies they desired to marry; and although a lifetime of experience had taught Mrs. Wickenden that very different principles obtained in the society which she had the privilege to serve, her early training was still sufficiently vivid to cause her an occasional sigh. Lady Roehampton was a great beauty, of course, and one knew what young men were – said Mrs. Wickenden, who had never come within three yards of a young man in her life; still, one couldn't help wishing that his Grace's fancy had lighted on a nice young lady, so they might look forward to a wedding in the chapel and eventually – though Mrs. Wickenden was far too much refined to say so – to a nursery once more at Chevron.

Somewhat to this effect did Mrs. Wickenden disburden herself to her sister-in-law, the wife of Wickenden the carpenter, who had come in to tea. She had once been stillroom-maid at Chevron, and was now Mrs. Wickenden's only friend and confidante. Together the two elderly women could stir their tea and discuss the affairs of Chevron up and down, inside and out. For Mrs. Wickenden could make no friends within the house. The housemaids – even the head housemaid – were beneath her; the cook was a *chef*, and, anyway, the 'kitchen people' were as separate as the Bandar-log; between herself and Miss Wace an avowed though inconvenient hostility existed, too complicated in its origins and ramifications to be detailed here; Button she considered pert and untrustworthy; Mrs. Vigeon and she were at daggers drawn; visiting maids, even Miss Hull, her crony, were ineligible for intimate confidences, since they formed no part of Chevron and Mrs. Wickenden's sense of the closed circle was at least as strong as Lucy's own; her sister-in-law, however, provided the ideal partner. Although not now of the house, she had once been of it, and had its workings at her finger-tips; moreover, she was allied through marriage and followed every event, large and small, with a faithful and passionate interest; finally, her discretion in the outside world was assured. She just allowed it to be known that no secret of Chevron was hid from her; but she never went further than that. Mrs. Wickenden, in consequence, said things to her which she scarcely allowed herself to think in the privacy of her own bedroom.

It was very pleasant, having tea in the housekeeper's room. It was a good tea – scones, plum-cake, Madeira cake, and several sorts of jam – all brought in and suitably disposed by a well-trained housemaid of the meaner sort. (Mrs. Wickenden was far more haughty and particular with the housemaid detailed to wait upon her than Lucy ever dared to be with Mrs. Wickenden.) Martha Wickenden much enjoyed the weekly teas to which she was invited by her glorious sister-in-law; not only did she relish the plum-cake, but she liked to feel herself associated with the lordly way in which the housekeeper rang the bell, said 'Bring some more coals,' rang it again for more hot water, and rang it finally that the curtains might be drawn. She liked to loll on the sofa and gaze at the photographs standing in their frames: Lucy in her wedding-dress; the late duke in the robes of the Garter; a Royal group with the King in the middle, wearing a Homburg hat, Lucy sitting beside him; Sebastian as a little boy; Sebastian and Viola as children, laughing on a toboggan in the snow; Sebastian, to-day, in uniform. The housekeeper never lolled. She sat prim and upright, jerking her shawl round her shoulders, for she was always chilly – a characteristic gesture, which interrupted the constant darting and stabbing of her crochet hook as inches of crochet lace dangled and lengthened with incredible rapidity. Sometimes she would have 'one of my headaches' – for thus did she always refer to them, prefaced by the possessive and almost affectionate pronoun – and then the darting of the hook would be suspended as she rubbed her forehead with a stump of menthol that lived in her work-basket, screwed into a tube of yellow wood. Mrs. Wickenden never allowed these distractions to interfere with her conversation. In a low, even, and mournful voice she rambled on, as one whose function is always to deplore. Listening to her, you would have thought that the very beauty of Chevron was tinged with a mortal melancholy, and that Sebastian and Viola were tragically doomed from birth. Sebastian was her darling. Viola she of course spoke of with fitting respect, but with slight reservation; for secretly she thought Viola haughty. But Sebastian! How often had she not crept into his nursery, despite the black looks of his nurse, whenever a cold had kept him in bed, and had amused him by the hour, making dolls for him out of wishbones, with sealing-wax heads and grey flannel cloaks. She had always been convinced that he would never reach manhood, and even now she maintained that he was not long for this world. Many a time had the carpenter's wife, who was of a more robust temperament (and moreover, was enjoying her tea), entered a word of protest, 'I'm sure, Jane, I never saw a better set-up young gentleman than his Grace,' but Jane would have none of it. 'You may think so, Martha,' she would reply, 'but you haven't heard him cough in his nursery as I have, winter after winter – oh, dear, something pitiful; and what with the draughts that come down these passages, and the cold striking up from these stone floors – there, they didn't think of those things in the old days; and now with this rackety life,' she added darkly, and Martha pursed her lips and nodded her head as she stirred her tea, for she knew what the allusion was to. It was the prelude to the most succulent moment of the whole afternoon. It meant that Jane, with many windy sighs, was about to embark on the topic of his Grace's infatuation.

Lady Roehampton was not a young woman; but she was still, though not without taking a certain amount of trouble, beautiful. This question of the middle-aged woman's beauty and desirability has never sufficiently been exploited by novelists. It is one of the minor dramas of life; yet who are we to call it minor, when to the women concerned it involves the whole purpose of their existence? Lady Roehampton, for instance, certainly thought she knew no other means of self-expression and believed that she desired none, though, as we shall presently see, she was to discover a human weakness within herself, which clashed uncomfortably with her scheme – but as for that, we must leave the story to take care of itself. In the meantime, we are concerned only with the Lady Roehampton who since the age of eighteen had been a professional beauty, wooed by some men thanks to sincere passion and by others thanks to sincere snobbishness, most suggestible of human frailties; the Lady Roehampton who had been mobbed in Rotten Row, and who by dint of sheer satiety had grown languid towards the compliments that had drenched her for so long that she took them as naturally as the rising and setting of the sun. Now she was arrived at middle age; and the compliments, though they still came automatically forth, had slightly changed their note; women said – ingenious women – 'No one would believe that your Margaret was eighteen'; and men said – ingenuous men – 'None of our young beauties can hold a candle to you'; and even as she absent-mindedly smiled, she winced. She neither relished nor appreciated this new note of wonderment which had crept into their expressions of admiration. It was one thing to be admired because one was so lovely, and quite another thing to be admired because one was still so lovely. She did not belong to the sort of woman who, half-way through her life, can change her manner and inaugurate a new existence; she possessed an art of her own, but that particular art was beyond her. Had she died at thirty, people would have exclaimed at the tragedy: they would have been better advised to exclaim at the tragedy of her living on to forty-two, the age when she caught her own fingers so badly in the trap she had set for Sebastian.

It was the last flare-up of her passing youth, compounded of sweet delirium and wild terrors. There were moments during that London season of nineteen hundred and six when she was either happier or more miserable than she had ever been in her life. Her relations with Sebastian would seem to have reached the crest of their perfection, until, as climbing in hilly country, yet another crest appeared and another, and still no limit came in sight. And everything that most delighted her was given to her now at the same time: the pageant of the Season, the full exciting existence in London, the crowds, the colour, the hot streets by day, the cool balconies at night, the flowers filling the rooms and the flower-girls with baskets at the street corners, the endless parties with people streaming in and out of doors and up and down stairs; the display, the luxury, the wealth, the elegance that flattered and satisfied her – and to crown all this, the knowledge that everywhere she would meet Sebastian, and that he would be at her side, vigilant, proprietary, perfectly decorous of course, but occasionally looking into her eyes with a long glance charged with the full message of their intimacy. She wanted nothing more. Intellectually, her head was as empty as it was beautiful. To Sylvia, as to most of her acquaintance, the life of pleasure was all in all; neither books, art, nor music meant anything to her except in so far as their topicality formed part of the social equipment. Sometimes she went to a picture-show, and frequently she was to be seen in her box at the Opera; but she gave to the pictures and to the music just about as much attention as she gave to the horses at Ascot. Books she never read at all, and indeed among her friends they were seldom discussed. A biography might possibly come up for argument, especially if it referred to someone they had known; but it was easy enough to pick up a little information from hearing other people talk; and then to say either that, in one's own opinion, Winston had rather overrated Lord Randolph, or else that Lady F. was really too much of a scandal-monger, and that her memoirs ought to be suppressed. One might, without too much effort, read the latest novel by H. G. Wells. But gossip, thank goodness, needed no brains beyond a certain shrewdness in human affairs. The gossip moreover was always of the most delectable kind, for not only did it concern people one knew intimately, but one enjoyed the additional savour of belonging to the very small band of the initiated. The freemasonry of Sylvia's particular set, as Lucy had rightly remembered for her reassurance, was jealously guarded. Thus to all appearances the Templecombes were the best of friends, but everybody within the set knew that Lord Templecombe had once found Harry Tremaine in Lady Templecombe's bedroom, and had not spoken to her except in public for twenty years. That had been a terrible affair, and was still remembered as the worst scandal of the 'eighties. Lord Templecombe had completely lost his head, and had behaved in an unheard-of way: he had threatened divorce, and it was said that he would have carried out his threat but for the personal intervention of the Prince of Wales. The great ladies of the day, in a panic – notably Lady L. and the Duchess of D., who between them ruled as dictators over society – had thrown in their weight also; they had severally sent for Templecombe, and in their darkened drawing-rooms had told him that, whatever his private sentiments might be, he could not sacrifice his class to such an exposure. '*Noblesse oblige*, my dear Eadred,' they had said; 'people like us do not exhibit their feelings; they do not divorce. Only the vulgar divorce.' They had expressed their sympathy with him; they were very sorry for him, but they had a duty to perform, and so had he. He bowed to them; he performed it. The Templecombes remained together, and no one in the outside world was any the wiser; what their private life, was, nobody troubled to enquire, so long as Lady L. and the Duchess of D. were satisfied. Standards had slackened a little since those severe days, but still the code prevailed; there was only one Commandment which mattered, and that was the eleventh. Similarly, everybody knew that when a discreet, one-horse brougham waited outside a certain door, one must not ring the bell, for the lady was otherwise engaged. Being satisfied with such things, as Sylvia was amply satisfied, it was very delightful to move daily among people as conversant as oneself.

An uncomfortable idea was put into her head: what did Sebastian think of it all? Julia Levison put the idea there, for besides being one of Sylvia's dearest friends she was also well known as owning the sharpest claws in London. Sylvia was disturbed, although she did not betray it. What *did* Sebastian think? Hitherto the question had not existed for her. 'Is it possible,' she thought, 'that I don't know what he is really like?' and Sebastian, with his charm, and his *chic*, and his extravagance, was suddenly presented to her as wholly inscrutable. She remembered that intent way he had of look-ing at her; she had always attributed to it the meaning she desired to find; but now she wondered. What was he turning over in his mind? treacherous things, inimical things? She remembered small encounters with him, in which she had come up against a blank obstinacy that defeated all her wiles; and according to Sylvia's creed a young man who resisted his mistress' wishes was an intractable young man indeed. When he said quietly that he was going to Chevron for a few days, for instance, she knew by experience that the battle was lost in advance; if he said he intended to go, he went. Sylvia had to accept it. Remembering this, she took some comfort in her perspicacity at having guessed his passion for Chevron. 'So I can't be such a fool,' she thought with the pathos of an unwonted humility, 'after all.' But her pride sagged again as she recognised that she never could get him to talk about Chevron. And if he withheld that from her, what else might he not withhold?

Then she dismissed her anxieties, for they were of a sort not normally within her province, and had been only artificially created by Mrs. Levison; Sylvia's conceptions of people were of a cruder and shallower nature than that. Still, she had been made to think; an unusual occupation for her; she had been made to notice. Henceforth, when they had lovers' quarrels, easily and deliciously though they might be mended, there was some element in those quarrels sharp enough to keep her on the alert, increasing his attraction for her and adding a per-sonal peril to the uncertainty of those rash days. Dissatisfied and dangerous by temperament, as she now acknowledged him to be, even in his most devoted moments, she knew that she held him not on a rope but on a length of cotton, a knowledge which stimulated even as it terrified her. Ah, that is the way to live, she exclaimed, and she soared to a height of excitement where she felt that she must shout and sing; then, falling down into the depths, she remembered that any day might take Sebastian from her, as any year might rob the beauty from her face.

Only one fly stuck embedded in her ointment, and that was the slight shade of disapproval with which she was regarded by the really exclusive hostesses. Of course she affected to sneer at these great ladies, saying that the calendars on their writing-tables had never been changed since eighteen-eighty; but all the same she was piqued. The Duchess of D. and Lady L. could not altogether ignore Lady Roehampton – if only for poor George Roehampton's sake – but they could limit their invitations to their larger parties, and could refrain from inviting her to those more intimate parties, where only twenty guests instead of a thousand were convened, and which were the little paradise of all those to whom the crown of worldly impeccability shone as the supreme jewel. Admission to them entailed certain definite qualifications. Birth – that goes without saying. Dignity – by dignity they meant virtue. Reserve – by reserve they meant a becoming abstention from publicity. Lady Roehampton fulfilled only the first of these requirements. As for virtue, it was true that she had kept strictly within the limits, and had never allowed herself to be compromised beyond a few rumours that had not as yet overleaped the palisade of a permissible intimacy; but, on the other hand, she was associated with a set that only loyalty to the Throne placed out of the reach of open criticism, so that the indignation of these dictators sought relief in criticism of a more personal nature: Sylvia Roehampton powders her face, they said; Sylvia Roehampton has been seen, undoubtedly rouged; Sylvia Roehampton was once seen driving in a hansom alone with Tommy Brand, that jaunty libertine; Sylvia Roehampton is not a person on whom our sanction can wholeheartedly be bestowed. Then as to reserve – Sylvia's qualifications fell pitiably short. It was not, of course, the poor woman's fault that she should be acclaimed as a professional beauty; not her fault that people should stand up to look at her when she entered a box at Covent Garden; but it *was* her fault that she should lend herself to such vulgar exhibitions as the imper-sonation of Queen Etheldreda in a pageant at Earl's Court. Such a thing had never been heard of before, and, so far as Lady L. and the Duchess of D. were concerned, it sealed her doom. Lady L. and the Duchess of D. decided that she must be mad. They had always mistrusted her, and now had an unan-swerable pretext for an avowed disapproval. Secretly, these austere tyrants seized with delight upon so estimable an excuse for censuring a member of the set they deprecated. It was easy enough for them to ignore people like Mrs. Levison, whom they dismissed as an adventuress, or Sir Adam, whom they dis-missed as a Jew. It was difficult, even for them, to ostracise somebody like Lucy, intense as their disapprobation might be; it had been difficult enough for them to mark the slight dif-ference in their cordiality towards Sylvia, with nothing but the tenuous film of Sylvia's face-powder floating between them and a natural acceptance of her position as Lady Roehampton. Their acutest problem was personified by people like Lucy and Sylvia, – actual renegades from a stricter standard, though balancing themselves still by skilful acrobatics upon the social tight-rope. Self-elected, self-imposed, Lady L. and the Duchess of D. assumed certain responsibilities towards society, even though the times were changing; and never forgot that they had certain canons of conduct to maintain. They were sincere enough to deplore that a figure labelled Lady Roehampton should transgress these canons. They were human enough to relish the opportunity that she afforded them.

Sylvia herself realised the mistake that she had made by appearing as Queen Etheldreda. The public pageant was a very different affair from the stately fancy-dress ball which had been given some time before by one of these great hostesses, and which still formed a topic of conversation; or dress-up parties in private houses. She had cut herself off for ever from the fragile hope she still nourished of figuring at the more exclusive parties at L. House in Park Lane or D. House in Piccadilly. She would still go to both in 'crushes,' but from the more rigorous gatherings she would be more rigorously than ever excluded. Queen Etheldreda – Queen of Beauty; her feminine vanity might be gratified; her social vanity was mortified; it had received its death-blow. She knew it, when she met the Duchess of D. dining with Lucy, and was given two fingers instead of three – she had never been given five – and was called Lady Roehampton instead of 'Sylvia.' 'What a success you have had!' said the duchess, putting up her lorgnon as though to scrutinise the remains of Sylvia's beauty; 'the *Daily Mail* this morning was full of your praises. Quite a public character you have become.' Sylvia's only wonder was that the duchess should condescend to mention the *Daily Mail* at all. Yet with one half of herself she did not regret the pageant. Mounted on a black charger belonging to Sebastian's regiment, she had paraded as Queen of Beauty; she had dismounted from her charger only to ascend the steps

under a dais, while around her were grouped the loveliest debu-
tantes of the season as maids of honour – Viola was amongst
them, very scornful, and poor Margaret perforce, as the Queen
of Beauty's daughter, though poor Margaret could not by any
stretch of the imagination be called a beauty – and below them
had stood the young men of fashion, dressed as heralds, with
tabard and trumpet, looking for all the world like the knaves in
a pack of cards. Sebastian had been one of them, coerced into
the role by Sylvia. The suit became him amazingly. The straight
lines of the tabard, and its brilliant red, black, and gold,
accorded amazingly with his black hair and olive complexion.
He had set his trumpet against his hip with a gesture that no
other of the young men could equal. When the moment came
for the heralds to blow a fanfare – a sham fanfare, for the actual
sound was produced by the regimental trumpeters concealed
behind the dais – he had put his trumpet to his lips as though to
proclaim the beauty of his mistress to the whole of mediaeval
London. That one moment, Sylvia felt, had been worth the cen-
sure of all the Dukes and Duchesses of D. since their creation in
1694.

Still, in more sober moments, she was irritated when
Sebastian was asked to small dinner-parties at D. House and
she was not. Pride forbade that she should express the true
origin of her irritation, so she took refuge in trumped-up
grievances. The duchess wanted to catch him for a daughter,
or a grand-daughter, she exclaimed; he was a simpleton not
to see through such transparent devices. Then her temper
would get the better of her, and she would upbraid him
frankly for going to parties where she was not invited. 'They
think you good enough, because you are an eligible young
man,' she would say; 'they don't think me good enough,

because I have compromised myself with you; I wonder at
you, for suffering such a slight to be put upon me for your
sake.' Sebastian, who by now was well-advised enough to disentangle truth from falsehood, only smiled, in the way that
most infuriated Sylvia. 'Very well, then, go!' she would say;
'go, or you will be late. Go, and enjoy yourself in your
respectable circles; I'm dining with Julia and Sir Adam, and
I dare say we shall have a more amusing evening than you
will. I don't envy you – stuffy, proper, strait-laced that you
are. That's your natural world ...' And so they would part;
but Sylvia, coming home that night, would unfasten her
jewels angrily and would cast them down upon her dressing-
table, raging inwardly at the tyranny exerted by those old
women, and snapping at her sleepy maid, who was usually
accustomed to find her mistress good-humoured and gay, if a
trifle capricious. Old, crushing sepulchres! so Sylvia would
think; old, crushing sepulchres, determined to enshrine
everything as it had always been! But she raged in vain, and
she knew it. Their smile or their frown sufficed to admit or
to banish. They were the last survivors of the old regime, and
they had never departed by an inch from their original standards. Their arrogance was as magnificent as it was
maddening. They refused even to be introduced to people
whom most people would have given their eyes to know.
Their insolence was intolerable – but they could not be
ignored. Fashionableness went for nothing, compared with
their hearse-like state. Brilliant though a social career might
be, in the long run it was always brought up short against the
wall of their severity. Few of Sylvia's personal friends could
get past them; and Sylvia, in moments of honesty, admitted
they made some of her friends look cheap; not only those of

her friends who were Jews or Americans, but people like . . . and Sylvia shrank at the names that came into her head. It was an uncomfortable admission. Sylvia took comfort in the thought that soon they would die off, and that there was no one of quite their calibre to take their place – those old Incorruptibles, in their black lace and their diamonds, who could set their disapproval even upon the choice of the King.

Lord Roehampton was considered no fit counterpart to his lovely wife. People tolerated him for her sake only, for he was in truth a dull, heavy man, with whom Lucy had every right to be bored as a neighbour at dinner; the only people whose company he really enjoyed were his trainer at Newmarket and the keeper on his Norfolk estate. In that company he could indulge himself in the only things – apart from his wife – he recognised as beautiful. He would, of course, have shied mistrustfully away from the word; still he got a private satisfaction out of watching his fillies cantering in the paddock, and his pheasants running on the outskirts of his woods. Standing there, with trainer or keeper, he would confine his remarks to the advantages that these animals or birds were likely to bring him. 'A sporting chance for the Oaks,' he would say; or 'We ought to equal last year's bag. But what about those damned foxes?' Nevertheless, those who appreciate the Lords Roehampton of England will readily believe that his brief grunts and utterances to the trainer and the keeper represented but a tithe of the pleasure he actually absorbed on a day spent in the paddock or tramping across the acres. Incapable though he was of saying so, he liked the green meadow with its white posts, the sensitive foals; the marriage of wood and cornfield, the turnip leaves holding the rain. He got a dumb satisfaction out of these things, which it never occurred to him to confide to anybody.

If his capacity for enjoyment was thus inarticulate and limited, his principles were equally simple and unexpressed. There were certain things which you did not do, and there was an end of it. You did not take the best place at your own shoot, you did not look over your neighbour's hand at cards, you did not open his letters, or put up with his committing adultery with your wife. These were things which everybody knew, and which consequently might be taken for granted. Lord Roehampton held very definite views about his wife. He was proud of having married the most beautiful woman in London, and, regarding her taste for parties and society as the natural foible of a creature designed by nature for all men's admiration, he took pleasure in indulging her in all the adjuncts of luxury necessary to her proper fulfilment. Jewels, dresses, furs – she could have whatever she wanted. Nobody should say that he did not appreciate his prize. He would even submit to spending the season in London, though his heart ached rather wistfully for Norfolk and the young corn on the particularly sunny days of May and June. Sylvia, however, rewarded his indulgence with great consideration, for she would often urge him to prolong his week-ends at home while she herself returned to London, to sail out again superbly on the ocean of festivities that were to him a weariness and an embarrassment. Why, she had even insisted upon going alone to the Court ball, so that he might not be defrauded of an important sale of short-horns down in Norfolk. There were few wives, he thought with real gratitude, who would do that. Yes, Sylvia was good to him, he thought – her dull old George – and standing upon the refuge waiting to cross Park Lane, he had seen her drive out of Stanhope Gate in her victoria with the smart, high-stepping cobs and James the tiger sitting very straight with folded arms upon the box, and his heart had swelled with emotion as he took off his hat. A nice turn-out, that, he had thought, watching the carriage bowl down Great Stanhope Street; and what a pretty thing it is, he thought, to see a lovely woman drive in London behind a well-matched pair. Lord Roehampton had no use for the motors that were beginning to invade the streets. He crossed into the Park and continued his walk, feeling that all the creases had been smoothed out of him. The Park was bright with tulips and the lilac-bushes near Rotten Row were all in flower; people were strolling or sitting under the trees, watching the carriages go by; it seemed to Lord Roehampton that everything was specially animated and gay, that the women were like moving flowers in their light frocks, and that the men in their black coats were an admirable foil, their spats whiter than usual, and their top-hats more than usually glossy. And this good-humour, he reflected, was all because he had seen Sylvia drive out of Stanhope Gate! He thought himself extremely lucky; how many men after twenty years of marriage could say as much? He was almost reconciled to being in London; he began to enjoy the sensation of all this life streaming round him; and, leaning over the railings, he watched an escort of Household Cavalry come trotting round the bend on their black horses, their accoutrements shining and jingling, their scarlet tunics brilliant above the immaculate pipe-clay of their breeches. A young officer rode with them, his sword sloped across his shoulder; Lord Roehampton recognised Sebastian. Nice boy, that, he thought; nice boy; and he sighed, for he had no son.

*

It was inconvenient for Sylvia that 'Sebastian's summer' should coincide with her daughter's coming-out. She had wondered whether she could invent any excuse to delay this ceremony by a year, but failed to find one: Margaret was eighteen and everybody knew it, and with all her daring Lady Roehampton was too well trained to break through the convention that a girl on the completion of her eighteen years was ripe for the feast and battle of the world. She would as soon have attempted to alter the date of Christmas. So she sighed and resigned herself. Nevertheless she was determined that Margaret should inconvenience her as little as possible, while preserving every appearance of the conscientious mother; and with this end in view she decided to devote an afternoon to establishing good relations between Margaret and several of her aunts, who had daughters of their own and might be expected to include Margaret in their parties where her mother's chaperonage would not be necessary. Fortunately, George approved of his sisters – who indeed were ladies of unimpeachable respectability – and would readily accept the idea that in their company, and in the company of her cousins, Margaret would meet people whose standards and morals were more suitable to her unsophisticated years than the outlook prevalent among her mother's friends. Sylvia tested him to see whether, on this subject, he was as sound as she hoped and anticipated.

'You see, George, dear, I am afraid I have been rather selfish. I ought to have realised that Margaret was growing up. I ought to have got into touch with people like the Wexfords – nice, old-fashioned, steady people who live in Cadogan Square, and give a ball once a year to try and work off another daughter – really one loses count; I believe it's the ninth

Wexford girl who comes out this year. Or is it only the eighth? And only the eldest one married, and to a parson at that. Anyhow, the Wexfords are just the sort of people who have their uses when one is bringing out a girl. Young men don't mind who gives the party – they don't mind, I mean, how stodgy their host and hostess are in themselves, so long as they get a party to go to, and can dance; and I must say I would rather that Margaret met her friends at the Wexfords, even if they are a bit dull, than always at Julia Levison's or Romola Cheyne's. Romola is quite careful, as a matter of fact, about what she says in front of girls, but one never knows how much they hear and notice that isn't intended for them. Besides, it's the general atmosphere that counts. You know what I mean, George. Now your sisters are such dears, I am sure they will help by letting Margaret go with them when you and I are simply obliged to dine at places that wouldn't amuse her. I must really go round leaving cards this afternoon, and I shall take her to tea with Clemmie when I have finished.'

'My dear,' said George mildly, 'you were saying the other day that you hadn't seen Clemmie for five years.'

'Nor I have – that's just why I must take Margaret to tea with her to-day. Clemmie's girl is just Margaret's age. By the way, George, what is her name?'

'Agatha,' said George, who often went to see his sisters when he had nothing better to do.

'Agatha. Of course. The girl with freckles. I had better go unpowdered,' said Lady Roehampton with a peal of laughter, 'or Clemmie will be shocked. And you really think, do you, George, that I ought to let Margaret go about with Clemmie rather than drag her always with us to people like Romola or Sir Adam? I expect you are right. One can't be too careful about a young girl. I won't tell Clemmie what you say, in so many words, or she might think I was apologising for our friends, but if she suggests rather adopting Margaret this season I won't say no. Dear George. You are always so wise. What should I do without you. Ring the bell, and I'll order the carriage.'

An hour later, Lady Roehampton, with Margaret at her side, drove away in her smart victoria. After some persuasion, for he still preferred horses to machinery, George had given her an electric brougham, but having obtained it she seldom used it. It lacked both the speed of a motor and the distinction of a carriage. It had other disadvantages. If one took it down to Ranelagh, its batteries were apt to run out, leaving it stuck on the middle of Kingston Hill. Then, after every stop, it started off again with a pounce that dislocated not only one's spine but the angle of one's hat – and, since one's hat was perched and pinned somewhat precariously on the top of one's coiffure, tilted forward over one's eyes, that was a serious matter. Sylvia did not often find herself in agreement with George – though for tactical reasons she sometimes pretended agreement – but over the question of electric brougham versus victoria they indubitably saw eye to eye. True, they approached the dispute from a slightly different point of view. George thought primarily of his horses and carriage, then of his wife, then of both together as a satisfactory whole. Sylvia thought of herself as a picture in a frame. She knew that a woman in a carriage is exceedingly becoming to a carriage: whereas George would have said that a carriage was exceedingly becoming to the woman who drove in it. Sylvia knew moreover that the greater and staider ladies, who, despite her affectation of modernity, excited her envy and emulation, clung obstinately to their barouche. Sylvia could not quite stomach a barouche. She could admire the barouche in which certain great ladies drove out, but she could not imagine herself driving in it. She compromised with a victoria.

There was no doubt that Lady Roehampton in her victoria, with her daughter beside her, presented an extremely pretty sight. She held a parasol over her head, and on the seat opposite lay her card-case and a pink leather address-book from Dreyfous. As they drove along, spanking through the Park, she extracted three cards in readiness, letting the little slip of tissue-paper flutter away over the side of the carriage; she turned down a corner and put them neatly together; on the larger card was engraved: The Countess of Roehampton, Lady Margaret Cairn; and down in the corner was the address: Roehampton House, Curzon Street. The smaller cards said: The Earl of Roehampton, and down in the corner: Carlton Club. Sylvia was very well satisfied. She enjoyed this leisurely business of driving through the Park; of stopping at various houses; of receiving the answer, 'Not at home'; of handing the cards to James the tiger, after rapidly pencilling 'So sorry to miss you'; of consulting her list for the next address; of rolling off again, on the silent rubber wheels, to the quick trot of her two little cobs. She liked the angle at which Bond the coachman wore his hat, and the delicate way he twirled his whip when about to turn a corner. And to-day she enjoyed it especially, for had she not some prospect of unloading Margaret on to her aunts, leaving herself a greater freedom for Sebastian?

Lord Roehampton had five sisters, who all seemed to have been brushed off the same stencil. They were all angular, erect, flat, and looked as though they had been born to sit behind a tea-table dispensing tea and refilling the teapot with water from a silver kettle. They all had long distinguished faces and remarkably beautiful hands. They adopted a severe style in dress, the effect of which was marred by the fact that their hair remained incorrigibly wispy round the back; no nets or slides could ever secure for them a neat nape. Rather caustic in their speech, it was evident that they were capable and energetic women, as fit to intimidate local government boards as to control the domestic economy of their own homes. There was no nonsense about them, nor would they stand any. What they thought of their lovely sister-in-law was never expressed, since their code permitted no outside criticism of their brother's wife, but it was sufficiently plain; and Sylvia on the rare occasions when she had been with them all assembled together, had felt that she sat surrounded by five grenadiers armed with upright pikes of disapproval. Fortunately for her she need seldom endure their scrutiny, since their social orbits rarely overlapped; at most, she might espy one of them at some big function, such as a ball at Devonshire House, when laughing behind her fan she would draw her escort's attention to the steel-grey satin and the diamond 'fender' of Lady Blanche or Lady Clementina moving stiffly through the throng; but at the more intimate gatherings which were the inner life of the London season – the little bridge-parties at Sir Adam's, the informal dinner-parties where the King came almost incognito and chuckled richly over his big cigar – she might be sure that no gaunt censor would be at hand to chill her happy irresponsibility.

Sylvia had diagnosed them rightly when she thought of them as in their element in the Wexford world. They all belonged to the same solid, territorial aristocracy that took no account of 'sets' or upstarts, jargon or crazes, but pursued their way and maintained their dignity with the weight and rumble of a family coach. They had genealogical tables at their fingers' ends; they thought more of a small old family than of a large new fortune; they were profoundly and genuinely shocked by the admission of Jews into society; they regarded the fast set, in so far as it comprised some people who by birth were entitled to inclusion in their own faction, as a real betrayal of the traditions of *esprit de corps*. Their solidarity was terrific. They had a way of speaking of one another which reduced everybody else to the position of a mere petitioner upon the doorstep. Too well-bred to be arrogant, too uninspired to sneer, they were simply so well convinced of their own unassailability that the conviction required no voicing, but betrayed itself quietly in glances, in topics, in the set of shoulders, the folding of hands, and in the serene assumption of certain standards and particular values as common to all. They moved all together, a large square block in the heart of English society, massive, majestic, and dull. In their own way they were as exclusive and as critical as the incorruptible *grandes dames* who were such thorns in Sylvia's side; the only difference between them was a difference of wealth and position; in outlook they were identical. Nothing but the chance of fortune differentiated Lady Blanche or Lady Clementina from Lady L. and the Duchess of D. For naturally all the daughters of this world could not aspire to brilliant marriages, but had to be content with the respect-worthy gentlemen whom England fortunately produced in such adequate supplies. Lord Roehampton's sisters, twenty years or so previously, realising that coronets and the nobler seats were not for them, had followed the example of many well-born but superfluous sisters in a similar position, and had one by one accorded their hands to various squires who were not sorry to acquire a wife with a handle to her name, and who in return were able to make her the mistress of some commodious Georgian mansion standing in its own park, and of a town-house with, possibly, a Doric portico. Thereafter the lady's life was marked out for her, as it were, by white posts with chains slung between them even as the carriage-drive of her country home; her future became reassuringly predictable; the first few years of her married life were spent in retirement, devoting herself to the production of an heir, of a younger brother or two if possible, and probably of several little girls whose own future, at that date, seemed not very hard to guess; this duty accomplished, she might hope for a period of yearly relaxation in London, ordered and increasingly stately as the natural frivolity of youth matured into the sobriety of complete matronhood; until we behold her, fulfilled in the person of Lady Clementina Burbidge, barricaded behind her tea-table and her sizzling kettle, dispensing tea to her afternoon callers with her debutante daughter in attendance to hand little plates of rock cake, bread-and-butter rolled into sausages, or buttered scones supposed to retain their warmth over a splash of hot water in the slop basin.

The very rooms in which they dwelt differed from Sylvia's rooms or the rooms of her friends. There, a certain fashion of expensive simplicity was beginning to make itself felt; a certain taste was arising, which tended to eliminate unnecessary objects. Here, the overcrowded rooms preserved the unhappy confusion of an earlier day. Little silver models of carriages and sedan-chairs, silver vinaigrettes, and diminutive silver fans, tiny baskets in silver filigree, littered the tables under the presiding rotundity of the lamp-shade. (Sylvia noticed, with

amusement, that no ash-trays were included among this rubbish.) Palms stood in each corner of the room, and among the
branches of the palms nestled family photographs, unframed,
but mounted upon a cardboard of imperishable stiffness; a
single shake, thought Sylvia, taking in every detail in the short
space between the door and the tea-table, a single shake would
bring down cascades of relations: Aunt Fanny in her bustle,
George in his sailor-suit, Ernestine about to bowl her hoop;
and one photograph of surprising beauty, Daisy the present
Dowager, a well-known Irish beauty, dressed in ermine from
top to toe, with her two little boys on a sleigh in a forest of
snow-clad firs, somewhere in the Carpathians; and then,
coming nearer home, Sylvia herself with Margaret, Sylvia
wearing a tweed cap and tailor-made skirt with a sailor tie,
Margaret in a pram, wearing a bonnet tied under the chin and
a pair of gloves that had thumbs but only a bag for the fingers.
It struck Sylvia as odd that she should figure in so intimate a
connection in so unfamiliar a drawing-room. She knew that
her photograph was there, not because her sister-in-law had
any affection for her, but because she figured (however unac-
ceptably) as one of the family. It was right that poor George's
wife should have her place among the palms.

Yes, certainly the room was overcrowded. There were too
many chairs, too many hassocks, too many small tables, too
much pampas grass in crane-necked vases, too many blinds
and curtains looped and festooned about the windows. The
whole effect was fusty, musty, and dusty. It needed destruction,
it needed air. The very satin was fastened to the chairs with
aggressive buttons. Everything had something else superim-
posed upon it; the overmantel bore its load of ornaments on
each bracket, the mantel-shelf itself was decked with a strip of

damask heavily fringed, the piano was covered over by a square
of Damascus velvet, on which more photographs and more
ornaments were insecurely balanced. In the centre of the room
stood a sociable, also buttoned to its cover; a sociable on
which two persons might sit, facing one another, but properly
divided by the arm and wriggle of the S. Sylvia remembered
that Romola Cheyne had once said that the S of a sociable
stood for Sex. That was the sort of joke that made the King
laugh, and kept him in a good temper.

When Lady Clementina heard 'Lady Roehampton!'
announced, she looked up expecting to see her own mother;
but it was no dowager that entered the room, but a radiant
Sylvia with Margaret in tow. Charm was so much second-
nature to Sylvia, that she must exert it even in her
sister-in-law's drawing-room. She rustled forward, avoiding the
obstacles, filling the air with unaccustomed scent; she was as
full of voluptuousness as a cooing pigeon. One could almost
believe that her soft generous curves bruised themselves
against the bony protuberances of the assembled ladies. For a
tea-party of ladies was in progress. Sylvia noted them all with
a skilled and rapid eye: Clementina herself; Ernestine;
Blanche; Lady Wexford in maroon velvet; Lady Porteviot; and
a handful of girls, all very gauche but very propitiatory, jumping up to prove themselves attentive, but gratefully subsiding
once more round the tea-table set apart for their especial use,
where their whispers and suppressed laughter testified to the
excellent understanding that existed amongst them. Sylvia
descended upon this gathering as a bird of paradise might wing
down upon an assembly of hens. She knew quite well that they
were startled and hostile, she knew too that they were hard
nuts to crack – no naïf sentimentality there, to be moved by

her beauty in a short cut! – nor was the conquest a very interesting one, but so intimately had she acquired the habit of
conquest that she must marshal all her powers against defeat,
for aesthetic reasons and in the cause of proper pride, quite
apart from the urgent practical motive she had in view. So she
started by taking it for granted that Lady Clementina would be
delighted to see her; enveloped the rigid form of her sister-in-
law in a voluminous and prolonged embrace; renewed it with
slight modifications for Ernestine and Blanche; extended a
cordial hand to Lady Wexford and Lady Porteviot, undeterred
by the chilliness with which it was received; beamed upon the
circle of girls; picked out her nieces and blew them a kiss; and
subsided upon the sofa beside Lady Clementina, retaining that
lady's hand in her own and patting it gently as it lay on her
knee.

This physical contact with Lady Roehampton was highly
distasteful to Lady Clementina; through the medium of her
hand she became aware of the extreme softness of Sylvia's
thigh under the thin silk of her dress, communicating to her a
suggestion of impropriety which was immediately associated in
her mind with the stories familiar to her – stories of Sylvia's
own affairs as of the fast set in which she lived. What was it
that Lady Porteviot always called her? pronouncing the a's
thin, with her north-country accent, 'That năsty făst woman,
my dear – sorry if she's your brother's wife – can't help that –
a năsty făst woman.' Lady Porteviot, from the altitudes above
her tightly upholstered bust, considered herself entitled to
make downright pronouncements, and indeed assumed the
position of dictator to the circle of ladies she frequented. She
was accustomed to being listened to with respect; her intimates
knew when to stop talking themselves in order to attend to her

words; and now here was Sylvia monopolising the conversation, chattering radiantly, appealing now to Ernestine and now to Lady Wexford for corroboration – 'I'm sure, dear Lady Wexford, you know what I mean – yes, I see you do' – turning her lovely head first to one lady and then to another, laughing, joking, and all the while clasping Lady Clementina's hand and bringing her eyes back to gaze at her as though she were the one object of her affection in the world. The girls had stopped whispering together; they gaped at Lady Roehampton, thinking that they had never seen anybody more fascinating, more animated, more self-possessed and altogether enviable. It was a real blow to them when Lady Clementina, seizing the first opportunity, fixed her daughter Agatha with an eye like an awl and said she was sure they would all like to go upstairs now to Agatha's sitting-room.

They went, of course, meekly, trooping out; and with their going Sylvia knew that she lost her only supporters. She had been quite well aware that she could play on their susceptibilities as upon the susceptibilities of young men. Now they were gone, and she confronted this stockade of unresponsive bosoms. She had managed difficult situations in her time; she had coaxed the King back into a good temper when he was in a bad one; she had steered coincident and resentful lovers into havens of mutual civility; situations such as these were well within her province; but a phalanx of women was a different matter. There was no hostility like that of women to a woman. But she had still got hold of Clemmie's hand. Clemmie was trying to wriggle it away. All Lady Roehampton's mischievousness rose up in the determination to retain it. So long as she held her hand, Clemmie couldn't pour out tea; and, according to Lady Roehampton's view of

Clemmie, Clemmie's function was to sit behind a teapot and pour it out; so, under the guise of sisterly affection, she would frustrate Clemmie. She continued to hold her hand and to pat it, meanwhile pouring forth a volume of amiable absurdities. Fancy, Lady Porteviot, she exclaimed, last time I saw Agatha she was in the schoolroom practising her scales, with chilblains and two plaits; now she is out, and what a lovely figure she has, Clemmie! she makes my poor Margaret look a lump beside her. Her poor Margaret, she continued, was scarcely enjoying her first season as much as she ought; and it's all my fault, she said, sighing; I should have kept up with the younger generation, but as one grows older one's friends grow older too, and the result is that Margaret doesn't know nearly enough people of her own age. Lady Clemmie looked cynically at her sister-in-law, but so outrageous a piece of nonsense deserved no comment and received none. Lady Roehampton proceeded to paint a sad picture of poor Margaret's plight at a ball. 'I know no young men to introduce to her,' she said; 'what a girl wants is a *start* – isn't that so, Ernestine? – but with neither brothers nor sisters it's so difficult. Now when I take her to the Court ball to-night she will simply trail about behind me all the time – and I'm dining out first and the poor child isn't invited, and will have to have her dinner at home all by herself. A cutlet on a tray. I shall pick her up afterwards, of course.' And she sighed again.

Lady Clementina began to be sorry for Margaret; no doubt Sylvia lost no opportunity of making the child feel she was a nuisance. She had no wish to oblige Sylvia, but the girl must be considered. Besides, it was most undesirable that poor George's daughter (Lord Roehampton was always 'poor George' to his sisters) should mix entirely with Sylvia's terrible friends. A mother with a young lover always at her side! The family must be thought of; what would Susan Darlington, and Julia Keswick, and Charlotte Grantham say if they knew that Clementina, Blanche, Ernestine, Ermyntrude, and Ada had done nothing to rescue and redeem their niece? And they certainly would know – these tyrannical old matriarchs who never came near London, but were informed of everything that went on there and ruled the family with a power and severity whose secret is known only to the deposed but tenacious Dowager. Lady Clementina, shaping that way herself, would not enjoy a scrutiny through Charlotte Grantham's lorgnon, nor the croak of that rasping old voice, 'Well, Clemmie; well, Clemmie? and what's this I hear? George's girl left to the Jews and to persons like that woman whose name I believe is Mrs. Cheyne? What's the meaning of it, Clemmie? eh? What have you all been about?'

Lady Clementina thereupon invited Margaret to stay in her house for a week. She did it as ungraciously as she could – which was very ungraciously indeed – but still she did it. She would take Margaret to the Palace with Agatha that evening. She would look after Margaret for Sylvia. For a week.

Sylvia rewarded her by instantly releasing her hand. Her thanks were profuse, and what Clemmie called 'gushing'. And now she must go, she exclaimed – hoping that her departure would not appear indecently precipitate, but now that she had gained her point she really could not endure the company of these old grenadiers any longer – she would send the carriage back with Margaret's things, she said, and Margaret's maid; 'dear, dear Clemmie, how kind you are,' she cried, embracing the gaunt form again and appealing to Lady Wexford and Lady Porteviot to say was Clemmie not kind? to which those ladies grimly assented; and then, lowering her veil, gathering up her belongings, her gloves, her boa, her cloak, she swept towards the door distributing radiant smiles to everybody. 'And now,' she thought as she tripped downstairs, 'let them say what they like about me, I've given their old tongues something to wag about for a week at least,' and looking at her watch she saw that she would not be more than an hour late for her appointment with her hairdresser.

Yes, she was indeed a beautiful woman, she decided, catching sight of herself in a long mirror as she came out of the cloakroom at Buckingham Palace. She was alone in the passage, but for the beef-eaters, and they affected her no more than so many pieces of furniture. She could take stock of herself in the mirror without any consciousness of men watching her; beefeaters were not men, they were effigies stuck down at intervals; no more men than sentries, or dummies in suits of armour. So she loitered, having come out of the cloak-room only to face an unexpected mirror that returned to her, full-length, the image of the complete woman she might have postulated from the head-and-shoulders revealed to her in the mirror propped on the cloak-room table. There, she had scrutinised a lovely head, something after the manner of Lely, she thought – having been told so innumerable times – and the bare shoulders, oyster satin, and pearls of Lely, all of which she affected on state occasions because she knew they accorded with her type of beauty. Here, in the long mirror, she saw herself not only as a kit-cat, but full-length: oyster satin flowing out at her feet, pearls vanishing into the valley between her breasts, pearls looped round her wrists, a rosy scarf tossed round her shoulders. She wore no tiara. The fact that Lady Roehampton wore no tiara at Court balls made other women say, with a half-deprecatory, half-envious laugh, that Lady Roehampton was an unconventional woman. Such daring was almost insolent. It was almost rude. But the Order of St. John of Jerusalem caught and held her rosy scarf.

Satisfied by the image that the mirror returned to her, she gave herself a little smile. Lady Roehampton's smile was famous; her lips parted slowly, and as though reluctantly, but with an extreme sweetness; and when the smile faded away, beholders said that it died like the closing chords of music. Poets had written about it; Browning, whom she had once met in a box at the Opera, had written a graceful compliment on the back of her programme. 'When Sylvia smiles,' it began. When Sylvia smiled it was indeed impossible to believe that Sylvia was an angel straight from Heaven. All the world of feminine voluptousness seemed to be gathered up and released in that one divine curving of the loosened lips. There was no humour in it, but there was an indescribable caress. It indicated that Sylvia thoroughly knew her most feminine business, and when Sylvia smiled nowadays people's thoughts turned, not without envy, towards Sebastian. No one ever saw Sylvia now without immediately thinking of Sebastian, for she was the kind of woman whose presence instantly suggests the thought of her lover and his ownership. Would he keep her? would she keep him? was she faithful to him? such were the questions that people asked themselves not only whenever they saw them together, but whenever they saw Lady Roehampton alone. Her past had been populous; Lord Roehampton – so they thought, but therein they erred – cared for nothing but racing; now she had caught the most notorious young man in London. How would it end? –

But meanwhile we are keeping the lady standing in the passage.

Her progress towards the ball-room was as well worth watching as her smile, and it was a pity that there should be only beef-eaters to watch it. But the beef-eaters gazed stonily at their halberds. The strains of a waltz dictated the rhythm of her steps, for she moved always harmoniously, with the carriage of a woman who has been accustomed to feel all eyes turned upon her. She moved without haste, and with seeming unconsciousness, as upright as an Egyptian who has borne burdens on her head, yet with the stateliness of a woman whose only burden has been a crown. She moved now, down the passage between the beef-eaters, as though she were in her right and natural surroundings, advancing towards a royal ball-room crowded with the fashion of London and the dignity of Empire, a ball-room where a lane would be made for her, in deference not so much to her worldly station as to her personal prerogative; but then that was her peculiar property, to move always as though her surroundings were right and natural, whether advancing in her satin and pearls down a corridor of Buckingham Palace, or emerging in her tweeds and brogues from a crofter's cottage, stooping under the low lintel, to take her place (on a shooting-stick) among the guns for an after-luncheon photograph of Lord Tomnoddy's party on his Perthshire moors. Whatever she did, she made her circumstances appear singularly apposite and becoming. The same applied to whatever she wore, for she was blessed with that enviable quality of investing every colour seen on her with a fresh significance; thus blue appeared more vividly blue, grey more subtly grey, black more intensely black, when affected by her; and tweeds or taffeta held their place as the only wear for woman, according as Lady Roehampton wore taffeta or tweeds. She had her imitators, who were surprised and chagrined to find that the same vestments on them did not produce the same effect.

A county family entering the passage just then saw her, and with a little thrill of excitement whispered her name. Father, mother, and daughter, they had 'arrived' at the big house in Belgrave Square for the season. An announcement to that effect had appeared in *The Times*, omitting to add that Lord and Lady O. were martyrising themselves for the sake of what they considered to be their duty towards their daughter. Of impeccable respectability and historic lineage, they had long looked forward with dread to this year when it would be necessary to transport themselves, their household, their carriages, and their plate up to London in May and devote themselves for three months to the task of taking their Alice 'out,' involving not only weariness for them, but also a constant irritating anxiety as to possible contact with things and people of whom they would disapprove. Careful as they might be of the houses where they would allow their Alice to go, society and manners had grown so lax – in their opinion – that the very nicest houses might be invaded by the objectionable. Here, for instance, even at Buckingham Palace, even at the Court ball, the first person they saw was a person to whom Lady O. could certainly not allow her Alice to speak. The notorious Lady Roehampton! That her very presence was demoralising was proved by the effect it produced on two out of the three members of the county family. Alice actually shivered with a dreadful envious rapture, as though at possibilities suddenly revealed; Lord O. stared, adjusted his broad red ribbon, and thought, 'Gad! that's a fine woman and no mistake.' Lady O. alone remained faithful to the family standard. She drew herself up, so that a diamond in her tiara came into line with a sconce and flashed a prismatic spot of light into the eye of a beef-eater and made him blink. Never, she thought, never! not if the King himself introduces her.

Lady Roehampton's entry into the ball-room created the stir which she accepted as her due. The foreign ambassador who bent to kiss her hand symbolised in his gesture the disposition of all the men who looked at her and drew slightly aside to make way. Her charm ripened, as always, before this homage. Crowded though the room was, and brilliantly diverse, she became a focus, filling the space around her with an aroma of graciousness that disengaged itself from her whole personality. Very slowly she moved about, eagerly attended, appearing scarcely to notice those who pressed their claims upon her, yet rewarding them all at length with a smile that singled each one out as the object of her special favour. Yet it is permitted to ask, having a novelist's privilege, what actually occupied her mind, behind an exterior of such exquisite confidence? Was she so well accustomed to the spirit of such gatherings that they could hold no glamour for her, such as they held for Lord and Lady O.'s Alice, up from the country? Uniforms, jewels, orders; names famous for past history or present achievement; wealth, government, representation, royalty – had this pageant indeed no power to stir her imagination? Was she too closely herself a part of it? Could she indeed give two fingers to the Viceroy-designate without thinking of the India that he would govern? Could she nod to the First Sea Lord while nothing more than 'Dear old Jacky!' brushed across her mind? Did she, in short, unlike Lord and Lady O.'s Alice, forget to associate

people with their historic or official labels? Did she not even
formulate to herself the thought, 'Here am I, the beautiful
Sylvia Roehampton, as famous in Paris as in London, painted
by every fashionable painter from Carolus Duran to Sargent,
entering the ball-room at a Court ball'? Did she take that, with
everything else, for granted?

Those, perhaps, are questions which cannot be answered;
chiefly because the person concerned, however helpful and
well-disposed, could herself have provided no answer. There
can be no doubt that the beautiful Sylvia would have looked
blankly at the inquisitive novelist. How does one answer a
man who asks one whether one is conscious of speaking one's
own language? 'He is speaking to me in English; I am replying
to him in English; he is Viceroy of India; I am the most beautiful woman in London' – the parallel seems obvious and futile.
Clearly, she never thought about such things; by the very
admission that she thought about them, the question would
have been automatically answered; the speaker of English
would have been revealed as a foreigner.

Meanwhile, very stately and gracious (M. de Soveral always
said he knew no other woman who could contrive to look
stately and voluptuous at the same time, so that you wondered
whether she were more *grande dame* or *grande amoureuse*), she
yielded herself up to the arms of young Ambermere and to the
rhythm of a waltz. Aware or not aware, she had no intention
of remaining in the crowd when the most desirable part of the
room was up towards the royal dais, and the dance seemed the
quickest method of making her way to where she wished to be.
Therefore she danced, and the dance served her well, for
presently she stood talking with the King, who, catching sight
of her, had beckoned to her to relieve his boredom, and was

now laughing with her while young Ambermere hung about in attendance and the rest of the room observed them out of one eye – the obsequious eye always cocked upon royalty – though they pretended to be doing nothing of the sort. Lady Roehampton was well known to be in the King's intimate set, and many were the looks of envy, disparagement, and criticism cast upon her as she stood easily swaying her fan and talking to the King and making him laugh. Many were the women who wished themselves in her shoes – the wives of civil servants, the young wives of territorial peers richer in birth than in elegance, the wives of Chilean secretaries of legation – but those who were honest with themselves must admit that they could not make as good a job of it as Lady Roehampton was making. Confronted with the King they would, in fact, have found themselves in extreme embarrassment. It was a delirious but a fearful situation; for the King, genial as he could be, was known to lose interest easily and to drum with irritable fingers upon the arm of his chair or upon the dinner-table. What a gulf there was between amusing the King and boring him! and, for a woman, all depended upon which side of the gulf she occupied. Life and death were in it. Now perhaps many a woman present to-night thought she could have swept a curtsey as luxuriant as Lady Roehampton's; but what woman would have backed herself to sustain that initial gesture with equal ease and success? No wonder they looked with envy and commented with satire. Lady Roehampton, conscious of their glances, could afford to relish their satire.

The Italian Ambassador and Marchesa Potini, coming within range of the royal eye, must be greeted by his Majesty; nothing less than an impulsive step forward and an outstretched hand would meet the demands of civility towards the

Italian Excellencies. Lady Roehampton, discreetly withdrawing, was perhaps slightly relieved by this intervention. Etiquette forbade that she should retire altogether, but she could remain, so to speak, in abeyance, whispering to young Ambermere, until diplomatic civilities should be over and she should be in request again or receive her dismissal. But Marchesa Potini showed no disposition to relinquish the King; a handsome, commanding Roman, her hair brushed upwards in eighteenth-century fashion to display her ears, which were remarkable for their smallness and exquisite modelling, she continued to talk with great determination in her husky voice, and already Lady Roehampton's experienced eye discerned the signs of boredom under the perfection of the royal manner. Not that the King could be called distrait; no, but he had begun to fiddle with the silver bracelet round his wrist. There was nothing for Sylvia to do but to draw the Potinis tactfully away.

They sat for a moment together on a sofa, all three of them, and Sebastian came up, bowed to the ambassadress, and asked Lady Roehampton for a dance. Through his gravity his eyes twinkled. The marchesa, far from insensible to the charm of handsome young men – and Sebastian undoubtedly looked very handsome in his blue and gold uniform, with the scarlet collar – the marchesa tapped him playfully with her fan. 'So here is our reprobate,' she said; 'and what wild story are we to hear next? Are you to risk your life again, or break another heart?'

Sebastian did not like this sort of conversation; it bored and embarrassed him. He stood smiling politely. Then Sylvia said, 'He must marry; mustn't he, marchesa? I am always telling him that he must marry, if only to annoy his heirs. There is his old uncle, whose life is poisoned by wondering whether he will ever succeed to Chevron or not. Then there are his cousins, who think about it even more, because they are younger and would have longer to enjoy it. Now if he would only marry, and produce an heir of his own, all those people could give up their speculations and think about something else. They could set about making a life for themselves, independent of Chevron. You must find a bride', she said to Sebastian, looking up at him with the mixture of roguery and mocking tenderness possible only between lovers in the restraining, stimulating presence of strangers.

'A bride!' said the marchesa, pronouncing it bry-eed, and looking fondly at Sebastian, in precisely that mood common to many people when they glance at the photograph of engaged couples in the newspaper and project themselves into a state of sexual indignation on behalf of one or the other party, a state of mind which can be summarised in the exclamation: 'He's not nearly good enough for her!' or else, 'What can have induced so attractive a young man to choose such a fright of a girl?' – a state of mind which finds a certain lickerish satisfaction only in the contemplation of a couple completely matched in the essentials of youth, swagger, and comeliness. 'A bride!' said the marchesa; 'and where, dear Lady Roehampton, will you find the duke a bride? Why will you hurry him into marriage? No, you must wait,' she said; 'his bride may be still in the schoolroom. A little girl with plaits. Why, who among our young ladies could you want him to marry?'

'Well, I want him to marry my daughter,' said Lady Roehampton lightly, 'but he's too obstinate: he won't be caught. His mother and I are both in despair about it. We are such old friends, and we should so enjoy sharing our grandchildren. But do you suppose this young man will listen? Not he. He laughs and looks on me as just another scheming mother. That's all the reward I get for my pains.' She laughed up at Sebastian, and caught the expression in his eyes. A shiver of pleasure ran through her. She asked no more of life than it was giving her at that moment – this combination of brilliance, flirtation, passion – and for an instant she forgot the thought that perpetually gnawed at her: if only I were younger! She was entirely happy. Presently she would tell Sebastian that she would be alone that night. No George, no Margaret. But not yet. She would keep him in suspense a little longer. She would prolong this hour in which he should seek her and she should evade him. So she departed with old Lord Wensleydale, who was hovering round her in a maudlin way, throwing Sebastian, as she went, a glance that was almost a grimace; and for quite half an hour afterwards, whenever she saw him working his way towards her, hastily accepted to dance with somebody else; thus, at the first Court ball of the season, giving a great deal of unexpected pleasure to people whom it was usually her policy to snub.

He caught her finally; and Lady O.'s Alice, sitting beside her mother – for nobody seemed inclined to ask her for a dance – whispered to her mother that there he was, the young man of whom they had heard so much. How spoilt he looked, and how scornful. But how romantic, so dark, in that uniform with the scarlet collar! and what a beautiful slender figure he had, and what long slim legs in the tight trousers with a gold stripe down the side. Alice's head brimmed with notions. But Lady O. looked disapprovingly at Sebastian, and instinctively her eyes sought Lady Roehampton, who was standing flirting with two other young men, scarcely replying to Sebastian's urgent but respectful request. Suddenly, however, she seemed to capitulate; put her hand on Sebastian's arm; abandoned the two young men; gave herself up to Sebastian, and swept away with him into the whirlpool of the dancers. Alice watched them go, and was quite taken aback when her mother said something tartly about the deterioration of the modern world.

IV

SYLVIA

Holding the views he did, Lord Roehampton was naturally upset when he received a packet containing some twenty letters addressed to his wife by Sebastian. At the first casual glance he saw enough to tell him everything, and with a quick movement he pushed the packet into a drawer of his writing-table and shut the drawer upon it as though upon a serpent that had bitten him. Then he sat back and stared at the drawer. All the reflections usual to a gentleman in that unfortunate situation incontinently began to course through his mind, and need not be repeated in detail here; honourable incredulity was followed by reluctant conviction, reluctant conviction by conventional indignation, conventional indignation by primitive rage, and primitive rage finally was cancelled by simple, human grief. Lord Roehampton stared at the drawer, a very unhappy man. Had Sylvia chanced to come in at that moment he would have spoken out, no doubt of it, then and there; as it was, he had time to collect himself, to take counsel with himself, and to decide that he must do nothing precipitately. After sitting for a long time sunk in his chair, he bestirred himself, slowly dragged up his keys out of his trouser pocket, selected the right one, bent forward, inserted the key, locked the drawer, restored the keys to his pocket, and went slowly upstairs.

Although he did not know much about himself, he did at any rate after fifty years of life recognise that his brain, considered as an instrument, was a leisurely and laborious affair. It required a very long time to absorb a new idea or to come to a decision; so that he could not help feeling it had been taken a very unfair advantage of, in that here it had abruptly been offered an entirely new and peculiarly distressing idea, and was being called upon to make a decision of the utmost import- ance. He ought to have been given warning, and no warning had been given. By the time he had reached the top of the stairs he had also reached the decision that as yet he must make no decision. He would take a week to think it over. He must first accustom himself to several truths: that Sylvia was unfaithful to him; that she had probably been unfaithful to him before; that at least one person – the sender of the let- ters – knew it. (It was not until the middle of the night that it dawned upon him that probably everybody knew it, had always known it, except himself. He remembered a joke to that effect, in a Flers et Caillavet play in Paris; the audience had laughed, and Romola Cheyne, who was with them, seeing him look puzzled, for his French was limited, had translated it for him; kind of her to bother, he had thought at the time, but now he wondered.) A good Conservative, he had the principle firmly fixed in him that nothing must be done in a hurry. The greater the consequence, the greater the need for deliberation. In the crumbling world of his private life, that axiom still held good; he reverted to it, after the first storms of rashness that had threatened to sweep him off his feet. 'A week to think it over.' The very phrase brought him a measure of reassurance; so far, the matter was private between himself and his drawer; no one need know what was going on between himself, his principles, his heart, and his conscience. He was well trained in the habit of reserve. Driving out to dinner with Sylvia in the brougham that night, no impulse assailed him to blow the brougham to pieces with the truth, as it might have assailed a less bridled man.

In the week that followed, he kept to his determination with comparatively little effort. Sebastian came twice to luncheon; he even came once to dine before a small dance, and took his hostess into dinner as was, indeed, inevitable. Lord Roehampton scarcely observed them, from his end of the table, as a man obsessed by personal jealousy would observe, for his concern was not with jealousy but with principle. It was not so much that he loved Sylvia, as that Sylvia was his wife. Sylvia was Lady Roehampton. She bore his name. Now that he had recovered from the first shock, he no longer thought of Sebastian in personal terms; Sebastian had become a symbol, an x. But as the personal element shrunk from Lord Roehampton's views, so, proportionately, did the impersonal determination increase. 'I won't stand any nonsense' was the rhythm now running in his head. 'My wife behaves herself, or she ceases to be my wife,' was another phrase he had coined for himself during those painful days, and which gave him great support and satisfaction. By the end of the week, he had really persuaded himself that his severity towards Sylvia was wholly directed towards Lady Roehampton.

At moments a sentimental remorse seized him, as he saw Sylvia going about her amusements unconscious of the trouble that was about to break over her head. He felt then as one might feel who, darkly standing in the wings, trains a revolver upon the laughing, triumphant, twirling queen of ballet. He would come up to her bedroom after he had had his breakfast and had read his *Times*, and would find her still lying in her wide bed littered with notes and household orders, directing her maid to lay out various costumes with their adjuncts, that she might choose what she would wear that day. And so, eight or ten selections might be displayed on chairs ranged round the room, complete with shoes, stockings, hat, veil, boa, and parasol, while Sylvia reclined in bed as Cleopatra upon her throne, scorning some, hesitating between others, losing her temper over this, weakening in favour of that, saying that she hated pink and could not imagine why she had ever ordered it, saying now that Worth was the only dressmaker who understood her, and now that Paquin could cut a bodice as nobody else; and finally, that she possessed nothing fit to wear, but supposed she must make shift with the tussore for to-day. It often happened that after standing and turning before her cheval-glass, completely dressed, she would declare that she could not possibly go out looking like that, and would change again from head to foot, for she would rather keep a luncheon-party waiting for three quarters of an hour, than fall below the standard of her own perfection. It was a worship, a rite, that she performed in the service of a double deity: her own beauty and the society that she decorated. As her husband watched her, seeing the little familiar gestures by which she twisted up an escaping curl, or pinned a bow so that it might nestle just under her ear, and heard her prattle of last night's ball – for in intimate life she was as good-humoured as a happy child – he felt nothing but tolerance towards this creature of frivolity and shameless vanity. Then he remembered that she would probably meet Sebastian wherever she was going, and his purpose again became firm within him.

The situation was complicated by a development in Margaret's affairs. Margaret had met a young painter who had fallen in love with her, and with whom she had fallen in love, and whom she now wished to marry. 'Where *can* she have met such a creature?' said Lady Roehampton, wringing her hands; 'I thought she was safe enough with Clemmie and Ernestine.' Apparently she had not been safe. She arrived at her parents' house one day, a radiant, different Margaret. Adrian had a great future before him, she said; and the hitherto lumpish girl pleaded with real inspiration. This eccentricity on the part of their daughter did much to draw Lord and Lady Roehampton together; Sylvia felt real gratitude towards George for his firmness, and George almost forgot his mortal disapproval of Sylvia when he saw how wholeheartedly she supported him. She retains *some* principles, he thought; she has not entirely lost her sense of decency. It was manifestly impossible that Margaret should be allowed to marry the creature. To begin with, he was illegitimate, and cheerfully said that he could produce no parents, having been left on the steps of the Foundling Hospital in a brown paper parcel, with the name 'Adrian' pinned to his shawl. 'But, my dear fellow ...,' said George; and though he restrained himself from completing the sentence, it was obvious that he meant, 'You can scarcely expect that to be good enough for our daughter.'

Margaret cried, and Lord Roehampton, who was sincerely fond of her, was much distressed. As most men would have done in the circumstances, he went out of the house leaving her to Sylvia. Sylvia hated bother of all kind, especially bother which interfered with her own arrangements; but she was patient with the girl, and, patting her shoulder, explained that certain sacrifices had to be made sometimes when one was born to a certain position – 'That's the penalty, you see, Margaret darling,' she said, 'and we all have to pay it in one form or another. It's a terrible thing to become *déclassée*, as you certainly would be if you married this poor boy – nice though he may be,' she added hastily. 'But if I don't mind?' said poor Margaret. 'You must think of your father and me, darling; it would break our hearts, I think; we've always been so ambitious for you. Besides, I thought the Wexford boy? ... now that would be a really nice marriage, and we could all be so happy together.' At that moment the Duchess of Hull was shown in – old, painted, and masterful. 'What's this I hear, Margaret?' she began at once; 'that you're engaged to Tony Wexford? Well, I congratulate you; it's a lovely place, I believe, and after all you aren't obliged to stay over in Ireland all the time.' These remarks produced a fresh outburst of tears from Margaret. 'What's wrong? What's wrong?' croaked the duchess; 'don't you like him, child? Oh, nonsense, you'll soon get over that. Don't you be such a little fool as to throw away the chance – eh, Sylvia?' 'Margaret thinks she wants to marry a painter,' said Sylvia, looking at her daughter with some compassion. 'What's that?' screamed the duchess; 'a painter? What painter? Who ever heard of such a thing? Sylvia

Roehampton's daughter marry a painter? But of course she won't. You marry Tony Wexford and we'll see what can be done about the painter afterwards,' she said, winking at Sylvia behind Margaret's back.

Margaret took her sorrows away, seeing that there was no help in either of her parents; but since she must confide in somebody she surveyed her friends in the search for a sympathetic ear. Her cousins were no good; they were far too sober and well brought-up. Until this event, Margaret had thought herself sober too, and obedient; but now she discovered the growlings of rebellion in her heart, was seriously shocked at herself, and desired an impartial confidante who would show her where the truth lay. It was no good consulting people like her cousins, when she knew in advance what they would say. Finally she decided upon Viola.

She had no idea what Viola's opinion would be. Viola was a dark horse. She had changed a great deal within the last few months. She allowed herself to be taken about like any other young lady of her age and position, but – perhaps because she was quiet and watchful – she gave people the uneasy feeling that she merely submitted herself to something which she disdained. Consequently she was not popular, in spite of her looks. Further, she was reputed 'clever,' and that was a serious disadvantage for a girl; 'though indeed,' said Mrs. Cheyne, 'I never can see where her cleverness comes in, for she hardly speaks at all. Dicky Ambermere says he can't get a word out of her.' Margaret went to consult Viola much as she might have gone to consult a witch. Accompanied by her maid, she walked up from Curzon Street to Grosvenor Square.

Viola was in. She took Margaret up to her own room,

having seen in the first minute that something was wrong. Margaret followed, feeling lumpish beside Viola's sleek grace; raw before Viola's quiet and reserve. How had Viola managed to do so much thinking in her eighteen years? But Viola made her sit down, and asked bluntly what was the matter.

Margaret's exposition was pitiably elementary and crude. Like most girls of her generation, she had always stayed in her place, her place being to believe whatever her elders told her. There had never been any freedom of discussion between them, nor had her mother, light-hearted and easy-going as she was, ever displayed the smallest interest in what Margaret thought, but took it for granted that Margaret should trail as a small tug in her wake – compliant, unobtrusive, and acquiescent. Unluckily for herself, Margaret took it for granted too, thinking herself very lucky not to have an irritable mother, as so many girls of her acquaintance had, but a lively, charming mother, who always joked and never scolded, seemed younger than the really young, and created far more fun out of everyday life than one could possibly have created for oneself. Margaret, up to that moment, had been very well contented. But now she was surprised to see how Viola, after quietly listening, took hold of her poor little story, used it, swelled it, juggled with it, erected it into a symbol, construed it, adopted it; she was dismayed, in fact, to see her difficulty pass into the possession of a strong mind. 'For what have our mothers thought of us, all these years?' said Viola; 'that we should make a good marriage, so that they might feel they had done their duty by us, and were rid of their responsibility with an added pride. A successful daughter plus an eligible son-in-law. Any other possibility never entered their heads – that we might consult our own tastes, for instance. They run like trains, on rails, and if you were to elope with your painter it would amount to a railway accident in their lives.'

'That's why,' said Margaret, groping, 'one can't.'

'On the contrary,' said Viola; 'no one will be killed, only shaken. Don't you see that their trains are made of card-board – put together out of every odd-and-end of prejudice and convention, decorated with a few streamers of tinsel, and labelled with pompous names? There's nothing real about them at all.'

'Oh yes,' said Margaret, shocked. 'They love us. That's real.'

'Love us! but do they? Yes, they love us, but they sacrifice us. To do them justice,' she added, 'they sacrifice themselves as well. There's not one of our fathers or mothers who wouldn't break their own hearts without hesitation if it came to a struggle between their desires and their convictions. Really,' she said, 'sometimes I think it magnificent. Like mar-tyrs going to the stake. Magnificent and absurd. But for what a creed!'

Margaret was staring at her in complete amazement.

'Viola! But what do you mean? Surely one must have some principles? One must consider one's ... well, one's class? Mother always brought me up to believe that, and I'm sure your mother did too. I always had it drummed into me. Not in so many words, perhaps; but it was always taken for granted. That's why I feel so badly now. You see, Adrian was in a paper parcel. One doesn't know who his parents were, and naturally father and mother don't like it. I quite see that. It's different for me, because I love him; but I suppose that ought not to count. Aunt Clemmie says one was not put into this world for self-indulgence.'

'Does your mother say that too?'

'I am sure she would say it. I know mother believes in doing one's duty. She opened two bazaars last week.'

'And was photographed, and given a bouquet of orchids?'

'No, they were malmaisons. – But Viola, I see you are laughing at me. You puzzle me dreadfully. I feel that you are full of ideas and express only half of them. It is very disturbing. It's like talking to a Socialist,' said poor Margaret.

'Have you ever talked to a Socialist?'

'No, of course not. But that is what I imagine it would be like. One would feel he was restraining himself – letting only a few drops come through, though a great Niagara was behind them. Dreadful people – wanting to upset everything. Aunt Clemmie explained it to me. Everything we believe in would go by the board. All decencies. All principles. Oh, Viola,' said Margaret, 'I do try so hard to keep my head. Between Adrian, and mother and father, and now you, I feel in a whirl. Adrian says that love is the only thing which matters. Father and mother say behaviour is the only thing which matters. Goodness knows what *you* say. You talk about cardboard trains, till I don't know where I am. What would Sebastian say?'

'Sebastian?' Viola looked as though Margaret had jerked her. She paused. 'Leave Sebastian out of this; Sebastian, I think, doesn't know his own mind. So far, he takes what he wants, and doesn't know why he is unhappy. He doesn't talk to me. I fancy he doesn't talk to anyone. He just lives, and tries not to think. People like us must never think, for fear of thinking ourselves out of existence. If Sebastian thought at all he would go back to Chevron.'

Viola could have said a great deal more about Sebastian, but she felt some reluctance to discuss him with Lady

Roehampton's daughter – for unlike the simple Margaret, she was well aware of the liaison between them. She changed the subject, therefore, but because her resentment was strong and bitter she still hovered secretly round it, saying: 'At least let us do our parents the justice of saying that they exact nothing from us which they would hesitate to exact from themselves. Your mother, for instance, would fling anybody aside rather than provoke a scandal. So would mine,' she added, for it sounded invidious to single out Margaret's mother; but she had already committed herself, and Margaret caught her up.

'My mother, Viola? A scandal? But who should she fling? There has never been any scandal about mother. You can't think how nice she is to father, even though their tastes are quite different. Anyway, how very seldom one hears of scandals in connection with people like us! It is always among the working-classes that those dreadful murders happen, or else in Naples.'

'Margaret, you really are delicious. I didn't mean to say anything against your mother, and I think the way she has brought you up is a great tribute to her moral sense. There! are you satisfied? Don't worry, my dear; I meant nothing, and it was only an imaginary case.'

But Margaret persisted. 'You did mean something, though perhaps not about my mother. Do you mean that people – the people we know – sometimes do things they oughtn't to do? Really awful things? The worst? Viola, tell me. I never thought of it before, but now I feel that perhaps things go on all the time which I don't know or notice. You seem to know a lot more than I do. – Oh dear,' she said, 'what *would* Aunt Clemmie say?'

Viola looked at her round, puzzled face. She felt very much inclined to enlighten Margaret. She felt inclined to say, 'Very well, if you want the truth, here it is. The society you live in is composed of people who are both dissolute and prudent. They want to have their fun, and they want to keep their position. They glitter on the surface, but underneath the surface they are stupid – too stupid to recognise their own motives. They know only a limited number of things about themselves: that they need plenty of money, and that they must be seen in the right places, associated with the right people. In spite of their efforts to turn themselves into painted images, they remain human somewhere, and must indulge in love-affairs, which sometimes are artificial, and sometimes inconveniently real. Whatever happens, the world must be served first. In spite of their brilliance, this creed necessarily makes them paltry and mean. Then they are envious, spiteful, and mercenary; arrogant and cold. As for us, their children, they leave us in complete ignorance of life, passing on to us only the ideas they think we should hold, and treat us with the utmost ruthlessness if we fail to conform.'

But Viola left this indictment unspoken. She thought privately that Margaret was very well suited to the future that Lady Roehampton desired for her; as the wife of Tony Wexford she would do admirably. In twenty years' time she would be setting nicely in the mould that had shaped Lady Wexford *mère*, Lady Porteviot, and her own aunts. Adrian was a freak that had somehow entered her life, and Viola moreover suspected that enterprising young painters were not unwilling to better their social position; for she could not imagine that an attractive young Bohemian like Adrian should really have fallen in love with Margaret. She had concealed from

Margaret the fact that she had seen him at the Café Royal, a place which she frequented in the strictest incognito. No, they were not, Viola thought, made for each other.

So she tried to repair the damage she had done, and Margaret went away disconsolate, having received some advice of which her mother would very heartily have approved, but feeling that Viola at the last moment had failed her. There was no hope in anybody. Viola had begun by criticising her parents – and in such terms, too, as Margaret had never heard before – but had ended by supporting them. What was poor Margaret to believe? She had never been so much aware of her own ignorance and inexperience. Her mother's gaiety depressed her now, and the usual chatter tinkled falsely in her ears; she found herself analysing and judging, instead of accepting everything with a fascinated admiration.

Leonard Anquetil would have been amused had he known how his leaven, transmitted through Viola, was working in the heavy girl he had seen at Chevron, but to whom he had not spoken a word. He knew it about six months later, for when Margaret had gone Viola sat down to her weekly letter; it reached him at Manaos, and diverted him greatly.

True to his self-imposed schedule, Lord Roehampton presented himself in Sylvia's room exactly as the week elapsed. That is to say, he had received the packet at three o'clock in the afternoon, and at three o'clock in the afternoon he tapped on Sylvia's door. His train was due to leave for Newmarket at four-fifteen. Sylvia was sitting in front of her mirror preparing to go out. They had had half a dozen people to luncheon; it had been a successful party; she had recorded vaguely how nice George could be as a host, in his simple way; she was feeling well-disposed towards George, principally because she had persuaded him to keep his Newmarket appointment instead of accompanying her to the Opera that night, and partly also because Margaret, officially engaged to Tony Wexford, was now on a visit to her aunt Ernestine. George had been a great help to her over that business, and it all served to put her in a good temper. So she smiled at him in the mirror as he came up behind her. She was pinning on her hat at the moment, and her maid was standing by with the pins, wearing an anxious expression and making little darts and pounces which on a less propitious day might have annoyed Sylvia, but which now she accepted without much notice, simply because she felt free and happy and in a good humour with all the world. No George, no Margaret; she could be quite fond of them now she was rid of them. Dear George; a good sort, conveniently dense, but a good sort, none the less, even though his collars were always too high for him and his bowler hat too small. 'Dear George,' she said aloud.

'You can go, Sheldon,' he said to the maid. 'Her ladyship will ring when she wants you.'

Sylvia sat round and stared at him; he, so mild, had never behaved in so arbitrary a way before. 'Dismissing my maid, George! but I'm getting ready to go out. Aren't you starting yourself? What on earth is the matter?'

She saw then that he looked very odd; he had taken off his London clothes and had changed into a tweed suit, but his face was flushed and he kept putting his hand up to his tie and taking it away again. He kept the other hand in the pocket of his jacket, fumbling with something in the pocket, half drawing it out and then thinking better of it and thrusting it back again. It seemed as though by his order to the maid he had temporarily emptied his cistern-full of determination, and was waiting for it to fill up before he should draw off some more. Meanwhile, he fixed Sylvia very hard with his gaze, and kept swallowing, so that the Adam's apple in his throat bulged uncomfortably against his collar and made him cough two or three times in a way which appeared to annoy him, as though he felt it to be foolish. An absurd idea occurred to Sylvia; 'he is going to be sick,' she thought; and then she thought, 'he has got some bad news to tell me,' and her mind flew to Margaret, for she knew that George would not waver thus over any bad news concerned with Sebastian. He would say straight out, 'I have just heard that Sebastian was hurt to-day playing polo,' or whatever the accident might be, so she cast that terror from her mind as soon as it had entered it, and at the same time she felt the blood leave her body as though it had all been drained suddenly away, such was the fear that she had had and such the relief in realising that it was unfounded. 'George?' she said, and going up to him she took hold of him by the coat lapels.

'It's that,' he said, moving away from her and throwing the packet of letters down upon the dressing-table.

A glance was enough for her.

'How long have you had these?'

'A week.'

'A week? And you said nothing? – Where did you get them, may I ask?'

'Post. Anonymous.'

'Well, what are you going to do?'

'That depends upon you.'

'Upon me? Do you want me to tell you that they're a forgery?'

'No. They're not a forgery.' The Chevron writing paper lay

open on the table, and the hot words spilt out in Sebastian's writing.

'Are you going to divorce me, George?' Absurdly her mind flew to the Templecombes.

'I've been thinking it over. At first I thought I must divorce you, but that would mean a terrible scandal. I don't think I could face it. Besides, I dislike the idea of exposing these things to publicity, it gives such a shocking example. I have decided that I shall not divorce you if you will do what I say.'

'And that is?'

'You must know what it is.'

'Give up Sebastian?'

'Naturally.'

'But, George,' she said, frightened of his hard look, appalled by this sudden catastrophe, desperately trying to find a way out, 'how can I – it isn't practicable – I shall meet him everywhere – and what should I say to Lucy? I could promise you that there shouldn't be anything more of . . . of that sort, but how can I give up seeing him altogether?'

'I have thought of that. We shall shut up this house and go down to Wymondham. You have had twenty years of this kind of life. I put up with it to please you; now you shall put up with Wymondham to please me.'

'Oh God, you've given me no time to think – won't it satisfy you if I swear to give him up as my lover?'

Lord Roehampton did not answer; he looked at her with an expression of hatred and contempt.

'George? You would be punishing me quite enough: I love him.'

'Leave that out, please; I don't want to know anything about your feelings.'

'Don't you even want to know what I shall feel about you if you break my heart and shut me up in the country? What sort of life do you suppose we shall have together? We shall be civil to each other in front of the servants, and in front of Margaret, but underneath I shall hate you. Be generous to me, George, and you shan't regret it. Let me keep him as a friend.'

'Sylvia, how can you make such a childish proposal? It only shows me how vain and irresponsible you are. You might be my daughter, not my wife. I see,' he continued, his grievance rising, 'that you have no appreciation of my generosity,' and now indeed he began to see himself as a man full of magnanimity which has been overlooked and tossed on one side, instead of being acknowledged with instant tears of remorse and gratitude. All the pompous solemnity latent in him was suddenly called out when Sylvia, as he conceived it, attempted to put him in the wrong. 'No other man,' he went on, 'would have given you a second chance. Another man would have turned you straight out of the house. And instead of thanking me – instead of going on your knees to me almost – you dare to plead with me, you dare to ask for further favours.'

'You might be a Victorian husband,' she cried, getting angry in her turn.

'Oh, my standards differ from yours, I daresay,' he answered; 'I've never been very up-to-date, I've only been content to let you enjoy yourself without noticing that you were fooling me, and now that I find you out and make you the most generous offer that any man in my position could make, you turn on me and imply that I am treating you harshly.'

'You are making an absurd fuss,' she said, trying to change the tone of the conversation; 'to hear you talk, one would think you had spent all your life in a cathedral close. Don't you know how people live? Of course you do. You don't refuse to go to Chevron because you know that Harry Tremaine is Lucy's lover, or refuse to dine with ...' but here again the name is so august that out of respect for the printer it must again pass unrecorded. 'So why, when I'm concerned, behave as though we were living in eighteen-fifty? Because I'm your wife, I suppose,' she scoffed, feeling meanwhile as though she were squealing with terror in a trap.

Something in her imitation of his pompous manner provoked a physical anger in him, an exasperation such as is aroused by a blow on the elbow; he took her by the wrists and shook her backwards and forwards, casting her finally down upon her bed. Gasping, shaken, she gazed at him in speechless terror; violence was an element that had never entered into her conception of life. The luxurious room, the soft bed, the silken coverlet, all gave the lie to such primitive conduct. In a world where manners were everything, what was left to cling to, once manners had gone by the board? once men began to treat their women as women, not as ladies? George himself was almost immediately as horrified as she. He stood over her for a moment, trembling with passion and frightened by his desire to murder; then as his training reasserted itself he awoke to a sense of shame and astonishment that such a scene could occur between people like himself and Sylvia. 'See what you've done,' he said; 'you turn me into a beast, you make me forget the decencies of ordinary behaviour. But I won't apologise. This is probably the first time there has ever been any honesty between us. We lived on the surface, we never knew anything about each other. You were nice enough to me, and God knows I wasn't difficult to manage. Don't cry like that,' he said roughly, for Sylvia had broken down and was sobbing into her pillows; 'I shan't take back a word I have said, for all your tears. You may be thankful that I spare you. I don't spare you for your own sake, or even for my own; you know my reasons. And there is Margaret. We must keep up the farce; we owe it to the child.'

He paused. His rage had sustained him, but now everything seemed to have become flat.

'What would Clemmie say, if she knew!' he said, wretchedly and absurdly.

He looked at his watch.

'Sylvia, I am going now. Try to pull yourself together. Don't let Sheldon see that you have been crying. Sylvia!' he said, touching her on the shoulder.

He got no reply but an inarticulate murmur.

'I shall expect you to be ready to leave London by the end of this week. Did you hear me?'

'I heard you,' she answered.

George had gone; she walked about her room, smiting herself with her fists on the forehead; she looked at the appointments of her dressing-table, wishing that her hair-brushes might be made of wood, instead of chased silver, so that she herself, conformably, might be a woman of humble birth, able to run away with her lover, obscurely, without a gong of scandal reverberating through the drawing-rooms of high society and echoing in a thousand suburban homes. She even paused in her pacing, to lift the hand-glass; she considered it, as in moments of the acutest tension one concentrates on a material object irrelevant to the true preoccupation; it was of Queen Anne design, of octagonal back – she noted the obtuse angles (rubbed smooth by age) – chased with a pattern of Chinese pagodas; she cast it down on the ground in the desire to smash it; but it failed to break, by reason of the thickness of the pile carpet. Mechanically she stooped to pick it up and turned it over, more dismayed by its failure to break than another woman equally superstitious would have been by the shattering of a mirror on a harsher floor. The glass, the carpet, swelled themselves out into symbols of a life she could not escape. Their respective solidity and thickness conquered her. She sank down on her bed and took her head between her hands.

This is the end, she thought, rocking backwards and forwards – for, from the first moment when George had thrown the packet down upon her dressing-table, she had known that the game was up. The lovely, delirious game played with Sebastian; in which her passions had been involved; and not only her passions, but also her last challenge to the encroaching years. She had loved Sebastian; she would never again have a lover. In those first moments after George's departure, she scarcely knew whether it was for Sebastian or her finished youth that she mourned. She had been beautiful since the age of seventeen. Since the age of seventeen she had been a Toast. Now for the first time she envisaged the years in which she would be merely Lord Roehampton's Wife. Norfolk, and the tenants' Christmas tree – her imagination, rushing, painted her future in the most, to her, repellent colours. But, as she sat rocking backwards and forwards, her clenched fists pressed against her head, everything reduced itself eventually to the fact that Sebastian was lost to her.

She picked up the letters and looked at them, putting them down again quickly as a few words here and there recalled the precious days and incidents of the past year. She wondered who was responsible for this disaster – what jealous or envious woman, rifling her writing-table, bribing a servant perhaps, to get an impression of her keys? All the great scandals were familiar to her; the scandal of the Templecombes, of course, and other stories – stories of angry women risking all their reputation to explore the pockets of a coat thrown down in too great haste; stories of ruthlessness, and of broken liaisons; stories of illegitimacy brutally revealed; stories of terrible scenes between unfaithful lovers, or between husbands and wives. Everybody in society knew of these dark patches on brilliant lives; everybody knew of the sacrifices made in the sacred name of *tenue*, and of the smiles amiably exchanged in public between mortal enemies. They prided themselves upon a social if not a moral conscience. And now the same tragedy had befallen her, and she must meet it in the same way as others had met it.

No alternative offered itself to her mind. She was too well-trained. People in their position – hers, Sebastian's, and George's – did not make an open scandal. It was, simply, unthinkable. Just as the populace knew nothing of the discreet, one-horse brougham that waited outside a certain door, just as the populace knew nothing of the breach that had existed for thirty years between Lord and Lady Templecombe, so must the populace know nothing of the triangular complication between Sebastian and Lord and Lady Roehampton. Each class was bound by different obligations. Sylvia, rocking on her bed and seeking to resolve the stone of desperation that had hardened until within the space of half an hour it petrified her whole mind, recollected the recent case of a man and a married woman who had plotted murder rather than escape together without sufficient financial provision. 'Sufficient financial provision' – that was the phrase used by the prosecuting counsel. Sylvia was surprised to find herself laughing aloud. How paltry a thing was money! how could lovers let such a thing stand in their way? How gladly would she endure privations for Sebastian's sake (or so she thought at the moment; but privation to Sylvia meant three instead of fifty thousand a year). But she was bound by far more rigorous a necessity: the creed of her class, of her code. Even Sheldon – in spite of the special, the quite particular, intimacy that existed between mistress and personal maid – 'body-servant,' didn't they call it? – must not know that anything was amiss. She stood up, replaced the unbroken mirror on the dressing-table, carefully repaired with powder and rouge any damage that her face had suffered, tidied her hair, and rang the bell.

Sheldon appeared; was informed that her mistress would not, after all, be going out till the evening; was dining early before the Opera and would dress at six; had a headache and would lie down till then; did not wish to be disturbed.

And if his Grace should call?

Lady Roehampton looked at Sheldon as though she had intended an impertinence; as indeed she had.

'I am not at home to anybody. Please draw the blinds. Turn down the bed. Put out a handkerchief dipped in eau de cologne. Take those lilies out of the room – they make my headache worse. Don't come back till six.'

Sheldon obeyed her instructions, then ran upstairs, jammed on her bonnet, and hurried off to Grosvenor Square, in the hopes of finding Miss Button at Chevron House. There had been a bust-up between her ladyship and his lordship; that was evident; and Sheldon meant to be the first in with the news.

*

At eight o'clock the curtain went up on *Tristan and Isolde*, before a house hushed into the proper frame of mind already by the Overture.

A house – the expression is inaccurate. Upper circles and gallery were full; the stalls and boxes but sparsely occupied. Into the stalls, people trickled in parties of two and four, tiptoeing in the semi-darkness; into the boxes, parties came with less circumspection, having no resentful feet to stumble over, no whispered apologies to make; they came in, with a gleam of light as the door opened, and took their places amid scarcely suppressed chatter and laughter. Sh-sh-sh, came from the circles and gallery, but the disturbers glanced round, although unseen, into the dim amphitheatre as though chidden by an intruder in their own home. As the first act wore on, these gleamings and rustlings diminished and subsided; the stalls filled up; and the house began to await the final chords of the orchestra and the turning-up of the lights, when the full splendour of Covent Garden in mid-season should be revealed.

How dark they were, those minutes filled by the rumble of impending tragedy! A doom-laden ship, – strange, accepted convention upon the stage – when everybody knew that the tiers around the house were filled by the galaxy of London fashion, light-hearted and care-free people who took this in the natural course of the things they had to do. Little clerks, putting aside half a crown out of a weekly wage of five-and-twenty shillings, felt no grievance; they merely awaited the turning up of the lights to admire a spectacle which was as much part of their evening's treat as the music itself. Dr. John Spedding, who had at last brought his wife Teresa to Covent

Garden because she gave him no peace until he consented to do so, and who, being himself a sincere lover of music, had taken his seat full of prejudice against this elegant performance, now found himself infected by the general atmosphere of luxury and sophistication, and leant back in his seat definitely enjoying the sensation that around him were hundreds of spoilt, leisured people, soon to be on show like regal animals or plumaged birds, well-accustomed and seemingly indifferent to excited gaze.

Teresa, at his side, could scarcely sit still, such was her impatience. She wriggled herself against him like a kitten, and whispered to know how soon the act would be over. She was terribly bored by King Mark. Hush, said the people behind them, and she subsided, giving herself up again to the warmth and the mysterious presence of all those men and women, nonchalant in their boxes between the dim pink lights of the sconces, which just permitted them to be seen, quiet, silent, and attentive. Teresa Spedding was frankly and childishly fascinated by high life. She had quite a collection of photographs which she had cut out of the newspapers and stuck into an album, so that she was confident she would be able to recognise many of these celebrities although she had never yet seen them in the flesh. She spent a great deal of her time wondering about them; had they any feelings, she wondered? did husbands and wives ever quarrel? did they know how many servants they had, or was all that left to a secretary? did they call the King sir or sire? And were they all dreadfully wicked? It excited her beyond measure to know that she was actually within reach of them: would brush against some of them as they left the building when the opera was over. If only one of them would slip and twist an ankle, so that John might push his way forward professionally – 'Allow me, Lady Warwick, I am a doctor –' and then a few weeks later would come an invitation on paper with a gilt embossed coronet, 'Dear Mrs. Spedding, it would give me so much pleasure if you and your husband would spend the following week-end with us at Warwick Castle.' Thus Teresa's mind galloped along, until she became aware that the orchestra was playing the finale, and that in a few moments everyone would begin to clap and the lights would go up.

The music ceased, applause broke out, and the curtain came magnificently down, but it must be raised again, and the singers must bow, twice, three times. 'Don't clap, John, don't clap,' implored Teresa, in agonies lest her husband's enthusiasm should swell the delaying noise; but like all evils it came to an end, the applause died away, the curtain remained finally lowered, and Covent Garden blazed suddenly into light. It was like the first day of Creation, let there be light, and there was light, thought Teresa, but hastily checked her irreverence. The whole house was full of movement; people were getting up in the stalls; conversation roared; the orchestra was creeping away through a trap-door. The great red velvet curtain alone hung motionless. But Teresa's eyes were devouring the boxes; she clutched John's arm, she pinched it; 'Oh John, look, there's Princess Patricia in the Royal box, and Lord Chesterfield talking to her – they say he's the best dressed man in London—' but Teresa had no time to linger over Lord Chesterfield; her eyes were roaming too greedily; like a child before a Christmas tree, she felt dazzled by the glitter and variety presented to her sight. Tier upon tier of boxes, those dark squares cut in a wall of light. Within them, visible to the waist, sat the queens of fashion and beauty – or so thought Teresa, undiscriminating between the rightful holder and the parvenue – dazzling in tiaras and *rivières*, resplendent in their satins and *décolletés*, they allowed their arms in long white gloves to repose on the velvet ledge, while a fan slowly waved, and their eyes slowly travelled over the house, to find and acknowledge a friend, many friends; and the well-bred minimum of attention was accorded to the men who with suitable gallantry leaned over the backs of their chairs. This, in truth, was the great world as Teresa had conceived it. She regretted only that the men were in ordinary evening dress; somehow she had imagined that they would all be in uniform. Still, the black and white was a good foil; and the ladies gave her no cause for complaint, so generously had they emptied the contents of their safes on to their persons: from head to waist they trickled in diamonds. But it was not so much the diamonds that dazzled Teresa, for those she had fully expected; what she had not foreseen was this coming and going, this interchange of groupings, this indication of familiarity; so that a young man but recently observed in one box appeared in another on the opposite side of the house, and lounged there in the same accepted way; and what delighted her almost beyond control was to see famous people stopping to chat together, Lord Curzon with Mr. Balfour down in the gangway, laughing together as they enjoyed a joke. Now her album of photographs served her well, for many were the personalities she could point out to John; 'Do you see, John?' she said, still squeezing his arm, 'there in the third box on the left, in the grand tier – there's Mrs. Asquith with the Duchess of Rutland – and in the next box there's Lady Savile and Sir Ernest Cassel, – look, they're talking to Mrs. Asquith now, across the partition – what do you think they're saying? – and there's the Marquis de Soveral with his little imperial – and oh John, look! in the box opposite them, that's Lady Roehampton surely? yes, it must be; I've seen her before, once in the Park –' and Teresa's excitement reached its height, as she contemplated the beauty through her opera-glasses and thought that nothing could ever be more exquisite than this apparition of the renowned Lady Roehampton in the framing of a grand tier box. What self-possession, she thought, was expressed in the set of the magnificent shoulders, emerging from clouds of tulle! how divinely her head was poised, under its crown of diamonds! how royally she sat, surveying the house while a faint smile played about her lips! how much Teresa envied her, so calm and languorous and queenly, without a care in the world! Even the impassive John agreed that she was a handsome woman. And now a young man entered the box, a dark, slim young man, and sat beside her for a moment, speaking to her, but she seemed scarcely to take any notice of him, but turned to another man instead, a foreigner evidently, who came in and bowed very low over her hand; and the dark, slim young man got up and went away.

After that moment in Sylvia's box there were only two people in the opera-house for Sebastian: himself and her. He had been flung abruptly into a storm of rage and revengefulness. He was very angry indeed, and deeply disturbed, more deeply disturbed than anything but intuition warranted. Sylvia had, after all, said very little; she might have been teasing him; but he knew it was not so. She had spoken in malice, not in jest. How mean of her, he thought, clenching his fists, to choose that moment, when he could not possibly ask for an explanation! But he would catch her; he would have it out with her;

he would insist on knowing what she meant. He felt that he would kill her if necessary; despair possessed him, as though everything had begun to break up without any warning at all. He was seized with a passionate longing for Anquetil; Anquetil whom he had rejected for Sylvia. This recollection of Anquetil struck him as very queer, here at Covent Garden. Where was Anquetil now, at this instant? – Only Sebastian's training and traditions saved him from betraying himself in public, but as he descended the stairs, and made his way back to the stalls, glancing up at Sylvia's rosy clouds, no one suspected anything wrong. A familar figure, he looked much the same as usual: slender, charming, elegant, slightly aloof perhaps, save when he smiled down at a woman with a persuasiveness that was almost unconscious, but his acquaintances would have experienced no small surprise had they been able to read his heart. For he was already visiting a complicated wrath on that lovely vision just above his head. He had been drugged – thus did he rage in his heart – he had wasted himself on her, she had fooled him, all his follies of the past year were due to her, she had transformed him into something that was not himself at all. Oh, she might elude him now; but let her wait till he had her to himself: he would revile her, he would tell her what he really thought of her and her like, then he would break away from her and she should never see him again. He would go back to Chevron; he would set out to look for Anquetil; he would make love to other women under her very nose. Such were the varying schemes that coursed through his mind. She had debased him already; very well, he would debase himself more. He knew, without undue conceit, that he could get any woman he wanted. Sylvia was jealous as he had reason to know: he would make her suffer all the tortures of jealousy. He would not care if she paid him back in the same coin; his love for her was dead, and nothing but the wish for revenge had taken its place.

He heard the bell ringing outside in the foyer; everybody stirred, irritated at being interrupted in their chatter and at the prospect of giving a more or less polite attention once more to the music; a general movement took place, as people sought their seats; the lights began to fade out, apologetically as it were, not suddenly and dictatorially, but so as to give the audience plenty of time (if they desired it) to re-enter the other mood. Sebastian was grateful for the darkness. He rejoined young Ambermere; the last whisperings and rustlings died away; the conductor rose up before his desk; glared menacingly over the heads of the orchestra; gave two sharp taps with his baton, and the intolerable sweetness of the violins took up the opening of the second act.

Sebastian had been grateful for the darkness, but he had reckoned without the music he was about to hear. The second act of *Tristan* is no fit fare for a young man unhappily in love.

In the shades of the grand tier, Sylvia sat appalled by what she had done. She had not intended to introduce her breach with Sebastian at all in that manner. She had on the contrary made up her mind – at the end of those dreadful hours after George had left her – to go to the opera as though nothing had happened, to force herself to forget, to give Sebastian no inkling that anything was wrong, but to invite him into her box and spend one last, brilliant evening with him, and on parting to tell him that she must see him alone on an urgent matter next day. With her sense of style, the notion could not fail to appeal to her; she had driven to the Opera with the real swagger of the aristocrat to the scaffold. She had been determined that if anybody could carry off such a feat, she could. And then, at her first sight of Sebastian, she had broken down, she had lashed out at him with the first words that came into her head, simply because she herself was suffering. He was dear to her, too dear; she could be cruel to herself only by being cruel to him.

What a reckless fool she had been! Not only had she fallen short of her own standards, but she had accomplished nothing save to set an inexorable Sebastian on her tracks. Should she slip out under cover of the music and the darkness? No, she was too proud to do that; she was not Lady Roehampton for nothing. She would see it through. If only this music would let her reflect for a moment, she desperately thought, while trying to steer amongst the seething waters and crashing rocks of her mind within; but far from allowing her to reflect, its insistence grew until it swelled into an echo of all her past joys with Sebastian, and tragically sounded the despair of her present misery. Dared she press her hands over her ears, to shut out this crescendo that like a wave gathered itself together and heaped itself curling higher and higher until the intolerable moment when it should break? Dared she? The lights were low – but still she might be seen. The instinct to preserve her dignity before the world was in her blood, in her bones: she might suffer, but she must endure.

He waylaid her as she was coming down the steps, enveloped in her cherry cloak, superb even amongst the decorative crowd that surged round her; and despite his anger some lines from *Cyrano* came into his head:

Elle fait de la grâce avec rien, elle fait
Tenir tout le divin dans un geste quelconque,
Et tu ne saurais pas, Vénus, monter en conque,
Ni toi, Diane, marcher dans les grands bois fleuris,
Comme elle monte en chaise et marche dans Paris!

but even as he identified the quotation, he scored an additional mark against her, that she should suggest the sugared
voluptuousness of *Cyrano* after the rich and passionate fire of
Tristan. He presented himself before her with perfect decorum,
a young man preparing to see a lady to her carriage, most correct. 'Let me get your carriage for you,' he said, and helped her
with her cloak, which was slipping from her shoulders. 'Lady
Roehampton's carriage,' he said to the functionary at the door.
'Just one minute, your Grace,' and the name was taken up
and bawled by the linkmen out into the street: 'Lady
Roe'ampton's kerridge! Lady Roe'ampton's kerridge!' and
there was a flutter among the little crowd of footmen, as Lady
Roehampton's James detached himself from the group and ran
away in his top-hat and hollow-sounding top-boots to look for
the carriage round the corner.

Other people were waiting for their carriages under the portico; amongst them, though Sylvia and Sebastian were
unaware of it, Lord and Lady O. and their Alice. Lady O. drew
her train aside and made signs to Alice, which Alice did not
in the least understand. For the first time in her life she paid
the minimum of attention to her mother and her signs. Lady
Roehampton and the duke were so much more worth looking
at! They epitomised for her all the life of the great and brilliant world; they had nothing upon earth to do except to
enjoy themselves and be ornamental. How beautiful Lady

Roehampton looked in the swirls of that cherry velvet! She envied them both from the bottom of her heart.

Then James ran up and touched his hat and said her ladyship's carriage was the next but one. Sylvia, gathering up her skirts, stepped delicately out as the horses drew up, tossing their heads against the bearing-reins, and James sprang forward, the rug over his arm, to open the door. It was a warm night and the window of the brougham was lowered. Sebastian leant in at it. He was bare-headed and extremely pale.

'Sylvia, I must see you.'

'Come to luncheon to-morrow.'

'No, to-night.'

'Really, Sebastian! George ...'

'Nonsense, George is at Newmarket. I shall follow you, in a quarter of an hour.'

'Lady Roe'ampton's kerridge stops the way!' shouted the linkman.

'You won't get in,' said Sylvia; 'I shall send the servants to bed.'

'You forget; I've got the key.'

'I shall put up the chain.'

'Then I shall ring the bell.'

'Lady Roe'ampton's kerridge stops the way!'

'Well, if you must – but for heaven's sake don't let anyone see you.'

'That's all you think of. – All right, James,' he said, stepping back.

It was a sight to see how James could twist himself up on to the box when the carriage was already in motion.

*

Half an hour later Sebastian let himself into the hall of Roehampton House. He heard the jingle of his hansom die away and the quick trot of the horse on the wooden pavement of Curzon Street. He felt cold and hot by turns, and a sharp pain kept stabbing through his head. Sylvia came out of the library as she heard him softly shut the door, and with a finger to her lips beckoned him into the room. A fire was burning, and one shaded lamp on a table. They both stood, facing one another. Sylvia still wore her cherry cloak flung about her, her beauty rising out of it as a painted portrait out of its drapery, but Sebastian noted with satisfaction that she was extremely nervous. She had taken up a paper-cutter and was tapping it on her nails. 'Are you quite crazy, Sebastian, to come here at this hour of the night?'

'It's not the first time,' he said, looking at her.

'Please say what you have got to say, and go away quickly. Don't speak too loudly; I think the servants have all gone to bed, but one can never be sure. However touchy and ridiculous you are, you can still show me a little consideration. What is the matter? Why don't you speak?'

But Sebastian remained silent. The words were strangled as they came to his lips. He was feeling so strongly that words were no use to him. Instead, his mind concentrated on a small, irrelevant object, so that it seemed that object was the only thing of importance to him in the world: a crystal rabbit of Chinese carving, standing on the table immediately beneath the lamp. The rays fell upon it, touching the crystal into little points of highlight; the nose, the ears, and one paw became little prisms, at which Sebastian stared. He had seen the rabbit a thousand times before; he had, in fact, given it to Sylvia himself; it was as familiar to him as the many other objects

152

which stood about upon the tables – the Celadon bowls, the jade ash-trays, the Fabergé cigarette-boxes, or the little jew-elled clocks from Cartier. From the rabbit his eyes travelled over the rest of the room, that room in which he had been a constant visitor, and which resembled so many other London rooms that he frequented, beautiful in their own way, but all equally impersonal, conventional, correct, with the grey pile carpet, the *petit point* chairs, the Romneys and the Raeburns, the big Coromandel screen, the mahogany doors, and all those objects disposed upon the tables – Christmas presents mostly, exchanged between so-called friends who in reality cared nothing for one another, but who unquestioningly followed the expensive fashion, giving one another these trinkets that were either cut in stone as hard as their own hearts, or mounted in enamel or ormolu as vain as their own protesta-tions. Romola Cheyne, he remembered, boasted that she had gone round the world commissioning Leygon to do up her new house for her, and had given a dinner party and a ball in it on the night of her return. He remembered this, staring again at the innocent crystal rabbit. He had almost forgotten what had brought him there; he was thinking only that the people he knew resembled the rooms they lived in – not vulgar, not showy; no; restrained rather, and in admirable taste, but hard, stereotyped, and meaningless.

Had not his own liaison with Sylvia been of that nature? He looked at her, standing by the fire, waiting for him to speak, so beautiful in her cherry cloak, so exquisitely in accordance with the refinement of her surroundings. Thus far at least he misread her as cruelly as Lady O.'s Alice and Teresa Spedding.

'George has found out,' she said.

She broke down then and wept, sinking on to the sofa and burying her face in her hands. For once in her life she forgot about her looks; her tiara went awry, most pitiable and grotesque; her tears dropped on to the velvet of her cloak. What would Lady O.'s Alice and Teresa Spedding have said, could they have seen her now! Sebastian himself was horrified; he had not thought her capable of such despair; he had so often upbraided her for her superficiality; had told her – cruelly enough – that in self-defence he would never give her all his heart. 'You know nothing about love,' he had said; it had been a joke between them – though a joke with a bitter edge to it – and he had never seen how wistfully she sometimes looked at him after he had teased her. She had not wanted him to know how much she loved him, even though by withholding that knowledge she had forced him to misjudge her. She had been afraid of making him feel a prisoner. Now there was no longer any reason for concealment. She put out her hand and groped for his head; he was kneeling beside her, and she hugged his head to her breast, weeping over him.

When she had recovered herself a little, they talked; Sebastian sprang up and walked about the room, for he could not endure to look at Sylvia in such ruin. 'But if you really care like that,' he said, 'tell George to go to hell; let him divorce you and come to me; we'll travel, we'll bury ourselves at Chevron; anything you like. Now that I've found out, I shall never doubt you again,' and he besought her, saying that happiness was not a thing to throw away for any consideration in the world. She sobbed again, even as she laughed at him; 'Sebastian, my darling, what are you saying? I'm an old woman – are you proposing to marry me? or are we to live together in open sin? Don't you see that marriage between us would be absurd? I could never face the ridicule ...' 'Then live with me,' he said; but she shook her head, 'Sebastian, you're young, you're crazy, you don't know the world; I couldn't face that scandal.'

'Well, but Sylvia,' he said, trying to be reasonable, 'you disconcert me completely: at one moment you tell me that the whole of your life comes to an end if we give each other up, and the next moment you tell me that you can't face the scandal. Is your reputation more precious to you than I am? Surely we have passed beyond social things. Life isn't entirely made up of parties. If I don't give a damn for the world, why should you?'

'I don't know, Sebastian,' she said miserably. 'I'm made like that, I suppose. What would happen to us if I lived with you? Everybody would fight shy of us, and I couldn't bear it. Despise me if you must. You have a great deal more courage than I have and you're more independent. Look how angry you were with me over Margaret's engagement. If I'd listened to you, I should have given her a cheque and told her to elope with Adrian. Oh, heavens,' she said, with a fresh burst of tears; 'don't tell me she loved that boy as I love you.'

He tried again to persuade her; he told her that she was making herself the victim of a system she herself and her equals had created. There seemed to him something incongruous between her grief, which was obviously genuine, and the false creed which forced her to suffer it. 'The moral aspect doesn't exist for you,' he said; 'if it did, I should have no right to urge you, I suppose, but you care nothing for George, you care only for the world. It's incomprehensible to me, Sylvia. I always knew that we were different. What would anything matter, so long as we had each other?'

'Sebastian, you talk like a boy.'

'And you – you talk like the most cynical of women. You've been brought up on the principle of old Octavia Hull: Thou shalt not be found out.'

'I have, I admit it, I'm not ashamed of it. People like us must not be found out. We owe it ...'

'Oh, Sylvia, spare me those phrases.'

'But they are true. Society is founded on them. We at the top ...'

'I never knew there was so much solidarity between you and the old women,' he said sardonically.

'I never knew it either – until it came to the point,' she replied. 'You know that I was never very careful; not strictly careful. I did rash things, like that Pageant, which compromised my position to a certain extent, but I risked it because I wanted to do it.'

'Oh, Sylvia!' he said, suddenly touched by her childishness.

'Well, you see for yourself,' she continued more confidently, encouraged by the softening in his tone and feeling that she had at last hit upon something to say in self-justification. 'I wasn't exactly a coward always, was I? I did show a certain independence? I went against George, over that. He didn't exactly forbid it, but he did say it was unbecoming, and I knew he was right. I knew a lot of people – people who mattered – would disapprove, but I did it all the same. And I suffered for it,' she added; 'oh yes, I suffered for it.'

He looked at her, gently, not scornfully, thinking that to her there was very little difference between one kind of suffering and another.

'So you see, Sebastian,' she went on, 'up to a point I have always been ready to take risks. But there comes a point beyond which one simply cannot go. It breaks my heart to lose you. I shall never be the same again.' She meant it.

'But you will still be Lady Roehampton, and I daresay that in a few years' time people will have forgotten all about the Pageant. Had I not better go now? The servants might see the light in the hall, and come down to find out who was here. They have never caught us yet, and it would be a pity if we were caught on the very night we were saying good-bye.'

V

TERESA

Lucy poured out her heart to Miss Wace. She took Wacey's loyalty and discretion absolutely as a matter of course, partly from years of habit, partly because it never occurred to her to regard Wacey as a human being at all, but rather as a repository for ill-temper, petty annoyance, temporary good-humour, or whatever mood she, Lucy, might happen to be in. Wacey in point of fact was entirely trustworthy. Her whole life was wrapped up in Chevron and in Lucy, for snobbish and emotional reasons, and Lucy's indiscretions sufficiently replaced any baby that might under different circumstances have nuzzled at Wacey's breast. Wacey had her friends, but it was not to them that she would repeat Lucy's confidences. Not likely. She got quite enough satisfaction out of wagging her head, pursing her mouth, and putting on a general air of I-could-an-I-would. An internal pride compensated her for any external boasting that she might thus forgo. The tap at her door, the almost surreptitious stealing-in of Lucy, was reward enough. She felt then like an old Nannie to whom her charge repairs in moments of distress.

Lucy sat at the schoolroom table – the schoolroom had long since been handed over to Wacey as her own domain – and twisted her pretty little hands unhappily on the dark-red, ink-stained cloth. 'I wish I knew what had happened, Wacey' – that was her refrain. Wacey knew very well to what she referred. 'He won't let me talk to him, Wacey. He doesn't see any of his friends. He comes here, and spends all his time with Wickenden and the estate people. You know that new circular saw that he has installed next to the forge? Well, he stands for hours with his hands in his pockets, watching the men cut up the wood as though it were human beings they were cutting. That's what Mrs. Cheyne said last week. He didn't know we were watching him. Yet in a way he seems quieter. He never does those mad things now – never arranges for those mad parties. In a way, I wish he would. It seemed normal for a young man with plenty of money. It worried me, but it didn't really worry me, if you know what I mean. It only worried me because I felt he wasn't really happy underneath. He wasn't doing it because he liked it. I wish he would do it again, and because he did like it, quite naturally,' said poor puzzled Lucy.

'He won't, though,' said Miss Wace, sagely; 'not now that he has had a Disappointment in Love.'

'Don't talk such nonsense, Wacey,' said Lucy, irritated; 'what do you know about disappointments in love? You don't imagine that he really cared about that baby-snatcher? Good gracious me, he was a year old when her daughter was born. I remember taking him with me when I went to see her in her cradle.' Lucy, by a queer unnecessary refinement of discretion, was becoming mixed as to her pronouns in her avoidance of proper names.

The confusion deepened as she went on. 'Her mother and I – her mother was still in bed – we used to make jokes about their marrying. I remember we used to discuss what church they should be married in. That was – oh dear,' Lucy sighed, 'in eighty-six. We wore bustles,' and Lucy, suddenly amused, went off into peals of laughter. 'What odd things one remembers! And how much more sensible we have become since those days! Would you believe it, Wacey, once I had a pair of sleeves of rainbow velvet with a white satin tight-fitting frock made by Worth, and a man seeing me struggling to go through a narrow doorway said, "Oh, duchess, surely you ought to wear only one sleeve at a time?" And then after that the sleeves became so tight that one could not put on one's little bonnet without undoing one's bodice. Isn't it incredible to think we could have suffered such things in the name of fashion?'

This was the mood in which Miss Wace adored Lucy; she could have listened for hours to such reminiscences. They evoked a dashing past which Miss Wace knew only by hearsay, since it had occurred long before Miss Wace's advent at Chevron; they indicated a period in which the great scandals, such as the Tranby Croft scandal, had taken place, and when the fashionable pastime had been bicycling round Battersea Park; a period when Miss Wace's father was still alive, and she had not been obliged to go out and earn her living. She adored Lucy for having led, at that time, much the same life as she was leading now. Of late, Miss Wace had observed, the duchess was much more readily inclined to such recollections of the past. It was as though she groped after something which was vanishing, something which had vanished – something which was already history.

'Fancy,' said Lucy, 'Sylvia and me in bustles! But how lovely she was! All the old men were mad about her. And all the young ones too. Whenever she appeared in a ballroom, there was a rush for her.'

'And for you, too, duchess,' said Miss Wace, loyally.

'Ah, well,' said Lucy, who did not altogether relish that 'too.' 'We used to go about a good deal together, certainly. And to think,' she reverted, 'that she should end by playing that trick on him! What do you think of that, Wacey? What do you think of that? When I remember him in his pelisse and Margaret sucking a comforter in her cradle!'

'I call it a Breach of Friendship,' Miss Wace pronounced.

'Rubbish,' said Lucy, turning on her; 'if a woman of her age can catch a young man of his, she has every right to do so. Not that I should care about it myself; I should think it undignified. But these women who have been beauties all their lives – they die hard, you know, Wacey. They can't resist it. They remember their old triumphs. But still, we don't know what has really happened, Wacey, do we? We only know that they don't see each other any more, and that she has gone off to Norfolk, and that he seems completely at a loose end. And now I hear that Lord Roehampton has got himself appointed governor of some province in Australia – or Africa perhaps it is – and that they are going off directly after their daughter's wedding.'

'Let me see – Lady Margaret is marrying Lord Wexford in the first week of November, I think,' murmured Miss Wace succulently; 'St. George's, Hanover Square; and that reminds me,' she added professionally, putting on a voice like an engagement block, 'Viola has an appointment next Thursday to try on her bridesmaid's frock.'

'Well, you'd better go with her, Wacey; I know you like that sort of thing. The procreation of children and all that. A wedding is nothing but an excuse for indulging in indecency under respectable guise. Oh, you needn't look down your nose. You know perfectly well that you would like to see a nursery at Chevron full of Sebastian's children. You know that when you come to Sebastian's wedding in the chapel, you will be thinking of the nursery all the time.'

Miss Wace did not appreciate such remarks, but Lucy was correct in her diagnosis all the same. The anticipation of Sebastian's marriage and its results were constant factors at the back of the minds of all the feminine population of Chevron. Miss Wace, Mrs. Wickenden, the housemaids, the scullery-maids, the still-room maid, the laundresses, and the wives of the men-servants all looked forward secretly and lasciviously to the day when his Grace's engagement should be announced. The essential secretiveness of their anticipation did not deter them from open discussion. But their discussion was based on other than the real grounds. It took the advertised form of an altruistic interest in Sebastian's welfare. Miss Wace, of course, held herself aloof from it, yet to her own friends she confided her dread lest Sebastian should become a Confirmed Bachelor. Mrs. Wickenden, of course, repaired to the sympathetic ear of her sister-in-law. The housemaids, scullery-maids, and laundresses chattered amongst themselves, unaware that each one of them projected herself into the position of his Grace's bride; turned over the trousseau as though it were her own; stood before the chapel altar and the white lilies in the great golden pots; imagined herself in a first-class carriage alone with Sebastian, *en route* for Spain or Egypt; lived through the intoxicating strangeness of the first night in the Paris Ritz. Any one of the housemaids, scullery-maids, or laundresses would have been sincerely and properly shocked by any suggestion of the kind. Their visions were all of a young lady, fair, innocent, and well-bred, who, shyly yielding to his Grace's pleading, involved herself deliciously and inextricably in the consequences of her murmured 'Yes'; for such was their ignorance and humility, that they were content to savour their own dreams through the medium of another. Their simple minds dwelt exclusively upon matrimony. Wacey and Mrs. Wickenden, certainly, were better advised, and derived a dangerous but agreeable titillation from their knowledge of Sebastian's affair with Lady Roehampton; they tasted their superiority, initiated as they were into the goings-on of the great world; nevertheless they shared the simple cravings of the lesser fry, the craving for romance, the feminine fulfilment of a wedding, the feudal desire for an heir – and, pushing their primitive sentimentality a step further, would willingly have wept over Sebastian's funeral and worshipped a baby master of Chevron in his cradle. Sebastian himself, unconscious of this stirring in the ant-heap of Chevron, went his own way and failed to gratify the visions of his mother and his dependents.

He had had one unfortunate experience; he did not want another. (But lions lie in wait for us round the corner of our path.) He was not broken by the loss of Sylvia, but he was made unhappy, uneasy; what worried him most was the knowledge that Sylvia was somewhere in the world, far harder hit than he himself. Whenever he could get to Chevron, he enjoyed hours of complete forgetfulness. His mother distressed herself unnecessarily. When he stood watching his new saw-mill, he was thinking simply of how cleanly the circular saw cut through the wood, knots and all; he was not thinking of Sylvia, who had never been associated with such things as saw-mills in his mind.

Chevron and Sylvia had always been kept quite separate. Only when he was in London did the uncomfortable thought of Sylvia return; he was always aware of the proximity of Curzon Street, even though he knew the blinds of Roehampton House were down – down, as for a death. Poor Sylvia! how much she must be hating her enforced retirement in Norfolk! How intolerably rural George would become! He wondered what Sylvia did all day. Sylvia's friends wondered too, and tried to sound Sebastian, but only Mrs. Cheyne dared to tackle him outright. Mrs. Cheyne was a woman of strong personality and vigorous courage; Sebastian admired and respected her, and she for her part entertained an almost maternal interest in the young man, an interest which was not lessened by the fact that he was rich, handsome, discontented, a duke, and the owner of Chevron. They understood each other very well. Mrs. Cheyne appeared to him as one of the few women of his acquaintance who had a real spaciousness in her nature; a woman who erred and aspired with a certain magnificence. She brought to everything the quality of the superlative. When she was worldly, it was on the grand scale. When she was mercenary, she challenged the richest fortunes. When she loved, it was in the highest quarters. When she admitted ambition, it was for the highest power. When she suffered, it would be on the plane of tragedy. Romola Cheyne, for all her hardness, all her materialism, was no mean soul.

She had, however, one weakness: she could not allow anyone to be better informed than herself. Whether it was politics, finance, or merely the affairs of her friends, the last word, the eventual bombshell of information, must proceed from her and no other. On the whole she preferred her information to be good; and although she was quite prepared to invent where she could not ascertain, she would first make an assault on the main and most reliable source of knowledge. Thus if she wanted to know exactly what had happened between Sylvia and Sebastian, she would ask either Sylvia or Sebastian; and Sylvia not being available it was on Sebastian that her attack was directed one evening, when he took her into dinner at her own house; 'Now tell me, Sebastian,' she said at once, 'what's this about Sylvia going off to the country in the middle of the season? She told me she needed a rest, but that's clearly nonsense; I never saw her looking better in her life. Sylvia would never coop herself up like that with old George, unless she had a good reason for it. What is it all about?'

Sebastian would have resented this questioning from anyone else, but there was something in Mrs. Cheyne's personality which made people not only endure but answer her questions. Besides, if one took her into one's confidence, there was more chance of enlisting her discretion than if, thwarted, she had to fall back upon her imagination. She was, moreover, a woman of great experience, to whom few explanations were necessary. 'Well,' said Sebastian, crumbling his bread, 'George found out and turned rusty.' It was a relief to him to say it. After those seven words, he knew that Mrs. Cheyne would press him no further. They were seven words more than he had spoken to anybody else, but Mrs. Cheyne was a woman who could fill in every detail for herself from an outline of seven words.

'So that's that,' said Mrs. Cheyne, but although she spoke briskly Sebastian felt that her briskness was neither unkindly nor unsympathetic.

He derived a curious comfort and support from this brief interchange with Mrs. Cheyne. The bond between them had strengthened by fifty per cent – a purely platonic bond, between a middle-aged woman who had a difficult position to maintain, and a young man whose problems were created entirely by his own temperament. Still, Sebastian thought, as he walked away from her house that night, she had suggested no solution to him. He was still in the position of having to work out his own salvation. Perhaps there was no solution. Perhaps he had really been condemned from the start to this unsatisfactory, searching, makeshift life. He wondered what had become of Anquetil. Anquetil, that stranger, had spoken a great many disquieting truths.

Moreover, Sebastian just then in that autumn of nineteen hundred and six was unhappy for other than personal reasons. Perhaps the excessive gaiety of his summer had disagreed with him. He had often envied Sylvia, who could take enjoyment frankly, and who, in her unanalytical way, assumed that he took it frankly also, despite her momentary anxieties as to a moodiness that she was quite incapable of understanding. Thus she would throw herself upon novelty in an uncritical spirit that was to Sebastian a source of mingled envy and disgust. Every craze of the moment rushed into her life like the waves of a tide filling her shallow pools; he remembered her many enthusiasms: her enthusiasm over the latest American millionaire – 'But, darling, you don't appreciate the *freshness* of his mind; we all appear to him like a lot of old waxworks; he told me so himself; such an amusing idea, I think; and he does so love our pictures and our houses; he's going to buy Eadred Temple-combe's "Red Boy," the Sir Joshua, you know; and last time he came to Wymondham he wanted to buy the whole house and move it brick by brick to America;' her enthusiasm over the Pageant; her enthusiasm over the Boston, and the youthful energy with which she had gone to d'Egville every afternoon for lessons. He had marvelled at her, even while he pretended to accord. But underneath it all he had worried. This American invasion; this Radical Government so unexpectedly returned at the General Election; this much talked-of Labour vote; these cartoons of John Bull looking over a wall at a bull labelled Labour; this new craze for publicity among the people he knew; this feverishness generally; this adulteration of society; this tendency on the part of young Wickenden to break away – what did it all mean? Did it mean that they were all riding for some smash? and would the smash, when it came, be constructive or destructive? But because such speculations were unsuitable, he had never imposed them upon Sylvia; he had never imposed them upon anybody; he had kept them to himself, and they had festered.

At moments he was overcome by the futility of his life. Flirtation was scarcely an adequate outlet for the energy of one-and-twenty. His mother, when he once incautiously said something of the sort to her, looked at him in amazement and asked what on earth he meant? 'I'm sure you do all that can be expected of you, darling. You run the estate; and then, think of all the time you spend in those tiresome barracks! Why, only the other day I heard Margot asking you to go to Cannes with her, and you said you couldn't, because you had to be at Windsor. I felt quite cross, knowing how much you would enjoy Cannes with Margot. Really, I don't see why you need reproach yourself.' But he continued to reproach himself. Every time he passed the two sentry-boxes in Whitehall and saw the two troopers sitting motionless on their motionless horses exposed to the silly admiring gaze of the passer-by, he hated himself for the authority he might exercise over those men. Every time he

met a detachment of his regiment, their red cloaks spread magnificently over the rumps of their horses, riding through the
mist of London down St. James's Street, he revolted against the
connection which linked him with such picturesque foolery. He
liked it, and he hated himself for liking it. He liked himself for
hating it, and hated himself for submitting to it. He could not
endure to look at the photograph of himself in uniform, with
the great black boots and the great white gauntlets; yet at the
same time, when Wacey, at his mother's request, presented him
with six copies of the photograph to sign for Mrs. Wickenden,
Mrs. Vigeon, Mrs. Diggs, Mrs. Hodder, the other Mrs. Wickenden, and Wacey herself, he sat down obediently and signed
them all with a suitable flourish.

That was on the occasion of his coming-of-age. His grandmother, and all his uncles with their wives, gathered at
Chevron. Sebastian liked his grandmother. He had sufficient
discrimination to respect in her a reality of which his mother
and her friends achieved only a thin imitation by the greatest
effort. His mother and her friends might be more amusing,
more up-to-date; they were certainly more fashionable; but the
Dowager Duchess carried an air of solid assurance which
belonged to a less uneasy age. That slightly raucous note of defiance was absent from her pronouncements. She did not protest;
she merely ignored. Nothing unpleasant ever ruffled her seren-
ity, because she simply failed to notice it. Darwin and the
Labour Party alike had passed unnoticed under the bulwark of
her mighty nose; the one in eighteen seventy-one, the other in
nineteen-six. She remained unaware that the Americans were
discovering Europe far more rapidly than the Europeans had
discovered America. The only event that had ever been known
to arouse her indignation was the death duty imposed by Sir

William Harcourt in the Radical Budget of eighteen-ninety-four. She had been forced to take notice of that; because her son, Sebastian's father, had been killed in the South African war in nineteen-hundred when Sebastian was fourteen years old; and she had read in the *Morning Post* that the duty payable on the Chevron estates would amount to one hundred thousand pounds' benefit to the Treasury. On that occasion the Dowager Duchess had startlingly and alarmingly emerged from her trance, had sent for her man of affairs, and had dictated a letter of protest to the Chancellor of the Exchequer. It was a dignified protest, but still it was a protest. It expounded the fallacy of impoverishing the great estates, and pointed out the increase of unemployment which must necessarily arise as a result of such taxation. It drew attention to the number of pensioners supported by the Chevron estate. It hinted that such pensions might in future be discontinued, reduced, or even thrown upon the charge of the Government. It indicated the necessity for the continuance of good relations between landowners, such as the lords of Chevron, and their people. It suggested that any disintegration of such good relations might be attended by the most disastrous consequences.

The Dowager Duchess was pleased with this composition. She sent for her surviving sons, Lord Geoffrey, Lord John, and Lord Richard, and commanded her man of affairs to read it aloud to them. The man of affairs, who in the solitary presence of the Dowager Duchess was the meekest and most sycophantic of mortals, recovered some degree of masculine self-esteem when confronted with these three male representatives of the House of Chevron. He was uncertain as to how they would regard his part in the affair of the letter; they might even consider that he had had no business to write it. But he was a poor man, with three children to support, and he could not be expected to go against the wishes of the Dowager Duchess. Thus he argued to himself, and hoped that Lord Geoffrey, Lord John, and Lord Richard would sympathise with his position. If the Dowager Duchess chose to make a fool of herself, it was no affair of his; he was there to do what he was told. To his surprise, and also to his relief, neither Lord Geoffrey, nor Lord John, nor Lord Richard, questioned his part for a moment. On the contrary, they entirely approved their mother's action. They applauded it as most timely and proper. With her, they settled down to await a satisfactory reply. With her, they exploded into a momentary indignation when a formal acknowledgement was returned by the Treasury saying that her Grace's communication had been received and would be passed on to the proper quarter. With her, they renewed their optimism. With her, they established a perennial grievance after a polite note came from the Treasury saying that the Chancellor quite understood her Grace's anxiety, but much regretted that no exception could be made for individual cases.

The Dowager Duchess never quite recovered from that outrage. It had, however, one definite effect upon her: it caused her to take Sebastian under her protection. She persisted in regarding him ever after as a victim of ill-treatment. In vain did Lucy explain that Sebastian — especially after a long minority — would have a more than adequate income; the Dowager Duchess continued to shake her snow-white head, and to console Lucy with the assurance that at her death her jointure of five thousand a year would revert to supplement Sebastian's budget. 'We useless old women,' she would say remorsefully. On Sebastian's birthday, and at the beginning of each school-term, she would send him a golden pound in a pill-box; and the pound, every time, would be accompanied by two separate notes; one to Sebastian, saying that, having had four sons of her own, she knew how schoolboys liked tips; the other to Lucy, saying she did not send more, because it was bad for boys to have too much pocket-money, but that she could not bear the idea of poor Sebastian going short. 'He must be able to keep up his position,' she wrote, 'among his schoolfellows.'

Sebastian, then, liked and appreciated his grandmother, and never treated her to any of his exhibitions of moodiness or ill-temper. His manner towards her was always full of consideration and courtesy. Lucy scoffed and called it his Little-Lord-Fauntleroy manner; but Sebastian only smiled and remained unmoved. The servants said that it was pretty to see them together. Sebastian's arm, indeed, was the only arm that the Dowager Duchess would accept on her annual peregrinations round the garden. Then she would stop frequently, because she was out of breath and would not admit it, in order to croak critically at some arrangement in the borders which she did not approve. 'Diggs never had any taste beyond begonias,' she croaked, pointing with her rubber-tipped stick at some grouping of tulips and forget-me-not; but Sebastian, in patient escort, knew that she was thinking of Diggs' father, and not of the present Diggs. He never pointed this out. He liked to encourage his grandmother in her memories of fifty years ago, when she had quarrelled with an earlier Diggs over the begonias. Lucy watched him, and told Wacey how odd he was. 'As sweet as honey with that old woman, and as cross as two sticks with the rest of us.' Wacey wagged her head, and said there was no Accounting for the Present Generation.

The presence of his grandmother alone reconciled Sebastian to his coming-of-age. He liked her rudeness, her interference, and her limitations. She was a rough, downright old woman, who said what she meant and meant what she said, and who had no pretty or even civilised affectations of opinion or behaviour. She said quite frankly that she regretted the abolition of slavery. It irritated her to know that an offending servant could give notice. Her personal habits were equally primitive, and by virtue of her position she assumed an equal right to them: if she wanted to spit, she spat; and since she suffered cruelly from eczema, she scratched her back quite frankly with an ivory hand on the end of a long stick, plunging it down the opening of her bodice after dinner; or, in the day-time, rubbed her shoulders against the back of her chair, performing both gestures with equal candour and vigour. A streak of coarseness in Sebastian's nature delighted in these displays and in the embarrassment which they produced in his mother. 'Really, Sebastian – she adores you – couldn't you suggest to her ...' 'But I don't want to suggest anything to her, Mother; don't you see that she lives in the eighteenth century?' 'No, I don't,' said Lucy tartly; 'I see only that she's extremely unpleasant and I'm glad I didn't ask anybody here outside the family to meet her.'

Sebastian talked to his grandmother about his distress. He knew that she would not sympathise, but he knew also that her lack of sympathy would come from deeper causes than that of his mother or his friends. Where, for instance, was the good in talking to Ambermere, who was in the same position as himself, but who was untroubled by anything save the pre-occupation of having as good a time as he possibly could? Where was the good of talking even to Mrs. Cheyne, who would simply tell him not to be silly? His grandmother would not dismiss him with such light evasions; she would hit him over the head with a bludgeon. That was exactly what

Sebastian wanted; he wanted to be stunned. But he wanted to be stunned by a real out-of-date conviction; not by a half-conviction shored up by desperate under-pinning on a threatened refuge. He wanted to be left lying, stunned, on the last rock, and hoped that he might die before he revived enough to feel the trembling of the foundations. His grandmother, to do her justice, gave him the hardest blows within her powers. 'Rubbish!' she said, when he had finished; 'I never heard such rubbish in all my life. Young men in my day didn't talk like that. Young men in my day were men. They hunted and they drank and they made love, and they didn't worry about doing their duty. They weren't so squeamish.' She scratched her back with the ivory hand. 'Don't you be so niminy-piminy, my boy. If you were born to certain rights, take 'em, and be thankful. Not that I approve of your mother and her ways. King or no King, I don't like those Jews; I saw a lot of their horrid names to-day, when I was looking through the Visitors' Book. She ought to have put the book away before I came, if she didn't want me to find out. They're no fit company for her or for you. I daresay they've been putting ideas into your head – perhaps they want you to go into business with them? A name like yours would be the making of them. Don't you listen. And don't have ideas. Ideas upset everything. Things are still quite pleasant, even to-day. Let 'em alone. Don't have ideas.'

'Things are all right for us, Grandmother.'

'Bless the boy! what else matters? We lead the country, don't we? People who lead deserve their privileges. What would happen to the country, I should like to know, if people at the top enjoyed no leisure? What would happen to the dressmakers, if your mother had no more pretty frocks? Besides, the country likes it. Don't you make any mistake about that. People must have something to look up to. It's good for 'em; gives 'em an ideal. They don't like to see a gentleman degrading himself.'

Well, thought Sebastian, that's honest! No qualms there! He liked his grandmother for being so uncompromising. He knew now what made him uneasy in the society of his mother and her friends. They were clinging on, with a sort of feverish obstinacy, to something they no longer quite believed in. The difference between them and the Dowager Duchess was that the Dowager Duchess admitted no flaw in her creed. They admitted none either, but were aware that rude, rough voices grumbled in the background. They tried therefore to disguise their insecurity with flash. Compared with that solid old monument, they were ever so slightly vulgar. She was less vulgar than they, for all her spitting and scratching.

Lucy frankly proclaimed her relief when the family party went away. She sank down on to a sofa, fanned herself, and said 'Ouf!' She said she could not have endured another day of Geoffrey's anecdotes, or of her mother-in-law's carping and barking, or of Lady John's crochet. Thank goodness, she said, they need never be invited all in a bunch again until Sebastian married. 'Or Viola,' said Sebastian, pulling at Sarah's ears. Lucy, in an access of dejection, said that she sometimes thought Viola would never marry. She was so odd. Meanwhile, the coming-of-age had been got over, and had passed, leaving no trace but a few charred marks where the fireworks had sputtered on the lawn – much to Diggs's disgust – a new piece of plate in the strong-room, and a Sargent drawing of Sebastian with an open shirt, a muscular throat, springing hair, and a fearless gaze. This drawing had been presented to Lucy by the tenants, and now hung in her sitting-room, balancing the Helleu etching of Viola, slightly tinted, in which long rounded curls descended to her shoulders and little tendrils of curl clustered about her ears. Sebastian had pointed out that Viola's hair was naturally straight, and that curling-tongs produced only a shapeless frizz, not a luxuriant and tender curve. Lucy had been annoyed by this remark, vaguely feeling in her unanalytical way that it threatened the pretence which she so greatly preferred to an unpleasant reality. She was always disquieted by her children's preference for truth. She had not sufficient intelligence to cope with it, or to argue; she simply registered her dislike, lost her temper, and dismissed their foible as a modern affectation, on a par with the works of Mr. H. G. Wells, whose novels, after one experience, she would no longer consent to read. What, she demanded, looking with affection at the Helleu, was the use of artists, if not to make people more beautiful than God had seen fit to make them? Did Sebastian suppose that Gainsborough's ladies had invariably possessed wavy hair and a perfect bust? No, said Sebastian; and dared to say, that Vandyck's Cavaliers certainly came home after a wet day's hunting with their love-locks pitifully straight and dank. But then, cried Lucy triumphantly, how much the greater artist was Vandyck, in that he gave us his Cavaliers always perfectly curled! No, said Sebastian again; how much more interesting, how much more true, how much more intimate, would be a portrait of Charles the First taken off his guard, as he was revealed to no one but to his hunting companions or his valet, before he offered himself, again restored to his official appearance. These arguments made Lucy cross, and only on rare occasions was Sebastian unwise enough to indulge in them. He knew that they served only to expose the unbridgeable gulf between his own generation and his mother's. Truth was a germ that should only surreptitiously be let loose on an unvaccinated world. Then, it might usefully breed, and kill.

Meanwhile, the pressure was too strong for him. He could attack Helleu as a symbol, but he could not shake himself wholly free.

*

Teresa Spedding and Sebastian were brought together in the clumsy way that often marks such apparently improbable but indubitably fore-ordained happenings. Life, as the novelists would have it, makes no allowance for such accidents. Yet in real life, as we all have reason to know, they occur. Lady Roehampton had spoken truly when, in those early days, she had said that things happened in a quick, odd succession. Sebastian certainly, at this period, desired no adventures of the amorous or any other sort. If he wanted anything, he wanted to be left alone to think things out. But to be left alone was beyond the reasonable hopes of any young man of his attractions and weakness. Life shapes itself, callous of our control, but proves itself to have been wise in the end. No doubt Teresa was necessary to Sebastian's development.

It may be remembered that Teresa, during a performance of *Tristan and Isolde*, had wished that Lady Warwick – innocent and unconscious victim in this matter – might slip at the exit and twist an ankle; Lady Warwick, however, had emerged unscathed; it was reserved for Sebastian himself to suffer the slight accident which complicated his life at a dangerous moment and gave him so disillusioning an insight into the workings of a world different from his own. Speculations as to the powers which flung Sebastian down on Teresa's very doorstep would be idle here and out of place; physical incidents are seldom worth dwelling on in fiction, however disagreeably large they may bulk in life; the sagacious novelist hurries on to the psychological situation thus adventitiously produced, skipping any explanation of an event which is indeed, by reasonable processes, inexplicable. Sebastian, then, alighting from a hansom which had not yet come completely to a standstill, tripped on the kerb and stumbled with a sprained ankle into the gutter. His impetuosity was no doubt to blame. He had espied a flower-seller with a basket of gardenias, and, poking up the trap-door of his cab, had enjoined the driver to stop; but, even as the horse responding to the sudden rein brought all four feet together and slid to its haunches on a wet pavement, he leapt from the step with the result above related. The startled flower-seller, scenting a tip, advanced with helpful hand. Sebastian, however, was beyond such easy aid; in short, he could not stand. Sitting helpless on the kerb, he produced two sovereigns and said he would take all the gardenias. Cabby and flower-girl, standing over him, contemplated him with a mixture of admiration and dismay. It was not everybody who could sprain an ankle and yet complete a purchase with such lavishness and coolness. The cabby exclaimed that the young toff had a nerve and no mistake. The flower-girl gasped, and hastily stuffed the sovereigns into the top of her boot. But clearly that was not an end of the matter: they could not leave the young toff sitting there. The street was not only wet, but empty; nothing but a brass plate beneath a doorbell promised relief. The flower-girl rang. Sebastian, with no premonitions as to what was being done to his life, felt himself being helped under the armpits into Dr. John Spedding's waiting-room.

It was not usual for Teresa to interfere with her husband's patients; it was, in fact, a point upon which John was firm. But on this occasion she decided that she might break the rule, for, gazing in boredom down from her drawing-room window, she had observed the accident and was already in the act of rushing downstairs when the door-bell tinkled and she realised that the obvious solution had occurred to the two other witnesses. Thus it came about that Teresa herself opened the door to Sebastian, and with her native but cultivated talent for recognition instantly identified him with the dark young man she had seen at the Opera in Lady Roehampton's box.

For the next half-hour Teresa was in torture. A friend of Lady Roehampton's beneath her roof! A potential opening to that great, that desirable world! – for we have already seen how Teresa's imagination could run on, and to what glittering visions it quickly led her. It mattered nothing that the young man's black coat and trousers – 'morning dress,' murmured Teresa – were stained with mud, or that his top-hat had turned to a lamentable object, retrieved by the cabby from the gutter where it had rolled, and gingerly deposited by cabby on tip-toe upon the console in the Speddings' little hall, among the visiting cards and the notice which said 'IN' and 'OUT.' The young man's accoutrements might be soiled, but the young man within them was a member of Lady Roehampton's world. That was enough for Teresa, who saw nothing ludicrous in his situation. He was a member of Lady Roehampton's world. But she didn't know his name.

John, fetched by the parlour-maid, who arrived with tardy dignity to answer the bell, came in his best bored professional manner from his consulting-room. Teresa ran to intercept him in the hall. It was necessary, it was essential, she tried to explain in a hot whisper – restrained because cabby and flower-girl were both still hovering about – that he should ascertain the name of his client. But John could be exasperating on such occasions. He merely put Teresa aside, in benign but dismissive fashion, and disappeared into the waiting-room, closing the door firmly and finally behind him. There was nothing left for Teresa to do but to go upstairs, and, twisting the lace curtains of her drawing-room windows, to spy upon the departure of their guest. John, she reflected, so solid, so comforting, in most emergencies of life, was in such matters not wholly reliable. He could not be made to realise their importance. When she tried to explain their importance to him, he was apt to laugh and to fondle her. 'You dear little snob,' he had said once; and Teresa had never forgotten it. It had shown her how little he appreciated the ambitions she nourished for his sake. Not for her own sake, of course; but just for the sake of transforming John from a humble South Kensington practitioner into London's fashionable doctor, the Mainstay of Mayfair. If John became the Mainstay of Mayfair, then Teresa would be willing to go to Mayfair parties, the help-mate of John Spedding – Sir John Spedding – 'such a help his splendid little wife has been to him in his career.' Teresa had mapped it all out, but for some reason John would not play up. That young man with his sprained ankle in the waiting-room – John would be sure to let him slip through his fingers. With sudden determination, Teresa ran downstairs again and listened at the keyhole till the men were ready to come out. Then she was discovered, as they say on the stage, putting the sporting prints straight in the hall.

That marked the beginning of Sebastian's friendship with the Speddings. The flower-girl with surprising honesty, before she left, dumped the gardenias on to the waiting-room table among the out-of-date *Punches* and *Illustrated London News*, and Sebastian gave them all to the doctor's pretty, sympathetic, fluttering little wife. After he had gone, Teresa, who knew what gardenias cost, totted them up with appraising and dazzled eyes. In her excitement and suspense she could do no more than put the gardenias in water – but two of them she pinned into her frock – for the young man had gone off with John in a four-wheeler, and so far, for all Teresa could make out, had given nothing but his address, 120 Grosvenor Square; no name; John, at any rate, had addressed him by no name, no title; just a curt 'I'll see you home,' and off they had gone together, in the growler, the young man hopping to it on one foot, unable to pretend that he could dispense with John's proffered hand. Teresa waited, not knowing – so little do we know ourselves, and Teresa being at best a self-deceptive young woman – whether it was the young man's anonymity or his personality that most allured her.

But when John returned, alone, she was not much wiser. She besieged John with questions, as John in his slyness had fully anticipated. He now took a mischievous delight in disappointing her. Where, he asked with a bland innocence, was the point in asking for the name of a casual client who paid for one's services in cash? A client who was helped into one's house by a cabby and a flower-girl, having sprained his ankle practically on one's doorstep, was not likely to become a regular patient should he chance to catch the mumps or the measles or to grow feverish with a common cold. Arrived at 120 Grosvenor Square, the young man had with suitable diffidence plunged his hand into his pocket, rattled the coins, and asked the doctor what he owed him. He had then limped into his house, supported by two footmen and followed by a butler, all in an appropriate state of concern at the mishap befallen their master; the door had closed behind him, and John had turned away. Teresa shook her small fists in her husband's face. Was he mad, was he *mad*, she demanded, to lose sight of such a patient without even ascertaining his name?

There was, however, such a thing as a Red Book, and Teresa, after she had exhausted her rage against an amused and unrepentant John, rushed to consult it. Running her finger down the page – 'here comes Brook Street,' 'here comes Carlos Place,' she discovered the owner of number 120. Then indeed her indignation against John mounted to the highest note. Chevron House! he had stood on the threshold of Chevron House, and had neglected even to see the duke to a sofa! Teresa wrung her hands, and her despair was sincere. She minded for John's sake as much as for her own – or so she thought, and what we think is, at least partially, what we are. If John would not help himself, then, she declared, she would abandon the uphill task of helping John. She was nearly in tears, but John only pulled at his pipe and smiled to himself as at a private joke. He loved Teresa, and in his eyes Teresa's foibles only added to her charms. It amused him to think that Teresa had briefly harboured a duke in her own house, and, outwitted, had let him go. John himself, all the time, had had a shrewd idea of Sebastian's identity. But he was not the man to press for the name of a patient who seemed reluctant to reveal it.

A ray of hope, a manifestation of Providence, however, gleamed for Teresa. She discovered that Sebastian's top-hat had been left in the hall.

On receipt of Mrs. Spedding's note – for Chevron House was not yet on the telephone – Sebastian came in person to fetch his hat. Why he came in person, instead of sending a servant, he scarcely knew; he knew only that he was bored at the moment; that he had met Mrs. Spedding's eyes; that they were full of query, excitement; that he was mortally sick of all the people of his acquaintance; that he wanted above all things to bury himself at Chevron; and that, failing that luxury which his regimental duties forbade, he must occupy his mind somehow, in order to forget Sylvia and the catastrophe which he had brought upon her. He was, indeed, in that unhappy frame of mind which succeeds upon an unfortunate love-affair unfortunately terminated. He did not like to think about Sylvia. His reason told him that he had been in no way to blame; but no one except a cad likes to reflect that he has been loved more than he has loved. It produces an uneasy though quite unreasonable sense of guilt. So Sebastian went himself to fetch his hat.

That second meeting between Sebastian and Teresa was unpropitious. He had given her no warning of his coming, but had caused himself to be announced by a flustered parlour-maid just as Teresa was settling down to pour out tea for her sister-in-law, up for the day by the cheap train from Dorking. Teresa, expecting her sister-in-law, had taken no pains with her appearance, but had dedicated herself – not altogether unwillingly – to a comfortable hour of gossip about John's family and of comparison between the prices at Whiteley's and John Barker's in the Winter White Sales – matters in which Mrs. Spedding and Mrs. Tolputt were equally interested. Sebastian's arrival, to say the least of it, was disconcerting; Teresa was pitiably at a loss to reconcile these two contradictory elements. Yet the balance was definitely on the triumphant side. How could it be otherwise? A duke dropping in to tea! So Teresa phrased it to herself – *comme si de rien n'était*, she added, having once passed an exam. in French, and having retained a few colloquialisms although she could not have sustained a conversation in French for more than one minute with any safety. A duke dropping in to tea! – and a frantic scramble ensued in her mind, while she introduced Sebastian to Mrs. Tolputt, as to how she could prevent Mrs. Tolputt from talking about pillow-cases, and at the same time could prevent Sebastian from betraying the extremely slight and distressingly accidental character of their acquaintance.

The opening was good. Teresa, agitated as she was, could see that. Mrs. Tolputt, as she herself would have expressed it, was knocked all of a heap. She had had no idea that Teresa carried on that sort of a life. Dukes, indeed! That would be a titbit to tell Mother to-morrow. Or should she catch an earlier train and go round to Mother's that evening? Mrs. Tolputt surreptitiously looked at her watch; it hung heavily, weighing down her keys, on her chatelaine. Teresa noted the glance, and, not wishing to press a precarious safety too far, suggested that Maud mustn't risk missing her train. Mrs. Tolputt was indignant. 'Surely, Teresa, you know that a cheap Day Ticket carries one up to the Theatre Train – eleven-forty, that is – why, you ought to know that, considering how often you and John, when you lived at Dorking . . .'

Teresa made a quick face at her sister-in-law, which Mrs. Tolputt, who prided herself upon being sharp at the uptake, was prompt to recognise. 'Ah, of course, it's so long since you and John lived at Dorking, you've forgotten. But would you believe me.' . . . She turned to Sebastian, and her eloquence was suddenly arrested because she was not sure whether she ought to address him as 'Your Grace' or 'Duke'; 'would you believe me,' she resumed, entering on a fresh lap and resolving that he should remain anonymous, 'would you believe me, I can get up to Town and back for one-and-thruppence. From Dorking on Wednesdays, that is. And believe me, Juke,' she cried, forgetting herself as her enthusiasm waxed, 'that's no mean consideration when the sales are on. I assure you, I make the price of my ticket over and over again. Those country shops, it's something dreadful, the way they stick it on. Believe me or not,' she said, excitedly, turning to Teresa and reverting to the tone of their conversation before Sebastian entered, 'Judd's would charge me ten shillings a pair for servants' sheets, where at Barker's I could get the same thing for seven-and-six. That's half-a-crown difference,' she said, turning to Sebastian, and emphasising her remark by striking the fingers of one hand into the palm of the other; 'half-a-crown difference! it may not sound much, I grant you, but repeated over and over again it comes to something in the year's budget, and that's a thing no man will ever realise – though you, Juke,' she said, suddenly recollecting herself, 'I daresay have never had to think of such things. – I expect, Teresa,' she said, turning to her dismayed sister-in-law, 'the juke has a housekeeper to think of such things for him – eh? – but I daresay you know more about his household affairs than I do, eh?' and she giggled, and buried her nose in a cup of tea.

The tea-drinking at any rate stemmed the flow of Mrs. Tolputt's volubility for the moment, but the consolation to Teresa was small, for she knew that Maud would be off again, no sooner than she had taken her nose out of the cup. She writhed as she thought that Sebastian might have come on any other day, when Maud was not there. And now he would certainly never come again. She kept glancing at him as he sat there, so sleek in his black London clothes – 'his hair is like patent leather,' she thought – his ebony stick laid on the ground beside him, his manner interested and deferential as he listened to Maud's outpourings. How beautifully grave he was! yet he must be bored, horrified, thought the agonised Teresa as she looked at her sister-in-law, so stout and homely and voluble, buttoned into her plum velvet bodice like the wife of any British tradesman. She noticed Maud's string bag, which, stuffed with bulky parcels, was reposing on the floor beside her, and contrasted its ungainliness with the elegance of Sebastian's stick. This contrast in the adjuncts they carried seemed to epitomise the difference between them. Oh, she thought, if only she could cover her eyes and stuff her fingers into her ears, that the misery of this scene might be excluded! No, he would certainly never come again.

But he did come again. When he took his leave, helping himself up by the back of his chair, leaning on his stick, he asked Teresa for permission to return. True, he made the excuse of wanting to thank the doctor. 'I am so sorry to have missed your husband ...' but Teresa knew very well that the doctor had nothing to do with it. It was she herself whom Sebastian wanted to see; she knew that by the way he looked at her, an unsmiling look, but intent, searching; the look, in fact, which Sebastian was apt to bend on all women, whether he meant anything by it or not. This time he did mean something by it. No one ever knew where the wind of Sebastian's caprice would blow next, though it was certainly very odd that it should have veered in the direction of Mrs. John Spedding. But he was bored; he had known too many different kinds of women and could appraise them all – women of fashion, prostitutes, dubious aspirants to social heights, fortune-hunters, sharks, toadies, and the light-mannered ladies of the stage – none of them held any more interest for him than the A.B.C.; but this pretty, silly little Teresa, who gazed at him with such puzzled admiring eyes, and who was evidently so much ashamed of her nice vulgar sister-in-law, might amuse him for a week, and at all events she would be a new experience, a type he had never learned before. It was perhaps a somewhat languid impulse, and not very complimentary to Teresa; but Sebastian was not in the humour for anything more creditable. Nor did he intend to do Teresa any harm. Sebastian was one of those charming but dangerous people who never do harm except by accident; such discontent as internally ate him away, remained his private knowledge; he never gave anything of himself beyond the things he could not help giving – his looks, his gravity, his slow smile, his caressing manner which, in conjunction with his aloofness, made him especially attractive and exasperating to women. In some complicated way, this sense of his own detachment persuaded him of their immunity. He was playing a game with a soft ball; a game in which nobody had any business to get hurt. The fact that they returned the ball at all, after his first preliminary throw, convinced him that they knew the game and its rules; after that, he settled down to play in earnest.

If Teresa was a new experience to Sebastian, Sebastian was no less of a new experience to Teresa. She was completely dazzled by him. His irruption into her life seemed not only fantastic, but unbelievable. All her standards were revolutionised; instead of the petty economies and 'managings' of her life, she contemplated his thoughtless extravagance; instead of her envious interest in the great, the notorious, or the socially eminent, she beheld his bored and casual familiarity; instead of the careful restrictions of middle-class codes and manners, she breathed the larger air of a laxer ease; instead of any rare little departure from the monotony of every day being regarded as an event, she came now into contact with one to whom such diversions were no more exciting than a bit of bread. She never succeeded in adjusting herself to his standards. The question of what Sebastian could or could not afford was always uppermost in her mind; she was horrified when he filled her rooms with orchids; she scolded him when he took her and John to the play in a box, and neglected to fill the fourth seat. 'Such a waste!' she exclaimed in real distress. She was disconcerted when he failed to be impressed by the things that aroused her easy enthusiasm, whether it was the beauty of a fashionable actress, or the turn-out of a carriage passing down the street; she thought him disrespectful, critical, and spoilt. Yet she adored him for it, and resolved endlessly that next time she also would be fastidious; would turn up her nose; would not give him the chance to laugh over her naïveté. Fortunately for herself, these resolutions broke down directly any strain was put upon them. Teresa could not pretend. She clapped her hands, she exclaimed with delight, she invited Sebastian's support, as soon as she saw something which pleased her, and only when it was too late did she remember that she had intended to play the fine lady. Then, having remembered, she would turn haughty, and haughty she would remain for perhaps a quarter of an hour. Sebastian, to his great delight, observed all these processes, and was enchanted by each one in turn. It amused him to watch her sparkling eyes, to feel the excited tug of her fingers on his sleeve; it amused him to answer in a light and derogatory tone; to see the quick jerk of reminder pass across her face; and then to note how her manner changed; how from 'Oh, look! look! how lovely!' she would put on a little air of the woman of the world and would pretend to be unmoved. He really had quite an affection for her, as one might have for a confiding, playful little animal, whom one alternately trained to do tricks and then summoned to jump snuggling upon one's knee. He deplored only that some of her tricks needed a great deal of coaxing. Thus he would have liked to listen to stories of Mrs. Tolputt, whose arrangements fascinated him, but Teresa naturally was incapable of reproducing Mrs. Tolputt – and indeed was extremely unwilling to do so, finding Sebastian's interest quite incomprehensible; the most that he could get was an occasional anecdote, given as an example of the indignities she was made to suffer. 'But why do you want to know?' she would say, when Sebastian asked whether Mr. Tolputt was a church-warden; 'as a matter of fact, he is, and they often dine with the Bishop. Well, not often, perhaps,' said Teresa, who was strictly truthful, 'but anyway once a year. John and I were asked once,' she added, 'when the Bishop heard that we were in Dorking.'

'Well?' said Sebastian, watching her. 'Did you enjoy it?'

'It was terrible – terrible!' said Teresa, suddenly hiding her face in her hands.

'Tell me,' said Sebastian.

'Maud lost a curl,' said Teresa, looking at him with round eyes.

'Lost a curl?'

'It fell into her soup. A false curl, you know. Oh, dreadful,' said Teresa. 'I didn't know where to look. I have never felt the same about the Bishop since. Imagine, – he laughed. Instead of looking away and pretending not to notice, he laughed. Such bad taste, I thought. But then, of course, he is an unmarried man.'

'And what did Mrs. Tolputt do?'

'That was the worst of all. She fished it out and held it up all dripping. She thought it a great joke. She wasn't a bit ashamed.'

'It seems to me that she behaved very sensibly.'

'What dreadful things you say, taking Maud's part like that. But of course it is my fault, for talking to you about things like false curls.'

'Because I am an unmarried man, like the Bishop? Tell me more about Mrs. Tolputt. When may I meet her again?'

'Now you are laughing at me, and it is very unkind of you. Tell me something about yourself instead. Tell me what it feels like to be you. Do you enjoy being yourself?'

'I enjoy being myself when you let me come to tea with you. I don't particularly enjoy it otherwise. Why should I?'

But Teresa was discreet and would not answer. Their friendship was still at a very tentative stage, and she bottled up many of the things she wanted to say to Sebastian, because her training had taught her that one must not be familiar with young men if one wishes to keep their respect. Sebastian saw through her gentility, and knew that not until he had made love to her would she treat him with any naturalness. He was, however, in no hurry to do so, knowing that this probationary period, when every meeting held the danger of avowal, was the most precious and tremulous of all; and that once it was over, a new phase was instantly entered, which brought its own delights, but which had lost a certain freshness, as surely as noon loses the freshness of the morning. He was therefore quite content to lounge on Teresa's sofa and listen to her prattle, contrasting her with other women and thinking how deliciously ingenuous she was, both in her confidences and in her reservations, without wishing to force the pace or to bring about a crisis which must alter their relations. If he wondered sometimes about her husband, he never asked her any questions. That was a matter which she must manage for herself. He did not even know whether the doctor was aware of the frequency of his visits.

'Why do you like coming here?' she asked him once; 'you who can go anywhere and meet anybody?'

He looked at her, but she was sincere; she was not trying to flirt with him. That was one of her charms for him: a double-edged phrase was unknown to her.

'Would you be surprised to hear that I prefer your company?'

'Very much surprised. I never told you, but once I saw you at the Opera. I saw you in Lady Roehampton's box.'

Sebastian got up and walked over to the window.

'In Lady Roehampton's box? That night? At *Tristan*? But how did you know it was Lady Roehampton?'

'She's very well known, isn't she, by sight?'

'I suppose so. Well, what of it?'

'Well, you can't prefer my company to Lady Roehampton's.'

'My dear Mrs. Spedding, you know nothing whatever about Lady Roehampton.'

Teresa felt terribly snubbed; Sebastian had suddenly become harsh and distant. She supposed that she ought not to have mentioned his friends. Evidently he thought of her as something quite separate, and with a chill at her heart she abandoned the dream that he would one night ask her to a dinner-party in Grosvenor Square. He was standing over at the window now, staring gloomily out into the street. 'Oh, I'm so sorry,' she said in her childish way, going up to him; 'of course I know nothing about Lady Roehampton, only she is so beautiful, isn't she? And I am sure she is very brilliant. – I just thought, how could you find anything in me when you were accustomed to people like that?'

For one instant the balance wavered as to whether Sebastian

would be irritated or touched by her humility. Then he looked down at her; saw her parted lips, her anxious eyes; and smiled. It was on the tip of his tongue to say that the less she knew of Lady Roehampton the better, but a retrospective loyalty to Sylvia restrained him. 'Never mind about that,' he said; 'I assure you, those people would very quickly lose their glamour for you if you knew them as I do. Let us talk about something else. All my friends are as alike as so many lumps of sugar.'

Dense young man! thought Teresa; doesn't he see that I only long for an opportunity of judging for myself? Doesn't he see how I am wasting my life, and my looks, and my social talents, tucked away in the society of doctors and solicitors and their wives? Very worthy people, but I was born for something better. Only give me a chance to prove it! Teresa was driven nearly frantic by Sebastian's stupidity, yet a mixture of shame and art- fulness prevented her from betraying what was always in her mind. She could not say to him frankly, 'Introduce me to your friends.' No, not even on the plea of helping John could she say that. So she hovered round the subject, unaware of how clearly Sebastian saw through her, and of the delight he took in teas- ing her, holding out some succulent morsel to her and then snatching it away as she advanced with outstretched hands to take it.

Still, her boldness grew. Every time she saw Sebastian she asked him at least one new question, as it were inadvertently, and added the reply to her stock of knowledge. Thus she ascer- tained that the fashionable world did not go to Henley, as she had always imagined, and also discovered the points for which Bridge was played in the houses of the rich Jews. Sebastian thoroughly enjoyed this would-be artless questioning; he would answer her gravely, knowing well that he made her mouth water with envy and curiosity, and all the time he would be thinking that he must cease tantalising the little thing, and must give her a taste of the life she so coveted. It was a shame to keep putting off the treat he could give her, when he could see that she was dying for the favour she dared not ask.

'By the way,' he said to his mother, 'who is coming to stay for Christmas?'

Lucy reeled off a list of names.

'I have invited two friends of my own.'

'Yes, darling? Who?'

'A doctor and his wife.'

'A doctor, Sebastian? Where on earth have you made friends with a doctor?'

'They are the people who picked me up when I sprained my ankle.'

'But, darling, will they go well with the party?'

'No, they won't go at all.'

'But, darling, what an extraordinary thing to do. You know how an unsuitable element can ruin a party. Couldn't you have asked them here for a week-end alone?'

'That wouldn't serve the purpose. The lady wants a glimpse into what I suspect she privately calls high life.'

'Oh, heavens, Sebastian, a vulgar little snob!'

'A snob, yes; she is eaten up with snobbishness, but she is not vulgar. She is, on the contrary, extremely genteel. And she is very pretty.'

Lucy groaned.

'And the doctor is really a very good fellow. Quiet, you know; sensible; slightly sarcastic; grizzled hair; pulls out his pipe, and looks on while other people talk.'

'Is he a snob too?'

'Oh, quite the reverse. I fancy his wife's snobbishness amuses him as much as it amuses me. Anyway, they are coming, and you must be nice to them. I will guarantee to take the lady off your hands most of the time.'

'Sebastian, do be careful. You will turn the poor creature's head, and then you will get bored with her and drop her. I begin to see how the thing stands. Won't you think better of it, and put them off? Say you found the house was already full – any excuse will do. It's really kinder.'

Sebastian laughed. 'Now, mother, you know you are not thinking at all of Mrs. Spedding or her broken heart. You are thinking only of your party, and of what a bore these people are going to be.'

'Well, I do think they will be a bore. Still, it is your house, and you always do what you want without consulting me. I have all the trouble and you have all the fun. I am really nothing but your housekeeper . . .' and the duchess went on in this vein for some time, getting into a tantrum; but seeing that Sebastian only watched her with a sardonic smile, she finally took herself off to vent her irritation on the faithful Wacey. Viola and Sebastian were left together.

'How much I adore mother, Viola; she's so ludicrously transparent. You, at any rate, will like Mrs. Spedding.'

'Mother seems to forget that all the people she had already asked were her friends and not yours.'

'Of course she forgot it. She has a convenient memory. Who were they? Sir Adam, Julia Levison, the Templecombes; I forget the rest. Anyhow, they will excite Mrs. Spedding.'

'Don't they excite you?'

'Do they excite *you*?'

'Me? I loathe them all.'

'So do I.'

Brother and sister were seldom alone together, and when they were alone they seldom talked, or talked only on practical and superficial subjects. Viola would always at any moment have been ready to draw nearer to her brother, but in common with everybody else she shrank from forcing any intimacy that he was not the first to invite. But now Sebastian was in an expansive mood; because he had been talking about Teresa, but had been compelled to talk in a more or less guarded way, he was in the mood to release himself even through other channels. Moreover, he was fond of Viola, in the uncomfortably remote manner of affection between brothers and sisters, and had often thought that when a convenient occasion presented itself he would take a little trouble to find out what Viola was really like. So, because it was a winter evening, and because he had been talking about Teresa; because they sat in the library before a great wood fire; because their mother had gone off in a huff, to their common amusement; because Henry lay twitching in his sleep, and Sarah lay in Sebastian's arms with her nose nuzzled under his chin while he pulled her ears – for all these reasons he responded when Viola said, 'Then why do you spend all your time amongst them?'

'Habit, I suppose. What else is there to do? One must get through life somehow.'

'But does it satisfy you, Sebastian?'

'Heavens, no. I don't suppose it satisfies anyone, except perhaps a sparrow-brain like mother. One is just caught in a machine, that's all, and one walks round with everybody else, nose to tail like a string of caterpillars. It saves trouble. There are boring moments and amusing moments – which I suppose is the most that one can ever hope to say about life – and one can be thankful if the amusing moments are in excess of the boring ones.'

'Amusing moments – I don't find many.'

'No, but then you are too serious,' said Sebastian, looking at her with an air of discovery. 'I have my pleasure-loving side, you see. It seems to have been left out of you. But I have my serious side too, and they quarrel inside me. Then I grumble, as I am doing now. Are you never amused?'

'Often, but not at the same kind of thing. Not at parties. Not at gossip. The lighted candle doesn't attract me.'

'You are a secret sort of person, Viola; if you disappeared completely one day, I should not be in the least surprised.'

'So are you a secret sort of person, Sebastian; you take a great deal of trouble to conceal yourself. I don't believe you care for a thing in the world but Chevron and Sarah, and certainly for no person.'

'Yet I have my friends.'

'Yes – women who grab you. Your men friends can thank circumstances that they know you at all. Tell me truly, have you ever met anyone that you really liked?'

Sebastian thought instantly of Anquetil, but he would not pronounce his name. 'Yes, one. Have you?'

Viola also thought of Anquetil, whose last letter was in her pocket. 'Yes, one.'

A slight awkwardness came between them, checking their confidences, for both of them wanted to say 'Who?' but their reticence prevented them. A log fell in the fire, sending out a shower of sparks. Sarah woke up and tried to lick Sebastian's chin; this not being allowed, she whimpered complainingly and went to sleep again with a sigh.

'How much longer do you suppose that people like us will last, Sebastian? – and places like Chevron.'

'How odd! I was thinking exactly the same thing.' Anquetil's presence was indeed very actively in the room. 'How can one tell? I suppose we are anachronisms already, though we may hold on for a generation or two longer. In the meantime, I don't see that we do much harm.'

'Or much good either. We are pretty negative.'

'Well, are we? I admit that I am not a particularly good specimen; but deplorably frivolous though you may think me, I do occasionally look into the welfare of the estate.'

'Don't be silly, Sebastian. I know you do. At heart I know you are never really happy except when you are talking to Wickenden or tramping about with Bassett. You were really born to be a squire, in breeches and gaiters, instead of running about London after pretty women whom you despise. You adore Chevron, and it would break your heart to see it turned into a national museum.'

'Well, naturally.'

'Yes, naturally. And that's our only justification. But don't let us sentimentalise ourselves. Do remember always that we are only a picturesque survival, even while we play at living still during the Wars of the Roses.'

'Mercy, Viola, I never knew you held these ideas.'

'Didn't you? I suspect that you hold them too, but haven't faced them. Too unpleasant. But I do admit that there is something to be said for Sebastian the Squire. I don't admit that there is anything to be said for Sebastian the Smart Young Man.'

'Or for mother? Or for Lady Templecombe? But tell me more about Sebastian the Squire. He interests me.'

'He interests me too. He is a real person. A real under-standing exists between him and Wickenden and Bassett. They speak the same language, even though Wickenden drops his aitches and Sebastian doesn't. They respect each other. And I'll say this in Sebastian's favour: that the day when Wickenden ceases to respect Sebastian will come sooner than the day when Sebastian ceases to respect Wickenden.'

'You're wrong there, Viola. They are interdependent. The Wickenden that Sebastian ceases to respect will no longer be the same Wickenden.'

'What you mean is, that Wickenden will be the first to break away from feudality, while Sebastian still remains bogged in it.'

'You go ahead faster than I do. I don't admit the fallacy of feudality. I look on it as a rock, on which we built not a palace and a hovel, but a manor-house and a cottage side by side. Chevron is big, but essentially it is only a bigger manor-house. That happened centuries ago, but it still holds good. Chevron and Wickenden's cottage have their roots in the same founda-tion. The same earthquake that destroys Chevron will destroy Wickenden's cottage.'

'Only it won't be an earthquake – not in England, England isn't seismic – it will be a gradual crumbling.'

'Perhaps. But the effect will be the same. They will both go down together.'

'But something else will be built in their place,' said Viola; 'something less glaringly discrepant.'

'Yes – two tenement buildings, alike in every particular,' said Sebastian bitterly.

'My poor Sebastian, you hate the idea, but you must resign yourself to it. You try to look on it dispassionately, I know, but you are a hundred years out of date. A hundred years only – we needn't go back to the Wars of the Roses. You are still living in the days when England was an agricultural and not an industrial country; when the population was smaller, and the tenant was really dependent upon his landlord, the employee upon his employer; when their relations were much more personal; when Wickenden's son didn't dream of finding a job anywhere but in the Chevron workshops; when Wickenden's job, like Sebastian's, was hereditary.'

'To-day he goes into the motor trade.'

'And Sebastian resents it.'

'But so does Wickenden. You forget that.'

'Wickenden, my dear, will die off. Wickenden and Sebastian both belong to the old order. There are too many young Wickendens now, – they can't all find employment in the Chevron shops. Naturally, Sebastian will cling on longer than the young Wickendens will. Sebastian is all right; he has a pleasant life; lots of money; he spends half his time in London; the other half he spends agreeably patronising his dependents, riding round his estate on a nice day, dispensing bounty, saying, "Yes, I will mend your roof" ...'

'And who do you propose as the mender of Wickenden's roof, if I no longer do it?'

'Wickenden himself. A Wickenden that need not be beholden to you or anybody else, except to an unseen employer – perhaps the State – who pays him a proper wage in exact proportion to the work he has done. No patronage, no subservience, no obligation.'

'But damn it, Viola, I pay Wickenden a proper wage. And I swear Wickenden has no sense of patronage or obligation towards me. Ask him. He wouldn't know what you meant.'

'No, but his son would.'

'That young Frank. That boy has no manners, no feeling for Chevron ...'

'Why should he have any? Chevron is your house, not his. You may respect Wickenden for identifying his interests with yours; I respect young Frank for insisting upon having interests of his own. It's a different point of view, Sebastian. We shall never agree.'

'I thought you loved Chevron as much as I do, Viola.'

'I do love Chevron. Something smashed inside me the day I realised that I mustn't cling on to Chevron. Little rootlets still push out, and I have to keep on tearing them up. It hurts me, but I do tear them up. I regard our love for Chevron as a weakness.'

'All love is a weakness, if it comes to that, in so far as it destroys some part of our independence. I don't see why the love of a place should be regarded as more of a weakness than the love of a person.'

'I think I know why, in this particular case. Your love for Chevron isn't pure. It includes the whole system on which Chevron is run. It includes Wickenden, and the carpenter's bench, and the painters' shop, and the forge, and the wood-cutters; and it includes your relationship to them.'

'I don't see that that matters,' muttered Sebastian sulkily. 'No, I'll tell you what I really think,' he added, rousing himself. 'I will agree with you that Chevron, and myself, and Wickenden, and the whole apparatus are nothing but a wax-work show, if you like. Present-day conditions have made us all rather meaningless. But I still think that that is a pity. I think we had evolved a good system on the whole, which made for a good understanding between class and class. Nothing will ever persuade me that the relations between the squire and the craftsman, or the squire and the labourer, or the squire and the farmer, don't contain the elements or decency and honesty and mutual respect. I wish only that civilisation could have developed along these lines. We have got away now from the day when we under-paid our labourers and cut off their ears and slit their noses for stealing a bit of wood, and we might have looked forward to an era when we could all have lived decently together, under a system peculiarly well suited to English people. But, as you say, there are now too many people. There is too much industrialism. My idyllic England vanishes. People like myself and Wickenden have got our backs to the wall. Naturally we don't like it.'

Viola laughed. 'Darling Sebastian, how well I foresee your old age – shut up inside the walls of Chevron, saying that the country has gone to the dogs, a good Tory to the last. What a pity you didn't live in eighteen-fifty.'

'Well, you've disposed of Sebastian the Squire. Now tell me about Sebastian the Smart Young Man.'

'I don't like him. I do like Sebastian the Squire, even though I disagree with him. But the Smart Young Man – no. He sins against himself, you see; he is a sham. He is very charming and good-looking, and he has perfect manners and dresses irreproachably. He does all the right things. He dances, he plays polo, he goes to race-meetings, he flirts – oh, how he flirts! He consorts with people he despises, but of course he never gives them an inkling of what he really thinks of them. He pretends to adopt their values, and does it very successfully. – Am I being a prig? Is it only because he is young and likes amusing himself?'

'Luckily he has a sister who tells him some home truths,' said Sebastian, making a wry face.

Lucy came in.

'Sitting in the dark, children?'

'We were having a very serious conversation,' said Sebastian, and he got up and kissed his mother, much to her surprise, for he was not usually demonstrative.

VI

TERESA

Chevron was even more beautiful in winter than in summer;
so Sebastian thought. (But then, whatever the season,
Sebastian always decided that it suited Chevron better than
any other season.) He had now been there for two days alone
with his mother and Viola, and, as usual, had forgotten all
about London and was deep in his Chevron mood. He had a
full day left, before the Christmas party arrived by the six
o'clock train. He had looked forward to this party, having
arranged in his own mind that matters should come to a head
between himself and Teresa, but now it merely irritated him to
think that by the evening the house would be full of people,
even though Teresa should be of their number. He had long
since discovered why he resented parties at Chevron, although
in his sardonic way he could enjoy them elsewhere; it was
because they forced him to mingle the two sides of himself, for
Sebastian was honest enough to dislike mixing his manners.
He could come to terms with himself only if he kept his two

selves sharply separate. Then he could manage to sustain himself by thinking that the one self redeemed the other. In this
way, since we first met him rebelliously sitting astride the roof,
had he tidied himself into compartments; but still parties at
Chevron had the same distressing effect, of confusing him by
pitting reality against unreality – one mood against the other.
The presence of Teresa would complicate matters. He was
clear-sighted enough to know well that he would play up to
Teresa; would consent to the rôle that she expected of him;
would hate himself for doing it; and would exaggerate out of
sheer exasperation. He wished by all his gods that he had not
invited Teresa.

Meanwhile, Teresa and the party were distant by twenty-five
miles of space and eight hours of time, and Sebastian, with
Sarah and Henry at his heels, was out in the park on a frosty
morning. For the moment he could afford to be happy.
Chevron was going about its business as usual, as though no dis-
cordant strangers were expected; the internal agitation of the
house was not here apparent; Sebastian could forget that within
doors his mother was interviewing the *chef*, Mrs. Wickenden
sorting out the sheets, Wacey struggling with the dinner-table,
Vigeon descending into the cellar, the groom of the chambers
going round the writing-tables with ink, pencils, and paper, the
stillroom-maid making scones in the stillroom. All that house-
keeping business concerned Sebastian not at all. He roamed
round the outer walls, meeting first a waggon charged with a
fallen tree, and appreciated the rounded rumps, like Spanish
chestnuts, of the straining horses; then he looked into the
slaughter-house, where Hodder the keeper was skinning a deer
slung by all four feet from a rafter; then he met two gardeners
pushing a handcart laden with beetroot and potatoes; then he

looked into the pimping-shed, where old Turnour was chopping faggots. Old Turnour, a frill of white beard edging his face, looked up, grinned cheerfully, and touched his hat, then went on with his chopping.

'Well, how are you keeping, Turnour? Nice weather, isn't it?'

'Nice enough, your Grace, but not seasonable, not seasonable.'

'Well, it's cold enough, Turnour; but I suppose you expect snow at Christmas?'

'Ah, the climate isn't what it was, your Grace; a Christmas without snow is onnatural.'

'I daresay we'll get it before we're done, Turnour.'

'Maybe, your Grace, but still the climate isn't what it was. Anyhow we're getting a touch of frost to set the sprouts. I had a nice lot of sprouts this year, your Grace, and it would have been a pity to lose them for lack of a touch of frost.'

'So it would, Turnour, a great pity. And how's the rheumatism?'

'Not onreasonably bad, your Grace, considering. But I'm getting on, and it tells.'

'Seventy-eight is it, Turnour?'

'Ah, your Grace has his late Grace's memory. Seventy-eight it is – seventy-nine come Easter.'

'Well, Turnour, there's a Christmas surprise for you and everybody on the estate – five shillings a week rise from the first of January.'

'No, your Grace, you don't say so?' said Turnour, desisting from his chopping to push back his hat and to stare; 'not that it won't be welcome to all, with prices going up as they do. Well, now!' said Turnour, still marvelling at this piece of fortune, 'if I haven't always said: a gentleman is a gentleman, but his Grace is a real gentleman. And here I get my words proven out of my mouth.'

'It isn't that, Turnour,' said Sebastian, compelled to honesty; 'only I can afford it, where others can't.'

'Ah, your Grace makes light of it. But it isn't all who would think of it, even them as can afford it. And your Grace pays a decent wage already, next to some. Thank you kindly, your Grace. My old woman will dance when she hears it; stiff joints or no.'

Sebastian smiled and nodded and walked away, with no very great satisfaction at his heart. He felt that he had received more gratitude, and had acquired more merit, than was his due. Five shillings a week meant thirteen pounds a year, and – say that he employed a hundred men – that meant thirteen hundred pounds a year; very little more than his mother would spend on a single ball; a negligible sum in his yearly budget. He felt ashamed. His conversation with Viola had shamed him. Money apart, he felt that his relationship with old Turnour was false. What did he really care for old Turnour's rheumatism? or for his age? or for the fact that he walked three miles at five o'clock every morning to his work, winter and summer, and three miles back every evening? Sebastian could stroll into the pimping-shed every now and then, and gossip with old Turnour in a friendly way for ten minutes, and he knew that old Turnour liked it, and retailed every word of the conversation to his old woman in the evening; but supposing that on a cold winter's night Sebastian had found his fire unlit, and, on ringing the bell, had been told by Vigeon that old Turnour had omitted to cut any faggots that day – would not he, Sebastian, have damned with rage, and demanded what old Turnour thought he was there for, if not to cut faggots? And would have thought himself a lenient master in that he did not sack Turnour without further enquiry. He walked on, unhappily shaking his head. Viola had upset him. Turnour's gratitude embarrassed him. He felt, rather, that it was he who should thank the old man for rising at five o'clock every morning and for walking three miles, that the bath should be hot by eight and the fires fed throughout the day.

But the morning was too lovely, and Sebastian too young, for his depression to last for long. He took his way across the park, throwing sticks for Henry to retrieve – Sarah did not care for sticks – and every now and then he turned round to look at the house which lay beneath him, spread out like a mediaeval village with its square turrets and its grey walls, its hundred chimneys sending blue threads up into the air. It was his; and he remembered Teresa's question, 'Tell me what it feels like to be you.' At that moment he knew exactly what it felt like to be himself.

The turf was white with frost, and each separate blade of grass stuck up, as brittle as an icicle. The grass crunched beneath his feet, and looking back across the plain he could see the track of his footsteps, making a dark line across the rime. Sarah stepped delicately, and from time to time she lay down to lick the balls of ice which gathered between her pads; Henry, who was made of coarser stuff, careered madly round and round in circles, galloping like a little horse, bounding over the tussocks, his ears flying, his feathers streaming. Sebastian cheered him on. He wished he could tear about like Henry. They came to the edge of the plain; Sebastian broke into a run down the slope; now they were in the valley; still they ran, startling the deer that nosed about among some armfuls of hay thrown down for them. They bounded away, the spaniels after them; they bounded up the slope, over the dead bracken, bouncing as though they had springs in their feet, their white scuts flashing between the trees. Sebastian stood still to watch; he felt so happy that he thought his heart would burst. Henry and Sarah, returning, dragging themselves on their bellies up to him, were astonished when they were not beaten.

By the morning of Christmas Eve, snow had fallen. Sebastian was amused by this, when he first looked out of his bedroom window and saw the white garden. He was amused, because Teresa would now see Chevron as she had expected to see it. 'Quite an old-fashioned Christmas,' she would say. He was in such a good temper that he could anticipate Teresa's careful platitudes with affection. He looked out at the familiar scene. Two gardeners were already sweeping the snow from the path. Swish, swish, went their black brooms, and the men moved after them, waddling from foot to foot, in a caricature of the scytheman's beautiful rhythm. The snow was powdery, and flew readily under the twiggy swish of the broom, heaping itself on either side in a low wedge-shaped rampart, clean and glittering; the yellow gravel of the path came through, streaked with thin semi-circles of snow between the brushings. Blackbirds walked over the lawn, printing the snow with their neat marks. Sebastian could not bear to remain indoors on such a morning; he pulled on a pair of trousers and a sweater; called to Sarah and Henry, who were still at the stage of stretching and yawning in their respective baskets – Sarah especially was always a slow waker, and liked to jump on to Sebastian's bed for five minutes' sentimentality before she was officially awake – and going downstairs he tried to get out into the garden, but was checked everywhere by fastened shutters and locked doors, for the indoor servants were not allowed into this part of the house so early, and had neither undone the fastenings nor pulled up the blinds. Sebastian tugged impatiently, unreasonably irritated with his servants for the efficiency with which they performed their duties. He was as irritated as when he sometimes arrived at Chevron without warning during the London season and found all the furniture piled into the middle of the rooms under dust-sheets. Then he grumbled at Mrs. Wickenden for the thoroughness that he really respected. At last he got out, having triumphed over the library shutters; Henry rushed in advance into the snow, tossing it up with his nose; Sarah followed more circumspectly, snuffing, looking back at Sebastian to know what this unfamiliar white grass might portend; they both ran, little brown shapes, snuffing, hither and thither, and Sebastian came after, at first reluctant to break the thick white carpet, then kicking it up with pleasure, seeing the powdery snow fluff up before his toe-caps as he kicked; and so he crossed the space to the path and the brushing gardeners, and taking a broom from one of the men he sent him off on other business.

A red ball of sun was coming up behind the trees; there was now a long stretch of path swept clear; Sebastian swept with such vigour that he constantly found himself outdistancing his companion. The cold air and the exercise made him tingle; his spirits rose; he chaffed the other man on his slow, steady progress. 'See if I don't clear my share in half the time, Godden.' 'All very well, your Grace; but your Grace hasn't got to work for all the rest of the day. Slow and steady – that's what keeps you going from breakfast to dinner.' Yet he knew that Godden was good-humoured and amused; amused, as any professional is amused, at the precipitate enthusiasm of the amateur. He looked up at the grey house; all the blinds were down, and he instantly despised his guests for being still asleep, in a rush of that superiority which afflicts all those who are astir earlier than other people. Then he remembered that his own windows alone, of all the bedrooms, looked onto the garden; and another rush of satisfaction took him, that he slept isolated in his fat tower, where no one could spy on him, and where for neighbours he had none but the portraits hanging on the walls of the unused state-rooms, or a Pontius Pilate who could no longer judge, on the tapestry in the chapel. How often, going to his room at night and leaning out to breathe the air from his window, had he felt himself in silent communion with Chevron, a communion which others were denied!

He liked the feel of the broom-handle in his hands, the wood polished by usage until it was as sleek and glossy as vellum. Even the knots in the wood were smooth. Sebastian had paused to straighten his back, and was running his fingers up and down the handle, enjoying the pleasant texture. Godden also paused, and watched him with a smile. 'Blisters coming, your Grace?' 'It takes more than that to give me blisters,' said Sebastian, injured by the asumption that his hands were soft, and he fell to his sweeping again, though he would have liked to stand still for a moment, gazing round at the glistening snow, sprinkled with diamonds, and at the low red sun just topping the trees, and at Henry and Sarah, who, mad with delight, were rushing round and round after one another.

Teresa decided that it would be suitable for her to make her first appearance at twelve o'clock that morning. Thus she would display no undue eagerness. She had arrived at Chevron determined to behave with the utmost caution; by no impetuous word would she betray her agitation, by no imprudent question would she expose her ignorance. She would be very quiet and self-contained, and, by carefully copying what other people did, she would manage to get through the three days of this thrilling, agonising, exquisite ordeal without shame or ridicule. Her manner should be reserved and dignified; she would allow nothing visibly to impress her; she would conduct herself as though staying at Chevron were quite the ordinary thing for her to do. Inwardly, of course, she was more flustered than she had ever been in her life. The size of Chevron, the luxury, the number of servants, the powdered footmen and their red velvet breeches, the great fires, the gold plate, the conversation, the fashionable company, their air of taking everything for granted – all this had far surpassed Teresa's expectations. Cinderella going to the ball was not more overwhelmed than she. 'Keep your head, keep your head,' she kept repeating to herself; 'don't give yourself away.' It was only when she had been shown to her bedroom before dinner, and was presently joined there by John, that she had let herself go. She had flown round the room, examining everything, clasping her hands in an ecstasy of delight. The familiar 'Oh, look, John! look!' came tumbling from her lips. The dressing-table, the washstand, the writing-table with its appointments, the vast fourposter on which some unseen hand had already laid out her clothes, the drawn curtains, the brightly burning fire, the muslin cushions, the couch with a chinchilla rug lying folded across it – all these things led Teresa from transport to transport. She lingered for a long time over the writing-table, fingering all its details. There was a printed card, gilt-edged, which said: 'POST ARRIVES 8 A.M., 4 P.M.; POST LEAVES 6 P.M. SUNDAYS: POST ARRIVES 8 A.M.; LEAVES 5 P.M. LUNCHEON 1.30. DINNER 8.30.' Nothing about breakfast; thank goodness, then, ladies were not expected to go down to breakfast. Then there were three different sizes of notepaper – 'Look, John! MacMichael's best vellum-laid,' said Teresa, showing it to him, 'and I know that costs a pound a ream' – but what fascinated Teresa above all, so that she could scarcely take her eyes from it, was the address, CHEVRON, under a ducal coronet. 'Just Chevron, John!' said Teresa; 'nothing else! no town, no county! You see, it's so well known. Just Chevron, England. If you addressed a letter like that, from any part of the world, it would get here,' and she sat staring at the sheet in her hand, remembering that she had once had a note from Sebastian on that paper, but had imagined that it was some special paper of his own, and now here it was, in quantities, in her own bedroom, all fair and unused; 'I must write to Maud and Mother,' said Teresa, privately resolving that she would send belated Christmas greetings to everybody she could think of; but she refrained from saying this to John – for she did observe a few little reticences towards him.

Nor was the writing-table the end of her delights, for everything in the room seemed to be marked with the sign of its ownership. Even the beribboned cosy which went over the hot-water can had the crossed C's and the coronet embroidered upon it; likewise the sheets, when Teresa turned down the counterpane to see; and they, furthermore, had a wide pink satin ribbon threaded through them. Teresa kept on exclaiming what all this must cost, 'and fancy, John,' she said, 'it isn't only one bedroom, but twenty-bedrooms, thirty bedrooms! so all this has to be provided twenty, thirty times over. But I don't like the duchess; do you, John? I'm sure she's very snappy in private life. Such a funny crumpled face, and I bet she dyes her hair. I wish Lady Roehampton was here. I don't like that Mrs. Levison either, though I know she's terribly smart – really the cream of the cream. I bet she has a tongue. And Lady Viola – she looks as cold as ice. Isn't it funny, John, that a nobody like Mrs. Levison should be so smart? You never can tell with these people, can you? They say that she is trying to set the fashion for women to dine alone with men in restaurants. I don't like that sort of thing; do you, John? Fast, I call it. Oh, dear, I do wish I had some jewels to put on for dinner. Do you think the ladies will wear their tiaras? No, perhaps not in a private house. Who do you think will take me in to dinner? I wish it could be the duke, but I suppose that's impossible, with all these ladies of title about. I must say, I think he was very nice when we arrived, and what dear little dogs he has; I daresay he thought we might be a bit shy. I wasn't; were you, John? One is all right so long as one doesn't put oneself forward, don't you think? What a lovely big room that was, and, oh! did you notice the flowers? Lilac, and roses! At Christmas! Do you think the duke would show us the hot-houses? Could I ask him, do you think? Or would it look silly?' So Teresa had run on, until it was time to dress for dinner, when a maid scared her by coming to ask if there was anything she wanted.

At home, when doing her packing, she had looked with some satisfaction upon her clothes. Nothing there that might not meet the critical eye of the Chevron housemaids! Except, perhaps, her bedroom slippers. She had scrutinised them, then had decided in their favour; they were a little worn on one side, certainly, but that might be overlooked, and really she could not ask John for any more money; he had given her a generous cheque already. But here, at Chevron, in this luxurious bed-room, her poor little chemises and her nightgown looked paltry; and as for the slippers, they had turned unaccountably shabby. She wondered if she should hide them away; but it was too late;

the housemaid had unpacked and had seen them. Teresa felt vexed. She regretted that she had given up her keys before dinner, when a footman came to ask her for them. But how could she have said that she would unpack her trunk herself? That would have revealed a woeful lack of *savoir faire*; and *savoir faire* for the moment was Teresa's god. She had given up her keys as though all her life she had been accustomed to have a maid; indeed, she had hoped that everybody within hearing would assume that she had brought her own maid, and that her retention of the keys was accidental. The Chevron housemaid was the only blot on Teresa's paradise.

Then she made a fresh discovery, which again scattered her regrets in the wind of her excitement. She discovered a nosegay upon her dressing-table: two orchids and a spray of maiden-hair fern. She flew into John's dressing-room next door, and there discovered the masculine counterpart: a buttonhole consisting of one exquisitely furled yellow rosebud. John by then was in his bath. She stood, cupping the rosebud within her hands as though it represented the total and final expression of everything refined and luxurious.

That had been last night. At dinner, the butler had thrown Teresa into a fresh fluster by saying to her, 'Champagne, m'lady?' After dinner they had sat upstairs, in the great drawing-room, surrounded by more lilac and more roses, and the family portraits had looked down on them from the walls, filling Teresa with curiosity and admiration; but as nobody else made any comment, she judged it prudent to make none either. She had felt acutely uncomfortable during the half-hour she sat up there alone with the ladies, for Teresa did not care for women at the best of times, and these ladies who addressed a few remarks to her out of good manners, but who could

certainly not fail to wish her out of the way, were especially not
calculated to put her at her ease. Click, clack, click, clack, went
their conversation, like so many knitting-needles, purl, plain,
purl, plain, achieving a complex pattern or references, cross-
references, Christian names, nicknames, and fleeting allusions;
until Teresa, unable to do anything but observe, came to the
conclusion that they thought their topics not merely the most
absorbing in the world, but, rather, the only possible topics. She
watched them wonderingly, much as Anquetil, also an outsider,
had once watched them, but her reflections were very different
from his. She envied, instead of scorning, their prodigious self-
sufficiency, their tacit exclusion of all the world outside their
own circle. She marvelled at the uniformity of their appearance: tall or short, stout or thin, young or old, there was an
indefinable resemblance, something in the metallic glance of
the eye, the hard line of the mouth, the movement of the
hands with their many rings and bangles. This glance of the eye
was peculiar; although penetrating, it had something of the
deadness of a fish's eye; glassy, as though a slight film obscured
the vision; and the eyelids moreover were sharply cut, as
though a narrowing tuck had been taken in them, still further
robbing the eyes of any open generosity they might once have
possessed. Altogether, Teresa thought that these ladies ought
properly to be sitting under glass cases in a museum, so fixed did
they appear, so far removed from any possible disorder; their
coiffures elaborate and perfect, their gowns so manifestly
expensive and yet so much a part of them, their manner so
secure from any conceivable bewilderment or confusion. Surely
no natural element would ever disturb that fine complacency;
no gale would dishevel that architectural hair, no passion
ravage those corseted busts. No passion, thought Teresa with an

exquisite shiver, but a chill and calculated wickedness. She did not criticise; she admired. She thought that they were like all the portraits by Sargent that she had ever seen – and she went to the Academy every year with John, so she had seen a good many – divine inhabitants of a world apart, for whom nothing sordid, nothing petty, and nothing painful had any existence at all; served by innumerable domestics, prepared for the day or the evening by innumerable maids, hairdressers, manicurists, beauty specialists, chiropodists, tailors, and dressmakers; sallying forth, scented and equipped, from their dressing-rooms, to consort as familiarly with the Great as she herself with Mrs. Tolputt.

Yet she was forced to admit that they did not seem to be saying anything worth saying.

She had expected their conversation to rival their appearance. She had expected to be dazzled by their wit and thrilled by their revelations. Try as she might, she had not been able to imagine what form their conversation would take; but had resigned herself humbly in anticipation, telling herself that she was in the position of a London child who had never seen the sea, or of a beggar suddenly promised a meal at Dieudonné's. She did not know what it would be like, only that it would be wonderful. And now she found that it differed very little from the conversation of her own acquaintances, only the references were to people she did not know, and the general assumptions were on a more extravagant scale. They even talked about their servants. 'Yes, my dear,' Lady Edward was saying, 'I have really had to get rid of the *chef* at last. We found he was using a hundred and forty-four dozen eggs a week.' They went into screams of laughter at phrases that Teresa (reluctantly) thought quite silly. In particular, there was one lady whose name Teresa did

not know, but who could not open her mouth without pronouncing some quite unintelligible words that instantly
provoked hilarity. Nevertheless, Teresa was interested. She supposed it must be some kind of jargon confined only to the most
exclusive circles, and the fact that it should be used in her presence gave her a sense of flattering privity. She tried to dismiss
the idea that it was really rather tiresome and affected, and that
it reminded her of nothing so much as of a secret language used
by herself and her fellows at school, which consisted in adding
the syllables 'jib' and 'job' to every alternate word. 'Are-jib you-
job going-jib to-job play-jib hockey-job to-jib day-job?' The
language had been known as Jib-job, and only the élite of the
school had been allowed to use it. This language of the élite of
London was apparently composed on much the same principle.
It consisted in adding an Italian termination to English words;
but as that termination was most frequently the termination of
Italian verbs of the first declension, and as it was tacked on to
English words irrespective of their being verbs, nouns, or adjec-
tives, it could not be said to be based on any very creditable
grammatical system. Smartness, Teresa couldn't help thinking,
was cheap at such a price. 'And after dinn-are, we might have
a little dans-are,' said this anonymous lady; a suggestion greeted
by exclamations of 'What a deevy idea, Florence! There's
nobody like Florence, is there, for deevy ideas like that?' The
critical faculty, raising its head for a second in Teresa, though
immediately stamped upon, suggested that there was nothing
very original or divine in the idea of dancing after dinner. But,
'How lovel-are!' cried Lucy, and suddenly recollecting her
obligations as a hostess, she added, 'You must tell Sebastian to
bring Mrs. Spedding as his partnerina.' All those searchlight
eyes were turned upon Teresa, modest in her corner. She was

just shrewd enough to realise that the duchess with a twinge of social conscience had remembered her, left out in the cold. Hitherto, nobody had addressed any word to her but some phrase such as, 'Do you live in London or the country, Mrs. Spedding?' a phrase which clearly could have no sequel but the actual timid reply. Now, thanks to Lucy's effort, Teresa became the momentary focus of interest. All the ladies took up Lucy's cue. They examined Teresa with a stare that was meant to be flattering, but which, in effect, was so patronising as to arouse Teresa's defiance. 'I'm afraid I don't dance,' she said, knowing that she danced extremely well; far better, probably, than all these ladies getting on in years. No sooner had she said it, than she wished to bite her tongue out for thus obeying an unregistered instinct. Involuntarily she had been rude; and, though half of her was pleased at daring to be rude, the other half was frightened. But their good manners were, apparently, not to be shaken. 'We don't believe that,' said Lucy with her light laugh; 'we just don't believe that – do we? I'm sure Mrs Spedding dansares like a ballerina. And anyway, if you won't let Sebastian bring you as a partnerina, I shall ask you to bring Sebastian as a partnerino. I'm sure you would never be so unkind as to refuse an anxious mother.'

After that, they had left Teresa in peace. She was at liberty to recover from the flutter into which they had thrown her. She could look round once more at the vast drawing-room, and, unobserved, could take in the details of the panelling with the frieze of mermaids and dolphins, tails coiled into tails, scales overlapping onto scales in Elizabethan extravagance; she could look at the portraits while the click-clack of the conversation crackled in the background of her consciousness; she could leap across the centuries from the painting of Edward the Sixth holding a rose between finger and thumb, to the silver-framed photograph on a table of Edward the Seventh in a Homburg hat, his foot lifted ready upon the step of his first Daimler. Teresa devoted a good deal of her attention to a furtive observation of the photographs. Thanks to her own private collection, she was able to identify most of them. There was Lady de T., very dark and lovely, sitting, in evening dress, on the ground in a wood, a scatter of faggots beside her. There was Lady A., seated on a Louis Quinze *bergère*, occupied with a spinning-wheel at which she was not looking – a favourite composition of Miss Alice Hughes. There were the three beautiful W. sisters leaning over a balcony with a poodle. 'For darling Lucy,' ran the inscription in a flowing feminine hand. There was Mrs. Langtry wrapped in furs, her profile turned to display her celebrated and lovely nose. There was Queen Alexandra wearing a crown, and Queen Alexandra wearing a bonnet, and Queen Alexandra surrounded by her grandchildren and dogs. There was the German Emperor in uniform, with an eagled helmet, his hands clasped on the hilt of his sword. These indications of intimacy sent associative shivers of delight down Teresa's susceptible backbone. She longed to prowl about the room alone, and savour the treasures that every table offered. But this, she told herself, was foolish. Was she not better employed in observing the flesh-and-blood that surrounded her? Photographs, after all, could be cut out of any illustrated paper. Teresa floated away on a dream. She considered the possibility of cutting out the next available photograph of the duchess; buying a silver frame for it; faking an inscription – 'For dear Teresa,' it would run; or would 'For dear Mrs. Spedding' be more probable and more convincing? 'Chevron, Christmas 1906' – and standing it upon her own drawing-room table for the benefit of Mrs. Tolputt and her friends. But what would John say? And what would she do if Sebastian unexpectedly came to call? Reluctantly she discarded the idea. The champagne must have gone to her head.

She decided that she did not like women. She felt much happier when the men came upstairs, and Sebastian immediately made his way to her side. She said again to John, that night in her bedroom, that Sebastian had been 'very nice.'

Now she lay in her vast bed, having breakfast on a tray. She had already written a great many letters, and had boxed them into a pack, like cards, putting on the top of the pile a letter addressed to the only other titled person she knew – the wife of a surgeon who had recently been knighted. She looked very pretty, breakfasting in bed as to the manner born, and felt as luxurious as a cat in the sun. John teased her by saying that she would now never be willing to return with him to the wrong end of the Cromwell Road. Outside the window, the snowflakes were falling silently; the great courtyard was all white, every battlement was outlined in snow, and every now and then came a soft plop, as men shovelled the snow off the roofs. 'Doesn't one feel,' said Teresa dreamily, 'that all this has been going on for hundreds and hundreds of years? – I mean, that the snow has fallen, and that men have gone up to shovel it off the roofs, and that it has fallen with that same soft sound, and that the flag has hung quite still, and that the clock has struck the hours. I wonder what Chevron is like in summer! I do hope the duke will ask us again.'

Poor Teresa. She tried to be so artful, and was really so artless. She did not know in the least which particular attributes in herself appealed to Sebastian, and which did not. She had no idea of how to treat Sebastian. When she finally appeared, very neatly dressed in the new tweed coat and skirt she had had made for the occasion, he came forward to greet her with a smile, but within an hour she had contrived to exasperate him beyond endurance. 'What do you think of this snow, Mrs. Spedding?' he had said; and going over to the window, Teresa had replied that it looked just like a Christmas card. It was precisely the response he had expected from her, but he caught a look of amusement on Lady Templecombe's face, and in an access of irritation had offered to show Teresa over the house. It was the readiest means of escape he could devise. She was his friend; he was responsible for her; he must get her away from these people who made her nervous and drove her into making a fool of herself. So he took her upstairs, away into safety. They wandered through the state rooms together.

Hitherto she had been more or less her natural self with Sebastian; her attempts at affectation had been brief and unsuccessful; but for weeks now, in anticipation of the Christmas visit, she had been schooling herself to be on her guard. So it was not the Teresa he knew who went round the house with him. It was a sedate Teresa, determined at all costs to appear unimpressed. Secretly, she was overcome by this new revelation of the splendours of Sebastian's home; she imagined that she traced a family likeness to him in every one of the pictures; she gasped at the sumptuous velvets, at the extravagance of the silver sconces, the silver tables; she longed to ask whose were the coats-of-arms represented in the heraldic windows; she longed to ask a thousand questions, to pour forth her admiration, her bewilderment, her ignorance; but she allowed herself to do none of these things. Instead, she strolled nonchalant and lackadaisical by his side, making pert remarks; 'Dear, dear!' she said, as they paused before a Titian of Diana and her nymphs surprised by Acteon, 'aren't you glad that your ancestresses didn't carry on in that way?' Still more unfortunately, she tried to ape the fashionable jargon. 'How you must love-are all these funny old rooms!' Sebastian clenched his fists in his pockets. He had not expected her to show any intelligent interest in the treasures of Chevron, but at least he had expected to enjoy the reaction of a naïf and unaccustomed mind; he had been prepared to laugh at her, fondly, affectionately, even though he knew that his motive in showing her his possessions was not a very estimable one. They were entirely at cross-purposes. Sebastian began to feel that this middle-class caution was the last thing he could tolerate. He wished that Romola Cheyne were his companion, or Lady Templecombe, or Julia Levison; or, rushing to the other extreme, old Turnour, or Godden. They would have been incapable of such airs and graces. What folly had possessed him, he wondered, to invite Teresa to Chevron? His world and hers could never meet. Old Turnour was a different matter; he liked old Turnour for talking about the frost and the sprouts; he appreciated the enormous, the vital importance of sprouts to old Turnour; he liked any reflection of a natural and practical nature, in character with the person who made it; thus he had liked Mrs. Tolputt for talking about the sales and the servants' sheets – but he remembered how Teresa had tried to interrupt her; he liked Lord Templecombe for saying at breakfast, 'Damn this bloody snow, Sebastian, can't you do something about it? Spoiling all my huntin'.' What he could not endure was the hypocrisy of Teresa's gentility. He liked her when she was, frankly and crudely, a snob. He could not bear people who pretended to be something that they were not. He decided that Teresa was nothing – neither practical, nor cultured, nor raw – and he determined there and then to dismiss her from his life for ever.

'Wacey,' he said, bursting into the schoolroom after this unfortunate expedition into the state-rooms was over, 'can I see the plan of the luncheon-table, please?'

The harassed Wacey produced it.

'Sorry,' said Sebastian, 'but this has got to be altered. I can't sit next to Mrs. Spedding. Be ingenious, Wacey. Shift everybody round.'

'But her Grace said ... ' Wacey began.

'Never mind what she said. Shift them round. Put me next to Lady Templecombe. Or can I come and have my luncheon with you in here?'

Wacey gasped at him. Was he mad? Was he simply in high spirits, as he sometimes was, when he came and teased her? or had something gone seriously wrong?

'I would much rather have my luncheon with you, Wacey. And my dinner, too. Can't I? just you and me and Viola? Then we could laugh together at everybody sitting solemnly downstairs.'

Miss Wace found the suitable formula. 'That would be very nice for me, but People in your Position have to Respect Appearances.'

'I seem to have heard that before,' said Sebastian, thinking of Sylvia. 'Do we really? But why? Why are people so careful of appearances? Mr. Anquetil, you know, Wacey, wouldn't give a fig for appearances.'

'There was a bit about Mr. Anquetil in the *Daily Mail*,' said Miss Wace.

'No?' said Sebastian, greedily. 'Was there? When? Show me.'

'I don't know that I've kept it,' said Miss Wace with caution.

'Nonsense, Wacey; you know you keep everything, even old

newspapers in case they should come in handy for lighting the fire. You were born to hoard. Produce it.'

Wacey rose and unlocked an enormous cupboard, where indeed, as Sebastian had implied, lay a pile of newspapers neatly folded. From these she drew a two-days-old copy of the *Daily Mail*.

'Adventurous Englishmen Missing,' he read. 'It is now three months since news has been received of a party which left Manaos in September in an attempt to discover the sources of the Upper Amazon. Mr. Leonard Anquetil, who will be remembered as a member of ... '

Sebastian put the paper down. He looked out at the snow falling past the window.

'Will this snow prevent the children from coming to the Christmas tree?' he asked irrelevantly.

'Only those who live far out,' replied Miss Wace, immediately well informed and brisk.

'Poor little devils! What a disappointment for them.'

'But Mrs. Wickenden sees to it that they get their toys and crackers just the same.'

'That isn't the same at all, Wacey, They miss their tea and their games. Do you think they like coming?'

'Of course they like coming,' said Miss Wace, shocked. 'It's the great treat of the year for them. They look forward to it, all the year through. So would you, if it was the only treat you had.'

'Yes,' said Sebastian, 'I expect I should. As it is, I find that treats always turn out to be disappointments. And now some of them won't be able to come at all.' He stared out at the falling snow; for one reason or another, he had forgotten the plan of the luncheon-table lying before him.

*

Matters went better between Teresa and Sebastian after luncheon. The morning is always an unpropitious time for emotional
relationships. Lovers, or potential lovers, ought never to meet
before the afternoon. Morning is bleak and un-erotic. During
luncheon, Sebastian had sat between Lady Templecombe and
Mrs. Levison, and had been bored by their conversation, which
was the replica of a conversation he had heard a thousand times
before. Once or twice he had caught Teresa's eye, and had again
imagined that a certain understanding ran between them – a
fallacy readily credited by any person temporarily deluded by
physical desire. Those airs and graces, he decided, were not the
true Teresa; they were but defences that she put up, as much
against the male in him as against the duke in him. He saw
them in a new light now, and was as leniently touched and
diverted by them as he had originally been by Teresa's
anguished efforts to control Mrs. Tolputt. In this mellower
mood, he perceived that Teresa's pretences were as much a part
of her as was Turnour's anxiety about his sprouts.

Still, he remained uneasily solicitous on Teresa's behalf; he
was disinclined to trust her for the rest of the afternoon with his
mother, Lady Templecombe, and the others. He proposed that
they should make a snow-man in the garden. This suggestion
was received with horror by all but Teresa herself and, unexpectedly, John; Teresa forgot herself and clapped her hands;
John took his pipe out of his mouth and said he hadn't made a
snow-man since he was a boy, by Jove! he hadn't. Lucy was all
too obviously relieved. She rapidly summed-up three bridge-
tables, and cast an approving look at Sebastian, who had thus
solved the problem of amusing his two incongruous friends for
the afternoon.

Snow had ceased to fall; it was freezing hard; the lying snow was in admirable condition. Sebastian, John, and Teresa went out in hearty spirits. Teresa, moreover, was looking deliciously pretty, dressed in a tight bolero of stamped velvet, a sealskin cap on her head, and her hands buried in a little sealskin muff. She tripped gaily between them, chattering, and turning her happy face from one to the other. This was better than London, she said; snow got so dreadfully dirty in London, and before you knew where you were it had all turned to slush. She chattered on, while John and Sebastian chose a site for their snow-man. But before they engaged on their work they must have imple-ments; so ambitious a snow-man as they projected could not be built by the unaided human hand. Sebastian and Teresa left John stamping among the snow while they went off to find the necessary shovels. Wooden shovels they must be – Sebastian knew from boyish experience that snow stuck to ordinary steel shovels – but he must find the shovels for himself, for he knew that on Christmas Eve the men would have knocked off work early. The door of the gardeners' bothy, indeed, was locked when they reached it. The discipline of childhood was still strong in Sebastian; he hesitated for an instant before the locked door; he went back to the days when Chevron, although officially his, was not his to treat in such high-handed manner; then, taking up a mallet with sudden determination, he broke down the door, and Teresa exclaimed in mixed dismay and admiration. Sebastian, while pleased with himself for showing off his strength and his mastership before Teresa, could not escape a private sense of guilt, as though he were still a little boy. Plunging into the dark bothy, stumbling over benches and mowing-machines in his search for the shovels he wanted, he remembered analogous defiances of law in years gone by, when no one but his mother and his nurse dared to reprove him; he

remembered getting out of the house at five on summer morn-
ings, climbing over the garden wall because he was not then
allowed the master-key that would unlock the wrought-iron
gates (he put his hand into his pocket now, and fingered the
key buried there); he remembered running across the park to
the kitchen garden; he remembered creeping under the nets to
eat the full, fresh strawberries with the dews of dawn still on
them; he remembered the way his fingers had got entangled in
the meshes, and how he had deliberately held up the nets for
the frightened thrushes to escape, having meanwhile an unpat-
riotic feeling about Chevron as he did it, for it was surely wrong
to let the thieving thrushes go. He remembered having once
stolen two peaches out of the hot-house. It was not quite so
criminal to eat fruit that grew in the open air – homely fruit:
but not hot-house fruit. He remembered how he had once met
Diggs the head-gardener carrying a basket of grapes, and how
he had begged for some grapes, but Diggs had drawn the basket
aside, saying, 'No, your Grace lied to me,' and how he had
never understood, to this day, what Diggs had meant. He was
sure that he had never lied – he hated lies; and even now, at the
age of twenty-one, he cherished a resentment against Diggs,
good servitor though Diggs undoubtedly was, all for that phrase
spoken thirteen years ago. So he felt glad that he should have
broken down the door of the bothy; it would annoy Diggs, but
Diggs would not be in a position to complain. And Wickenden
would have to mend it. His Grace could do what he liked with
his own. Meanwhile, he had found the shovels.

It was not a snow-man that they made, but a snow-lady. She
was all complete, even to the buttons down the front of her
bodice, and the bun at the back of her head, and the hat tilted
over her nose, and two pebbles for eyes. They laughed a great

deal over the making of her, while the sun that Sebastian had seen climb up over the trees in the morning sank slowly down into the trees on the opposite side of the lawn, the same red ball that it had been all day. Absolute stillness reigned, the stillness which comes with a heavy fall of snow, and which to Sebastian, the country-bred, seemed expected and in the right order; but which Teresa, the little Cockney, thought unnatural, and which, she maintained, could only portend a storm. Sebastian scoffed at her, but amiably, very different from his sulky monosyllables of the morning. 'A storm! This snow, unless we get a sudden thaw, will lie for days; to-morrow you will see the whole village out, tobogganing in the park. Our snow-lady will have an icicle dripping from the end of her nose.' They worked on, putting the finishing touches in the fading daylight, all three of them in good humour, their shouts and their laughter ringing over the snow and echoing back from the walls of the house. Even the taciturn John expanded; he displayed himself as quite a competent sculptor, modelling the lady's bust and paring away the snow at her waist, till Sebastian cried out that if he made her any more like an hourglass she would snap in half; while Teresa arranged the lady's train on the ground, and scolloped the snow into flounces. Kneeling on the ground, her face glowing beneath her sealskin cap, she laughed up at Sebastian as she beat her hands together to shake the snow from her gloves; he thought only how pretty she was, how charming, and had no longer the slightest desire for the company of Mrs. Levison or Lady Templecombe.

'In a few moments we must go and give the children their presents,' said Lucy, after tea. 'You will have to make up the bridge-tables without me. I can cut in when I come back. What a nuisance these entertainments are, but I suppose one must put up with them.'

'What children are they, Lucy, dear?'

'Only the estate children. We have a tree for them, of course, every Christmas. It means that we can never dine in the Hall on Christmas Eve, and I used to be so terribly afraid that Sebastian and Viola would catch something. Really I don't know that it is a very good plan to spoil poor children like this; it only gives them a taste for things they can't have; but it is very difficult to stop something which has always been an institution.'

'In my opinion,' said Mrs. Levison, who had neither estates nor children on them, but had always maintained herself somewhat precariously by her wits, 'we do a great deal too much for such people. We educate their children for them for nothing – and I don't believe they want to be educated, half the time – we keep the hospitals for them entirely out of charity, we give them warm old clothes and almshouses: what more do they want? Alfred Rothschild even gives the bus-drivers a pair of gloves and a brace of pheasants for Christmas.'

'We always give our beaters a hare and a pheasant each, after every shoot,' said Lady Templecombe, self-righteously.

'They've earned it, too,' said Lord Templecombe, unexpectedly; 'how would you like to go plunging through hedges and brambles from morning to night, tearing all your clothes?'

'Now, Eadred, you know they enjoy it,' said Lucy, with her light laugh. 'You're as bad as Sebastian: do you know what he has done now? Given every man on the estate a rise of five shillings a week this Christmas. Did you ever hear of such a thing?'

'My dear boy!' said Lord Templecombe, screwing in his

eyeglass to stare at Sebastian, 'what made you do that?' Not my business, of course, but it's a great mistake. A great mistake. Spoils the market for other people less fortunate than yourself. Besides, they won't appreciate it. They'll only expect more.'

They all looked at Sebastian as though he had committed a crime.

Vigeon, followed by two footmen carrying trays, came in to clear away the tea.

'The children are quite ready, when your Grace is ready,' he said in a low voice to Lucy.

'Oh, heavens! then we must go,' said Lucy, getting up off the sofa. 'Let's get it over quickly. I always believe in getting boring things over quickly. And I always believe in doing things well if you do them at all. I always change into my prettiest frock for the children; I'm sure they like it. Anyway, their mothers do. Come along, Viola. Come along, Sebastian. You must both support me.'

Teresa took an enormous decision; she knew that none of the other ladies would want to go to the Christmas tree, but partly because she dreaded being left alone with them, and partly also because she so desperately wanted to see the ceremony of the tree, she resolved to abandon her policy of imitating what other people did. 'May I come too, duchess? You see, I don't play bridge ...'

The roar of voices and the stamping of feet in the hall ceased abruptly as the door opened to admit the duchess and her party. The hall was full of children, and there, on the dais, in isolated splendour, stood the great tree, shining with a hundred candles and glittering with a hundred baubles of coloured glass. Silver tinsel ran in and out of its dark boughs; tufts of cotton-wool suggested snow-flakes; the pot was swathed in cotton-wool; and a spangled doll, a fairy queen with a crescent in her hair, gloriously crowned the topmost spike. Toys were heaped upon the table; a hamper of oranges and a hamper of rosy apples stood ready on either side, the lids thrown back. The children seethed excitedly in the body of the hall, even while the Chevron housemaids flitted about, trying to marshal them into order. The mothers sat grouped round the blazing fire, many of them with babies on their knees, but as Lucy entered they all rose, and some of them curtseyed, and a murmur ran round the hall, and some of the little boys, who had been carefully primed, saluted.

Now that Lucy was actually in the presence of her audience, standing above them on the step, all trace of boredom vanished from her manner. She believed, as she had said, in doing things well if you did them at all; moreover, she was not insensible to the favour she was conferring, or to the dramatic quality of her own appearance, backed by the shining tree that cast an aureole of light round her fair head and sparkled on the diamonds at her breast. She paused for a moment, surveying the mob of children, while the last murmurs and shufflings quieted down; then she spoke. Her clear voice rang out, in the formula she had used for the past five-and-twenty years: 'Well, children, I hope you have all had a nice tea?'

More murmurs; here and there one could distinguish a 'Yes, thank you, your Grace.'

Lucy pursued, after rewarding them all with a bright smile, 'And now I expect you all want your presents?'

Here Mrs. Wickenden came forward; she had been hovering in the background, waiting for Lucy to give this signal. The estate children's treat was always a great day in Mrs.

Wickenden's calendar. She came forward now with a long list
in her hand.

'Should I read out the names, your Grace?'

'Yes, please, Mrs. Wickenden, would you?'

For five-and-twenty years the list had been read out by the
housekeeper, whether Mrs. Wickenden or her predecessor, but
that little ceremony was never omitted. Mrs. Wickenden would
not have believed her ears had she heard Lucy say, 'No, I'll read
it myself.' So now, clearing her throat and carefully settling her
spectacles, she advanced to the edge of the step and began calling up the children one by one. They were listed in families,
from the eldest to the youngest, and the families were arranged
in strict order, the butler's children coming first, then the head-
carpenter's, then the head-gardener's, and so down to the
children of the man who swept up the leaves in the park. Each
child detached itself from the rows and came up to the step as
its name was called out; the little boys wore thick suits of dark
tweed, the little girls wore frocks of pink, mauve, blue, or green
voile. An elder sister sometimes had a younger brother by the
hand. Lucy, stooping very graciously to bestow the present into
eager hands, had a kind word for all. 'Why, Doris, what a big
girl you are growing! ... Now, Jacky, if I give you this lovely
knife, you must promise not to cut your mother's furniture ...
And so this is the new baby, Mrs. Hodder?' – Lucy was very
quick at picking up the names – 'let me see, how old is he now?
seven months? only *four* months! well, he *is* a fine boy, you
must be very proud of him, and here is a lovely rattle for him.
He must wait a few years before he gets a knife, mustn't he?' –
this was a joke that, however often repeated, never failed to
arouse laughter. Mrs. Wickenden stood by, beaming; yet she
kept a sharp watch on the children's manners: 'Say thank you

to her Grace, Maggie; Bob, you've forgotten your salute; now touch your forehead nicely to her Grace,' and Lucy herself in the midst of her benevolence could preserve discipline too, saying, 'Well, if you won't say thank you for your knife, Jacky, I shall have to take it away from you.' Sebastian, listening, was slightly embarrassed to hear the children reproved in this way; he tried to tell himself that his mother and Mrs. Wickenden were probably quite right; his discomfort would have been less-ened, however, had he been able to convince himself that his mother did not really enjoy doing it. He and Viola had their share in the ceremony; they presented an apple, an orange, and a cracker to each child after Lucy had given the toy. Here, again, Mrs. Wickenden supervised and intervened, taking the forgetful child by the shoulders and turning it round; 'Look, Stanley, his Grace and Lady Viola have something for you, too.'

But every now and then there was no response to the name called out, and after a suitable hesitation there would come a murmur from amongst the mothers round the fire, and Mrs. Wickenden would say, 'Not here?' and would turn with the explanation to Lucy, 'Mumps, your Grace,' or else, 'They live too far out, your Grace, to get here through the snow.'

Teresa was spell-bound. She stood modestly to one side, fas-cinated by the lights, by the great hall, by the rows and rows of faces, by this list of names that never seemed to come to an end. She noticed, too, how many families there were of the same name, Hodders and Goddens and Bassetts and Reynolds. 'Feudal!' she kept saying to herself; 'really feudal!' It was a source of enormous satisfaction to her to be standing on the dais with Lucy, Sebastian and Viola; she felt privileged and ele-vated; though had she overheard the whispers round the fire her vainglory might have received a check. The mothers had been so anxious to know who the stranger was, for her Grace was not usually accompanied by a guest, and they had enquired of the Chevron housemaids, who stood amongst them in their quality of part-hostesses, dandling the babies in their arms. But the housemaids had sniffed. 'A Mrs. Spedding,' they said; 'wife of a doctor,' and poor Teresa had unwittingly provided a disappointment.

The last present had been given, the last apple, the last orange, and the last cracker: Lucy was preparing to make her little farewell speech. A threat of rowdiness had to be suppressed, for the impatient children had already begun to pull their crackers, hob-nailed boots clattered on the stone floor, and one or two of the little boys had loosed off a pistol with deafening caps; so 'Hush, children!' cried Mrs. Wickenden, holding up her hand, and the noise subsided. 'Well, children,' Lucy began again, 'I hope you all like your presents, and now I hope you will all have a good game, and so I'll say good-bye till next year. Good-bye, children, goodnight, good-bye to you all.'

Vigeon rose very stately in the body of the hall.

'Three cheers for her Grace, children!' he cried. 'Now lift the roof! Hip, hip . . .'

'Hooray!' they shouted, lifting the roof.

'And again for his Grace. Hip, hip . . .'

'Hooray!'

'And for Lady Viola. Hip, hip . . .'

Teresa blinked the tears back from her eyes. How beautiful it was! How young, how handsome, how patrician were Viola and Sebastian! How the children must adore them!

'Hooray!'

Bang went a cracker. Lucy made her escape. Sebastian

slipped round the tree to his sister. 'Shall we stay and play games with them, Viola?'

'But what about Mrs. Spedding?'

'Oh, she can stay too.'

They all stayed. Vigeon had already wound up the gramophone, and its enormous trumpet brayed forth, but the children were in no mood to listen even to Dan Leno. They wanted to make as much noise as possible themselves. If they were to be controlled at all, regular games must be organised. Sebastian and Viola knew all about this, for they had always been allowed to stay behind with the children, and Sebastian indeed had always been puzzled as a little boy by 'Nuts in May,' because, as he explained to his nurse, nuts grew in September, not in May.

The housemaids were admirable hostesses. They wore their best black dresses; enjoyed their role thoroughly; knew all the children by name; were inventive and competent; could produce enough chairs for 'Musical Chairs,' or a clean handkerchief for 'I wrote-a-letter-to-my-love,' or a thick honest scarf for 'Blindman's Buff'; in fact, anything that was wanted. Mr. Vigeon was a terrible Blindman. He had to be saved a dozen times from falling into the fire. He plunged about, his arms whirling, so that one scarcely dared to creep up and poke him in the back or tweak his coat-tails, he was so quick on his feet and could nip round so fast. He caught his Grace, who was too daring – he had always been too daring, even as a little boy – and everyone stood round breathlessly while he felt his Grace's head and nose, and finally gave the pronouncement right. There were shrieks of laughter when his Grace blundered into the panelling and caught one of the heraldic leopards; felt its tail very carefully, right up to the tip; and then said, 'Mrs. Wickenden.' Then they wanted to play 'Hunt the Slipper,' but Mrs. Vigeon said it was too cold for the children to sit on the stone floor. So they played 'Musical Chairs' instead, with Mr. Vigeon working the gramophone very ingeniously; his Grace and Mrs. Spedding were left in last, and had an exciting scramble over the last chair, which ended in their both sitting down on it together and trying to crowd each other off. By now everyone was in very high spirits, and even Mrs. Wickenden forgot to reprove the children for lacking in respect to his Grace. They played 'Nuts in May,' swaying in two long lines up and down the hall after the invidious business of picking sides had been completed; Mr. Vigeon had picked one side and Mrs. Wickenden the other, as befitted their dignity. Mr. Vigeon had very gallantly picked Mrs. Spedding, and Mrs. Wickenden had retaliated by picking his Grace. So Teresa and Sebastian were ranged opposite to one another, each with their hands clasped by the hot little hands of two excited children. Teresa was conscious of a strange agitation, which in her innocence she ascribed to the general ferment of the evening; Sebastian, just as much troubled but less innocent, watched her closely; this intimacy with her, in the midst of their apparent frivolity, was of the very nature that whipped his taste. Ever since they fetched the shovels out of the bothy, ever since they made the snow-lady, he had been wooing Teresa, not very openly as yet, but still more openly than he had hitherto dared. Now he laughed at her gaily, as his enemy on the opposite side; she saw his laughing face across the gap that separated them. And, since such humours are contagious, the line of children and servants rocked backwards and forwards, taking Sebastian and Teresa as on a tide with them, and as they rocked they sang:

'Who will you have for nuts in May? nuts in May? nuts in May?'

'We'll have Mrs. Spedding for nuts in May, nuts in May, nuts in May. We'll have Mrs. Spedding for nuts in May, all on a frosty morning.'

'And who will you send to fetch her away? fetch her away? fetch her away?'

'We'll send his Grace to fetch her away, fetch her away, fetch her away. We'll send his Grace to fetch her away, all on a frosty morning.'

A handkerchief was laid down in the middle, and Sebastian and Teresa advanced amidst much laughter to pit their strength.

'It isn't fair!' cried Teresa, resisting the many hands that pushed her forward.

'Nonsense,' said Sebastian firmly; 'all's fair ...' and he looked at her, but did not complete the sentence.

They joined hands across the handkerchief; there was a brief struggle, and Sebastian pulled her easily over to his side. She came, panting, laughing, submissive; looking at her captor while everybody applauded. For the first time in their acquaintance she was frightened of him; for the first time in their acquaintance he was sure of her. Viola observed them; she sized up the situation; she felt sorry for Teresa, sorrier for John Spedding. But, of course, it was no good trying to interfere with Sebastian.

Sebastian himself was well aware of this. He had been circumspect, he had been forbearing, but now he was bent on hunting Teresa down, and nothing could stop him. He turned everything into a circumstance that drew her closer to him, and he did it with a certainty and a recklessness that swept her along with him on his crazy course. The control was entirely in his hands. All through the maze of children he seemed to be chasing her, so that she found him always behind her, or beside her, or facing her, where she least expected him, mocking her lightly, or alternating his gaiety with a smouldering look that disturbed her to some unexplored region of her soul. Everything piled up for Teresa: the new experience of Chevron, the lights of the Christmas-tree, the shouting of the children, the fantasy, the improbability, the sense of this young man burning his way towards her, a remorseless young man who would spare her nothing – all this turned Sebastian from the most unhoped toy that she had ever had into an urgent but still undefinable terror. He saw the fright in her eyes, and, skilled in reading the signs, exulted. How ludicrously he was misled, he had yet to learn.

Meanwhile they played. They played the childish games, with the adult game lying behind them. They played 'Oranges and Lemons,' with Sebastian and Viola making the arch; they let a dozen children pass, but snatched Teresa, as she tried to slip past them, and for the first time Sebastian felt Teresa's small body imprisoned in his arms. He could feel her heart beating against his ribs. She, for her part, clipped between brother and sister, turned laughing and dizzy in her imprisonment from one to the other, seeing Viola's grave brows bent inquiringly towards her, and Sebastian's eyes dark with a question that exacted an answer. 'Oranges?' said Sebastian. 'Lemons?' said Viola, and Teresa knew that she must take her place in the string of children behind one or the other. 'Lemons,' she said, casting Viola a glance that was an appeal. It was as though she had said, 'Save me from him!' divining that in this cold, secretive girl she might hope for some masonic, feminine support; but at the same time the oranges that Sebastian offered her seemed luscious and warm, opposed to the sour lemons of Viola's following. The very colour of the fruits, which in her sensitive state she visualised, seemed symbolic: the reddish fire of the orange, the unripe yellow of the lemon. Yet 'Lemons!' she said, and took her place behind Viola, in a gesture that repudiated all that Sebastian had to offer.

Still he would not let her go, for her defiance had only served to stimulate him; he persecuted her, softly, stealthily, even when the Christmas-tree caught fire and the hall was suddenly filled with the acrid scent of burning fir. One of the candles had burnt out, and the little candle-clip had tipped over; the hall-boy, who had been left in charge with a damp sponge on the end of a pole, had been tempted by the games to desert his post, thinking that no one would notice – he was only fourteen, so there was some excuse for him – a flare resulted; everyone rushed to help; fire-buckets were brought and the water flung sizzling over the conflagration; this happened nearly every year, but still for some reason Vigeon's theory of discipline refused to accept the fact that a hall-boy aged fourteen was not a suitable person to be left in charge of a Christmas-tree whilst other fun was in progress. No harm was done, only a little excitement added to the general excitement; and Sebastian's hand had caught Teresa's wrist and had pulled it away from a blazing patch of cotton-wool. No further harm. But somehow the incident broke up the games. The guilty hall-boy ran off to lay the table for the servants' hall supper; a baby by the fire woke up and began to squall; Mrs. Wickenden realised that she was tired; mothers remembered that they were faced with a long trudge home through the snow; a sudden weariness descended upon the children; the housemaids bethought themselves of the hot-water cans they must fill; it occurred to Sebastian that it was time to dress for dinner; and

Vigeon finally put an end to the jollity by calling upon everybody to sing 'For he's a jolly good fellow.' Sebastian stood on the step between Viola and Teresa while they sang it. He did not enjoy it as his mother would have enjoyed it, but he endured it as inevitable. Teresa was again compelled to blink the tears back from her eyes.

'Mrs. Spedding, do come and talk to me. You don't play Bridge, neither do I – at least, not when I can do anything better. Let's go and wander through the house. We'll take a candle. Look – they're all settled down. No one will notice. Let's creep away. Shall you be cold?' Impetuous, he caught up a cloak thrown down on the back of a sofa.

'But that is your mother's cloak.'

'Never mind.' He put it round her shoulders. It was of gold tissue lined with sable. Teresa's feminine eye had appraised it already, earlier in the evening. The soft fur caressed her bare shoulders. It seemed fitting that Sebastian should swathe her in such a garment; but still she cast a glance at John, conscientiously sorting the cards in his hand. John had let drop a hint to her that he was a little alarmed by the high stakes they played for. He hoped that he would not lose more than he could afford. Poor John, who had given her fifty pounds to spend on clothes, in anticipation of this party! Poor John. But the sable was warm and soft to her bare skin; she had never felt just such a caress before; Sebastian opened the door for her, and she passed through it into the dark galleries, hoping that the other women had seen them go, hoping that John had not looked up.

Sebastian carried a three-branched candlestick in his hand; it lit up his face, but left the rooms in shadow. He proved to be in a mellow mood, neither sarcastic, nor excited, nor scoffing; but dreamy, as though he had plenty of time before him, and were disposed to betray something of himself as he had never done to Teresa before. They sauntered down the long gallery, talking softly, and every now and then Sebastian would pause before a picture, and, holding up the candlestick, would make some comment or recount some anecdote, while the three little spears of light flickered over the stomacher of a lady or the beard of a king. Then the gilding of the frame came to life, and the face looked gravely down at them, until, moving on, they left the portrait to re-enter the darkness, and woke some other image out of its painted sleep. There was now no friction between them, as there had been in the morning, when Sebastian was irritable and Teresa cautious. They talked naturally but softly, lowering their voices almost to a murmur out of respect for the hushed and sleeping rooms, where the moonlight spread in chequered lakes across the boards and the muting hand of the centuries seemed to have laid itself gently over the clamour of life. They breathed the air of a world that was completely withdrawn from reality – a world of which Sebastian was a natural inhabitant and to which he had admitted Teresa as by the unlocking of a door. She felt that with a princely generosity he had now shown her all his jewels. He had shown her his friends – and, though Sebastian might not value his friends, Teresa valued them extremely – he had shown her his boyishness and simplicity; now by leading her into this enchantment he had revealed another aspect of himself, the most secret, the most romantic of all. For it goes without saying that Sebastian was the essence of romance in Teresa's eyes. Whether he came to tea with her in the Cromwell Road out of the mysterious background of his

London life, or sat at the head of his table half-hidden by the plate and the orchids, or laughed as he tossed the snow, or murmured in the moonlit rooms, it appeared to her in turn that he could play no other part. And now, seeing him in the crowning magic of the moon and the ancient rooms, she thought that she at last saw him in the round. She could put all the pieces together; he was, triumphantly, a unity. Out of the jumble of her impressions emerged a perfectly clear figure. She had her moment of revelation; she experienced the ecstatic shock of truly apprehending a work of art.

So, at least, thought Teresa; except that she did not put it to herself in terms of apprehending works of art. Sebastian was wiser, and colder. He had estimated – and, up to a certain point, with accuracy – the effect that the dark galleries would have upon Teresa. When he chose, his technique could be faultless; it was faultless now. (He was not really to blame for his miscalculation of one essential particular.) He was very gentle with Teresa, warning her not to stumble over a step, holding the tapestry aside that she might pass beneath; he was protective, though impersonal: the stories he told her were just such as would lead her deeper into this poetic world where reality ceased to have any weight. He wanted her to feel that he and she were its only inhabitants, and that it was their possession, for them to re-enter at any moment which left them alone together. So gradually he began to speak of the people they had deserted in the drawing-room – 'chattering magpies,' said Sebastian – and of the difference between herself and them, speaking with eloquence because he had half-persuaded himself that he believed what he was saying. Teresa believed it too. With her final putting-together of Sebastian, she had come to the sustaining conviction that she 'understood' him. He must know it, she thought; for otherwise he would not have led her away into this beautiful, secret house of his. Her reverent adoration of him became slightly maternal.

Despite their lingering, they had wandered through two galleries and found themselves now in Queen Elizabeth's Bedroom, where the great four-poster of silver and flamingo satin towered to the ceiling and the outlines of the famous silver furniture gleamed dimly in a ray of the moon. Sebastian went to the window and pulled back the curtains. He knew that this was the moment for which the whole day had been but a preparation, yet he almost forgot Teresa and his wary plotting in the first shock of the beauty that met his eyes. The white garden lay in the full flood of the moon. The dark room was suddenly irradiated; the figures on the tapestry seemed to stir, the bed was full of shadows, the bosses on the silver shone, the polished floor became a lake of silver light. Softly he blew out his candles, and as their three spears of gold vanished, the room was given up entirely to that argent radiance. Teresa's gold cloak turned silver too as she slipped into the embrasure of the window and leant there by his side. They were both silent, now gazing through the lattices into the white garden, now turning to let their eyes roam and search the recesses of the beautiful room. Teresa's arm, escaping from the cloak, lay along the window-sill. Sebastian recollected himself; he remembered the purpose with which he had brought her there; his desire revived – but he was a little shocked to discover that his delight in Chevron, ever renewed, could eclipse even for a moment his desire for a woman – it was, however, not too late to repair the mistake; his hand stole out, and he laid it upon hers.

Teresa also came to her senses as his touch recalled her. She looked at him in some surprise. She had been weaving a dream about him, in which she saw him straying endlessly as a wraith among this incredible beauty. That moment in which she fancied she saw him in the round had been very valuable and illuminating to her. But it had slightly accentuated his unreality. On the whole, in spite of her maternal impulse when she told herself that she 'understood' him, it had helped to make him into something more of a peep-show, something more definitely apart from herself. As his romance increased, so did his reality diminish. So now, when his slim fingers closed upon her hand, she was surprised, and baffled, and could not relate the physical contact with the image she had formed of him.

They were once again at cross-purposes.

He leant towards her, and, to her intense perplexity, began to pour words of love into her ear. 'Teresa,' he said, in a tone she had never heard him use, just as she had never heard him use her Christian name; and she found that he was speaking of the great shadowy bed, and of his desire for her body, and of their solitude and safety, and of the loveliness and suitability of the hour. 'They will be stuck at their bridge until at least midnight,' he said, and proceeded to paint a picture of the joys that might be theirs for years to come. But the immediate moment was the most urgent, he said. The snow outside, the moonlight, their isolation; he pleaded all this in fulfilment of his desire. Her mind flew to John, sitting in the great drawing-room, playing bridge for stakes which he knew were beyond his means; John, whom she had persuaded against his will to come to Chevron for Christmas; John, who had given her a cheque for fifty pounds; John, who had searchingly asked her once whether there was 'nothing wrong' between herself and this young duke, and had instantly, almost apologetically, accepted her indignant denial. She pushed Sebastian away. She almost hated him. 'You must be mad,' she said, 'if you think I am that sort of woman.' Sebastian, in his turn, was equally perplexed. Had he not spent all his life among women who made light of such infidelities? Besides, had he not seen the adoration in Teresa's eyes? 'Teresa,' he said, 'don't waste our time. Don't pretend. You know I am in love with you, and I believe you are in love with me – why make any bones about it?' Teresa put her hands over her ears to shut out the sudden voicing of this crude and shocking creed. 'John!' she cried in a low voice, as though she were crying for help. 'John!' said Sebastian, taken aback; the very mention of her husband at such a moment struck him as an error of taste. 'Why, John knows all about it, you may be sure; else, he would never have consented to bring you here.' 'What?' said Teresa, taking her hands away and staring at him in real amazement; 'you think that? You think that John knew you were in love with me, and condoned it? You believe that? You think that John and I are that sort of person?' 'Oh,' said Sebastian, maddened into exasperation, 'don't go on saying "that sort of woman," and "that sort of person"; it means nothing at all.' 'But it does mean something,' said Teresa, suddenly discovering a great many things about herself, and feeling firmer than she had ever felt before; 'it means that John and I love each other, and that when we married we intended to go on loving each other, and to be faithful to one another, and that that is the way we understand marriage. I know that it is not the way you understand it – you and your friends. I am sorry if I gave you the impression that I was in love with you. I don't think I ever was, and if I had been I should have asked you to go away and never see me again. I was dazzled by you, I admired you, I used to watch you and think about you, in a way I almost worshipped you, I don't mind admitting it, but that is not the same as being in love.'

She paused for breath after rapidly delivering this little speech. She clutched the cloak about her and fixed Sebastian with a distressed but courageous gaze. 'I don't want to hurt you,' she said more gently, 'but I must tell you exactly how it is. I suppose it is as difficult for you to understand our ideas as it is for us to understand yours. I know what you are thinking – you are disgusted with me, and you are wondering why you ever wasted your time over a conventional little *bourgeoise* like me. To tell you the truth, I used to wonder too. To tell you even more of the truth, I knew I attracted you and I was pleased. But I never took it seriously. If I had taken it seriously I should have told John at once. But I didn't take it seriously, and anyway I was weak, because you represented everything I had always longed for. I am being so frank with you because I want you to understand. Perhaps I never really thought about it very much; I was so excited about you, and when you asked me to Chevron I nearly died of joy. There, now, you know all the depths of my silliness. You were offering me sweets, and I took them. But I love John, and he's my husband.'

'And if you did not love him?' asked Sebastian curiously.

'It would still be the same,' said Teresa; 'marriage is marriage, isn't it? – not in your world, perhaps, but in mine – and I should hold on to that. Not one of my relations would ever speak to me again if I were unfaithful to John. Surely you must know that?'

Sebastian could not sympathise with these sentiments. He had acknowledged her dignity when she first spoke, but now she seemed to have switched over from something fundamental to something contemptible. Love was one thing; middle-class virtue was another. This was as bad as Sylvia Roehampton, who could sacrifice him and herself to her social position. Sebastian was angry, because he saw his caprice broken against a rock. Was he never to find moral courage anywhere in the world, he demanded? It now seemed to him that that was the only quality worth having. (Reference has already been made, perhaps too frequently, to the intemperate nature of his moods.) He had tried the most fashionable society, and he had tried the middle-class, and in both his plunging spirit had got stuck in the glue of convention and hypocrisy. The conventions differed – Sylvia had not hesitated to give herself to him – but the hypocrisy remained the same. He raved and stormed. He tried anger, only too unfeigned; and he tried persuasion, but neither could move Teresa. She was grieved, she was sorry, but she was softly stubborn; she even appeared incapable of understanding half he said. Indeed, he poured out such a torrent that no one but himself could have followed his arguments; no one, that is, who had not grown up as he had grown up, with the sense of being caught and condemned to a prearranged existence; who had not alternately struggled against his bonds and then drawn them tighter around him; who had not loved his good things and despised himself for loving them; who had not tried to solace himself with pleasures and with women who meant nothing to him; who had not wavered, in unhappy confusion, between an outward rôle that was almost forced upon him, and the inward passion for Chevron that was the one stable and worthy thing in his life. It was not surprising that Teresa should be puzzled by the abuse that he poured upon her or by the bitterness that he heaped upon himself.

The big clock, striking overhead, abruptly reminded her of her absence. What would John think, what would they all think? she cried. 'We must go,' she cried, tugging at him; she was frightened now by this scene that had taken place between them; she only wanted to get back to safety and to John. 'Do come,' she implored. Sebastian would not move; he leant against the window-sill, looking wild and indifferent to earthly pleadings. 'Please!' she cried childishly; and desperately added, 'I can't leave you here alone, but I must get back.' She made the only appeal that meant anything to her; it was an unfortunate choice. 'Do think of me,' she said; 'think of John, think of my reputation.' At that Sebastian laughed. The contrast between her plea and his own feelings was – or seemed to him – too ironically discrepant. 'Your reputation?' he said; 'what does your reputation matter? You timid, virtuous wife!' The inner know-ledge that he was behaving not only badly but histrionically increased his obstinacy. He was acutely ashamed of himself, since, for the first time in his life, he saw himself through other eyes; and saw his selfishness, his self-indulgence, his arrogance, his futile philandering, for what they were worth. Still he would not give way. He was as childish as she; for he was in what Wacey would have called a Regular State; and when people get into Regular States all the problems of their life rise up and join forces with their immediate sorrow. He had wanted Teresa; he had been thwarted by Teresa; so he remembered that he had wanted Sylvia and had been thwarted by Sylvia, and so by a natural process he had remembered everything else – Chevron, and his hatred of his friends, and the shackles that had been tied round him like ribbons in his cradle, and the sarcasm of Leonard Anquetil. 'You shan't go,' he said, making a movement towards Teresa.

She escaped him; she fled out of the beautiful room, leaving her cloak where it fell, lying in a pool of moonlight. Sebastian stared at it after she had gone. Its wrinkled gold was turned to silver. Its sable lining was as dark as the shadows within the great bed. It was as empty and as crumpled as everything that he had ever desired.

VII

ANQUETIL

Five years had passed, when, for the second time in this chronicle, but for probably the thousandth time in her life, Lucy again poured out her heart to Miss Wace. But it was in a mood of hopefulness, not of despair, that she now sought Wacey in the schoolroom. 'I really think something may come of it, Wacey!' she said in triumph, but sinking her voice as though she feared lest some malignant spirit should overhear. 'They were playing tennis together all yesterday afternoon, and now he has taken her for a walk in the park. Don't you think that looks as though he intended something? You know how he hates girls as a rule. Of course, I daren't ask him. If I did, he might kick up his heels and be off. He might go and join Viola, or worse. You know how he hates to be watched or questioned. He might ruin all our hopes. She's a nice girl, Wacey. Not pretty, but perhaps that's all the better. She's well-born enough to make up for any lack of looks; she's docile, and quite obviously she adores him. And I daresay I could do something about her clothes, once her old frump of a mother is out of the way. Why don't you say anything, Wacey? You're as dumb as a fish.'

Lucy took herself off to Mrs. Levison, leaving Miss Wace to mourn the prospective bride's homely appearance. All her hopes of a Radiant Young Couple were vanishing. The girl was definitely plain, and Miss Wace could not believe that Sebastian was in love with her. There was a great difference between Radiant Young Couples and Settling Down. Sebastian meant to settle down. That was Miss Wace's reading of it. She sighed.

Mrs. Levison took a more sensible point of view. 'If I were you, Lucy,' she said, 'I should be delighted. You'll never have any trouble with that girl, and that's about the best one can say of any daughter-in-law. I don't see why you shouldn't continue to live here after they're married. You know quite well that you wouldn't like to leave Chevron, Lucy, and the alternative would be the Dower House or Sir Adam. You've never been able to make up your mind about Sir Adam in all these years, and now you may be glad you didn't. If you play your cards cleverly you may get everything your own way. Sebastian doesn't seem to notice much what happens – I sometimes think, you know, that Sylvia did him more harm than any of us realised at the time – and the girl will never dare to lift a finger against you. She'll have her babies to keep her quiet. She looks a good breeder,' said Mrs. Levison, coarsely, 'and I daresay Sebastian will make her thoroughly miserable, so between motherhood and worry she oughtn't to give you much trouble.'

'You always had a lot of good sense, Julia,' said the duchess.

'Whereas,' continued Mrs. Levison, developing her theme, 'a lively, pretty daughter-in-law would put your nose completely out of joint. For one thing, Sebastian might be in love with her, and then he would support her in everything against you. Out you would go, my dear. He doesn't care a rap for this girl, and once he is married he will be only too glad to shut his eyes to anything that goes on. You would hate to play second fiddle, Lucy.'

'Yes, I should,' said Lucy frankly. 'After all, Julia, we're not getting any younger, and one likes to hold on to whatever one has got. With so much Socialism about, one doesn't know what may happen; and now the King is dead I expect it will get worse; I always felt that he kept things together somehow,' she said vaguely. 'Oh dear,' she said, 'how things are breaking up. There's Romola gone to China, and Sylvia disappeared out of our lives, and Harry has become a bore, and people are quite disagreeable about Sir Adam now that he no longer has the King behind him, and now, of course, the Court will become as dull as ditch-water.'

'Poor things,' said Mrs. Levison, apparently referring to the new sovereigns; 'we must all do what we can to help them.'

'Yes,' said Lucy dubiously. She was not sure how far King George and Queen Mary would relish Julia's assistance. 'In the meantime, what will become of us? Eadred Templecombe says England is going to the dogs. It really looks like it, when girls like Viola can defy their own mothers and go off to live by themselves in London. I always knew that I ought to have taken a firm line about that, and told her that I would wash my hands of her for ever, but Sebastian took her part and I was helpless. Heaven only knows what she does in London, or what kind of people she sees. All self-respect seems to be going out of the world, Sebastian has some extraordinary theory that people are becoming more honest towards themselves. All I can say is that we may not have been honest, but we did at least know how to behave, It is all very puzzling. Naturally one wants to hold on to anything one can.'

'Anyway, you may be thankful you have plenty of money,' said Mrs. Levison, with the bitter note that always came into her voice when she spoke of other people's fortunes.

'For the moment, but one wonders how long one will be allowed to keep it. There are terrible rumours flying about. Sebastian is a perfect fool. He is almost as bad as Viola. He says he is going to join the Socialist party. A Socialist duke! Did you ever hear of such a thing? If we don't all hold together and support our own class, where shall we be? That's what I say to him. But Sebastian has always been odd. Do you remember that dreadful time two years ago, when he threatened to marry the keeper's daughter? I never knew whether he really meant it or not. And lately I have heard that he has been seen about with some little model he has picked up in Chelsea.'

'The sooner he gets engaged to Alice, the better,' said Mrs. Levison firmly.

'I quite agree. I am on tenterhooks whenever that girl is in the house,' said Lucy. 'Whenever Sebastian comes into my room I look up to see whether he has got anything to tell me, but he always throws himself down on the sofa with the *Tatler*. But still I do think there is something in it. He has never shown any interest in a girl before – a girl of his own class, I mean, of course; I don't count the keeper's daughter. But now he has made me invite Alice for three week-ends running.'

'And you have to endure her parents, my poor Lucy!'

'I know. They aren't much trouble. Lord O. talks to Sebastian about his farms. And Lady O. amuses me. She is torn in half between her desire that her Alice shall marry Sebastian and her intense disapproval of the rest of us. She tries so hard to be civil, and it does go so obviously against the grain! She is used only to people like the Wexfords and the Porteviots. Did I tell you what Potini said to me last night? You know how tiresome he is with his views on the English character? Well, he said to me, "*Ma petite duchesse*" – he always calls me that – "*ma petite duchesse*, in Lady O. you have the English terrrrritorial arrristocracy personified. Look at her bosom – it is like two turnips. Look at her teeth – they are like twelve sarsen stones."'

Mrs. Levison gave her scream of exaggerated amusement, the scream which had been responsible for half her success in a society to which she did not properly belong. But, indeed, Lucy's mimicry had been exact.

'Oh, Lucy, you are *impayable*! Dear me, it makes me sad when I remember how the poor dear King used to enjoy your imitations. You were one of the few people who could always keep him amused. How awful it is to think that all those good times are over. We shall be like a flock of sheep, leaderless.' No one could expect Mrs. Levison's metaphors about sheep to be realistically very accurate. 'We shall have to make a little temple of our own, out of our ruins. You and Romola between you – when Romola comes back – must build it. We must hold the fort, mustn't we, Lucy?' She glanced at Lucy, and, shrewdly perceiving that this thesis was unwelcome, changed the subject. Not in vain had she always relied upon her wits. 'Meanwhile, of course, there is the Coronation to be got over before things can become normal again, but engagements don't wait for coronations, do they, Lucy? There is no reason why the engagement shouldn't be announced at once. There would be plenty of time left' – by plenty of time left, Mrs. Levison meant plenty of time before the end of the season – 'plenty of time left for the wedding to take place. The Coronation isn't till the twenty-second of June. It would be nice if you could get them married in, say, the first week of July.'

Lucy thought, too, that it would be very nice. Meanwhile, it was necessary that Sebastian should make up his mind. There was the whole difference between an unspoken proposal and a spoken one. Lucy, with her vague apprehensions of disturbances in the air and her distress over the breaking-up of her own set, felt that she would give much to get her own family affairs settled. She had always lived in the dread that Sebastian would make some terrible or eccentric marriage or would involve himself permanently in some hopeless liaison; but now the advent of Lady O.'s Alice seemed to promise a solution that, to Lucy, would be like sinking back into a comfortable armchair. She could not pretend that Sebastian was very ardent in his courtship. He pursued it, indeed, with the utmost languor; but he did pursue it. That was the main thing. He made his mother renew her invitation to Alice over and over again – an invitation which, needless to say, was always accepted – and when Alice was at Chevron he dutifully appropriated her; took her off for walks and rides; allowed her to play with the puppies of Sarah and Henry, while Sarah and Henry soberly looked on; conceded that she was 'good with dogs,' and consulted her as to the new golf-course he was planning. Lucy could not imagine that his interest in so dull and meek a girl could have any source other than a desire for marriage. Like Miss Wace, she could not believe that Sebastian was in love.

She clung to Sebastian as the only hope she had left in life. She was beginning to feel her age, and the things of her youth were beginning to shrink all round her. It was unpleasant to observe the alteration in values. Viola, for instance – so recently as in nineteen hundred and six Viola had allowed herself to be taken to all the right parties, but in nineteen hundred and ten Viola had rebelled; on one unforgettable evening at Chevron, after dinner, she had announced that she had taken a flat in London. 'You prevented me from going to Cambridge, mother, but you can't prevent me from doing this. I'm of age.' That phrase had entered Lucy's soul as a dagger. She had never heard it before as applied to a girl; she had heard it only as applied to young men, in connection with festivities, and fireworks, and tenants' balls, and the presentation of silver salvers, engraved with a double column of names. Then it was due and proper; on the lips of a girl it was unforeseen; it was immodest. But it was also unanswerable. Lucy's authority shrivelled as muslin in a fire. And as her legal authority shrivelled, so did her personal authority turn suddenly into a thing which had never enjoyed any real existence. She could do nothing but stammer and weep before Viola's cold, though regretful, logic. She had appealed to all the standards within her range. 'If you won't think of me,' she had said, 'think at least of your position and the example you are setting!' Viola had smiled, patiently but inexorably. 'Oh, darling mother!' she had said, 'all that rubbish!' To Lucy it was not rubbish; it was the very bricks of life. In her anguish she had revealed some of the secrets of those who would not sin against their code. 'Look at the Templecombes,' she had said; 'twenty years of misery rather than give a bad example to the world. Remember Lavender Garrow, who went off with Caryl Thorpe, and was never heard of again. That was all the reward she got for her independence.' 'But,' Viola had said, 'I don't want to go off with anybody. I only want to lead my own life.' 'That's almost worse,' Lucy had groaned; 'up to a certain point, people can sympathise with lovers – only, of course, they can never be received – but for a woman to go off with herself is unheard of. People won't understand. You will lose caste, Viola, utterly. You will never be invited anywhere. You will bring shame on me and on Sebastian. What excuse shall we be able to give, when people ask us where you have gone to?' At this point Sebastian had failed her. He had ceased pulling Sarah's ears; had allowed Sarah to fall with a flop on the floor, much to her indignation; and had stood up with his back to the library fire. 'I entirely sympathise with Viola, mother,' he had said; 'I think she has every right to lead her own life, as she says, if she wants to. She happens to have her own money, but if she hadn't I should certainly give her a sufficient income. I wish I had her courage, and I envy it. She won't be stifled by you, or by Chevron. She wants to be a separate person, and not just a piece fitted into a picture. As to the example she is giving, I hope a lot of girls will follow it. When you are eighty,' he had said, squashing himself down into the same armchair as his mother and putting his arm round her shoulders, 'you will dodder and say how proud you were of your daughter.'

Lucy was not yet eighty – far from it; and she was not yet proud of her daughter. Indeed, so far was she from proud, that she continued to make so many excuses for Viola's absence that her friends began to wonder whether there was not, in fact, some very discreditable reason for Viola's unusual behaviour. '*Qui s'excuse*,' said the new Duchess of D., '*s'accuse*,' and Viola was struck off the list. Lucy was thereby justified in her prediction, to her mingled grief and satisfaction. It was a consolation to be able to say 'I told you so!' but a mortification to go unaccompanied by a daughter to D. House. It was still more of a mortification to find that Viola did not care.

Still, she had Sebastian. Sebastian had not yet broken loose.

He grumbled and he rumbled, with a noise like an approaching storm; but, then, he had done that ever since the age of sixteen. Lucy sighed as she remembered how poor Sylvia Roehampton had said that Sebastian sulky was irresistible. Sebastian had sulked, at intervals, for years. She had always been a little bit in awe of him. Perhaps she might be thankful now that he should have released his mood in periodic sulks, spread over so many years, rather than affect docility like Viola, and then suddenly break away as Viola had broken. 'I'm of age.' Sebastian had never said that, or anything analogous. His obstinacies had always been much softer, much more in keeping with the traditions that Lucy understood; at moments, certainly, he had been tiresome; he had given her frights, as when he threatened to marry the keeper's daughter; but he had never done anything beyond the natural extravagance of a spoilt young man. His worst threat was to join the Socialist party; and Lucy could generally dismiss that as too impossible to offer any very serious danger. She had, too, a comfortable, old-fashioned conviction that marriage would cure him of such fantasies. They were included, even for Lucy, in the category that Miss Wace labelled Wild Oats.

She wondered about Sebastian, but, being a woman, her speculations were confined to the adventures he had had with women. The greater adventure of his mind was of no interest to her. She had scarcely suspected his true perplexities; or, if she had noticed their outward signs in his sudden reticences, his ill-humour, his cutting remarks, she had at once attributed them to some love affair gone wrong. Lucy's imagination could not move outside that orbit. She had all the inquisitiveness of a woman about a man's life, even when that man happened to be her son. Honey would have seemed less sweet than any revelation from Sebastian about himself; but as no revelation was ever forthcoming she had to be content with such pictures as she could secretly make. From her point of view, Sylvia had certainly been the most satisfactory of Sebastian's affairs; for, out of her own experience, she could build up a very detailed reproduction of the relations between them. She had dwelt with an almost incestuous pleasure upon the vision of her son in the rôle of Sylvia's lover. But what of the other women Sebastian had known? What, for instance, of the little model he was said to have picked up in Chelsea?

The little model was, in reality, the fourth of Sebastian's experiments. Looking back over his life, he saw that it took shape, and that, out of the welter, four experiments emerged. (The crowd of other women counted for nothing; they had been merely incidents; inevitable, nauseating in retrospect, and, above all, tedious.) Only four women had made any mark on him; and, now that he could contemplate them detachedly, he observed with interest and surprise that each one had been drawn from a different caste – Sylvia; Teresa; the keeper's daughter; and now the little model. Not one of them had given him satisfaction. He had been defeated by Sylvia's code; defeated by Teresa's; the keeper's daughter – a desperate expedient, undertaken in a moment of revolt against both the upper and the middle classes – had ruffled his sensibilities from the start by her personal habits. In vain had he told himself that such things ought not to matter. They did matter. She was a good girl, a wholesome girl, a friendly, sensible girl, whom he had first noticed going the rounds with a pail of boiled meal for his young pheasants; but she had dropped her aitches and she had sucked her teeth, and Sebastian, examining himself severely, had come to the conclusion that he would wince too acutely whenever she was presented to his friends. He was thankful, at least, that he had withdrawn from that experiment before he could possibly be said to have behaved badly. He had gone through a period of the blackest despair when he realised how tyrannically he – even he! – was bound by custom. He scorned himself for being no better than Sylvia or Teresa: they had their codes, and he had his; they were all prisoners, bound in hoops of iron. He wondered sceptically what Viola would make of her new freedom. 'But Viola is tougher than I,' he thought in his dejection; 'I am too soft ever to carry my struggles through to their conclusion.' He felt, indeed, that he fiddled inconclusively at everything he undertook.

Then, at Viola's flat, he had met Phil, his little model. Before he knew what was happening – such was the exaggeration of his moods – Sebastian somersaulted into a championship of Bohemia. The full torrent of excitement in his new discovery poured over Viola, towards whom since her emancipation he had relaxed something of his reserve. He did not specifically mention Phil, but all his lyricism extolled the independence of the artist; the gaiety, the moral courage, of the happy-go-lucky life. Viola listened, made no comment, smiled at him, guessed with great exactitude what had taken place, and privately prophesied exactly how the new whim was likely to end. Meanwhile, Sebastian trod on air; he thought that he had found his salvation; he had broken the bounds of his own world; he thought that he had discovered everything that was disenfranchised, liberal, free of spirit. His conviction was increased by the fact that, until his advent, Phil had led what is known as a virtuous life; was not in the least impressed by his worldly assets; and gave herself to him without any fuss, within twenty-four hours of their meeting, simply because he had taken her fancy. All this she explained to him in the frankest language, adding that the moment she tired of him she would throw him out. Sebastian, who was not accustomed to be treated in this way, delighted in such discourse. Lying on her divan amid the ruins of their supper, he prodded her on from statement to statement, from revelation to revelation. She had run away from home when she was seventeen; she had served in an A.B.C. shop; and there, Augustus John had seen her.

'Well, and what then?'

'He painted me. He said I was his type.' So she was, with her black hair cut square; her red, generous mouth; her thick white throat; and brilliant colours; especially when she crouched, gipsy-like, over her guitar.

'And what then?'

'Lots of other people painted me.'

'But you never lived with any of them?'

'*You* ought to know that I didn't.'

'Why not?'

'I didn't like them enough. I was awfully hard up at times, too.'

'What do you mean by hard up?'

'Well, I hadn't enough to eat.'

'Literally?'

'Literally.'

'You were hungry?'

'Horribly hungry. I used to faint.'

For the first time it dawned upon Sebastian that people, other than the rheumy old women who sat under arches selling matches, did not have enough to eat. He remembered the meals at Chevron; the endless meals that he had sat through.

'You used to faint? From hunger?' he said incredulously.

His incredulity made her laugh. 'But of course. Lots of people do. Whenever I was flush, I used to bring people back here and give them a meal.'

'What sort of a meal?'

'Oh, eggs – sardines – sausages. It depended. When I was very flush there might be a bit of cold meat.'

'And didn't they do the same for you when you weren't flush?'

'Of course they did. We all helped each other. Only, sometimes we were all down and out at the same time. But why do you want to know? It's all very sordid, and not very interesting. It's only interesting to you because it's something you've never known.'

'That,' said Sebastian gravely, 'is the essence of romance.'

Phil stared. 'Oh, you're too clever for me. You wouldn't think it romantic if you knew it. But don't let us talk about all that. I don't have to worry about that kind of thing now.'

'You never will again,' said Sebastian resolutely.

'Oh yes,' said Phil lightly; 'when you're tired of me, or I'm tired of you. But why bother about the future? Let's put on the gramophone. Let's dance. Let's do something. Or shall we go out?' 'Go out' meant the Café Royal. 'We might meet Viola.'

'Is Viola often there?' asked Sebastian with curiosity. The truth about Viola's life was gradually, very gradually, becoming apparent to him.

'Oh yes,' said Phil unconcernedly; 'she's been there for years. She used to go under another name. We used to call her Lisa, because she looked so smooth – like the Gioconda, you know. But since she came to live in London she goes under her own name. I can't think why she ever bothered to conceal it. Everybody knew quite well who she was.'

Sebastian recoiled before the task of explaining to Phil why Viola should have troubled to conceal her name. Such explanations, as he had already learnt, meant less than nothing to Phil. He wished that his mother could have heard some of her comments in the days when he had been so ill-advised as to endeavour to explain certain things to her.

'Don't let us go out,' he said, though there were times when he liked sitting at the café in her company. 'I like talking to you.' It was true. He wondered now how he could ever have endured the conversation of Mrs. Levison or the Duchess of D. Phil was rough and frank, when she was neither frivolous nor sensuous; she had brought herself up in a hard school, reinforcing her native candour. Beside her, he felt that his own experience had been banked with cushions. She had estimated him shrewdly when she compared him to the princess who felt the pea through four-and-twenty mattresses. He had to adjust himself to her scheme of values, for nothing that he said made the slightest impression upon her. Physically fragile, she was spiritually tough; she had made up her mind, long ago – she was now twenty-two – as to what she considered worth while or not worth while; and her judgement was extraordinarily pure. Sebastian was guiltless of a lover's delusion when he decided that her nature was without dross. The best in him had recognised the best in her. Her taste, too, in letters, art, or music, though uneducated, was direct and right; the second-rate, to her thinking, was excluded from consideration; in those matters, as in life, no compromise was possible. But often her lack of sentimentality hurt him, even while it braced him; he could not grow accustomed to her unflinching brutality. 'But I like the truth,' she said when he upbraided her; 'facts are facts, why shirk them?' Yes, facts were facts to her, as sprouts were sprouts to old Turnour, or winter sales to Mrs. Tolputt, or reputation to Sylvia. 'You won't love me for ever,' she said, 'so I may as well make up my mind to it now. And I suppose I shan't love you for ever, though for the moment I could almost believe it. You and I are as different as chalk from cheese' – that was one of her favourite, stereotyped phrases, that contrasted so oddly with her independent nature. 'One day I shall love somebody of my own sort. Then I shall probably stick to him till I die. I love you, but you aren't my sort. You love me, but I'm not your sort. We can't help it. Why worry? Why not enjoy the present? We may all be dead to-morrow, or there may be a war, or an earthquake,' she added vaguely; 'personally, I don't much care whether I live or die – do you? What I like better than anything, is driving with you in that racing motor of yours; then I feel we might be dashed to death at any moment. I think one never enjoys life so much as when it becomes dangerous. Meantime, I love you like anything,' she said, putting her arms round him as though to make up in passion what she had lacked in tenderness, 'and that's enough for me; it makes me feel like a real thing, a tree, or a stone; a thing that you can see and touch and hold; a thing which you know doesn't exist only in your imagination. It may be gone to-morrow, but it's here to-day – here now, *now*,' she said, holding him closer and emphasising the word as though inspired by some superstitious terror to catch the second even as it ticked away.

Sebastian had exulted; he thought he had found the thing for which he had been searching ever since Sylvia first aroused him. He adopted Phil's standards, Phil's expressions; while their connection lasted, she really did something to break down his conventions, to loosen the inevitable rigidity of his creed. Things which he had thought important she swept aside as cobwebs. Any form of punctiliousness provoked her laughter; any sense of social obligation, her impatience and derision. Thus if Sebastian had an appointment, she would compel him to break it, so that telephone messages frequently went to various ladies, saying that Sebastian much regretted he was unable to come to luncheon, or tea, or dinner, after all; and instead of fulfilling his engagement he would picnic with Phil in her studio, or would take her in his car, down to Kew or Richmond. At first, such was his intoxication that he enjoyed these truancies, regarding them as an act of defiance, a snap of the fingers; he loved Phil the more for her power to make him do things which outraged all his upbringing. Sylvia had never been able to make him do anything he did not want, or to prevent him from doing anything he proposed to do. But after a while Phil's laxness of conduct began to irritate him. The habit of courtesy was too deeply rooted in him; also he liked a certain order in his life; when he had made a plan he liked to adhere to it; Phil's harum-scarum methods really went too sharply against his grain. Then the extreme disorder of her life began to jar upon him; he would arrive at her studio at four o'clock in the afternoon, to find her having breakfast, while the dirty plates of last night's supper had not yet been cleared away and a thick film of dust lay over everything. Phil was incapable of understanding his distaste. 'You're so correct,' she would sneer at him. According to her ideas, one ate when one was hungry, slept when one was drowsy, dressed when one felt inclined, sat up all night if so disposed, threw letters into the fire if not in the mood to answer them, turned people out of the house if one had had enough of them. 'Get out now,' he had heard her say to her friends; 'I'm sick of you.' When he remonstrated, she pointed out with perfect truth that her friends did not mind.

They were 'her sort,' and they were used to her. They knew that she meant no offence, and so took none. Her complete frank-ness as to her relations with himself also embarrassed him; he had been accustomed to people who, whatever their private lives, observed the decencies in public; no one seeing him and Sylvia together could have suspected anything but friendship between them, but Phil treated him quite openly as her lover when her friends had invaded the studio; she kissed him impetuously, lavished endearments on him, and came to nestle beside him on the divan, or to sit on his knee. Sebastian felt that, since she was not a prostitute, she should not behave like one. He could not be angry with her, for he knew that under this distressingly frank surface she owned the most honest soul he had ever known, save Leonard Anquetil's, but gradually he was coming to the conclusion that his excursion into Bohemia had not been a success. Birds of a different feather had best remain apart. At any rate – even though she made him break his engagements – she would let him go as soon as he gave any indication of his wish to do so. It had always been understood that no obligation existed on either side. Phil would never seek to hold him against his will. She might grieve – he shrank from that thought – but she was gallant, she was proud; she would not whine; she would tell him to go, and get it over quickly. She would wave to him before shutting her door behind him, even though she might then throw herself down on the divan and weep, and tear the cushions with her teeth. It was this very conviction which held him and made him hesitate.

Sebastian was scrupulous, and certain accepted conventions had forced him to satisfy his conscience. 'Would you marry me, if I asked you to?' he had said one day. She had shouted with instant laughter. 'Darling, precious Sebastian, I've been waiting for that very question. I knew you would feel obliged to ask it. You're a gentleman, and you've seduced an innocent girl – isn't that the position? Well, my answer is no, a thousand times no, thank you very much. What! me a duchess, and having to live in your horrible old house, and dress for dinner every night, and produce an heir, and kow-tow to all your old aunts and grandmothers, and give orders to a lot of servants, and never call my soul my own again? Not me! Besides, my dear, you wouldn't like it any better than I should. I shouldn't fit in. No; when the time comes you'll marry some tidy miss who'll do her duty by you. You can ask me to your wedding if you like. Where will it be? Westminster Abbey? I should like to see you in uniform, very handsome. Now we've got that over. Admit you're relieved?'

Sebastian was relieved. He loved her with redoubled ardour.

Still, the day came when he could bear it no longer. As he had foreseen, she made no fuss. She accepted his going as she had accepted his coming. She refused his suggestion that he should settle a thousand a year upon her; and made him feel that thereby, though not by his desertion, he had offered her an insult. Just before their parting, a lot of things came out and found the air. He discovered that his orderliness had irked her just as much as her disorder had irked him. 'We could never have hit it off for long. There was never anything but love to keep us together.' In those two sad, wise little phrases she summed up the tragedy of much striving towards happiness.

For a time he was very miserable. Nothing but common sense restrained him from going back to her. Then, true to his temperament, he pulled himself out of his slough and went to the opposite extreme. He looked round for his tidy miss. He pitched upon the dullest, nicest, and plainest girl he could find; he pitched upon Lord and Lady O.'s Alice.

He did not like Lord and Lady O.'s Alice; he almost hated her. He hated her for being so exactly what she ought to have been. Familiar with the family joke of Miss Wace's habit of neat labels, he lacerated himself by labelling her as Miss Wace would have labelled. 'The Perfect Wife,' he said; 'Eminently Suitable.' There was no denying that Alice was very suitable indeed; she had a profound understanding of Chevron – which Sebastian bitterly resented, even while he conceded it; – she had a real genius for gaining the confidence of people like the man Bassett; she understood Sebastian, the fundamental Sebastian, as neither Sylvia, nor Teresa, nor Phil, had ever understood him. Yet such was his perversity, that the greater her understanding and the sharper his recognition of her advantages, the more he disliked her. Several times she was nearly responsible for sending him back to Phil and her slipshod ways, when it seemed to him preferable that Phil should turn the whole of Chevron upside down rather than that Alice should carry on its orderly and hierarchical government. Alice, for him, symbolised defeat; she symbolised the final renunciation of his independence, the admission that he had found no way of escape, the fulfilment of all Anquetil's predictions. If he married Alice, he would be able to foresee what he would be doing on any given date for the remaining years of his life. Thus he thought, taking a grim pleasure in the intolerable prospect. Sebastian was very grim in those months after his parting with Phil. Sullenly, he made everything as bad for himself as possible. With his own hands he was weaving the sacrificial wreaths for the altar.

*

Possibly he had been affected by the opening of the new regime, feeling, like everybody else, that with the death of the King a definite era had closed down and that the future was big with excitement and uncertainty. Possibly it affected him contrariwise, driving him to seek security at the very moment when his adventurous spirit might have welcomed the offer of a fresh opportunity. In order to comfort himself, as much as to disquiet his mother, he advertised his democratic theories; announced his intention of ranging himself with the Socialists; denounced Privilege in all its forms; swore loudly that nothing would induce him to take part in the mumbo-jumbo of the imminent Coronation. Yet all the time – such was his weakness – his actions betrayed his words. Alice alone was evidence of that. Sebastian, as Anquetil had said, had been born a prisoner; and his chains were dear to him, although he might pretend to strive against them.

'Excuse me, your Grace. Should I send your Grace's robes to the cleaners?'

'Robes? What robes?'

'The Coronation robes, your Grace.'

'Why, has the moth got into the ermine?'

The valet looked shocked. He reprovingly corrected Sebastian's inaccurate nomenclature.

'Certainly not, your Grace. The miniver is kept in camphor, and aired twice a year.'

'About all it deserves. Then why send it to the cleaners?'

'The lining seems a bit soiled, your Grace, round the neck. Your Grace's grandfather, the tenth duke, used it at the Coronation of Queen Victoria.'

'I'm not going to the Coronation.'

'No, your Grace. But should I send the robes all the same?'

*

Sebastian went to the Coronation. He was called at seven o'clock on the morning of June the twenty-second; clouds hung about, and in spite of the mild softness of the summer morning, the hour seemed bleak. Looking out of the window, pulling on the white breeches of his uniform, Sebastian thought how much better such a morning would have suited the isles of Western Scotland than the iron railings of Grosvenor Square. But it was vain to think of the isles of Western Scotland, and the good days that he had enjoyed there, when he was hemmed in by such paraphernalia of pomp and circumstance. His robes spread their red velvet and miniver over the back of a chair; his coronet and gloves stood ready on a neighbouring table. His valet, attaining the apotheosis of a valet's life, hovered round him with tunic and boots, ready to pull, to adjust, to button. His coach waited at the door – the old family coach, which had conveyed its owner to the coronation of Queen Anne, all the Georges, William the Fourth, and Queen Victoria; the family coach, with a huge coat of arms emblazoned on the panels, silver handles, and silver springs coiled in the shape of a snake. On the high, fringed box sat the old coachman who had taught Sebastian to ride, happy to be re-established in his natural function if only for one day – for, recently, he had been parted from his horses and trained as a chauffeur. Sebastian looked down on the coach, and imagined it rumbling up from Chevron on the previous day, an incongruous object, provoking a derisive curiosity in the suburbs of Bromley, even as his motor had provoked a derisive curiosity not many years before. Lord! he thought, have I really got to drive in that hearse? and incredulously he looked down upon the two footmen, who in their state liveries were now standing upon the pavement, sheepish yet self-important, mistrustfully eyeing the rumble into which they must presently spring. Sebastian suddenly became aware of his own body. He saw it, he felt it, as a bolster stuffed with straw, a Guy, which must be hung with velvet robes and put into that grotesque survival of a conveyance, there to comport itself with such dignity as it might muster, and eventually to take part in an organised performance with hundreds of other similar bodies, all moving in a solemn, rehearsed, and empty ritual. No doubt, thought Sebastian, in his room at Buckingham Palace the King is waking too. But, since his valet was taking the matter seriously, Sebastian must likewise treat it with becoming decorum. He allowed the crimson cloak to be hung about his shoulders; he received his gloves and his coronet with a suitable gravity. The valet surveyed his master, not only with satisfaction but also with admiration. The smug and healthy snobbishness of the British race was rampant. His Grace was a master whom it was a pleasure to dress. His natural elegance made buttons shine more brightly, breeches appear more dazzlingly white, the polish on boots rival the sheen on his hair. Plate-powder, pipe-clay, and blacking had found a worthy ally. So thought the valet; but Sebastian, glancing at himself in the long mirror before he left the room, thought that the mirror returned the reflection of a character in the pantomime. He was bored, he was disgusted; he wished that he might be casting a Jock Scott into the Tay.

Down on the landing he was confronted by a group of women; the housemaids, the kitchenmaids, had all assembled to see him start. Perforce, Sebastian had to smile, while in his awkwardness he gathered up his robes as a girl gathered up her first long dress. A whisper of appreciation ran over the group; eyes bulged; the housemaids and the kitchenmaids felt that they had been associated with the fringe of some unattainable mystery. The entire collection, at that moment, was more or less in love with his Grace; some of them, denizens of the basement, had never set eyes on him before, and now, seeing him in full panoply, vaguely imagined that that was his ordinary appearance. It would have been no surprise to them to learn that his Grace strode over the golf-links in coronation robes. Unwittingly, Sebastian misled several hearts; he knew nothing of the regrets eating at the heart of Mrs. Wickenden, and even of Miss Wace, marooned down at Chevron. After his shy and deprecatory smile of acknowledgement he rapidly continued his descent of the stairs, unaware of the billowing of his crimson robes behind him or of the corresponding emotion in the breast of his dependents. What a fool he must look – that was his only thought, so far as he had a thought about himself at all.

On the pavement a small crowd had collected; coronations happened but seldom, and the spectacle of a coach in Grosvenor Square was not of common occurrence. Sebastian, holding his coronet under his arm, making it seem as much like an umbrella as possible, had to endure the curious stare while the footmen bungled clumsily with the unfamiliar step, pinching their fingers on its many hinges, before the step was let down and he could enter the coach and be shut into the privacy of the strange and musty upholstering. He sat back with a sigh, not of relief, but of respite. For half an hour at least he was shut, alone, into this dark, swaying box; half an hour at least must elapse before he was called upon to continue his part in this fantastic pageant. The sense of unreality had never oppressed him so strongly since Sylvia had included him as a herald in the pageant at Earl's Court.

But Sebastian was young enough for his boyhood to be real to him. The coach had not lumbered into Berkeley Square before he was leaning forward, examining the fittings, trying the window blinds to see if they would pull – but the silk was rotten; his finger went through it – sniffing the camphor, touching the old seats, opening the flap of the pockets, turning this way and that to look out at the familiar streets slowly passing the window. He had often climbed into the coach as a little boy, enjoying the musty smell, jumping up and down to make the coach rock upon its exaggerated springs; had often been reproved by his nurse for so doing – 'Now come along, Sebastian; if you don't come along at once I'll tell her Grace – dawdling in that nasty old carriage' – but in those forbidden games he had never foreseen the day when he would actually drive in the coach to the trot of his own horses, with the old coachman on the box, and two footmen hanging uneasily on to the straps of the rumble. Even as he peered, and pulled, and explored, and sniffed, he wondered what the coachman and the footmen thought of it. He decided, and rightly, that they probably rejoiced in the possession of a coach and a master who drove in it to the Coronation. They certainly esteemed such privileges much more than he. He could well imagine the polishings and furbishings and brushings and boastings that had gone on down there, at Chevron, and the ceremony of departure when the coach finally rumbled away on the cobbles of the stable-yard; he wondered whether Sarah and Henry had attended and had barked; he could well imagine the gathering of the estate people, headed by Diggs and Wickenden, and probably reinforced by all those stolid and unattractive children who came to the Christmas tree. Dear Chevron! thought Sebastian, suddenly and sentimentally overcome by the smell of the camphor. He put his hand into an unexplored pocket, half expecting to find there the forgotten mask of his great-grandmother.

Then he sat back again, reclined, and gave himself up to the rhythm of his progress. It seemed very slow, and stately, after the accustomed speed of his motor. Life seemed suddenly to have slowed up again. This drive in the coach was an experience; a strange experience, in that the whole timing of life seemed to have altered and to have gone back to what once it was. There was no hurry; he knew that when he drew near to Westminster Abbey a way would be made for him. He thought of Phil. Would she have taken a camp-stool, and waited for hours among the crowd? Crowds, so the papers told him, had been waiting all night, though the crowds were not so great as had been expected, a fact which was gravely explained by the *Times* as owing to the popularity of picture-palaces; why, asked the *Times*, should people wait in the streets when they could see the sights that evening for threepence? But Phil would not be there; Kings, coaches, and coronations meant nothing to her. She would be slopping round her studio in that tattered old Chinese coat, forgetful of any coronation; entertaining Sebastian's successor, perhaps; frying bacon for breakfast, and filling the studio with the reek of burnt lard. She might even be sitting down to strike a chord or two on her guitar. Her invincible gaiety was as liable to break out at seven in the morning as at any other time. Teresa, on the other hand, would give anything – save her virtue – to get a good view. He regretted, ironically, that Chevron House was not in Carlton House Terrace; he might have offered Teresa a window with a balcony. Her cheap little soul would not have arisen to the gesture of refusal. Then he came to the others. Alice? Alice would be in the Abbey, bearing the Queen's train. Before long he would have to decide whether he intended to marry Alice or not. Sylvia? – he found, unexpectedly, that he shrank from seeing

Sylvia again. He had not seen her for five years. But he knew that Lord Roehampton was back from his five-years term of service as Governor, and so, he supposed, he would see Sylvia among the ranks of the peeresses.

His life passed him by as slowly as the familiar streets passed the windows of the swaying coach. The rockings of the springs lulled him into a resuscitation of his childhood. The closed-in atmosphere induced a retrospection of his more recent years. The past, both distant and immediate, became oppressive. He noticed that there was no handle on the inside of the door. So he could not get out, even if he wished! He leant forward to lower the window. It stuck. The family coach itself had entered into the conspiracy to imprison him and to deny him air.

Sebastian's coach drew up with commendable swagger at the West Door of the Abbey. On his way, he had passed numerous peers and peeresses who, having abandoned their carriages or cars, were hastening on foot in their robes and feathers down the damp of Victoria Street – for a fine, drizzling rain had now begun to fall. Sebastian looked with amusement at the unusual sight presented by these ladies and gentlemen in their finery at nine o'clock in the morning; the sobriety of Victoria Street was transformed into an appearance of gaudiness and dissipation. He espied the Templecombes; Lady Templecombe was grasping her skirts with one hand, and the feathers in her hair trembled unhappily in the breeze. Sebastian was glad that he was not obliged to walk, but that the Earl Marshal's pass secured him a way through. At the gates of the Abbey he had to face a larger crowd than had speeded his departure at Grosvenor Square, but here at least he had the comfort of reflecting that the personal interest was negligible; no one in the crowd had had time to ask the footmen whose coach it was; he could sweep hurriedly into the Abbey without a whisper murmuring his name to the spires of Parliament or the reverberations of Big Ben. He had become merely a participant. He had ceased to be himself.

Within the Vestibule, all was quiet and dignity. Such business as reigned was conducted in the hush that befitted so august an occasion and so venerable a fane. Some officer, detailed for the job, approached Sebastian, received his name, and instantly preceded him, soft-footed, to the allotted place. Sebastian looked round, and nodded to the men he knew. He no longer felt so self-conscious, in the company of other men attired as he himself was attired. He straightened his shoulders beneath the heavy cloak. He even felt inadequately dressed, in so far as these men – older men – all displayed the insignia of some Order, which he, by his youth, was denied. There was the Duke of Northumberland with the Garter; Lord Waterford with the Star of St. Patrick. They were all men of a certain age and experience; Sebastian either knew them personally, or had heard them speaking in the House of Lords. He felt apologetic for his youth, and for the rank which entitled him to a place in their midst. Young boys, their pages, in white and scarlet dress, clung closely behind them; and Sebastian himself felt that such a rôle would have become him better than the active rôle he had to play. His own page joined him; a little cousin, an Eton boy; joined him with evident relief at his arrival, and took his coronet from him, tucking it under his arm much as he might have secured a passed ball at football. Sebastian smiled at him with sympathy. He was a shiny-cheeked little boy, more delighted by the special permission which had released him from school than by the privilege of attending the Coronation.

Sebastian looked round again as he waited. There on the table lay the Regalia; there stood the great Officers of State; there stood the Archbishops of Canterbury and York, and seven bishops with their great lawn sleeves; many peers, and a number of Gentlemen-at-Arms. They were waiting for the moment when the pieces of the Regalia should be delivered to them, passing first from the hands of the Lord Chamberlain of the Household to the hands of the Lord High Constable, and from the hands of the Lord High Constable to the hands of the Lord Great Chamberlain, and from the hands of the Lord Great Chamberlain to the hands of the peer or prelate destined to bear them in the procession. The crown of Edward the Confessor lay there; the orb, the sceptre; the golden spurs; the swords of justice; Curtana, the sword of mercy. They seemed to Sebastian to hold about as much significance as the staves of a Tarot pack, yet something within him responded to these strange emblems of centuries and sovereignty. He looked with humorous but affectionate proprietorship at the crabbed, mediaeval little object which would fall to his own lot; and remembering that the hands of his ancestors had likewise closed upon it, wondered whether they also had had a moment's anxiety lest they should drop it? Had old Sebastian, the first duke, following Queen Elizabeth up the aisle of this same Abbey, borne it as cautiously and looked forward as anxiously to the moment when he should restore it safely to its keeper? Sebastian stared at the little object, which he alone had the right to carry; and as he stared he felt the long line of his ancestors rise up and stand about him like ghosts, pointing their fingers at him and saying that there was no escape.

*

In the body of the Abbey, the assembled congregation passed the time as best they might by watching the arrival of the distinguished guests. They saw the Royal Representatives escorted to their seats in the Choir; the German Crown Prince and Princess were there, the Archduke Charles Francis Joseph of Austria, the Grand Duke Boris Vladimirovitch, Prince Chakrabhongs of Pitsanulok, and Dejasmatch Kassa of Ethiopia. The Ethiopian wore a bristling lion's mane swathed about his head-dress, which tickled the face of his neighbour in the next choir-stall every time he turned his head to observe the movements of some fresh dignitary taking up his position. This misfortune, however, was concealed from the gaze of the smaller fry in the body of the Abbey. It was revealed only to the privileged few assembled in the Royal Box and the Transepts. These privileged few beguiled the time likewise by observing the arrival, the hushed and almost stealthy arrival, of the forerunners of the main ceremony. They had, indeed, need of something to beguile the time. Most of them had been in their places since eight o'clock. They were already beginning to look dubiously at the little greasy packets of sandwiches that they had brought with them. They were already beginning to wonder about the practicability of other, more intimate, arrangements. Meanwhile, they could solace themselves by taking in the details of those preparations which had closed the Abbey for so many days while carpenters in their aprons went about, and the vast space, now murmurous with the strains of the organ, had echoed only to the tap of hammers on tin-tacks. The light at first was dim, falling only from the high windows of the clerestory; some hours passed before the golden lights in the candelabra began to pale and the shadows to lessen, revealing many motionless figures, such as those of the Yeomen of the

Guard in the nave, who hitherto had gone almost unperceived. There was indeed much to notice, and the eye strayed alternately from the overhead architectural splendours of vault and column to the tiny figures moving across the floor, stiff as dolls in their multi-coloured robes. The blue-and-silver of the velvet hangings, the blue mantle of the Prince of Wales, the grey heron-plumes in his cap, the silks of the Indian princes, the lozenges on a herald's tabard, the crimson of the peers and peeresses massed in the transepts, the motley of a jewelled window, the silence of the Throne, the slight stir, the absence of voices, the swell of the organ, the hushed arrivals, the sense of expectancy – all blended together into one immense and confused significance. It is to be doubted whether one person in that whole assembly had a clear thought in his head. Rather, words and their associations marched in a grand chain, giving hand to hand: England, Shakespeare, Elizabeth, London; Westminster, the docks, India, the Cutty Sark, England; England, Gloucestershire, John of Gaunt; Magna Carta, Cromwell, England. Vague, inexplicable epithets flitted across the mind, familiar even in their unfamiliarity: Unicorn Pursuivant, Portcullis, Rouge Dragon, Black Rod, O'Conor Don, the Lord of the Isles, Macgillycuddy of the Reeks. What did all those words mean? What could they possibly mean to a foreigner? What could they mean to Dejasmatch Kassa of Ethiopia, whose lion's mane was even now tickling the face of his neighbour? No more than the war-dances of Dejasmatch Kassa could mean to the King of England. The organisation of a planet was a very strange thing indeed.

So thought Sebastian, bearing his little mediaeval object in the train of the King. Somewhere in the galleries above him was a choir five hundred strong, shouting, 'Vivat! vivat Rex

Georgius!' as the procession came up the narrow path of the blue carpet and paused for a moment before the empty thrones. There was the King, in his Robe of State, the Cap of State upon his head, escorted by Bishops, his train borne by eight young pages, flanked by twenty Gentlemen-at-Arms, and assisted – indeed, he had need of assistance, thought Sebastian – by the Master of the Robes. There was the tiny figure of Lord Roberts, and the towering figure of Lord Kitchener. There were the Standards, hanging limp on their poles. There was the Queen – but enough. The ceremony had begun.

Sebastian stood, carefully holding his little object. He must stand as still as a statue, his heavy cloak flowing out round him; he must not turn his head, nor show by any relaxation of muscle that he lived. He was like a piece in a game of chess; he must move, woodenly, to the square next prescribed for him. But his eyes might wander. They wandered; they found Alice among the flock of girls round the Queen's train; they found Sylvia, as beautiful as ever, among the peeresses. She was look-ing at him, and their eyes met across the church, searching each other for some sign of change after these five years. This was the moment that Sebastian had dreaded; now that it had come his heart remained dead; neither Alice nor Sylvia had any power to restore him to reality. He imagined that all life had been suffocated for ever within him, stifled under the mag-nificence of ceremonial and the shroud of his crimson cloak. Since he had consented to lend himself to this mummery, he allowed a spirit of complete abnegation to possess him; hence-forward he would stand woodenly, move woodenly; go where he was bidden; bow; respond, according to what was expected of him; a terrible passivity overwhelmed him, and he accepted it with fatalistic superstition. He had never felt so lost, so forlorn, yet at the same time so resigned, as in that moment when he gave up his freedom. He recognised the moment as having an immense importance for him. Westminster, and the lords temporal and spiritual, had beaten him. (But even then, it seemed to him a huge paraphernalia to have set in motion for that pitiable purpose.) He would marry Alice. He would propose to her at the Russian ballet on Saturday; Prince Igor should furnish a fitting accompaniment. He would fulfil Anquetil's prophecy, even to the last detail. He would cease to struggle. He would satisfy Society, his mother, and the ghosts of his ancestors who had stood where he was standing now.

Meanwhile, the pageant went superbly forward from rite to rite. The undoubted King of this Realm had been presented to his people at each point of the compass, and at each point of the compass had been recognised with loud and repeated acclamations and with the blare of trumpets echoing against the stones from the pavement to the roof. The waiting Altar had received the Bible, the paten, and the chalice. Zadok the priest and Nathan the prophet had been invoked, and the crowning of Solomon recalled. Four Knights of the Garter had raised a canopy of cloth of gold over the King. Oil from the Ampulla, poured from the beak of the little golden eagle, had anointed his head, his breast, and his hands. His hands had been dried with cotton wool. The white tunic of the Colobium Sindonis and the golden pall of the Supertunica had replaced his robes of state, revealing the mark of sunburn at the back of his neck. The golden spurs had touched his heels; the Armill had been flung about his shoulders; the Sword had been girded on and redeemed with one hundred shillings in a red velvet bag; the Orb, the Ring, and the Sceptres had been delivered to him; the Lord of the Manor of Worksop had offered a glove. The Crown had been placed upon his head, the trumpets and drums had sounded, the people had cried God save the King.

And at the moment when the Queen was crowned the peeresses had likewise put on their coronets, in a single gesture of exquisite beauty, their white arms rising with a sound like the rushing of birds' wings and a proud arching like the arching of the neck of a swan. Then out came the little mirrors, and, with furtive peeps in that cluster of femininity, hands had stolen upwards again to adjust, to straighten. Many dowagers, looking down from the galleries above, tut-tutted. In their day, they said, ladies were not in the habit of producing mirrors in public. It was easy to see, they said, that the reign of Edward the Seventh was over and the days of decent behaviour ended.

Everybody streamed out of the Abbey, greatly relieved. They were tired, but how impressive it had been! and, thank heaven, no one had thrown a bomb. Groups of lords and ladies stood about, chattering while they waited for their carriages. Incongruous sights were to be observed: one backwoodsman peer had put on a straw hat which contrasted oddly with his robes, another had wrapped his coronet in a piece of newspaper. Someone was saying that old Lord— had placed his sandwiches loose in his coronet and had upset them all, over his head, at the moment of the crowning.

One by one the coaches, carriages, and cars rolled up and rolled away. Sebastian found himself once more shut into his musty box, alone. He was exhausted, not so much by the long hours of waiting and of standing, as by the spiritual catastrophe which had befallen him and from which he felt that he would never recover. Vainly he told himself that he had been defeated by mere symbolism: it was by the reality behind that symbolism that he had been defeated. He must remember that. It was important. The reality behind the symbolism.

He pressed his hands to his head, where his coronet had weighed upon it.

Then a block in the traffic caused the coach to stop, and glancing idly out of the window into the faces of the crowd that lined the streets Sebastian looked straight into the eyes of Leonard Anquetil. He recognised him instantly, though he had not seen him for six years. There was no mistaking that strange countenance, pitted with the blue gunpowder, scarred by the sword-cut; a countenance sallow and sarcastic between the two black puffs of hair. Anquetil wore no hat, and his clothes might have been the clothes of an artisan. His hands were plunged into his pockets. He had the air of a street urchin who has wriggled his way to the front to look at the passing show. He had not aged at all; he looked hard and healthy; his mouth had lost its bitter twist; he looked extraordinarily happy. Sebastian frantically sought the door-handle before he remembered that it was not there. He turned, tore away the little flap, and banged on the tiny window at the back with such violence that he broke it. Through the shivered glass he could see the four white silk calves of the two footmen. Air rushed into the coach. He shouted to the white silk calves, remembering, as he did so, the way that one had shouted to the cabby through the trap door in the roof of a hansom. 'Open the door,' he said; 'open the door!' In dismay, thinking his master must be ill, Wilfrid clambered down and hurried round to struggle with the unwieldy fastenings. The traffic in front had moved on, and a policeman, concerned with his duty but still anxious to conciliate a young peer who drove in so magnificent a coach, came up to see what had occasioned the delay. 'Get in,' said Sebastian, craning forward and gesticulating; 'get in; we can't hold up the traffic for ever. Never mind the step,' he said impatiently to the footman, who was groping after it; 'I daresay Mr. Anquetil can do without it.' Mr. Anquetil could. A jump took him into the coach; Wilfrid slammed the door, and Sebastian proceeded on his way with Anquetil beside him.

'Well,' said Anquetil surveying his companion, 'you're very smart to be sure, and what a pretty bauble,' he added, picking up Sebastian's coronet and turning it round and round in his strong hands. 'Strawberry leaves. Ermine. Balls.' He put it down again on the seat opposite. 'How very delightful to see you after these long years.'

The complete conventionality of the phrase relaxed Sebastian's tension as nothing else could have relaxed it. He laughed as he had not laughed since he last played with Henry and Sarah. 'Oh, Leonard, Leonard!' he said then, putting his hand over his eyes and shaking his head helplessly because he had no words. He was flooded by an inexplicable happiness. 'Oh, Leonard,' he said, 'why did you desert me?'

'Lama sabachthani?' said Anquetil.

'Lama sabachthani.' The coach rolled on. 'What have you been doing? The *Daily Mail* said that you were missing. Then there was a little paragraph in the *Times* to say that you were found. What have you been doing, all this time?'

'And you?' said Anquetil; 'what have you been doing?'

'Nothing,' said Sebastian, picking up his coronet; 'nothing!' He ran his fingers over the outline of the strawberry leaves. 'It's an awful thing, Leonard, to have been born a duke; a paralysing thing. It doesn't give one a fair chance. Better, far better, to have been born the son of a fisherman. I had just resigned myself to my fate.'

'Just? How long ago?'

'Two hours ago.'

'During the Coronation? In Westminster Abbey?'

'During the Coronation. In Westminster Abbey. Leonard! pull me out of it. But for you, I'm lost.'

'My poor Sebastian. Crushed under the weight of that beautiful cloak?' He touched it. 'Lost in a forest of tradition?'

'You understand it. You can't know anything about it, yet you understand it. You understand both sides.'

'Our all too infrequent conversations,' said Anquetil suddenly, 'always seem to take place under unusual circumstances.'

'Last time, we sat on the roofs of Chevron.'

'Sebastian,' said Anquetil, 'take care. You are letting yourself be misled by a symbol.'

'Am I?' said Sebastian, startled. 'But isn't symbolism always backed up by reality?'

'Yes,' said Anquetil; 'that's the danger of symbolism.' The coach rolled on. 'I ought to tell you,' said Anquetil, 'that I am going to marry your sister.'

'Marry Viola?'

'Yes. I arrived in England yesterday; I asked her to marry me last night.'

'But you don't know her.'

'We have written to each other once a week for six years.'

'Oh,' said Sebastian enlightened; 'that explains a great deal.'

'But we are not going to marry,' said Anquetil rapidly, 'for three years. I am leaving England again next week. If you like, you can come with me. I repeat the invitation I made six years ago.'

284

'I always imagined,' said Sebastian, 'that once you had finished discovering the sources of the Amazon you would go into politics.'

'No politics for me yet. I'm not ripe.'

'If you're not ripe, then what about me?'

'You? Ripe! You've scarcely flowered into blossom, let alone set your fruit. You've never come into contact with life at all. Come with me, and learn that life is a stone for the teeth to bite on. Then after three years you may perhaps come back with some sense of proportion. Or there may be a war, by then, which will kill you off. I've no doubt that you would behave with great gallantry; and I'll even admit that Tradition, by which you set such store, will serve you then in the stead of experience. In the meantime, will you come?'

'Chevron!' said Sebastian in the throes of a last struggle.

'You'll be a better master to Chevron.'

'All right,' said Sebastian. 'I'll come.'

The coach came to a standstill in Grosvenor Square.

VIRAGO MODERN CLASSICS

The first Virago Modern Classic, *Frost in May* by Antonia White, was published in 1978. It launched a list dedicated to the celebration of women writers and to the rediscovery and reprinting of their works. Its aim was, and is, to demonstrate the existence of a female tradition in literature, and to broaden the sometimes narrow definition of a 'classic' which has often led to the neglect of interesting books. Published with new introductions by some of today's best writers, the books are chosen for many reasons: they may be great works of literature; they may be wonderful period pieces; they may reveal particular aspects of women's lives; they may be classics of comedy, storytelling, letter-writing or autobiography.

'The Virago Modern Classics list is wonderful. It's quite simply one of the best and most essential things that has happened in publishing in our time. I hate to think where we'd be without it' – *Ali Smith*

'A continuingly magnificent imprint' – *Joanna Trollope*

'The Virago Modern Classics have reshaped literary history and enriched the reading of us all. No library is complete without them' – *Margaret Drabble*

'The writers are formidable, the production handsome. The whole enterprise is thoroughly grand' – *Louise Erdrich*

'The Virago Modern Classics are one of the best things in Britain today' – *Alison Lurie*

Good news for everyone writing and reading today' – *Hilary Mantel*

'Masterful works' – *Vogue*

ALL PASSION SPENT
Vita Sackville-West

Introduced by Joanna Lumley

When Lady Slane was young, she nurtured a secret, burning ambition: to become an artist. She became, instead, the dutiful wife of a great statesman, and mother to six children.

In her widowhood she finally defies her family. Her children, all over sixty, have planned for her to spend her remaining days quietly, as a paying guest of each of them in turn. Much to their dismay, Lady Slane rents a small house in Hampstead and chooses to live independently, free from her past. She revels in her new-found freedom, living the life she forfeited seventy years earlier to the conventions of a Victorian marriage, and attracts an odd assortment of companions. Among them is Mr FitzGeorge, an eccentric millionaire who met her in India, when she was very young and very lovely . . .

First published in 1931, *All Passion Spent* is the fictional companion to her friend Virginia Woolf's
A Room of One's Own.

NO SIGNPOSTS IN THE SEA

Vita Sackville-West

Introduced by Victoria Glendinning

Published the year before her death, this haunting, elegiac tale
is Vita Sackville-West's final novel.

Edmund Carr is at sea in more ways than one. An eminent
journalist and self-made man, he has recently discovered that
he has only a short time to live. Leaving his job on a Fleet
Street paper, he takes a passage on a cruise ship where he
knows that Laura, a beautiful and intelligent widow whom he
secretly admires, will be a fellow passenger.

Exhilarated by the distant vista of exotic islands never to be
visited and his conversations with Laura, Edmund finds
himself rethinking all his values. A voyage on many levels,
those long purposeless days at sea find Edmund relinquishing
the past as he discovers the joys and the pain of a love he is
simultaneously determined to conceal.

'A moving and original book . . . her final testament'
Victoria Glendinning

You can order other Virago titles through our website: *www.virago.co.uk* or by using the order form below

☐ All Passion Spent	Vita Sackville-West	£8.99
☐ No Signposts in the Sea	Vita Sackville-West	£9.99
☐ South Riding	Winifred Holtby	£8.99
☐ The Return of the Soldier	Rebecca West	£9.99
☐ The Fountain Overflows	Rebecca West	£10.99

The prices shown above are correct at time of going to press. However, the publishers reserve the right to increase prices on covers from those previously advertised, without further notice.

───────────────── 🍎 ─────────────────

Please allow for postage and packing: **Free UK delivery.**
Europe: add 25% of retail price; Rest of World: 45% of retail price.

To order any of the above or any other Virago titles, please call our credit card orderline or fill in this coupon and send/fax it to:

Virago, PO Box 121, Kettering, Northants NN14 4ZQ
Fax: 01832 733076   Tel: 01832 737526
Email: aspenhouse@FSBDial.co.uk

☐ I enclose a UK bank cheque made payable to Virago for £
☐ Please charge £   to my Visa/Delta/Maestro

Expiry Date ☐☐☐☐   Maestro Issue No. ☐☐

NAME (BLOCK LETTERS please) ....
ADDRESS ....

....
....

Postcode .... Telephone ....

Signature ....

Please allow 28 days for delivery within the UK. Offer subject to price and availability.